REVENGE

&

REDEMPTION

REVENGE

&

REDEMPTION

BY ROBERT M. COOPER

Mr. Cooper is grateful for permission to use the following: the photograph of the rifleman on the book cover by Dreamwalker Films; the picture of the Civil War boots by Union Drummer Boy Gettysburg; the drawing of "The Cowboy with the Rifle" by John Shaffer; the photographs of the Henry rifles by Henry Repeating Arms.

DEDICATION

For their inspiration, William Charles Cooper (1853–1940), James Roy Cooper (1881–1970), Jess Ralph Cooper (1915–1985), and in honor of Chloteal Bonner Cooper (1945–), my loving wife of 53 years.

ACKNOWLEDGEMENTS

I'm grateful for the help of a longtime friend, Robert Langley. After finishing the story, I knew it needed constructive criticism. Because we talked regularly for many years, Bob knew I was writing a book. He liked Westerns and asked to read it, so I sent him the first few chapters. Through his feedback, I was impressed by his editing skills. He also had a youthful exposure to farming and cattle, enabling him to relate to and make suggestions that improved the story. We exchanged numerous emails for months, and Bob stayed committed. Without his input, I would not be as proud of the story. I also thank Carolyn Cahill and Bill Bonner for constructive proofreading and story suggestions.

Table of Contents

Chapter 1: Running For His Life

It was a few minutes past midnight on the first of July 1877. Only ninety minutes earlier, Luke Garrelts committed a crime punishable by hanging. He's a twenty-eight-year-old West Texas cowboy who led an exemplary life until last night. He's seventy miles north of Amarillo, fleeing his crime on a quarter horse he named Smokey fourteen years ago when Smokey was two. They're headed north to the Panhandle of Oklahoma, known as No Man's Land; it's roughly twenty miles ahead.[1]

Smokey is sweating a soapy white lather, and his stride is getting shorter. Luke has pushed Smokey out of fear that a sheriff's posse could be close behind. If one is, he has only two choices: outrun or engage them in a shootout. Luke wonders, *Might the fear of hostiles keep a posse from following me into No Man's Land?* He quickly decides that a large group of men is not the easy target Indian warriors look for.

Luke knows he should switch Smokey with a ten-year-old gelding named Fury, which he bought one year ago, specifically for this getaway. Fury carries a lightweight canvas packsaddle with two pouches on either side to hold their provisions, which are not much. Fury is tethered to Smokey by a lasso wrapped around the saddle horn. Luke is concerned that switching saddles would allow a posse to catch up, so he decides to let Smokey press on until he can find a safe place.

Luke worries about where they could hide on the prairie. He decides a dry arroyo (a gully created by rushing rainwater) wide enough to ride in would be ideal. Luke doesn't want a posse to find his trail, but if they do, it will lead them into a trap. He thinks the perfect place for an ambush would be a sharp turn where the deep, narrow creek bed makes it difficult to turn a horse around. A posse would slow down and bunch up if they could not see around the bend. He'd ride a safe distance past a turn like that, leave the horses, and return to the rim, where he'd easily pick them off from above.

For the past thirty minutes, Luke listened to the rumbling of thunder from behind that was gaining on him. He hasn't looked back because of the need to stay focused on avoiding obstacles ahead. A sudden downward blast of cold air bends the mesquite branches like willow limbs and churns up a cloud of dust, grass, leaves, limbs, and twigs. He slows Smokey to a much-needed walk and leans forward to reduce the force of the wind.

Spooked by something airborne, Smokey bolts sideways a few steps, and Luke calms him with a stern "whoa boy" and firm reassuring pats on his neck. He suspects it was a limb and looks back at Fury, now only a half-step behind. Luke is satisfied that Fury and the packsaddle are okay. He momentarily freezes as lightning reveals the ominous sight of a massive, towering, glowing storm in the clear night sky. It looks to be only a few miles behind, and its incredible size makes it unavoidable. He thinks. *If it's moving at the speed of a galloping horse, it will reach us in a few minutes!* Luke has experience with summer storms in West Texas, Oklahoma, and Kansas. This one appears taller, broader, brighter, and louder than any in his memory. He decides a storm of this size could be a mixed blessing.

Earlier in the evening, at about ten-thirty, Luke took a man's life. It wasn't the first time he had done that; however, in the Civil War, killing wasn't illegal. Luke knows someone saw him leaving town just as flames from the fire he set erupted from the front door of the Addison Cattle Company office. If the sheriff believed the fire was arson rather than accidental, he'd quickly deputize a posse, so his head start could be as little as twenty minutes.

Luke is concerned that a good tracker will quickly pick up their trail by looking for hoof prints made at full gallop. Luke wonders, *If they bring extra horses, the chase could continue until I outsmart them or vice versa. If they get within rifle range, hopefully, they'll fire a few warning shots before shooting to kill. After the first gunshot, I'll immediately find cover, scatter the horses, and prepare for a shootout to the death. I'm sure tracking will become more difficult and slower as the approaching clouds block the moonlight. So, it's unlikely they can catch up unless they've brought torches for night tracking; however, torches would be useless in a rainstorm.*

As he predicted, the storm's leading edge is over them within minutes. Lightning makes it easier for him and Smokey to pick a path free of trees and gullies; however, it also makes tracking easier. Luke always got out his rain ponchos in preparation for a soaking rainstorm, but he didn't want to give up lead time this time.

Within another mile, the wind switches from a cold northern to a pleasant, warm southern gale, and the gut of the storm is over him, but it hasn't started raining. The nonstop lightning bolts create enough light for him to see at a reasonable distance. He rides more closely to the occasional mesquite groves and leans forward to lower his silhouette. Smokey knows if he bends back a branch that snaps back on Luke, he'll be in trouble, so he keeps a safe distance from the low branches.

The gale sends a tree limb flying over Luke's and Smokey's heads. He spins backward to see if it hit Fury. It did not, but simultaneously, a series of lightning bolts brightened the sky long enough for Luke to look across Coyote Canyon. He sees the dark figures of five riders, moving in a single file, without extra horses or torches. Luke thinks, *Those men probably saw me; they're hoping I haven't seen them and are trying to beat me to the far end of the canyon.*

Coyote Canyon is several miles long and nearly a quarter mile wide along most of its length. It drains thousands of acres of prairie. The canyon walls are steep, with large rocks outcropping near the bottom, making it slow and extremely dangerous to cross even when dry.

Because tracking is slow, Luke guesses the posse gambled on him turning toward Colorado and believed taking the west side of the canyon would be a shortcut to catch up with him. However, he isn't going to Colorado, so their horses increase the distance between them with every stride.

Luke recalls a newspaper article about a man who watched his friend and horse drown in Coyote Canyon following a monster rainstorm. He expects someone in the posse to know that story, so they will not try to cross until it becomes a small creek in another mile or more. By then, the storm should be upon them, delivering the advantage Luke hopes for, and the posse will be even further behind.

Since Luke only saw five riders, he thinks, *If I must, taking a stand may not be fatal; few men have my skills with a rifle. However, if the original posse was ten men, and they split up before the canyon, the second posse could arrive in time to catch me in a crossfire. It's best to press on; hopefully, the storm will improve my chances, but I must stay mentally prepared for a gunfight.*

Smokey has cooled down, breathing normally and trotting almost effortlessly due to the wind providing a hefty push. A nearby coyote or feral dog yelps from being pelted by marble-sized hail. Luke quickly reins Smokey under the branches of a sprawling tree, performs a flying dismount, and pulls two waterproof ponchos out of Fury's packsaddle. He maneuvers the horses close to the tree trunk and covers their heads with the horse poncho to cushion the hail. He stands between them, grips both sides of the poncho, and pulls their heads beside him.

The hail gets larger but not round; it's lumpy, irregular-shaped, thumb-sized chunks. Those not slowed by first hitting a tree branch are painful and make the horses flinch. The hail gradually gets smaller over the next ten minutes until it's pea-sized. Luke decides they must go and throws the poncho over Smokey. It covers him from the top of his neck to his tail with a hole for the saddle. Luke sticks his head through the hole in his poncho, grabs the saddlehorn with one hand, and swings up into the saddle, and they leave the protection of the tree.

Other than the packsaddle, Fury has no protection from the weather. There's enough ice to affect their footing, so Luke lets Smokey walk until he can no longer see the ice reflecting the lightning bolts.

Before long, the rainstorm Luke hoped for was upon them. Visibility is about fifty feet, and the air is so full of water that he humorously wonders if anyone has drowned while on horseback.

Wind-driven rain is pounding him, and he thinks, *This amount of rain should fill our tracks.*

After thirty minutes, the wind isn't as noticeable, but the thick clouds continue producing lightning and heavy rainfall. During lightning flashes, the prairie looks like an endless lake, and Luke thinks, *This deluge will be talked about for years.* Water has filled the buffalo wallows, making it impossible to know where they are. He worries that one of the horses could step into the side of a deep wallow and slip, so he lets Smokey pick a path he's comfortable with and mosey.

Because visibility is limited, Luke prefers hiding in the rainstorm and decides to drift along with it. He ties a half knot in the reins and drops them on Smokey's neck. Smoky knows it means he's to maintain the pace and direction. After thirty minutes, Luke decides to loop back to see if the rain is covering their trail, and he's happy to find that it is. That observation makes him think, *A posse that's tired, wet, cold, probably hungry, and doesn't have a trail to follow might decide to return home. Even if only two men did, my chance of surviving a shootout is a safe bet.*

Luke decides to estimate how many miles they've gone since leaving Addison. When the moonlight was good, he galloped Smokey to where Fury was waiting. With Fury in tow, he alternated, cantering Smokey at a fast pace for fifteen minutes, followed by a slow trot for five minutes or until he got his wind back. Luke believes they've covered about twenty miles. But in the last few hours, they had only gone about five miles due to the storm. Despite the waterproof poncho, he is dripping wet and uncomfortable. Luke looks at his watch but can't see the hands. He guesses it's close to two o'clock and thinks, *In another four hours, at dawn, I must find a place to hide, rest, and eat.*

With his situation improving, Luke stops worrying about the posse to reflect on his time in the Addison Cattle Company office. He thinks, *My getaway has turned out better than I thought, thanks to good planning, preparation, and execution. The lessons I learned at Appomattox were to remain calm, no matter the distraction, and execute the plan without hesitation. I know Jordan has longed to hear of Tom Addison's death. As for me, it's satisfying to avenge the death of my brother-in-law.*

Tom's bedroom was dark, and I was in a hurry, so I paid little attention to the denomination of the bills and the coins in the gun safe. The pillowcase I put them in felt like it weighed ten pounds or more. The tightly packed bundles of bills were all the same size and bound with a paper ribbon. Because the bundles were so stiff, the bills had to be uncirculated, like the ones I sometimes get in a *bank. They must be from a bank, train, or coach holdup. If they were all $1 bills, the amount would be good but not great. I suppose Mr. Addison had not deposited the bills, fearing the serial numbers would identify them as stolen. To avoid that, he could have exchanged them for pesos in Mexico and then for greenbacks in the U.S.*

Smokey's front hoof slips into a deep wallow. Smokey's response jars Luke enough to stop his reminiscing about Tom Addison's office. Curious if Fury avoided the unseeable hazard, Luke briefly looks back at him and the packsaddle and takes a moment to review his provision planning. The packsaddle included a saddle pad, a cooking kit, and a large canteen. He threw in clothes, a homemade first aid kit, toiletries, apples, two ponchos, enough hardtack and jerky for a five to six-day ride to Kansas City, and a hundred dollars in cash in one and two-dollar bills from his farm savings account in Amarillo.

His getaway plan assumed a posse would not give up their chase for several days. So, he'd avoid nosey people by staying off roads and out of towns with a telegraph line. His navigation plan was to use his military-issue compass and an old map. However, if he met a local, he would inquire about the location of the closest town. He hopes to come across farms and ranches in Kansas and buy fresh eggs and garden vegetables.

Luke knows he must be able to give a logical reason for being off the beaten path. He'll say, "I'm checking with cattle ranches, hoping to find a job as a cattle driver." Luke plans to ramble about his experience working for King Ranch and over-educate the questioner about cattle drives and markets. He'll try to dominate the conversation by explaining how, for eight years, he and a dozen to sixteen cowboys herded over 2,000 head of cattle up the Chisholm Trail to the Kansas City or Dodge City stockyards each spring.[2] From South Texas, the trips usually took three months, depending on the weather, water, and grass conditions. The cattle are auctioned, loaded on railcars, and taken to Chicago and New York City meat-packing plants. In Kansas City or Dodge, a steer was worth four times more than the same steer in South Texas. The remarkable disparity was due to wealthy individuals in the East willing to pay a high price for a Texas steak. Luke thinks, *If I can waste their time listening to my boring details, which they likely care nothing about, I can discourage most from asking open-ended questions.*

Luke looks up and sighs when the clouds begin showering him with lukewarm water. He removes his hat, tips his head back, opens his mouth, and lets the rain massage his face and wet his whistle. His boyish enjoyment doesn't last long because Smokey stops abruptly at the edge of a creek out of its banks. Luke dismounts to wade in and evaluate the depth and current. He thinks, *The posse will eventually come to the canyon's end and try to pick up my trail. If they get lucky and follow me to this creek, they will split up to go in both directions.* Upstream looks to be from the north, so he verbally coaxes Smokey to wade in, which he reluctantly does.

The lack of moonlight makes walking in a coal-black stream dangerous, so Luke lets them poke along close to the water's edge. Occasionally, they stop and wait for him to decide if it's safe to go ahead. Smokey cannot overcome the discomfort of being unable to see where he's stepping and tries to sneak out. Luke scolds him, and in response, Smokey turns his ears toward Luke and protests with a whinny and a long look back. But Smokey obeys, and before long, Luke relaxes enough to drift into a state of semi-consciousness; he's halfway between being awake and asleep, and he begins to reminisce.

For the next thirty minutes, Luke recollects and summarizes the circumstances and history that got him into this remarkably undesirable situation. *Fourteen months earlier, in April of last year, his half-sister Jordan Booth sent a letter to his farm. In it, she said, "Luke, an assassin killed Jesse on the eleventh of April. I need your help. It was the work of Tom Addison, owner of the Addison Cattle Company and Ranch. I want to meet where no one can see us. Love, Jordan."*

Fortunately, he was just a week from leaving for the King Ranch spring cattle drive. He wrote back on the eighteenth of April, saying, "I can meet with you on the thirtieth of April. There is no need to confirm if you can meet me five miles south of Amarillo at a crossroad called Okie's Road Home. Love, Luke." While waiting to meet with him on the 30th, Jordan felt safer staying at the Champion Hotel in Amarillo.

Jordan was noticeably nervous, upset, and tired when they met at the crossroads. He wondered if she was concerned that he'd try to discourage her from seeking revenge. As soon as they found a place to talk, he told her that since reading her letter, he had fixated on Tom Addison paying for Jesse's death.

Watching Jordan fight back the anguish of explaining her loss and desire for revenge broke his heart. A very evil man had instigated the assassination of the love of her life. Then Tom made sure she had no choice but to sell the ranch to him. Tom's offer was less than the market value for pastureland. He placed no value on the improvements, nor was she allowed to sell off or remove them.

At Jesse's funeral, two widows shared how they lost their husbands and farms to Tom Addison. Their stories were just like what happened to Jordan and Jesse. When several ranchers and potential buyers told Jordan they feared what Tom would do if they bid on her property, Jordan knew the only bid she'd get would be Tom's.

Jordan said the undertaker had the answer to her most important question: Jesse was shot in the back by a Sharps rifle at a considerable distance. She'd never know the assassin's name, but the shooter was likely one of Tom's hired guns. The county sheriff never investigated these land-grab murders after the first man to request an investigation had met with a tragic accident. And lastly, because the mayor and sheriff met with Tom daily, it was clear that Tom owned them, so it was easy for him to get away with murder.

Tom did not try to disguise his eagerness to own the J&J. When Tom's attorney hand-delivered a buyout offer at noon the day following Jesse's death, Jordan knew that Tom knew when Jesse would die.

During their seven years of married life, Luke visited Jordan and Jesse each year for a week. He watched the ranch grow to over twenty-five hundred acres, and the work gave them a common cause and a sense of pride. They loved their ranch and named it the "J&J" for Jesse & Jordan in the second year of operation.

The J&J was three miles north and a half mile west of Addison, which was about halfway between Amarillo and the Oklahoma Panhandle. They started with just six hundred acres, a herd of thirty Hereford cows, and a lazy, old bull that checked the cows only once in the late morning.

Each time he visited Jordan and Jesse, he noticed their herd had grown. Jesse bought and fenced more property and bought more heifers, sheep, pigs, chickens, ducks, and rabbits. He cultivated a half-acre with a single bottom plow to make Jordan a vegetable garden, which she irrigated by diverting the overflow from an adjacent lake kept brim-full by an artesian well.

Unfortunately, the J&J was adjacent to the Addison ranch, and Tom wanted it. Jordan said Tom began badgering Jesse about selling the J&J six months earlier. Jesse told Tom the J&J meant more to them than money. To ruin them financially, Tom sent riders at night to stampede the cattle, cut fences, and set fire to the pastures. Jordan said news of Tom's demise would give many families peace of mind, like an answer to their prayers. Luke was seething with a desire to kill Tom Addison. However, Jordan thought it was wise to put some time and space between Jesse's and Tom's deaths. She asked him to wait at least a year.

He had asked Jordan to tell him every detail she could recall about Mr. Addison and the city. She reminded him that the town sat at the intersection of two stagecoach routes. The north-south route had a telegraph line to Amarillo. Tom's Cattle Company office was in a two-story building in the center of town, and he lived on the second floor. She said Tom was about five feet six inches tall and balding, with a full white beard. He was in his late seventies and was infirm due to age-related afflictions. He moved into his office years earlier after his wife divorced him. At the time of their divorce, she confided to close friends that she couldn't live worrying about her friends thinking she was complicit with Tom. The sheriff reported that she died at home a few days after the divorce from a blow to the head caused by falling into the stone fireplace. It was a questionable finding because she was a healthy, physical, and capable woman.

Jordan said Tom hired former Huntsville prisoners to protect him and do his dirty work. She knew he had three in town who walked Main Street as though they owned it. They purposely walked right at her, and she had to jump out of their way to avoid a collision. That outraged Jesse, and he called them Addison's mad dogs. Their failings were that they drank too much whiskey while playing poker in the hotel dining room every night. Most evenings, they were "three sheets to the wind" by midnight and slept it off, draped over a dinner table or on the floor.

After describing everything she thought would help, Jordan said she would return to the hotel to pack and leave on the A.T.&S.F. the following day. She had picked Kansas City to start over because it was a large city with employment opportunities. While waiting for their meeting on the thirtieth, Jordan had closed on the ranch and prepared for the train trip. She bought two derringer pistols and sewed pockets in her clothing and baggage liners to hide half the closing money.

From their conversations about Kansas City, Jordan knew that the Cattlemen's Inn was his favorite, so she sent a telegram requesting a reservation. After closing, she wired half the money to a Western Union account in Kansas City. Jordan didn't want to look like a dowager on the train. So, she planned to dress in her most worn, inexpensive clothing and carry about $5 in liberty dollars and small coins in a tattered carpet bag.

He worried that Jordan could become involved if he got caught, so he asked if anyone in her circle of friends knew of their relationship. She said she had been careful that no one other than her husband, JR, learned of their half-sibling relationship. She asked JR to tell anyone who inquired that she had no living blood relatives. All the others who once knew, such as their parents and Jesse, were dead.

The first time they met, thirteen years ago, Jordan had convinced him it would simplify her life by pretending they were not related. After her mother passed, gossip about her working in the livery at her father's side became hurtful. Jordan felt their parentage had too many details and players for anyone to keep straight and would provide fodder for more rumors. Fearing that, Jordan asked him to help her keep their relationship clandestine.

After she moved to Kansas City, they exchanged monthly letters without return addresses, so he knew she had started working as a bank cashier. She was careful not to talk about herself, where she came from, or what brought her there. A co-worker said her reticence had earned her the Tight-Lipped West Texas Widow title.

After six months, she became manager of the cashiers and small loan department and married the bank's owner, J.R. McMann. She joined a church and became a Sunday School teacher, but was not yet a mother, which concerned Luke; however, he didn't know how to discuss it. He decided that her standing in the community and concealing their relationship would keep her above suspicion.

However, finding the money in Tom Addison's gun safe created a problem he didn't expect. How would he get it to Jordan without either of them getting caught? His plan was simple: deposit it in his name and transfer it to Jordan slowly over time, but he had no idea how to execute it safely. He hoped Jordan's banking experience would be helpful, but if getting it in a bank right away couldn't be done safely, he'd hide it until he could.

Luke began reflecting on his foster parents, Myron and Phoebe Garrelts, and his upbringing. *Phoebe waited until he was ten to tell him that his father, Herbert Langley, and his mother, Naomi, had abandoned him. After leaving them, Herbert died in a barroom shootout in northwest Oklahoma only a few weeks later. Without financial means, Naomi asked Phoebe to raise him. Phoebe was six years older and unable to conceive, so she was thrilled to get a beautiful one-year-old baby boy. Fortunately for him, Myron was ten years older than Phoebe and owned a respectable wheat farm five miles south of Amarillo.*

Myron and Phoebe insisted that he graduate from eighth grade and be an acolyte in their church. Myron taught him wheat farming, caring for animals, hard work, maintenance and repair, guns and hunting, survival skills, judgment, bravery, and helping those in need. Phoebe taught him gratitude, respect for others and himself, kindness, hygiene, the importance of laughter, fun, and joy, and to follow his passions. Growing up, he earned respect in the community by working during the wheat harvest for most of the folks he knew from church.

His problem with farming was his dislike for plowing, planting, and harvesting. He loved horses and gravitated to a livery and blacksmith shop in Amarillo owned by Frank Weiner. He worked part-time for Frank, earning enough to buy Smokey. Frank taught him how to communicate verbally and non-verbally with Smokey, read his body language, and tend to Smokey's needs before his own.

When he was fifteen, Myron and Phoebe died in a runaway buckboard accident, and he inherited their farm. He talked a neighbor named Bill Boyer into sharecropping his property. In that same year, 1864, he received a letter from Jordan, and being eager to meet her, rode Smokey 300 miles to Fort Worth.

Luke spent a week with Jordan, learning about his mother from Jordan's dad. Then he returned home to tell Mr. Boyer he was leaving to fight in the War Between the States. Slavery had bitterly divided the country, and he thought both sides were less than honest because northern newspapers called it the "Great Rebellion" and southern papers the "War for Southern Independence."[3]

He was proud to have served on the winning side. But ending the war didn't end slavery; it took the 13th Amendment to make slavery illegal in the Re-United States of America.[4] Texans who fought to abolish slavery were frowned upon as traitors. So, when he returned home, he was careful not to mention or display anything that would indicate on which side he fought.

The eight years he spent working cattle drives fulfilled his childhood dreams, and the time passed quickly. When not on a cattle drive, he lived on his farm and made good money rounding up and breaking free-range mustangs.

Jordan was three years younger; her father was James Snider. James told him that after his mother, Naomi, gave him to Phoebe, she moved to Fort Worth and worked as a waitress until she married James. When Jordan was almost three, Naomi died from a rabid skunk bite she got while hanging up laundry.

Needing to know where Jordan was at every minute, James made her stay at his side. He worried the boys would not come courting because Jordan preferred to work in the shop rather than associate with girls her age. By her fourteenth birthday, she managed the inventory, handled the cash, was the janitor, prepared their meals, and helped board horses.

Jordan's father died from a horse kick to the head six months before she and Jesse married. Immediately after her father's death, Jordan sold the livery and went to work in a local clothing store; she was only eighteen. As luck would have it, Jesse went into the store to buy new trousers before leaving on a long cattle drive and asked Jordan to dinner. It was love at first sight, and he returned to Fort Worth to date her for a few weeks before they married. They didn't wait long before buying the first six hundred acres with the money from selling her father's business, Jesse's savings, and a bank loan.

Smokey is still wading uncomfortably in two feet of creek water. He suddenly kicks one leg backward twice, and Fury jumps out of the way. The lasso snaps painfully across Luke's groin and ends his reminiscing. He settles the horses verbally and investigates the stream to see what could have caused Smokey's reaction. Luke sees a snake swimming away and assumes it's a rattler or copperhead that probably bit Smokey close to his hock.

The incident reminds Luke of the many hidden perils they will encounter on the 500 miles to Kansas City, made worse by traveling off the main roads. But he believes his time on cattle drives exposed him to nearly every possible danger.

Luke is confident there will be a warrant for Tom's killer. He imagines it will offer a sizable reward for information leading to the arrest and conviction of the person(s) guilty. When a poster like that appears in all the newspapers, he knows that bounty hunters and law officers will be on the prowl, and he'll look suspicious enough to be questioned and searched.

Luke worries that they won't turn him in for the reward if he gets caught off guard. Upon finding the money, they'd shoot him and run. Because of that, a gunfight to the death seemed more practical than surrendering, even against several men.

Luke thinks, *If I can make it to Kansas City, it seems unlikely that folks up there would be motivated by a Texas warrant. They would assume the guilty party would flee to Mexico, out of the jurisdiction of the Texas Rangers.*

After the snake incident, Luke lets the horses plod along for a mile or more in the swollen creek. He wants to believe the posse has lost his trail and returned home. He hears the distant sound of a train coming from behind and decides it must be a prairie twister because there's no railway nearby. Very quickly, the rumbling, roaring, and whirring sound becomes so loud and the wind so powerful that Luke becomes alarmed. He gets the horses out of the creek, finds an area with thick grass, and has them lie back-to-back.

The roar turns painful, like standing next to several locomotives at full speed, and the air swirls with dirt and vegetation. He pulls his neck scarf over his nose and mouth, stuffs his hat in Fury's packsaddle, lies face down between their heads, wraps his arms around their foreheads, and recites the Twenty-

Third Psalm.[5] He pulls their heads close to him to protect their eyes with his arms and upper body.When he feels his lower body lifting off the ground, he tightens his hold and brings his knees under his chin, and soon, the sensation goes away.

By the time he finishes the Psalm for the second time, the worst has passed, and Luke thinks, *A tornado this size will make headlines if it hits a town.* He has trouble standing without leaning into the wind. Luke tells the horses to get up; they're unharmed but noticeably shaken. They snort, swish their tails, and will not move, so he talks to them, strokes their foreheads and necks, and gives them time to recover from the experience.

Because they are still jumpy, he walks with them along the edge of the creek and hand-feeds sliced apples he had intended for himself. He walks less than a mile and comes upon a large stretch of ground stripped of trees, shrubs, and prairie grass. An unimaginable force has gouged a shallow trench that curves northeast into the darkness. In places, it's nearly fifty paces wide, and rain is ponding at the bottom. Luke recalls an old-timer telling him about an enormous storm that created a scene similar to what he was observing.

Luke follows the trail for a half mile and is stunned by the sight of a half-naked, partially dismembered human body. Luke bends down to take a closer look. The body has a sheriff's badge pinned to a leather vest. He believes this man must have been in the posse he saw earlier. Upon close inspection, the man's skin is missing in places; his face is so disfigured that his mother wouldn't recognize him. Luke thinks, *This fellow was picked up by the wind, pelted and speared by debris, and dragged along the ground for quite a while.*

Luke mounts up and searches in larger circles until he finds four more men and five horses in the same atrocious condition. He picks up two large canteens but nothing else.

Riding away, Luke tells the horses, "Boys, that twister did us a favor; otherwise, that posse might have shot me full of holes." Luke reconsiders the possibility of the posse splitting up before the canyon. He thinks, *If there is a second posse, they would have lost my trail by now and would be trying to regroup. When they find the bodies, they'll return to Addison.*

Luke is satisfied that he does not worry about a posse for the rest of the day, hopefully for another day or two. He comes across a healthy patch of bluestem grass and stops to switch saddles and for the horses to graze. His Waltham-made "soldier's pocket watch" shows it's three-thirty, but he questions its accuracy due to being almost underwater during the storm.

Luke's mind and body are numb from the continuous adrenaline rush, plus he didn't sleep well the previous two nights. He believes the Oklahoma Panhandle is ten to fifteen miles away, and he'll reach it by daybreak. He will not cross it until they've rested. To be comfortable, he decides to let Fury walk until dawn.

After thirty minutes, the storm outruns them and goes northeast, and in another hour, they encounter dry ground. In the dim light of dawn and a clear horizon, Luke can see the sails and tail of a windmill in the distance. He stops short of the farmhouse and sees no chimney smoke.

Then he scanned the outbuildings and wondered why no one was up doing chores. He noticed prairie schooner tracks in the sandy loam leading toward the home. He rode to the front gate and saw many shoe prints of various sizes made by five people loading the wagon. He believed they left the previous day and planned to be gone for a while.

Luke reins Fury to a stop in front of two sliding barn doors. Above the doors is a board with "2-Handles" burned into it. Luke slides one door partially open for the horses to walk in. He removes their saddles and bridles, goes to the back of the barn, and opens another sliding door. It opens to a corral holding a few cows and calves. He sees a windmill spinning slowly and pumping water into a cement trough that extends into the barn. The trough's overflow runs a hundred paces to a small creek passing through the corral. He closes the back door, finds two horse stalls with mangers, and pours a half bucket of oats into each.

He takes a staircase to the hayloft and tosses prairie hay into both horse stalls through openings in the floor. Smokey and Fury are nickering and appear very content, and he decides to spend the night in the loft. He opens the large, hinged doors at each end to flush out the musty air. The rising sun lights up the loft, and Luke lays his wet bedding and clothing on the horse's poncho. While Luke eats hardtack and jerky, irate barn swallows protest his presence from their mud nests, sticking to the rafters. For a bed, he spreads his small poncho over a pile of hay. A mother raccoon with four babies becomes fed up with Luke's activities, and the belligerent swallows. For more privacy, she leaves carrying her babies one at a time, in her mouth, down the staircase.

Though exhausted, Luke plans the next day while cleaning and oiling his rifle. He's aware that the Oklahoma Territory is not yet a state because the government has designated it for Indian reservations. Luke knows that more than fifty tribes were relocated there by military force. The last time he crossed the Panhandle was in '74; he was with three cattle drive friends. They were concerned about stories of small bands of roaming Indians holding up "trespassers" for anything of value. So, they crossed the thirty-five-mile stretch riding at a pace that did not make them an easy target. This time, he must be even less of a target. Since both horses have a fast and comfortable cantor, they could make it to Kansas in three hours. Switching horses is when he's most vulnerable, so he'll make only one quick switch after an hour and a half when he's halfway across. The switch should take about fifteen minutes, but he'll try to find a safe place where he can take extra time to let them cool down, catch their breath, and drink.

Luke thinks, *After I cross the Panhandle, I must protect the horses from becoming overly tired and possibly injuring themselves. I'll probably cover more miles if I trot them for an hour, followed by fifteen minutes of rest. If I ride each horse five times and take a full hour for lunch, that'll be thirteen hours, leaving me eleven hours for breakfast, dinner, tending to the horses, and sleep. My success depends on the horses being well-nourished and healthy, so we'll rest when we come across a good stand of grass, clear water, or both. With good weather and luck, I can travel one hundred miles daily by riding at a comfortable pace of ten miles per hour and be in Kansas City in five days.*

Luke dries and oils his Colt revolver and falls asleep with it on his belly.

Chapter 2: Luke Meets Charlie Bonner
July 1st Continues

After only a few hours of sleep, Luke sits up, looks around, remembers where he is, and falls asleep again. He sleeps until one o'clock in the afternoon. For breakfast, Luke had hardtack, jerky, and the warm contents sucked out of eggs gathered from under six chickens that squawked in disgust. He fills the canteens with well water, readies the horses, takes the money out of the pillowcase, and repacks it in the saddlebag. Luke is pleased that half the bills are tens and twenties, making him anxious to know the exact amount.

It's two o'clock; before leaving 2-Handles, he enters the house and drops six $1 Liberty coins in a Mason jar on the kitchen countertop. Luke sees no evidence of boys in the family and wonders, *Is that why this home is so tidy and clean?* Guessing that they have a neighbor checking on the livestock, he wants to leave before having to explain his reason for being there.

Riding out of the farmyard, Luke looks at his compass, picks out a feature on the horizon that aligns with due north, and reins Smokey in that direction. He's feeling safe but knows it's not wise to be overconfident. If the five men he found last night were the entire posse, a search party would not be organized for several days. Since they'd have little or no trail to follow, it could take several more days to find the bodies and return to Addison. If that was true, a second posse seemed unlikely.

On the other hand, opening the gun safe would trigger an arrest warrant. If that happened today, it would be on the telegraph wires and in every law and newspaper office within 500 miles of Amarillo by evening. In that event, he'll need to change his travel plan. He would consider taking a less populated route through Nebraska to South Dakota and back to Kansas City, possibly even traveling at night and hiding during the day.

Because a warrant creates such a big problem, Luke has a change of mind. He decides it would be worth the risk to go into towns, to get a newspaper, and even read wanted posters on the front of the sheriff's office. It would also provide an opportunity to buy food and horse treats. Luke even considers stopping by the public horseshoe pits where old-timers gather with their newspapers to discuss politics and current events. If questioned, he will say he's an out-of-work cattle drover, considering bounty hunting, and willing to pursue whichever occurs first.

Luke recalls soldiers shredded by cannon fire at Appomattox and compares them to the mutilated posse. He thinks, *The man with the badge had to be the sheriff or an undersheriff. The well-dressed man could have been the mayor. The other three were probably convicts who worked for Tom Addison, and perhaps they were the security guards Jesse called Addison's mad dogs. Though war deaths could be gruesome, that tornado was a more horrific way to die, and those five deserved every second of it.*

Within a mile, Luke sees a weather-beaten sign he can't read. He's sure it marks the boundary between Texas and the Oklahoma Territory. Because of some strange government decision, the Oklahoma Panhandle became public property. Because it could not be privately owned, it got the name "No Man's Land." The boundary between the Texas and Oklahoma Panhandles isn't well-marked, so fenced land in the Panhandle would appear to be privately owned Texas property. Therefore, farmers and ranchers commonly encroached on the public land when fencing their property. Naming the farm 2-Handles was a clever way to make an honest point that the owner had done that.

While crossing the Panhandle, Luke synchronizes with each horse's gait and looks like a man in a high-speed rocking chair. He begins to reminisce about the days leading up to June 30th.

On June 26th, he camped in a thicket of mesquite, which he had passed many times during his visits with Jordan and Jesse. It was two miles north of Addison and a quarter mile off the main road, and it wasn't on the J&J. He had ridden through Addison several times but never had a reason to stop. Now, he was interested in finding the best way to enter Tom's office.

Assuming the town would be asleep, he walked Fury through Addison the following evening at ten o'clock. It had not grown; there were still about ten buildings on each side of the road. The main crossroad led to the livery and blacksmith businesses east of town. Luke figures Tom built them there so the prevailing north and south winds wouldn't carry the manure odor into town.

As Jordan had described, Tom's office was a two-story building in the middle of town with a large Addison Cattle Company sign over the front door. But the Western Union sign mounted on the side of the building was a detail she hadn't mentioned.

He saw a short man reading by the light of a kerosene lantern in the Addison office. Jordan often referred to Tom as a mean little bastard, so his slight stature was consistent with her description.

He recalled riding from one end of town to another and not seeing anyone other than three men playing cards in the hotel's dining room. If someone had seen him, he would have been impossible to describe.

Jordan described the hotel as a two-story building with a ten-table dining room on the first floor and guest rooms on the first and second floors. She said the hotel served beer and whiskey with meals because the town did not have a saloon.

The U.S. Post Office was brick, but all the other buildings were stand-alone, clapboard structures painted white. Again, they fit Jordan's characterization of Tom's control over the city.

Jordan believed Tom had a Napoleon Complex, and growing his ranch and town to his specifications was how he "scratched that itch."

The next evening, he repeated his surveillance but rode Smokey, a shorter, stouter horse than Fury. He slumped and wore no hat to appear shorter. He rode even slower and closer to Tom's office windows this time. He saw a balding man wearing glasses, asleep in a high-backed chair behind an oversized desk with a tall, expensive-looking, glass kerosene lamp. He noticed the breezeway between the adjacent buildings would be wide enough to hide Smokey while dealing with Tom. When he rode out of town, he decided the next night, Saturday, the thirtieth of June, would be Tom Addison's last.

Smokey accidentally steps on an abandoned gopher hole, home to a hive of ground-nesting yellow jackets. Immediately, the black and yellow demons stream out of the hole and quickly catch up with them.[6] Luke is only half-awake and doesn't know the wasps are circling their heads. They decide to attack Smokey's ears, and he bucks to let Luke know he has a problem. Luke reflexively shouts, "Go, boy!" Smokey is at full gallop in two strides, and Fury is trying to pass them. Within a quarter mile, they've all been stung a few times; the yellow jackets give up their pursuit, and Luke slows Smokey to a trot.

Luke looks at his watch; it's nearly three o'clock, so it's time to switch horses. He continues until he finds a small ravine deep enough to hide in. He's comfortable taking a thirty-minute break for the horses to catch their breath, cool down, eat the last of his apples, and drink two canteens of water from his hat.

After another hour and a half, Luke believes they could be five miles into Kansas, so he slows Fury to a walk to let him cool down. A few miles later, he sees a healthy patch of prairie grass and stops for them to drink the last of the water and graze while he switches saddles. After thirty minutes, they leave, with Smokey trotting slowly. In another thirty minutes, he comes across a well-traveled road and thinks, *This must be the road to Dodge City that I took returning home after the cattle-drive to Dodge three years ago. I'll ride a half mile north, turn east, and ride parallel to it toward Dodge City.*

From his left, he hears someone trying to get his attention. Luke's first reaction is to retrieve his rifle. He looks through tightly squinted eyes at a small wooden house on wheels. As it gets closer, he can see an older man in a suit and bow tie with a short double-barreled shotgun lying across his lap, the kind used by the man who rode "shotgun" on a stagecoach. Luke decides the stranger is not a threat; his frown turns into a smile, and he slides the rifle back into its scabbard.

The wagon driver asks, "Where are you headed? Are you in a hurry?"

Luke answers, "To Kansas City, and I'm not in a hurry."

"That's a long way from here. We're headed home to Dodge, and we'll be stopping to make some sales. If you don't mind, we'd like to tag along with you for a while," the wagon driver says.

"I'm not in a hurry, but I'm trying to take the most direct route," Luke says, pretending there is a better way to Kansas City than taking this road.

"Son, there's no better road to Dodge City than this one. I've used it for years. It runs straight into Dodge, then to Wichita and Kansas City, but I no longer go that far."

"All right, you've convinced me, but can your big sorrel keep up with us, pulling that big rig?" Luke asks.

"If you don't mind slowing down a little, she can. We'd sure enjoy your company for a few miles."

"All right, my name is Luke Garrelts. This palomino is Smokey, and the sorrel looking in the back of your wagon is Fury."

"Nice to meet you all. My name is on the signs on both sides of my wagon, Charlie Bonner's Kitchenware," he says proudly. "The nag pulling this rig is Ginger."

"When you said, 'We instead of I,' I thought you had someone inside the enclosure. What all do you sell?" Luke inquires.

"Just about everything you'd find in a nice kitchen. If I don't have it, I can get it. I sell to farms, ranches, and city dwellers. In the cities, I park on the main street through town and let word of mouth bring in customers," Charlie says.

Luke asks, "My horses would like a drink; can you spare some water?"

"Sure, Ginger would like a drink, too. Do your horses prefer carrots or apples?" Charlie asks.

"Apples, but I want to pay you for them," Luke insists.

"That's unnecessary; I don't have that many," Charlie says.

After the "water and apples" break, they ride at a fast walk, with Charlie dominating the conversation. After an hour, Charlie asks, "Luke, would you consider camping with me? Normally, I spend the night in the safety of a livery or farmstead. But you strike me as a man who can defend himself; I'd feel safe camping with you anywhere."

"Sure, I'd like to camp with you," Luke says. "I'd like to find a campsite before sunset."

"Good, that'll leave me enough daylight to make dinner," Charlie says.

Thirty minutes later, Luke notices the tops of a stand of healthy-looking trees peeking over a bluff a short distance off the road. He points to them and says, "I'll check those out. There must be a reason there are so many healthy trees." When he returns, he tells Charlie, "I found a pond that must be spring-fed. A lush stand of bluestem surrounds it, and the water is clear, cool, and tastes great."

"I've heard enough; let's go," Charlie says. When they arrive, Charlie says, "Well, I'll be; I've been going right past this for years, never realizing this little oasis was here."

"Yeah, this is better than I had hoped for," Luke says.

They turn their horses loose to graze and drink, and Luke builds a small fire with dead limbs lying beneath the cottonwood trees. Fifteen feet upwind from the fire, Luke places his gear in a half-circle on the horse poncho, with the bedroll in the middle. He refills the canteens at the spring and returns for a meal of hardtack and jerky.

When Charlie sees Luke about to eat a biscuit, he says, "Hold on there. Give me twenty minutes, and you can have my world-famous salt pork and beans."

"That sounds delicious; I'll wait. How about throwing in a few of my biscuits to bulk it up? I'm starving!" Luke shouts.

"Excellent idea," Charlie responds.

"While you're cooking, I'll go back to the pond and wash up, maybe swim. A flour sack with biscuits and jerky is next to my saddle. Use as many as you want," Luke says as he leaves for the pond with his saddlebag.

When Luke returns, Charlie says, "Those clean clothes must feel good."

"They do!" responded Luke.

Charlie asks, "Did you get into that storm that cut across the Texas Panhandle last night?"

"Yes, but we only caught the edge of it and some light rain; it was moving fast," Luke says.

"I heard about it this morning from a fella from Amarillo headed to Denver," Charlie said.

"What did he say about it?" Luke asks.

"Just that it looked like a killer storm. He thought he was lucky to have been on the west side of it and headed northwest while it was going northeast. He said he didn't even get rained on."

"Yeah, I'd call that very lucky, and I was, too," Luke says.

Charlie hands Luke a twelve-inch diameter dinner plate and a soup spoon and says, "Take all you want; there's more than enough for both of us."

While scooping a large serving out of the kettle, Luke asks, "How can a quarter horse pull what looks like a house on a prairie schooner?"

Charlie says, "I can explain that, but it's a long story."

"That's okay. I have no place to go," Luke says.

Charlie says, "Okay, I'll start with Doris and Amy; they're my wife, daughter, and the most important people in my life; Ginger is next. Third in line are my customers. They expect me to carry new and improved products, and I try hard to please them. By doing that, I've spoiled them in a good way. My profit grew as farms, ranches, and small towns sprang up. Over time, I could earn more money and travel less.

"A significant factor is that roads are much better and not as hard on the wagon or the horses. However, should I break down, help will come in an hour or less. I knew a one-horse wagon would be more profitable and less troublesome, so I was anxious to experiment. In the 40s and 50s, the typical four-foot-wide by ten-foot-long prairie schooner weighed 1,400 pounds and was built to carry 2,000 pounds of cargo. Its hefty design enabled it to endure a six-month trip of over 2,000 miles to western Oregon or northern California, traversing rugged terrain with mountain ranges and rivers.

"Twenty years ago, I had one of those big rigs to carry several weeks of cast iron inventory, and I had two Clydesdales. If one got sick or lame, I could limp home; that happened a few times. My customers no longer ask about cast iron, so I quit carrying it. That was a significant weight reduction. I still sell cast iron from my home, and I'll deliver it if I get an order by letter or telegram. Enamelware is what women want. My pots, pans, dishes, cups, and containers are enamel-covered tin and copper. I also carry tin-covered copper and brass items. My eating utensils are tin; my knives and ladles are steel."

"Do you carry porcelain products?" Luke asks.

"Oh, hell no! They're too fragile. I couldn't afford the breakage. Besides, people who want dinner place settings to impress their guests would never consider buying from me.

"Typically, I'm on the road five days and four nights per week from the beginning of wheat harvest in mid-June through mid-September. Most of my customers are within a hundred or so miles of Dodge and have a general idea of when they'll see me next. I have two markets, rural and small cities. Large cities have businesses that compete with mine. I tell my customers that I'm willing to beat their prices. But after October, people won't wait until next June or July for me to deliver.

"My customers are friends of mine and always seem to be very happy to see me. I stop at farms and ranches next to the main roads, but typically only twice a season unless I have something they've ordered. Sometimes, when they see me coming, they will come out, not buy anything, but invite me to dinner. They always invite me to stay the night in their barn if they have one. I like a barn because we're out of the weather, and Ginger can eat plenty of hay. I typically don't go to farms that aren't on the beaten path, and I can't waste my time stopping at a farm that looks too run-down to afford new kitchenware. I'm sure you've heard the expression, 'Time is money."

"Usually, after dinner, I get invited to breakfast. I have a pent-up need to talk, and isolated folks want to hear what's happening in the country. Many have never been further away from home than the nearest town. Several of them heard about the beginning and end of the North-South War from me. Their faces tell me they enjoy hearing me talk. So, I keep on for as long as they'll listen; it's their decision when I shut up.

"When I leave home, I'll have an assortment of products weighing close to 150 pounds. It could be more if I received orders from customers living along my routes. Around harvest, I leave home with as much as 300 pounds. To protect my inventory, I have always slept with the wagon. Initially, I slept on the ground, but eventually, my old bones couldn't take it. So, I put a five-foot-long by two-and-a-half-foot-wide kid's mattress on the right side of the back half. The size is okay because I sleep with my pants and boots on, just in case. Other than the space for the mattress, it's tight in there. The carriage seat has leaf springs; it's very comfortable, and I've learned to sleep on it. The center aisle is only one and a half feet wide, with storage on both sides extending back to the mattress.

"I learned to travel light. For example, I keep the water barrel only half full and carry snacks for Ginger. I don't need to take a lot of water and feed. Ginger has learned to eat a big breakfast and dinner. I barter with the liveries to get a better deal than paying their posted prices, and farmers and ranchers won't let me pay for hay and water.

"I changed the wagon's design once I realized a lumbering prairie schooner and two horses were much more than I needed. About ten years ago, I disassembled a ten-footer during the winter.

I cut the hickory and oak frame members in half, and the very hefty ones even more."

Luke asks, "Where did you do that?"

"In my barn, on a long-legged bench I built. A friend owned a five-foot whipsaw; we sawed 'em. I found that a glued dowel made the best wood joint, so I didn't reuse the bracing steel and lag screws.

"I reused the sideboards; they're the structural members of the enclosure. The non-structural wood, like the siding and roof shingles, is cottonwood; it's lightweight and sturdy. I use screws and rubber-based glue to secure and weatherproof the shingles.

"The enamel-coated items chip easily. To keep that from happening, I sewed pockets in canvas panels and hung them along the sides and rafters. The height from the floor to the rafters is four and a half feet. I store stuff in the rafter space. Luke, you would have to bend almost double to get around.

"I installed deluxe carriage axles and wheels. I put two-inch-wide metal rims on them to keep the wheels from sinking too deep into soft dirt. To keep the rim from falling off due to a significant temperature change, I used screws to attach the rim to the wheel. Other than the anchor screw, the other screw holes in the metal rim are half-inch-long expansion slots; you get the idea.

"I had to get rid of the heavy single-tongue harness. I chose a lightweight, double-tongue, like on a buckboard. Excluding the enclosure, I cut the wagon's weight to about 600 pounds. What I had was a very well-built buckboard. Most buckboards weigh 400 pounds and can carry up to 800 pounds; that's twice their weight.

"The siding and shingles for the enclosure added 200 pounds. As I previously said, I usually leave Dodge with 150 pounds of merchandise. Me, including personal items, food, water, and horse treats, is another 350 pounds. So, leaving Dodge, my downsized prairie schooner weighs about 1,300 pounds, and it'll get lighter as I make sales. Now, I want you to remember the 1,300-pound number for later."

"Okay," Luke says.

"When I was experimenting, I wrote to a master carriage maker in Cleveland, Ohio, to pick his brain.[7] This fellow spent his life studying horses that pulled wheeled transportation. He sent me a book that said that the industry uses a rule of thumb when designing wagons. He said a fit horse could pull a wagon one and a half times its weight for five to six hours by pulling for fifty minutes, followed by a ten-minute rest break. During the break, the horse must have access to water, be able to graze, and be fed their favorite treats. Old Ginger is a big girl; she weighs about 1,400 pounds. When you divide the wagon's weight by Ginger's, you'll get a number considerably less than the rule of thumb of one-and-a-half. That Schaefer guy claimed a force of only ten percent of a wagon's weight is needed to keep it moving on level ground. So, old Ginger thinks she's only pulling 130 to 140 pounds on a good road. A rider and saddle weigh more; not having that weight bouncing on her back must be less stressful."

Luke says, "Take a breath; I have two questions. How did you get into the business, and why are you two days from home on a Sunday evening?"

"Like father, like son," Charlie says. "My father was a traveling tinsmith, a tinker. My mother died when I was a boy, and I grew up at my dad's side, wandering through the countryside. Over time, as kitchen items became more affordable, people preferred buying new ones rather than repairing old ones. For a while, Dad did both, but he eventually quit the tinning business. This business is the only trade I know. I never saw one day of school. Dad taught me to read, write, and do simple math.

"So, why am I not home on a Sunday night? The four weeks right after harvest are a unique opportunity. Wheat harvest in

South Kansas is somewhat predictable. Give or take a couple of weeks, wheat harvest begins in the last two weeks of June and finishes in the first two weeks of July. After harvest, farmers have more money than they'll have all year, and they go to town eager to buy the things they've been putting off. All the businesses compete for that money, so I must pay attention to when harvest occurs each year and be ready to pounce when the time is right. For example, I doubled up on merchandise when I left Dodge last Sunday. I've had eight good days, and I may sell out before I get home two days from now. It's been stressful, and I'm tired and anxious to be home. However, I'll probably rest for one day, restock, and leave the next morning headed east. In a couple of more weeks, sales will return to normal. I'll return to working only on weekdays and visiting the more rural locations."

Luke asks, "What do you do during the months you're not on the road?"

Charlie says, "Doris and I own a little farm a half mile past the edge of Dodge. We have a barn for two horses and a milk cow, a small coop for a dozen chickens, several rabbit cages, fifty acres of pasture, and a half-acre garden. A darn good water well with a windmill irrigates the garden. We enjoy it, and it's profitable.

"I sell from home in the offseason, from early September to a week after wheat harvest begins in Southwest Kansas. I keep my wagon in the barn, where I can make improvements and repairs. I take the signs off and mount them in our front yard for advertising. During the winter, the Jacob Bromwell Company in Chicago, which manufactures the products I sell, sends out its new catalog.[8] After ordering inventory and wiring the money, it's shipped to Dodge on the Santa Fe. Back in the day, it came by stage, or a third party transported it, or I traveled to Wichita. I wouldn't want to do that today.

"Nice of you to sit through all of that. I'm not a man of few words. When I get wound up, it's hard for me to stop. Amy, my teenage daughter, is kind of like that."

Luke says, "You don't need to apologize. I enjoyed listening to you explain all of that. I would have never guessed that you didn't attend school. You strike me as a clever and inventive man and perhaps a little long in the tooth to have a teenage daughter."

Charlie replies, "I was forty-three when I married Doris in '65; her daughter Amy was five. I knew Doris' husband, Owen. He left to fight in the war when it started in '61. He died at the Battle of Gettysburg in '64. I lost my wife to consumption a few years earlier. I liked stopping at Doris' home because she was beautiful and enjoyable. You can figure out the rest."

Luke asks, "How does the future of your business look?"

"A hardware store is among the first businesses to spring up as a town matures, so progress tends to hurt my sales. A mail-order company called Montgomery Ward sent out thousands of catalogs listing hundreds of products at very reasonable prices. They buy an enormous amount of every product, so their prices are much lower than mine. That outfit is beginning to affect my sales, and I fear I've only seen the tip of that iceberg.

"This telephone invention will let folks talk directly to the factory or Montgomery Ward and place orders. To maintain profitability, we'd need to move further west, where railroads and modern communication may lag by three to five years, like Wyoming, Idaho, and Montana. But we're too old for that, so I'll quit traveling when my sales taper off, but I'll continue to sell from home. I'll have to find other sources of income. I'll probably make a second garden, get more chickens and ducks, make a brooder house, and add eggs and fryers to our product line. I may keep a few sheep in the pasture. Sheep provide two paydays: their lambs and their wool. Oh, and when they get old, I can sell lamb chops."

Luke says, "Sheep will keep the yard around your house and pasture trimmed up and well kept. Their droppings are small enough to fall through the grass, dry up, and become toys for dung beetles; that beats the heck out of cow pies and road apples."

"I can tell there is a little farm boy in you," Charlie says laughingly. "I've thought about planting more fruit and pecan trees, doubling our garden's size, and installing another irrigation windmill."

"How deep are your wells?" Luke asks.

"The well-digger found water at sixty feet, the same as at our home," Charlie says.

"How productive is the formation?" Luke asks.

"Since the pump never loses suction, the formation can produce more than the pump can lift. Based on the water level change in the storage tank, I figured out the pump can deliver three gallons per minute in a ten-mile-per-hour wind, but the wind doesn't always blow. I know the tank holds 2,400 gallons brim-full, so based on my observation, we average a little more than half that, around 1,500 gallons per day. Doubling our current workload means we'll have to hire full-time help during the summer, probably a strong kid. In our twilight years, we'll continue to make the decisions about planting, fertilizing, irrigation, and harvest, but we'll hire someone young and strong to do the bending, picking, and lifting that we can't."

"I understand your need for help; a bushel basket full of any vegetable is heavy!" Luke says.

"In season, Doris and Amy turn a pretty penny selling fresh garden vegetables and the pies and cobblers they make from the pecans, apples, peaches, and cherries the orchard provides. Out of season, they sell dried fruit, jams, jellies, and preserves; they are hard workers." Charlie leans back, stretches his upper body, yawns, and confesses, "All this thinking and talking has tired me out."

Luke asks, "Before we wash the dishes, I have one more question, and you can keep it short if you want. How have you managed to keep your scalp for all these years?"

"My scalp has not been worthy of a lodge pole for years. By staying on the well-traveled roads, I've avoided the hostile ones. Whenever friendly Indians stopped me, they reciprocated my respect. To be safe, I removed my hat so they could see the sun reflecting off my bald head. They liked my wares, especially the knives, and paid with U.S. currency! Our government breaking the treaties is what stirred up their raiding parties. How the military has treated them is comparable to poking a stick in a wasp nest. Fortunately, I never encountered Indians intent on killing me to get even with the government."

Luke says, "You have a different perspective than most."

"Yes, fearful people will shoot first," Charlie says.

Luke looks at his pocket watch and says, "Holy smoke, it's almost ten o'clock. Charlie, I know why farm folks invite you to join them for dinner; you're their entertainment."

Luke heads for the pond after gathering the cooking pot, plates, cups, and spoons. Charlie leads the way with a kerosene lantern, a dishcloth, and a towel. Luke washes and dries everything in the light of the moon while Charlie takes off with the lantern to find a bellowing bullfrog that he plans to stick with his four-inch pocketknife. Charlie is unsuccessful and, on their way back to their campsite, asks Luke, "Have you ever had frog legs?"

"Just once," Luke replies.

"So, you didn't like them?"

"I did, but they taste just like chicken. If I want something that tastes like chicken, I walk out to the coop and wring a neck. A chicken has a lot more meat."

"That's true," Charlie says. "But the frog's legs are free."

Charlie puts his cookware in the back of the wagon, relieves himself on a cottonwood tree a short distance away, climbs in the wagon, and says goodnight. Luke believes Charlie's snoring is loud enough to scare off predatory creatures. Luke walks into the middle of the cottonwood trees and squats while the horses watch.

Luke washes up at the pond, breaks off a small green branch, returns to the campsite, removes his boots, places his Colt single-action revolver on his belly, his Henry rifle at his side, and pulls a light blanket and the small poncho over him. Before falling asleep, he chews on the cottonwood branch to make a toothbrush and a pick. Smokey's and Fury's bellies are full of bluestem, and they show up to hear him say goodnight and sniff his bean farts.

Following a good night's sleep, Luke is eager to get going. Charlie is still asleep despite the horses' neighing and the aroma of fresh coffee and leftover hot pork and beans. After filling the water barrel at the pond, he realizes he can't hear Charlie's snoring and decides to look in on him. When Luke peers over the tailgate, Charlie is on his back, his eyes wide open, his face ashen white, and he has a death grip on a Buntline Special with a rifle stock. He feels Charlie's neck for a pulse, but there is none, so he closes Charlie's eyes and pulls the blanket over his face.

Luke recalls Charlie talking about his wife and daughter in Dodge. He feels obligated to get Charlie to his family. Dodge is over a hundred miles away, making it two long days over a well-traveled road. He thinks, *The road is not the safest way for me to travel, but it's the quickest way to get there, and the sooner I get started, the better.*

Luke remembers Charlie saying he didn't carry a lot of feed for Ginger. Concerned that he may have trouble finding enough grass, he cuts thirty pounds of bluestem with his big sheath knife, piles it on the horse poncho, rolls it up, and ties it to the wagon's side.

Luke puts the saddles and all his gear on Smokey and Fury to lower the wagon's weight. After harnessing Ginger and tying Fury to the back of the wagon with a halter he found hanging there, he sets out for Dodge; Smokey is walking on the right side of the wagon.

Chapter 3: Luke Meets Charlie's Family
July 2nd & 3rd

About noontime, Luke comes across a weather-beaten sign pointing down and to the right, with "Dodge City 90" barely visible. Charlie's unusual wagon draws some comments, but most folks only look at it and smile. Luke thinks, *Several riders could have been bounty hunters, but they didn't even give me a long look. A kitchenware peddler probably doesn't fit the mold of a murderer and arsonist.*

One family inquired if he had kerosene to sell, to which he replied, "Nope." He's surprised by Ginger's ability to pull the wagon at her age. He watches her and decides that years of experience have taught her how to conserve energy by avoiding difficult road conditions requiring more effort. Because Charlie must be at a funeral home in Dodge by tomorrow, Luke knows Smokey and Fury must help Ginger. It has been years since Smokey was in a buckboard harness, but Luke's sure he'll do fine. When he bought Fury, the seller claimed he was harness broken; Luke will soon know if that's true. He recalls Charlie saying a horse can pull one and a half times its weight, and the wagon is lighter due to sales. Luke calculates that the wagon's weight plus his could be nearly 1,400 pounds. Since both of his horses weigh about 1,200 pounds, they are well within the rule-of-thumb ratio and far more fit than the typical quarter horse.

Luke guesses that pulling the wagon requires a lot less effort than cantering. He decides that after lunch, he'll have his horses pull for two hours with a fifteen-minute break after their first hour and a thirty-minute break at the switch. Luke is pleased they do nearly as well as Ginger when given the opportunity. The difference is that they don't foresee places on the road where pulling is more difficult and have time to correct. He knows that with time, they will learn how to avoid difficult road conditions.

During the afternoon, between breaks and the switch, Luke gets in catnaps to help with his lack of sleep. It's six o'clock when Fury finishes his second hour in the harness. Luke decides to make Dodge by tomorrow; each horse must pull for one more hour before stopping for the night.

It's ten o'clock when Luke reins Fury a hundred paces off the road so passing night travelers won't disturb them. Luke divides half of the bluestem into thirds, feeds it with green beans and sweet potatoes from the feed box, and uses two of Charlie's boiling pots for drinking water for Smokey and Fury. Luke ties the horses to three sides of the wagon. He knows Smokey will get restless, whiny, and snort if someone approaches. After another meal of hardtack and jerky, Luke makes his bed under the wagon. He sleeps with a weapon in each hand and thinks about the size of the steak he'll order in Dodge City.

In the morning chill, he tries to roll over, but a lump of something behind his back won't let him. He knows it's there to take advantage of his body heat. With his right hand, he flips the poncho and rolls out from under the wagon. He stands with his Colt pointed to where he believes the critter is, and then he hears the unmistakable rattling sound. When he sees it slither across the top of the poncho, he flips it to cut off the rattler's escape. Then he drags the poncho fifty feet away from the horses. He carefully unfolds it, revealing a six-footer in the striking position and daring Luke to come closer. He aims his Colt revolver from the hip and shoots its head. Then he thinks, *It's been a while since I've had rattler for breakfast.*

He looks at Smokey and says, "SMOKEY, you know better than to let that cold-blooded devil slither up next to me. How about stomping around and stepping on it the next time that happens?

For God's sake, you're wearing steel shoes, and if you got bit, you're too BIG to get sick." While Luke is scolding him, Smokey shakes his head up and down and neighs as if he understands. "Yeah, you know what I'm talking about," Luke says critically.

Their breakfast is hardtack, jerky, and leftover bluestem; he left the big rattler for the vultures and crows. Luke wastes no time with Ginger starting in the harness. By noon, Luke passes a road sign showing Dodge is only twenty-five miles away.

A traveler going west asks, "Where's Charlie?"

Luke replies, "He's in the back!"

The fellow answers, "Well, wake him up... he'll have plenty of time to sleep when he's dead!"

"I'll be sure to tell him!" Luke shouts back.

After taking their hour-long break for lunch at the best grass Luke had seen in a while, they were back on the road with Fury in the harness. After Fury's two hours of duty, Ginger pulls for the second time that day. Ginger's pace is smoother than his horses, and he thinks it's because she's bigger. The hot, boring ride and lack of stimulation are the ideal conditions for Luke to drift away from the present and replay the unforgettable night of June 30th.

He left Fury hidden, packed, and ready to go in the thicket north of Addison. He considered cutting Western Union's telegraph line, but worried that a downed line could trigger an alarm somewhere. He decides that destroying their office equipment will do more long-term damage.

He had taken the cross-country shortcut and reached the north edge of Addison at ten p.m. without seeing a soul. He dismounted and walked Smokey to the breezeway between the Cattle Company office and the adjacent building that looked to be vacant. He wrapped the reins loosely around the saddle horn, knowing Smokey would quietly wait until he returned.

He walked to the front door of the Cattle Company office and peered through the window. Tom was asleep with his chin on his chest. Luke tried turning the locked doorknob; then, he tapped on the glass until Tom looked over his glasses and waved. He suspected Tom's eyesight was so bad that he assumed the knock was one of his security guards. Tom opened the door without noticing who had awakened him. He returned to his desk, picked up the document he had been reading before he fell asleep, and asked about the time. Without hesitation, he struck the back of Tom's head with the butt of his Colt, and Tom fell backward into his chair, unconscious.

He extinguished the kerosene lantern and tied Tom's hands, knees, and feet. Then he gagged, blindfolded, lowered him to the floor, and turned him on his belly. He searched the desk and file cabinet but found nothing of value. It took less than a minute to see that the Western Union's telegrapher had left nothing of value.

He quietly walked up the narrow, creaky staircase to the second floor. He found only one room with nothing in it but hunting trophies hanging on the perimeter walls. Remembering that Jordan said Tom lived in his office, he returned downstairs, thinking he had missed something. He found Tom's bedroom by opening a door he hadn't tried earlier because he thought it was the office's back door to the outhouse. The room's only window supplied enough moonlight to see everything. A couch and a side chair, a four-poster bed, a wardrobe with open doors, a full-length mirror, a table with a washbasin, and a gun safe next to the window. He remembers being surprised that the key was in the safe's lock. He recalls thinking that only an absent-minded old man, fearing he might lose the key, would not lock it up. Maybe it was left unlocked because it contained nothing of value.

His second surprise came when he opened the safe door as far as it would go and turned it sideways for the moon to light the inside. It was practically empty except for a Sharps rifle with a scope, five rows of neatly stacked paper-bound bundles of U.S. currency, and a ceramic bowl with gold coins. He took a pillowcase off a bed pillow to hold the coins and bills. It was less than half full, so he tied the loose end in a half knot.

The empty safe gave him the idea of using it as Tom's coffin. While searching for valuables, he had come across two one-gallon kerosene cans in a broom and mop closet. At the time, it crossed his mind to use them to burn down the office, which would also destroy the telegraph equipment.

He had initially planned to slit Tom's throat and ride off. If he got lucky, no one would find Tom until morning. That plan provided a lot of getaway time, whereas a fire might get someone's attention before he was out of town. Though far riskier, he preferred setting the office on fire with Tom in the gun safe. It was gratifying, and perhaps the gruesome death would send a message to men of Tom's ilk.

He remembers being excited about the plan. He removed the rifle, laid the safe back so the opening faced the ceiling, and slid it to the center of the room. He gathered up Tom, still unconscious, and lowered him into the safe.

Tom was not a big man, and the safe was more than adequate. He pulled off Tom's blindfold and poured a pitcher full of water on his face, which had been sitting on the washbasin. While Tom opened his eyes and regained consciousness, he raised the door vertically. He waited until Tom knew where he was, positioned his face less than a foot from Tom's, glared directly into his eyes, and said, "Welcome to hell; Jesse Booth sends his regards." Tom's pleading, tearful eyes, sweat-gushing brow, and desperate grunting were all the confession Luke needed. He closed the safe door, locked it, put the key in his shirt pocket, placed the pillowcase next to the front door, got the kerosene cans, and returned to the bedroom. He remembered hearing old Tom kicking the bottom of the safe. He kicked the end of the safe where Tom's head was, and the kicking stopped. He wished he had had time to stay and torment him.

He opened the bedroom window and emptied one can of kerosene over the pieces of furniture, but not the safe. He then splashed the contents of the second can on Western Union's office furniture and poured a trail leading to the bedroom. He disassembled the kerosene table lamp and poured its contents on the desk and file cabinet. He picked up the pillowcase, opened the door, looked up and down the street, and, seeing no one, took a match from his shirt pocket, stroked it on the back of his leg, and flicked it ten feet into the center of Tom's desk. He waited long enough to see a small blaze spread quickly to the bedroom. To feed the fire, he left the front door open.

He walked to Smokey in no hurry, like a security guard. He stuffed the pillowcase into one side of the saddlebag, buckled the belts holding the flap closed, mounted Smokey, and let him walk out of town. As he passed the last building, he turned and took a last look at Addison.

The glow of the fire lit up the street, and he could make out a man at the other end of town walking quickly toward the Cattle Company office. He told Smokey, "Let's go, boy," and he was at full gallop within seconds. He remembers hearing five gunshots intended to wake up the town. He doubted a sleepy town would respond fast enough to save anything in the Cattle Company building or the adjacent buildings. Smokey covered the two miles to Fury's hiding place in less than five minutes. Luke took only seconds to untie Fury and flee north from the Mesquite hideout at full gallop. He remembers leaving the main road to avoid running into a night traveler.

Luke was patting himself on the back and wondering how Tom died. Did he roast slowly, suffocate, or have a massive heart attack while begging for mercy? It was satisfying that Tom knew Jesse was reaching out from the grave to end his life. He preferred that Tom die as he did rather than being found slumped over his desk with his throat slit. Tom's bizarre death should make for eye-catching newspaper headlines, exciting gossip, and welcomed news for those he made suffer. A quick death would have been merciful; the despicable Tom Addison did not deserve mercy.

Ginger sees the familiar community watering trough at the edge of Dodge. She stops abruptly, popping Luke's neck, startling him, and ending his replaying of Tom Addison's last excruciating minutes. Smokey hears Ginger making a sucking sound that he recognizes and hurries to her side. Luke is only half awake but enough to imagine the pleasure he'll get from telling Jordan about Tom Addison's uniquely agonizing demise, and Tom knowing that Jesse got revenge. Then he wonders, *Will she read about it in the Kansas City paper before I can tell her?* Luke climbs down and takes a moment to stretch and gather his senses. He unties Fury, tells him to join the others, and gets the last horse treats. After cutting them in half and hand-feeding the slices, he dunks his head in the trough to rinse off the trail dust.

Luke remembers where to find the sheriff's office and the city-wide prohibition of concealed firearms. Luke introduces himself to Sheriff Bartholemew Masterson, who prefers to be called Bat.[9] He explains that Charlie Bonner died in his sleep two nights ago. Bat asks for more details, and Luke says they met over a hundred miles west of Dodge about this same time two days ago. They camped together, and Charlie passed away sometime during the night. When he found Charlie, he closed his eyes and pulled the blanket over his head. Luke says, "During the evening, Charlie talked about his family in Dodge. I felt obligated to get him back home as soon as possible."

Bat says, "You're a good man, Luke Garrelts. I've known Doris and Amy for years. Delivering bad news comes with this job; I'll tell them. Our funeral parlor is at the end of town; you can follow me there. After delivering the bad news, I'll meet you there."

Bat leaves for Doris' home, and Luke follows until Bat points at the funeral home. He goes inside, meets the undertaker, Barry Stiff, and explains the situation. Barry immediately asks if he knew when Charlie passed away.

Luke says, "Sometime between ten tonight and six tomorrow morning, he will have been dead for two days. When I checked his pulse and closed his eyes, he was still warm to the touch, so he must have died closer to six. It was a cool morning, but he was in his wagon, fully dressed, on a thin mattress, and covered with a heavy wool blanket."

Barry says, "I can make an educated guess when we get him out of the wagon. I'll get a box his size, but I'll need your help getting him in it."

While Luke opens the tailgate and uncovers Charlie, Barry returns, dragging an open-top pine box. They slide Charlie off the wagon and lower him into his casket. Rigor mortis has not dissipated, so Charlie is helping. The casket fits him perfectly, and they carry it into the parlor and set it on a large, substantial viewing table.

Barry says, "Based on his rigor and bloat, I think he died well before six that morning. I hope Doris is okay with having his funeral tomorrow. I'm completely out of embalming fluid. If not buried by tomorrow, I'll have to strip him naked and immerse him in a barrel of alcohol."

Barry begins by prying the Buntline Special from Charlie's right hand. Then he straightens his clothing, brushes his hair, sprays on cologne, and dabs his cheeks and lips with rouge to make him look a little less dead. Meanwhile, Luke waits outside, and after twenty minutes, Charlie's wife, Doris, and her daughter, Amy, arrive in a buckboard with Bat following behind.

After brief introductions, Doris and Luke enter the parlor while Amy makes a beeline for the back of Charlie's wagon. Doris takes Charlie's hand and cries, "How did my Charlie die?"

Luke says, "Ma'am, I met your husband two days ago, a little more than a hundred miles west of town. After riding together for an hour, he invited me to camp with him. Charlie made a pot of salt pork and beans that we shared while he talked about the two of you, his business, and the wagon. I probably kept him up too late by asking so many questions. I found him extremely interesting. Before going to sleep, he said he'd had a long, exhausting week and was looking forward to getting home. His heart must have stopped. He passed away painlessly because I'm a light sleeper, and I didn't hear him cry out; he was only fifty feet away."

Doris starts weeping and says, "When Bat told me he had passed, I was sure it was his heart; I blame myself."

Amy returns from the wagon with Charlie's cash box. She opens it, counts the money, and says, "Gosh, Dad had $315." She looks at Luke and says, "It didn't look like you tried to find where Dad kept this money. Given that he was on his way home, you had to know he had money somewhere."

"I respected your father. Stealing from him never entered my mind. I couldn't live with myself if I did that," Luke says.

Amy says, "Your morals are rare in these parts. We're very fortunate that you and Dad met. You had a choice and decided to be noble without even knowing us. You could have ransacked

Dad's wagon, found the cash, and left him there! God bless you for bringing Dad home."

Doris has been listening and says, "Charlie was an excellent judge of character. He wouldn't have camped with you unless he believed you were a good man."

Barry asks Bat to join him while he discusses funeral arrangements with Doris. Barry tells Doris, "Before you leave today, I want you to empty Charlie's pockets and get the pistol he was clutching." Then he explains to Doris what he told Luke about not having embalming flu and suggests they schedule it at ten a.m. because of the heat. Doris agrees, and Barry asks Bat to have his men spread the word about the funeral.

Bat says, "I'll get on it right now," and leaves.

Barry asks Doris if she has any funeral preferences. She asks Barry to talk to their pastor about a eulogy and to ask the church choir director to sing "Old Rugged Cross" and "Amazing Grace."

Barry says, "I'll be glad to do that, and I'm sure they will also."

Doris gets the pistol from Barry, removes the personal items from Charlie's clothing, and rejoins Luke and Amy, who have been getting to know each other by talking about Charlie. Doris sees Luke's road-weary appearance and asks if he can join Amy and her for dinner. She says she'd like to hear more about Charlie's last day.

Luke says, "Ma'am, I'd happily accommodate you, and home cooking would be fantastic. But first, I need to check into The Dodge House, get my horses to the livery, and clean up. After that, I'll get directions to your place from Bat and bring your horse and wagon home."

Doris says, "We're not waiting that long for dinner. I have the best place in town for you to get cleaned up and spend the night."

Amy says, "I'll be glad to wash your clothes while you get cleaned up. You can use Dad's toiletries and wear his clothes while yours are drying on the clothesline.

"That's too good to turn down," Luke says. "Where can I stable my horses?"

"In the barn with ours," Doris says.

Luke thinks, *I must be the luckiest twenty-eight-year-old man alive! Charlie said his stepdaughter is a teenager; if so, she seems a lot more mature than her age would suggest.*

Amy is a tall girl at five feet six inches. She's the same height and looks like her mother. She has light-brown hair that slowly turns golden blond toward the end of her shoulder-length ponytail. She has bright, crystal-blue eyes, a gorgeous smile, perfect teeth, a physique sculpted by physical work, a youthful and energetic disposition, and a quick mind.

Luke follows Doris and Amy from the funeral parlor to their farmstead, which is a half mile away. The women help Luke carry his gear into an enclosed porch at the back of the house that serves as a utility room. The porch's three exterior walls are boarded halfway up, with a small mesh wire screen above. There's a doorway on the back wall that leads into the kitchen.

The porch has a small hand pump and a large sink, both mounted on a sturdy table with a mirror hanging above. Lined against the walls are a cream separator, a corn sheller, a sizeable double-door storage cabinet, a long table to clean and prepare wild game and vegetables, a washboard, a pile of dirty clothes, and a burlap bag stuffed with old rags for their dog's bed.

Amy starts a fire in a large brick fireplace on a small flagstone patio next to the back porch. She grabs two two-gallon milk buckets beside the cream separator, fills them with water, and sets them on a grate over the fire. Luke is arranging his possessions and wondering how he'll bathe privately. Soon, Doris drags a copper tub through the porch to the patio and pushes it against the siding. Then she brings a mattress, places it between the corn sheller and the separator, and tosses the dog's bed on the patio. The Shepard-Collie mix circles his bed, sniffing it and wondering what he's done wrong.

Amy places Charlie's razor, comb, scissors, clothing items, a bar of yucca soap, and two large towels on the food prep table. After shaving and while waiting for Amy to finish heating the water, Luke falls asleep. Amy awakens him with a tap on the shoulder, says, "Your bath awaits," and leaves, closing the door behind her.

Luke strips next to the tub, steps in, goes underwater, and holds his breath as long as possible to extend the refreshing sensation. Amy has put something in the bathwater with the fragrance of a flower he can't name.

Amy shouts from the porch, "How is it?"

"Indescribable!" Luke shouts. "You can go back in the kitchen now." Luke is six inches taller than Charlie, so his clothes don't cover Luke's ankles and wrists. His weight varies from 170 to 180, depending on the kind of work he's been doing. He's flat-bellied and ruggedly handsome, with black hair, olive skin, and dark eyes. He carries himself confidently but without conceit and turns the heads of women of all ages. His attire portends caution, but his ubiquitous smile conveys that he's approachable.

Luke has a thick steak, mashed potatoes, gravy, green beans, squash, biscuits, radishes, onions, and watermelon, and asks for milk to wash it down. After finishing his second helping, Doris says, "Most cowboys coming into Dodge go straight to the famous Long Branch Saloon. They spend their pay on whiskey, poker, and chuck-a-luck. The fun ends when someone gets shot."

Luke says, "My dad died in a bar shootout when I was a year old. After the war, I went into a few bars out of curiosity, and my experiences were not good. I don't like the taste of whiskey. After losing a few hands of poker, I realized I would have to lose a lot to learn how to beat a professional card player. Chuck-a-luck is guessing the outcome of thrown dice. The odds of doing that aren't good; fools and drunks will play it until they're broke. Once, a gunfight broke out at the opposite end of a saloon, where I stopped to have a quick beer. I had to leave by the back door when bullets started flying. I felt lucky to get out alive; one man didn't.

"The buffalo skinners stink so bad their backsides complain, and the women cover up their lack of bathing with cheap perfume. Around the spittoons, the floor is slippery. I watched a drunk returning from the privy lose footing and take down two other drunks. Those memories are what keep me from going to the Long Branch. I like beer, but I can get a colder beer in a hotel dining room where they wash the mugs after each use. It's cheaper there, and I don't choke on cigar smoke. I can order a meal and talk with someone who isn't drunk. I was here in seventy-four at the end of a cattle drive. Due to Dodge's newspaper reputation, I got my pay and headed home the same day."

Doris says, "So, you only drink beer in a hotel dining room and don't gamble or frequent saloons? Please give me your halo before bedtime; I'll polish it. It shouldn't take long to clean off the little tarnish you put on it."

Amy says, "Dodge has changed since seventy-four. In seventy-five, Wyatt Earp left Wichita and joined our police force. He cleaned out the troublemakers in only a few months."

Luke says, "I read about that. My theory on gunslingers is that they'd rather leave town than face their huckleberry. I read articles that quoted Bat Masterson saying that Wyatt was every gunslinger's huckleberry. News like that makes cowards out of troublemakers."

"Tell us a little about yourself," Doris says.

"Okay, I already told you my father died when I was one. My mother asked her older sister to raise me before moving to Fort Worth. My foster parents were wonderful people and raised me as their own. They passed away in sixty-four; I was fifteen and inherited their farm. I knew from my first wheat harvest at age eight that farming wasn't for me. I found pulling the legs off grasshoppers more interesting than anything about harvest. I was desperate to find something exciting, so I found a good man to farm my land and joined the North in late sixty-four. The war was over in April of the next year. I returned to the farm and worked for my sharecropper; how peculiar is that?"

"Why did you fight for the North?" Doris asks.

"I know why you asked; Texas was proslavery.[10] My parents were extremely opposed to slavery, which they believed was the real cause of the war."

Doris looks at Amy and says, "That was Owen's reason for fighting for the North." Doris looks at Luke and says, "Owen was my first husband, Amy's father. I interrupted you; I don't think you had finished."

Luke says, "Where was I...a school friend and I entertained ourselves between cattle drives by rounding up and saddle-breaking free-range mustangs. That lasted a few years until he broke both legs on the same ride and took a job in town. So, in sixty-eight, I read an article in the Amarillo paper about King Ranch hiring cattle drivers. I telegraphed my qualifications, and they hired me. King Ranch is over forty miles southwest of Corpus Christi, the biggest ranch in Texas. They pay $2 per day to drive cattle to Kansas City. That's about a one-hundred-day journey, so it's good money, and they feed me on the trail. I've worked spring cattle drives for eight years and was their lead drover from 1872 through 1875; that position paid $3 per day. I didn't work for King Ranch last year or this year for personal reasons.

"Seventy-four was the only year King Ranch brought cattle to Dodge by the Western Trail. That's because the rainfall and grass reports must be good to bring cattle up through West Texas. If we brought them to Dodge in a typical year, the cattle would spend a few weeks in a feedlot regaining the weight they lost along the way. Driving them up the Shawnee Trail to Kansas City through eastern Oklahoma and the Kansas Flint Hills takes longer, but fields of lush bluestem and spring-fed creeks are abundant. So, for King Ranch, the Shawnee Trail was the preferred route.

"Cattle drives and breaking mustangs are for young men; I can't continue doing those things. I could live on what my farm makes, but I don't want to spend the rest of my life praying for rain and doubting the Lord is listening. The time spent with my brother-in-law and King Ranch taught me a lot about range cattle. I've considered selling my farm, buying some pasture, a few cows, and growing a small herd into a sizable cattle operation."

Doris says, "I can see you doing that. Don't ever give up chasing your dream. Were you coming to Dodge to find work?"

"No, I'm headed to Kansas City to work in the stockyards and spend time with my sister. I'll eventually return to my roots; perhaps farming will be more appealing the third time, though I doubt it."

Amy is disappointed that he's not looking for work in Dodge. She wants to discuss local opportunities, but she knows Luke is capable of more than a day job around town. Luke says, "Your home and farm are well-maintained; your pride of ownership is plain to see. Charlie only used superlatives when talking about you all, and now I see why. He told me how hard you all work in the garden and selling vegetables and baked goods around town."

Amy says, "Mom and Dad created something out of nothing, like a painter starting with a blank canvas. This farm was a pasture when I first saw it. What you see today is a monument to their hard work and love for one another."

Luke interrupts, "I witnessed that with my sister and her husband."

Amy continues, "I like working in the garden, watching Mother Nature do her thing, and turning what she produces into products people need and enjoy. My reward is more than money; selling to cheerful, thankful customers makes me feel good; it's addictive! I know all the decent people in Dodge, and they say our produce and baked goods are the best."

"I wish I felt that way about wheat farming," Luke says. "Doris, you mentioned earlier that you blamed yourself for Charlie's heart attack. Why is that?"

Doris says, "Charlie suffered chest pain that required bed rest in the last few years. Each episode seemed like it was getting a little worse. I was suspicious it was a heart problem of some kind. We went to St. Louis at the end of his selling season two years ago to meet with a heart specialist. He called Charlie's condition angina pectoris. He said it was a man's disease, thought to be due to stress, not contagious, and would likely become more severe with time. He offered no treatment other than rest and slowing down, which wasn't easy for Charlie. You were with him long enough to see that he stayed wound up tighter than an eight-day clock.

"We sell out of our home eight to nine months of the year, and he talked about selling full-time from home. You said Charlie talked about his business, so he must have mentioned that the weeks after the wheat harvest are the most profitable. Maybe as much as half of his entire year in only three to four weeks. As I always do, when he left on Sunday a week ago, I prayed that he'd return. I suppose you answered that prayer. Amy and I have talked about Charlie being in the short rows of life, so we are not shocked by his death, but that doesn't make our loss any less painful."

Luke says, "I experienced what a pleasure he was; I know you will be reminded of him often. You must think of tomorrow as though you are sending Charlie off on a long sales trip, and you will see him again one day." Doris and Amy are silent for a while.

After dinner, Luke helps Amy with the dishes despite Doris telling him to sit and relax. When they finish, he thanks the women for all they've done and says, "Goodnight." Luke plunks down on his porch bed and quickly falls asleep. While he sleeps, the women wash and hang his clothes out to dry.

Luke awakens in the wee hours to someone tapping on his shoulder and hair tickling his face with the same fragrant smell as his bathwater. Then Amy whispers, "I couldn't sleep, so I decided to see if you were."

Luke couldn't remember being at such a loss for words. He sits up, looks at Amy, and says, "Why can't you sleep?"

"It's your fault; you charmed me so much tonight that I can't sleep." Luke believes Amy is emotionally vulnerable and needs to talk, though he's not disappointed that she showed up.

A bright, low-hanging crescent moon lights up the room. Amy talks comfortably about her life and how they plan to manage things without Charlie. Luke can tell they knew Charlie's last day was not far off and had mentally prepared for it. Luke carefully answers Amy's questions by sharing details about his childhood, parents, core beliefs, ambitions, likes, dislikes, love of horses, and cowboy life. But he avoids discussing why he's going to Kansas City.

Amy says, "Excluding your war and King Ranch experiences, we had similar childhoods: our parents taught the same values."

Luke says, "I came to that conclusion while you were talking. Which last name do you use?"

Amy answers, "Bonner, although my father's last name was Bushnell. When Mom took Dad's last name, I followed suit."

Luke says, "I asked because I was born a Langley and raised by Garrelts. When asked my name at school and around town, I said, "Luke Garrelts," and it stuck."

Amy is dying to know if Luke has a girlfriend, but doesn't want him to think she's husband-hunting, so she asks no probing questions. Luke says, "I've enjoyed our conversation, but I need more sleep. Excuse me for saying goodnight."

Amy says, "Same for me, goodnight," and returns to her room.

Chapter 4: Charlie's Funeral
July 4th

Luke wakes up a little after sunrise and sees his clothes folded and stacked on the prep table. He dresses, brushes his teeth, combs his hair, goes to the outhouse, washes his hands, and walks into the kitchen.

"Did you sleep well?" Doris asks before turning toward the stove to tend to her frying pan.

"Yes, I had a good night. I woke up only once," Luke says as he looks at Amy with raised eyebrows and a smile.

Amy blushes noticeably and says, "Good morning, Luke," as sweetly as he's ever heard it.

As Luke sits down, Doris asks, "Will you go to the funeral? It's scheduled for ten o'clock to beat the heat. We have a family plot on Boot Hill. It's only a short buckboard ride away."

"I'll be glad to," is Luke's response.

To elevate the mood, Amy quips, "If we want to beat the rush and get a good seat, we must leave here by nine-thirty." Doris smiles and shakes her head, approving of Amy's lightheartedness to lessen the sadness.

On the way to Boot Hill, Amy tells Luke she wants to reward him for bringing her father home. Luke refuses to accept a reward for simply doing the right thing.

Hearing that conversation, Doris says, "That's very admirable of you. Instead of giving you cash, we'll take you to Brotherton's Clothing store right after the interment to get you some new clothes. We couldn't help noticing you could use some new ones when we washed them last night."

Luke knows she's right and decides she would be insulted if he refused her generous offer. He says, "I would appreciate that very much, but will the stores be open on the Fourth of July?"

Doris says, "Today is Wednesday, a regular workday for store owners. The activities planned by the city will draw customers to town beginning around noon. They'd be silly to keep their doors closed, but some do. I know Brotherton's will be open."

The gathering outside the small church surprises Luke. He thinks, *Charlie's funeral has drawn quite a crowd on such short notice; he and Doris must have been well-liked and respected by the community. The* crowd of over sixty squeezes into the little chapel, and some attendees are standing. Due to the group size and the heat and humidity, Barry and Reverend Cross discuss shortening the service and interment before entering.

Barry recites his generic funeral comments, adding that there was insufficient time to organize a post-interment reception. He says, "Charlie would say, 'Your time is better spent enjoying the holiday festivities with family and friends.' Doris and Amy asked me to thank you all for attending this morning."

Reverend Cross eulogizes Charlie for ten minutes, followed by the choir director, Gladys Goodnight, singing "Amazing Grace." Barry turns to Luke and asks, "Luke, since you're the last person to be with Charlie, is there anything you can add?"

Luke shakes his head, signifying that he will, smiles, stands, and says, "I believe my evening with Charlie Bonner was God's way of rewarding me." Luke points up and says, "The Man above pulling the strings knew I was a good listener, so He picked me." Muffled laughter interrupts Luke, and he pauses for the audience to quiet down. "Charlie loved to talk about his prized possessions, the two women in his life. My foster parents raised me, and I lost them as a teenager. Charlie awakened me to the fact that a family is one of God's precious gifts. I could see that Charlie's love was unbounded, and I thought how lucky I would be to feel that way someday. We talked well into the evening, and I found him smart, sincere, honest, kind, generous, and entertaining. He slept in the wagon, and his snoring rattled the inventory so much that it kept predators at bay. If the Lord lets Charlie continue snoring in Heaven, no one will ever again rest in peace." Everyone laughs and is charmed by Luke's sincerity and humor.

Bat Masterson puts his arm around Luke and says, "Damn, that was great." Doris and Amy are on either side of him, and they get on their tiptoes and kiss him on the cheeks. Luke is glad he came. Barry asks the pastor for a closing prayer, which he keeps brief. Then Barry announces the location of the interment.

Due to the heat, only a few close friends attend the interment, and Charlie is lowered into the ground while Mrs. Goodnight sings "Old Rugged Cross." After the Reverend Cross's final prayer, Doris and Amy thanked everyone for their attendance and took Luke to Brotherton's. Doris buys Luke two long-sleeved white shirts with blue stripes, two pairs of Levi Strauss denim trousers, five pairs of socks, and a rust-colored vest and matching jacket. Amy buys him black knee-high boots, a wide-brimmed black hat, two bright red neck scarves, and leather gloves. The women enjoy purchasing the clothing, and Luke looks more handsome each time he emerges from the dressing room; they spend $36.

Doris says, "Now you need a close shave and a fresh haircut; let's go to Marvin's barbershop."

Luke says, "I know I can't talk YOU out of anything, so let's go."

Marve walks around Luke and asks how he'd like it cut. Luke says, "I like it a couple of inches long in the back; trim up my mustache, the sideburns to mid-ear, and after that, whatever you think will look good. "

Marve says, "What if I left some chin and jawline whiskers?"

Luke says, "If you think it will look good, okay."

Marve says, "Anything I do will look good on you." Both women approve of Marv's opinion by nodding their heads with one eyebrow raised. After a hot towel to soften his whiskers, Marve shaves him and splashes on an alcohol-based aftershave that stings like the dickens but makes him smell delicious. They want to show him off, so they take him to the Dodge Hotel Dining Room and sit at the center table. He orders two slices of apple pie and milk. Amy watches without taking her eyes off him for even a second.

Chapter 5: Luke Likes Amy's Advice
July 4th continues

When they return to Doris' farm, Amy invites Luke to join her on the front porch for lemonade. There's a gentle south breeze, and they're shaded from the sun by the roof's overhang. Amy shows up barefoot with two glasses of lemonade. She's wearing a lightweight summer skirt hemmed up at her knees and a white short-sleeved blouse, missing the top two buttons, and no bra. Seeing Amy, Luke takes off his new boots and vest and unbuttons the top three buttons of his shirt. They sit on the porch floor facing each other and chatting while Luke disassembles and cleans his Henry rifle and Colt pistol, seldom looking at either.

Amy asks, "How long do you plan to stay in Dodge?"

"I need to leave in the morning," Luke says.

"Why can't you stay for a few days? I want to get to know you better, and we like your company," she confides.

"The feeling is mutual, but I have some important family business to see to in Kansas City," he says.

"What kind of business?" she inquires.

Luke pauses and says, "It's with my half-sister. It's about a subject I can't put in a telegram or a letter. We write often, but I haven't seen her in over a year. Sorry, I'm not able to be more open. If I were to tell you more, I'd have to start telling half-truths or lying. If you ever learned the truth, you would think it didn't bother me to lie to you, and that's not true. I admire you too much to ruin our friendship. I want to apologize for being too tired to talk much last night. I enjoyed our conversation and would like to get to know you better. Would you consider joining me tonight for more moonlit conversation on the patio?"

Amy says, "I like you too, and I'm not going to badger you, but I don't like not understanding your problem. It's a long way to

Kansas City, like 350 miles. So, it's four days on horseback and less safe than taking the Santa Fe."

Luke says, "The train is quicker but expensive."

"Heck, I'll loan you the money," Amy says.

Luke says, "You've cornered me. So, I'll tell you a little more. I prefer to avoid public transportation. Perhaps I should not have told you that."

Amy sat quietly before suggesting, "Why don't you take Dad's wagon? If you also plan to avoid hotels, the wagon will keep you from sleeping on the ground, and the seat, with its leaf springs and backrest, is way more comfortable than a saddle. Dad would drop the reins and sleep while old Ginger plodded along. Before I forget, you can count on me showing up tonight."

"Great, I'll hear you if you knock quietly; when poked, I jump," Luke says.

"I didn't think you jumped last night," she says.

"My heart did," Luke says. "It wasn't expecting anyone."

"Oh, I'm sorry," Amy says.

Luke says, "I agree; your father's wagon would make for a safer and easier trip. I found that to be true while bringing him home. What if I stayed in Kansas City for several weeks?"

"Mom and I are not going to be using it. We've already talked about selling it. She plans to put the wagon signs out by the road and sell out of her home. If you're not back here in a few months or decide never to return, you can ship the wagon and Ginger on the train."

"I need to come back," Luke says.

"Why is that?" Amy asks.

"On the day we arrived, Fury's head was bobbing, so I watched, and he was limping on his right front hoof. I found a stone wedged underneath his shoe that I couldn't get out without causing him pain, so I found a nail puller in your barn and removed the shoe. If it's okay, I'd like to leave him here."

Amy thinks, *Thank you, Fury,* and says, "We'd love to have Fury as our guest. I'll watch his hoof; does it need a liniment?"

"No, I don't think so. The hoof should heal quickly with rest and no riding for a week."

"Okay, I'd like to use your father's wagon for the next four to six weeks, but I insist on having Doris' approval."

"I'll talk to her about you using it in the morning. Now, think about this: a traveling salesman is a great cover. And if you'd let me come along, it would be even more convincing." Luke is surprised and pleased by Amy's suggestion. He thinks, *Amy is willing to go out on a limb to advance our relationship. So am I, but until she knows my situation, it's not fair to her; there's a possibility I could end up a jailbird or dead.*

Luke drinks Amy's lemonade and says, "A wagon trip to Kansas City will be at least a week long. It'll be tiring and hot with dusty days and sleepless nights. Except in the cities, good food, bathing, and lemonade aren't possible. I don't want to put you through that. When I return to Dodge, I promise to stay long enough for us to decide about a long-term relationship. At that time, I will tell you everything about this "thing" I'd rather keep to myself for now. Then you can decide what to do about me."

Amy says, "I'll hold you to that. Say, you must clean those guns a lot; you've only looked at them a few times."

"Yep, every few days, whether I fire them or not, and when they get wet," Luke says.

Amy wants more alone time with Luke, so she gets enough whisky in Doris to send her to bed early and keep her there until morning. So, while Doris is in town at the feed and tack store, Amy gets two whisky bottles out of the cupboard. She pours both contents into one bottle and puts tea in the empty one; then, she tells Luke her plan.

After dinner, Amy gets three one-ounce whiskey tumblers and begins a series of toasts to her father. After each, they click glasses and empty them in one gulp. Amy refills Doris' tumbler with whiskey, and Luke fills theirs with tea. After six toasts, Doris is almost cross-eyed, and Amy guides her to the bedroom.

Luke thinks, *This girl is clever beyond her years. If I married her, she would keep me on my toes. I wonder how old she is.*

After getting Doris into bed, Amy changes into a cotton nightgown and goes to the back porch, but Luke isn't there. Then she remembered he said he would be on the patio. She finds him in one of the four reclining chairs that Charlie made. To get his attention, she knocks twice on the back of a chair, draws it close to Luke, and asks, "Is there danger waiting for you in Kansas City?"

"No, my concern is getting there. I'll feel safe when I get there. I know my way around the city and have a few friends besides my sister. I worked on several cattle drives to the stockyards. After getting paid, I'd usually stay a week to rest and regain lost weight before returning home."

"Why do you drive cattle from South Texas to Kansas City rather than Dodge?" Amy asks.

Luke explains the economics of Kansas City over Dodge, and Amy says, "That's interesting; I didn't know that folks back East would pay so much for a Texas steak. They have a lot more money than folks around here. Are cattle drives dangerous?" Amy asks.

"They can be at times."

"Like what?" she asks.

Luke says, "Good men have died trying to turn and stop two thousand stampeding longhorns in a thunderstorm or a hailstorm. Lightning can start a prairie fire with the same results. Fending off cattle rustlers; negotiating safe passage through Indian land;

avoiding rattlers, copperheads, and cottonmouths; fording a raging river; finding safe drinking water; disease, sickness, and serious injury; infrequent bathing and dirty laundry. Perhaps the most dangerous is food poisoning from Cookie's chuck wagon concoctions; his stews didn't always have fresh kills."

"You make driving cattle sound risky," Amy says with a look of concern.

"After a few years, I knew how to deal with most of those problems," Luke says. "My experiences helped me to understand the significant loss of life experienced by pioneers naive to the perils of the 2,000-mile trek on the Oregon Trail. The estimated death rate was one out of every ten. A clever journalist said the Oregon Trail is the longest cemetery in the U.S."[11]

"I believe taking Charlie's wagon to Kansas City is an excellent idea. It would give me an unquestionable reason for being alone on the road, whereas riding Smokey would not. I'm flattered by how much you trust me."

"If you stop in towns, old ladies will gather around the wagon and ask about Charlie. I get asked if I knew Dad had a widow waiting for him in every town." Answering 'No' to that cleverly worded question plays right into a gossip's hands because they can say, "Amy told me she didn't know that her father had girlfriends all over Kansas."

Luke says, "A gossip will make up a story out of jealousy; their objective is to besmirch whomever it's about."

"Charlie was an easy target because he was gone most of the summer," Amy says.

Luke is concerned about getting Doris' okay and says, "I need to leave by mid-morning. That doesn't give you much time to get your mother's approval."

"I think Mom likes you too much to say, 'no.'"

"I hope so. Tomorrow will be a long day; I need to get some sleep."

"Would you allow me to join you until morning?" Amy asks.

"If you agree not to talk so I can sleep, then okay," Luke says. He remembers Charlie saying Amy was five in 1865, so he knows she's seventeen or eighteen. He decides to test her truthfulness. "Charlie said you were a teenager. How old are you?" Luke asks.

"Almost eighteen," Amy answers.

"What's almost? What's the date?" Luke asks.

"It's next month, the twenty-first day of August."

"You ARE a girl beyond your years," Luke says.

"Thanks, I'll take that as a compliment, and I PROMISE to let you sleep. So, how old are YOU?" Amy asks inquisitively.

"I'm twenty-eight," Luke answers proudly. "My stepmother didn't know my exact birthday, so she celebrated it on March eleven, her birthday, which was fine with me." Luke goes inside, undresses, lies on the mattress, turns his back to Amy, pulls the trailing edge of the cover forward, and says, "Jump in." Without hesitation, Amy snuggles in; her heart is pounding. Luke flips the cover backward over them but remains quiet due to being aroused by Amy's warm body pressing against his and the scent of her perfume. She is no less affected by her first experience of sleeping beside a man, one she finds irresistible.

When the dawn lights up the porch, Amy kisses Luke softly on the shoulder and says, "See you at breakfast." As she gets up, her thin nightgown is transparent, revealing the outline of her sculptured, firm, youthful body. The bed sheet is wrapped around Amy's leg, and she must hold the pose long enough for Luke to unwrap it and ask himself, *Should I delay my trip to Kansas City?*

Chapter 6: Amy Gets Doris' Approval
July 5th

Amy is in the kitchen frying bacon, boiling coffee, and chopping up vegetables for a stew that Luke will take on his trip. She wants the aroma of coffee and bacon to stimulate Doris' brain enough to jolt her awake. Amy is mulling over how she'll convince Doris to let Luke take the wagon to Kansas City.

Believing that honesty is the best policy, she tells Doris she thinks Luke might be a good catch. She'll explain that loaning the wagon for a few weeks is another way to show their appreciation, and he will return because of Fury's stone bruise. Amy decides she will follow Doris to the chicken coop. Along the way, she'll suggest that Doris might drop a few eggs in her condition, so it's better to let her do the gathering.

Amy doesn't have to wait long for Doris to come into the kitchen, holding her head and saying, "I'll go get the damn eggs."

Amy says, "I think I'd better go with you, Mom. You look a little unsteady this morning." Doris faces a significant challenge staying on the narrow stone walkway about one hundred steps to the chicken coop. Once there, Amy says, "Mom, only eight of our chickens are laying, so by my math, we now have four fryers. If you accidentally drop a couple of eggs, there may not be enough; Luke has a big appetite."

Doris agrees, and Amy slowly gathers them by carefully placing them in a sling she makes by holding up the bottom of her blouse with one hand. She tells Doris of her conversation with Luke. When she finds where the eighth fertile chicken is nesting, she asks Doris what she thinks. Doris says, "I also like Luke, and I understand why you'd like to get to know him better."

Amy says, "After you went to bed, we talked on the back patio for about three hours. If you and Dad had had a son, you would have raised him like Luke."

Doris says, "We won't miss the wagon for a few weeks, and I trust him. And I like helping him through a rough patch, so tell him to use it."

Amy thinks, *That was easy.*

When they return from gathering eggs, they find Luke at the kitchen table, drinking coffee and smiling. Doris talks nonstop about what he needs for the trip to Kansas City. Amy gives Luke a subtle "yes" nod to let him know he has Doris' approval.

After enjoying Amy's breakfast of scrambled eggs, bacon, fried potatoes, buttermilk biscuits, and coffee, Luke and Doris prepared the wagon for his trip. They replaced Charlie's mattress and bedding with the one Luke slept on for the last two nights. Then they filled the kerosene can and topped off the coffee, sugar, salt, and flour tins. Luke fills the water barrel while Doris goes to the root cellar and returns with four half-full feed sacks of sweet potatoes, apples, carrots, and green beans, which she places in Ginger's feed box next to the water barrel. Then, Doris disappears into the barn and returns carrying a water bucket, a feed bag for Smokey, and a twenty-five-pound bag of oats.

Luke says, "I don't think you have forgotten a thing; Smokey will enjoy this trip."

Amy filled the wagon's containers with garden vegetables, biscuits, jerky, hard-boiled eggs, rice and beans, cornmeal, and a pot of stew she'd worked on for two hours. Luke and Amy carry the containers to the wagon, and Doris places them in the spaces Charlie crafted for each.

Amy says, "I want to show you something I doubt you would ever find." She drops the tailgate and rolls the mattress forward, and Luke gets a faint whiff of Amy's perfume. He breathes deeply through his nostrils while closing his eyes and mentally pictures her in the see-through nightgown. Amy puts her index finger through a knothole in the corner of the floor and lifts a one-foot by two-foot piece of false flooring that perfectly matches the rest. Then she says, "This is where Dad kept his cash box and, at times, expensive silver items that he delivered to his wealthy customers."

Luke says, "How clever," but he gives no hint of being excited about the hidden compartment.

Luke goes to the porch and returns to the wagon with what he wants to take on the trip. He tosses his bedroll on the mattress and stows his rifle, bandolier, old boots, and saddle bag with his new clothes and toiletries beneath the driver's seat. Luke leaves Smokey's tack and the packsaddle in the corner of the back porch. He hopes they will remind Amy of him every time she walks past. It's nine o'clock, and he's anxious to leave.

Doris approaches the two and says, "Luke, this road forks about a half mile out of town; take the south route. Charlie always said it was better, and more importantly, the Cavalry out of Fort Dodge patrols it. If I remember correctly, it's 150 miles to Wichita."

"Except for the cavalry patrols, that's what I remember," Luke says.

Doris says, "Oh, I forgot you've been here before. It's not my old age; it's from drinking to Amy's tributes to my dear Charlie last night."

Luke tells the women, "I plan to make fifty miles daily by keeping the horses fresh. Each horse will take four turns pulling the wagon. Each turn will last approximately one hour and fifteen minutes, depending on road conditions, followed by a fifteen-minute break. During the switch, they'll rest, graze, and drink, and I'll hand-feed some treats. Our lunch break will be on the fourth switch for a full hour. Their eight turns add up to ten hours on the road. They'll stay fresh and rested because they'll only pull a light load for five hours a day; walking next to the wagon for them isn't much harder than standing." Luke says, "I hope to average five miles per hour or better, and if all goes well, we'll be in Wichita by late afternoon on the third day."

Amy has been adding up Luke's travel time and, with concern in her voice, says, "You'll be on the road almost THIRTEEN hours a day!"

"Yeah, well, I don't have much else to do with my time. The story about the race between the hare and the tortoise taught me that slow and steady wins the race," Luke says with a big grin. "However, if we haven't made fifty miles and their energy is good at the end of the day, we may go longer."

Doris says, "That plan will be good for Ginger. She will have a lighter-than-usual load, get to rest, and have something to eat and drink frequently; she'll do well."

Luke says, "Ginger's days may be a little longer than she's used to, but probably less work overall. If I see her tiring in her fourth turn, I'll cut it short and let Smokey make up the time. Rest assured that I'll care for Ginger like she's mine."

Seeing all they have done so quickly, Luke says, "Ladies, I'm overwhelmed by all you have done for me and allowing me to use your wagon. I have more than enough provisions to get past Wichita. It will be nice not to have hardtack and jerky three times a day."

Doris asks Luke if the wagon should have more inventory. Luke says, "I think it's about right. If asked, I plan to say I'm going to Kansas City to restock. Therefore, I want the inventory to appear as if it is low. Also, I don't plan to spend time trying to sell."

Amy looks at him piercingly with bright blue eyes and says, "When you can, please send me a telegram. I'd like to know where you are and that you're okay."

Luke smiles and says, "I'll do my best to send you a telegram at Wichita, Topeka, and Kansas City. And I'll not leave Wichita and Topeka until I receive your return message. In Kansas City, I'll be staying at the Cattlemen's Inn. The owners are Ray and Virginia Simms; they're good friends." Amy gives Luke a kiss that will linger in his memory until he sees her again; Doris is surprised by her public display of affection.

Luke climbs into the wagon, unwraps the reins from the brake handle, flicks his wrists so that the reins fall gently on Ginger's back, and clicks his tongue. Ginger leans into the harness and begins slowly pulling away. Doris's collie, Daisy, chases the wagon and yaps at the left rear wheel. When Luke gets to the road leading into Dodge, he looks back to where he left the women, and they're standing right where he left them, waving. He stands and returns their wave by waving his hat. Daisy gives up her chase and circles back to Doris' side.

He turns around and settles in for a long day. Smokey is walking on the right side of the wagon, and Luke begins talking to him. Smokey's ears turn toward Luke, and he veers closer because he doesn't want to miss a word.

When Luke gets to where the road forks, he takes the south fork and sees a faded "Wichita 150" sign pointed in the wrong direction. His pocket watch says it's almost ten o'clock, and because of the late start, he decides to take the lunch break during the third shift, which will be about two-thirty. He plans to cut their one-hour break in half and should camp at about ten o'clock. The sun will have set, but with clear skies, he'll have enough moonlight to care for the horses.

Luke is eager to find out exactly how much is in the saddlebag. Based on what he saw when transferring the bundles from the pillowcase at 2-Handles, he believes it could be significant. The day passes without incident, and twilight has almost petered out when Luke sees a sign shot full of holes with "Wichita 100" written on it. He congratulated himself on estimating the distance they would cover.

He decides it's time to find a place for the night where the rig will be out of sight. Within a mile, he spots a small hill on the right that rises abruptly. When he gets behind it, he stands on the wagon seat and convinces himself that the wagon is not visible from the road. He knows Smokey and Ginger won't wander off, and he lets them graze on the grass and sets out both buckets filled with water.

He's anxious to eat and count the money. He warms a half bowl of stew over the kerosene lantern and crumbles two butter biscuits into it to soak up the juices. He replaces the lid on the boiling pot and ties it down using a wire Amy designed to keep it from sliding off.

Luke ties his grass-eating security guards to each end of the wagon. Then he gets the saddlebag from under the wagon seat, walks bent over and sideways back to the mattress. Then he removes the clothes, dumps the bundles, and stacks them by denomination. All the bundles are the same size.

BILLS	
$1 =	600
$2 =	800
$5 =	2,000
$10 =	3,000
$20 =	26,000
($32,400)	

He counts the number of bills in one of the $20 bundles; it has one hundred. He counts six bundles of $1 bills and writes 600 on the wagon floor with one of Charlie's pencils. He counts four bundles of $2 bills and writes 800; four bundles of $5 bills and writes 2,000; three bundles of $10 bills and writes 3,000; thirteen bundles of $20 bills and writes 26,000. He sums the numbers and circles the total.

Luke decides he'll put the money in his old cavalry boots. He retrieves them from under the seat and drops the key to Tom's gun safe into one of them. Luke makes two equal-sized stacks and puts a stack in each boot, leaving plenty of room to stuff in Charlie's dirty socks and drawers. Then he slides the  boots to the back of the compartment and puts the rest of Charlie's dirty clothes and polishing rags in front. To let him know if anyone opens the false flooring, he places three barely noticeable pebbles in the narrow gap between the boards that will fall when opened. He puts his clean clothes back into the saddlebag and returns it underneath the wagon seat.

Luke calculates the value of the gold coins in the same way. He

COINS	
$1 =	68
$5 =	130
$10 =	150
$20 =	140
($488)	

counts sixty-eight Liberty coins and writes $68 on the floor, twenty-six half-eagles for $130, fifteen eagles for $150, and seven double eagles for $140. He sums and circles the total and puts $88 in his pocket and saddlebag for spending money, and the remaining $400 in Charlie's cash box. Luke snuggles the cash box among the merchandise.

Luke's plan in Wichita is to exchange the coins for paper money and get a bank receipt. If he got held up before getting there, even a not-so-bright robber would know he should have a lot of cash because of his low inventory. So, he'll sacrifice the $400 to keep a robber from looking for more, he hopes.

He rubs the numbers until they disappear and tries to sleep. But he can only think about the money and can't wait to tell Jordan. Since the road conditions and the temperature had made for a relatively easy day for the horses, he thought they should rest well and be ready for an early start.

Chapter 7: Luke Meets The 7th Cavalry
July 6th

Luke is on the road by seven-thirty with Ginger in the harness. Within an hour, he comes upon a shack leaning to the north so much it would fall over without timbers bracing it at forty-five degrees. Hanging on the windmill is a sign with "watter 1$" scribbled and barely visible. When Luke gets closer, he sees a skinny man standing on the porch with a pipe; his long white hair and beard are flowing in the breeze. He wears no shirt or shoes, and the pant legs of the tattered bib coveralls are rolled up to mid-calf. He has one hand inside his pants, and the other scratches the ears of the mastiff at his side. The image does not incentivize a potential customer to stop for water.

As Luke passes the windmill, he shouts, "Howdy," and the dog barks, but the owner doesn't respond. Luke thinks, *"The old codger is deaf, or he's the only person who doesn't like Charlie."*

At their hour-long, midday stop, Luke has set out water buckets and is hand-feeding the horses when he sees what appears to be a cavalry troop approaching from the east. Within minutes, ten 7th Cavalry soldiers and four Clydesdales pulling a heavily built munitions wagon are looking at him. A young officer, trying to be authoritarian and intimidating, addresses Luke from his saddle sternly, saying, "I'm Second Lieutenant Joel Jackson. Sir, please state your name, destination, and business."

Luke says, "Howdy, I'm Luke Garrelts. I'm headed to Kansas City to visit my little sister."

"What does she do there?" the lieutenant asks.

"She works in a bank that her husband owns," Luke answers.

"What's his name?"

"It's J.R. McMann, and he owns the Commerce Bank," Luke answers. "Please don't ask me where it is. I haven't seen my sister in over a year. She married JR about nine months ago."

"I've heard that McMann name before. And I've seen this wagon often and talked to Charlie a few times. Why is it in your possession?" Luke explains the situation, and the lieutenant says, "You did the right thing taking him home."

"I don't deserve much credit because Dodge was right on my way." Luke wants the lieutenant to stop asking questions, so he asks, "What can you tell me about Colonel Custer up in Montana last year?"

"Well, sir, officially, not much, but I talked to a man who helped clean up the battlefield. He said the Indians did disgusting, almost unimaginable, things to the dead and dying soldiers spread over a battlefield of fifty acres. Custer's troops must have been overwhelmed and retreated in panic. The military doesn't want the truth of that battle known because it would encourage the Indians and tarnish Custer's reputation as a legendary Indian fighter. Sitting Bull set a trap for Custer along the Little Big Horn River; Crazy Horse was his second in command. There are no Chieftains more revered than those two; they're considered big medicine. That battle is called "Custer's Last Stand" by the Plains Tribes. For a long time, the Indians have been incensed over the government taking land granted to them in their Relocation Treaties. The government rubbed salt in the wound by making that land available to the railroads and settlers, the same people the Indians wanted off their land! Sending CUSTER up there to protect gold miners prospecting on the Sioux, Cheyenne, and Arapaho reservations stirred things up. Custer made the mistake of splitting up his troops and leading two hundred men into a massacre where the Indians outnumbered them ten to one. After the battle, the warriors returned to loot, scalp, and mutilate the soldiers' bodies."

Luke says, "Eventually, an English-speaking Indian with firsthand knowledge will spill the beans to a newspaper reporter, and Custer's Last Stand will make headlines nationwide."

"I imagine so," laments the lieutenant. "But there is more to the story. Crazy Horse ran around the Montana Territory, encouraging all the tribes to engage us in skirmishes. We got payback for the Little Bighorn at the Battle of Wolf Mountain in January.[12] Crazy Horse and 500 Braves got their butts kicked, but somehow Crazy Horse slipped away. The government has made life so miserable for the Cheyenne that Crazy Horse surrendered in Nebraska two months ago. Sitting Bull got tired of being chased, and his bunch hid somewhere in Canada for a while, but they're back now. Because Sitting Bull is the chief of the Sioux and their holy man, they'll do whatever he says."

Luke doesn't want the lieutenant, whose job is to look for trouble by asking questions, to read or hear about the problem at Addison. He thinks, *If the lieutenant goes to Dodge, he might ask Bat Masterson about me because I have Charlie's wagon. And the lieutenant might decide to visit Doris and Amy to verify my story. If so, he'd learn I was from the Amarillo area, left a lame horse, and met Charlie one hundred miles west of Dodge. The lieutenant could piece together a timeline that would make me a suspect.* Fearing that possibility, he asks, "Are you all headed to Dodge City?"

"No, we're not; we're out of Fort Dodge. We're returning to the garrison. We're not allowed to go into the city. Every time a soldier romances a dance hall girl in the Long Branch, a jealous, liquored-up gunslinger starts a fight, which never ends well for the soldier. Those bastards do it to brag about the number of notches on their pistol grips."

Luke is relieved to hear the lieutenant's answer and says, "Your big wagon makes me think you've been gone for a while."

"Yep, we have. We're finishing an expedition to turn back Indians headed to a big powwow in South Dakota on the Sioux reservation. We're supposed to escort them back to their reservation. We went as far east as Fort Riley, circled into Nebraska, and then back down to Wichita. There are Indians everywhere, but we can't catch them. They have fast ponies, and they're damn good horsemen. If we catch any, they'll have to be snoozing. I'm supposed to take second offenders to jail. I'm not sure how I'll know; they're damn sure not going to tell me. All the forts have expeditions out doing this reconnaissance-type operation."

"How big of a deal is this powwow?" Luke asks.

"It's big; I expect all the tribes will go. So, the Apache, Arapaho, Cherokee, Cheyenne, Choctaw, Comanche, Creek, Crow, Chickasaw, Kiowa, Kickapoo, Osage, Pawnee, Ponca, Tonkawa, Sioux, Sauk, Fox, Kansas, Kaw, Dakota, Seminole, Shawnee, Black Feet, Iowa, and Ottawa will be there. And there will be many smaller, lesser-known tribes."

"So, what's the purpose of the powwow?" Luke asks.

"To talk about a whole string of grievances with the U.S. Government. Besides the government taking back land promised in many treaties with tribal leaders following the Relocation Act of 1830, they've done nothing to stop the massive immigration of European settlers squatting on their reservations. The government expects them to stay on their new land, adopt the culture of white settlers, and befriend trespassers. We aim to see that they do that; it's not easy for them or us. (An Author's comment: *According to the census, the U.S. population increased from 5.3 to 76.2 million between 1800 and 1900.*)[13]

"The enormous herds of buffalo, often a mile wide, no longer exist. Who would have thought that was possible? It's sad; it makes the Indians crazy, and I can't blame them." (Author's note: *The buffalo population of more than 60 million in the late 1700s was down to less than 1,800 by 1900.)*[14]

Luke says, "It doesn't help for Buffalo Bill Cody to tell his hunting parties that every time they kill a buffalo, they kill an Indian."

"Yeah, the newspapers quoted him saying something like that. Then I heard Cody denied it and blamed some colonel or general," the lieutenant says. "When the chiefs agreed to the treaties, they didn't foresee the abuse that would befall them. Their resistance amounts to skirmishes intended to run off trespassers, but that doesn't work. I understand their frustration and why they're planning to have a powwow.

"The Indians know they can't defeat the U.S. Military. They don't have cannons, enough rifles, or an unlimited supply of ammunition and men. They have tried suing for breaking the treaties and our strict policies and punishment. But they won't win a battle in any court of law; they're in a no-win situation. Have you encountered Indians since leaving Dodge?"

Luke says, "I've not seen any hide or hair of an Indian. I heard Indians stay off this road because y'all patrol it regularly."

"Yeah, until the South Dakota powwow came up, we patrolled it weekly from Wichita to Dodge City. I know this road like the back of my hand. After listening to that fellow who had clean-up duty at Little Bighorn, I'm glad we didn't engage a war party. Otherwise, I'd be short a few men. They are fierce fighters and now have Henry rifles for Chrissake! The rumor is they are better shots on horseback than most cavalrymen standing flat-footed."

"Say, before you go, have you bought a newspaper in the past few days?" Luke asks.

"I don't waste time reading newspapers; they're full of shit," the lieutenant says. "Before we leave, I need to check your wagon. I don't believe you've lied to me, but my superior expects me to be thorough. You could have an Indian or two hiding in there."

Luke replies, "I understand."

The lieutenant points at one of the men and then to the wagon. The guy climbs in the back, pokes around for less than a minute, and returns to the lieutenant, saying, "As the signs say, he sells housewares."

"I appreciate your honesty, Mr. Garrelts, and I hope you have a safe trip to Kansas City," the lieutenant says sincerely.

"Likewise," says Luke.

The lieutenant announces, "Mount up!" And seconds later, he barks, "Move 'em out!"

Luke is glad they're gone. He refills the horses' water buckets and finishes hand-feeding sweet potato slices and carrots. Luke eats the last of Amy's stew, three big buttermilk biscuits, carrots, and radishes. He decides to spend the night at one of the roadside businesses, believing the added safety will be relaxing. The lieutenant has caused him to be a little behind schedule, but they should make fifty miles by seven o'clock with four more turns in the harness. If Smokey performs well on his last turn, he could extend it by thirty minutes.

Luke passes an attractive roadside business at about six o'clock. With plenty of daylight remaining and Smokey showing no fatigue, he decides to go a few more miles before stopping for the night. Shortly after seven, he comes across a road sign on his right with "Wichita 50" and thinks, *The horses have done well; it's time to stop.*

A run-down relay station is a quarter mile ahead on the left side of the road. Luke would have believed it abandoned had a swayback draft horse not been watching them. Smokey is tired, so

Luke decides to talk to someone about staying there. He has no sooner said, "Whoa, when he sees a gimpy codger with an eye patch, shotgun, and a German Shepard with a grey face.

The old man says, "Hello there, my name is Roscoe Moore, and the name of that fleabag that's going to sniff your butt as soon as you climb down is My Dog. I didn't waste much time thinking about a name for him. My Dog doesn't know come here from sic 'em, but he's a good companion and keeps my feet warm on a cold night. The Belgian's name is Caesar; he enjoys having company. I've seen this rig before; where's Charlie?" Luke tells Roscoe the same story he told the lieutenant, introduces the three of them, and asks if they can spend the night with Caesar.

Roscoe says, "Sure, the water is one dollar for each horse. Open the big gate at the back, and there are eighty acres of fenced pasture for them to graze on." Then Luke offers to share Amy's jerky, biscuits, and vegetables.

Roscoe says, "I'd be happy to share your grub. Do you have coffee beans?"

"I do," Luke says.

"Oh, good. I'll grind some and make a big pot to have enough for breakfast."

During dinner, Luke asks, "Would you believe I've never taken a stagecoach anywhere?"

"Well, you're young. Coaches are for older folks, widows, women with small children, and rich folks with a bug up their ass," Roscoe said.

"This place must have been a very nice relay station at one time, right?" Luke asks.

Roscoe says, "Yep, this was a Home Station. The difference is that we offered rooms and meals; the relays didn't. I started as a Whip, but after a couple of bullet holes and hemorrhoids the size of plums, they made me a Hostler. I did that until the pain of arthritis and the dang horses stepping on my broken toes became intolerable. The owners felt sorry for me and made me the Keeper.

"This place was shut down by Santa Fe laying rails between Dodge and Wichita. It took less than a year to end stagecoach service, and the Southwestern Stage Company sold it. The buyer acquired it for almost nothing and attempted to operate it as a hotel and restaurant, but it wasn't profitable. Now, it's just a watering hole and rest stop.

"The outfit that bought this place sent a young fellow here over a year ago to haul off everything of value. He told me I could stay here as a security guard until the next owner ran me off. He did me a favor and left old Caesar, so I'd have transportation. You don't work for the new owner, do you?"

"Oh, no," Luke says, realizing Roscoe doesn't remember his story about how he got Charlie's wagon.

"Good, I have no place to go. I've been getting along by keeping that old windmill pumping and charging a buck for water. I feel like I'm just hanging around here waiting to die."

"Cheer up; I'm thrilled you're here. Do you have any recent newspapers?" Luke asks.

Roscoe says, "When I remember, I will ask customers if they have a Wichita or Kansas City paper. If they do, it's nothing but political puke! So, you're interested in the news?"

"Yeah, I like knowing what's happening in the country."

"That's because you have a future, and you're smart," the innkeeper says.

Luke says, "I'm road-weary and need sleep. But I'll sleep better if I wash up first. Is it okay if I take a bath in the horse tank?"

Roscoe says, "Help yourself. My water well is great, and the windmill keeps the horse tank brim-full, but it's cold. I'm out here alone, without much company, so I don't need much bathing. If you get naked, Caesar will likely stare."

Luke feels safe in the corral because he's out of sight behind the big relay station. Smokey and Ginger return from grazing to drink, and he cuts several apples in half for them. He closes the gate to the pasture, tells Smokey to be on guard for strangers, lowers the lantern's wick, and goes to sleep thinking of Amy.

When Luke lets the horses out to graze the following morning, Roscoe says, "I'll fry bacon for both of us, and I have leftover coffee I can reheat."

"Good, I have hard-boiled eggs, a cheese wedge, and biscuits. With your bacon, I'll make you a couple of bacon, egg, and cheese biscuits; you'll love 'em."

After breakfast, while Luke cleans his rifle, Roscoe asks, "Are you any good with that over fifty paces?"

"Pretty good; why do you ask?" Luke says.

"A half dozen crows sit on the fence and eat more of my garden vegetables than I do. And to entertain themselves, they pester Caesar. Would you kill them for me?" Roscoe asks.

"I can shoot one, but the others will fly off," Luke says.

"They'll come back," Roscoe says.

"Yes, but I won't be here," Luke says. "You could build some clever ground snares, set them in your garden, and bait them with their favorite vegetable."

"Go ahead and plug one of the bastards, and I'll try your snare idea on the rest," Roscoe says.

One crow is on the ground a minute later, and the rest are long gone. After harnessing Ginger, Luke gives Roscoe ten $1 Liberty gold coins.

When Roscoe asks, "What's all this for?"

Luke says, "Should I return, I want you to be in business and selling garden vegetables." Before heading out, Luke throws My Dog a chunk of jerky, which he catches in mid-air and swallows without chewing.

As they leave, Roscoe shouts, "We'll be here waiting for you. My dog and I like your company, and I think Caesar is in love!"

Remembering his twilight bath in the horse tank with Caesar hovering right over him, Luke laughs, slaps his thigh, and says, "Until we meet again, you take care!" He couldn't help but think about the nice old man's lonely existence. But on the other hand, the place is so full of memories that there's probably no place he'd rather be.

Chapter 8: Luke Reads About The Fire
July 7th

Luke hopes to arrive in Wichita by late afternoon. The traffic is primarily wagons. After holding back at first, Luke feels obligated to be friendly, and he returns the odd Kansas gesture that says, "Hello." It's performed without enthusiasm by dipping one's head forward and pointing an index finger to the sky. One traveler recognized the wagon and waved excitedly, but slowly dropped his hand as they passed. Luke thinks, *I know he's wondering why I'm in Charlie's wagon.*

A man who looks to be Charlie's age reins in two big horses to a slow stop and asks, "Who in the hell are you? And where's Charlie?"

"Charlie is with his Maker," Luke answered.

"Well, shoot, I'm so sorry to hear that. Charlie was a good man and a friend, but he owed me five bucks. There's a widow in Wichita who's going to be disappointed."

"Because his wife is letting me use his wagon. I'll pay off his debt," Luke says.

"Oh, I like that. I'm Jake Cloud, and I'll take your money. It'll be nice not to spend the rest of my life bitchin' about Charlie owing me five bucks. Why did Doris let you use the wagon?"

Luke says, "I'll save you time listening to a long-winded story. I was with Charlie when he died and took him a hundred miles to his home. So, you know Amy and Doris?" Luke asks.

"Oh, I've known them since Amy was a little girl. I even knew Doris' first husband, Amy's father. I've often broken bread with Charlie's family; two sweeter women do not exist. I'm glad we met, but I must keep this rig moving," Jake says.

"Can you catch a Half Eagle?" Luke asks.

"If I can't, I'll scratch it out of the dirt," Jake answers.

Luke throws it underhanded; Jake snatches it out of the air and says, "Thanks; I'll tell Doris you settled Charlie's debt, and I'll ask her and Amy to dinner."

"That will be money well spent," Luke says.

Luke arrives at a livery at the end of town at half past six. He tells the owner he'd like to sleep in his wagon to protect his property.

The owner says, "This isn't the first time this rig has been in my corral; where's Charlie?"

"He passed away a week ago. His widow loaned it to me for a round trip to Kansas City. I left Dodge the day after his funeral, on the morning of the fifth."

"Dang, I'm sorry to hear that. There's no charge to sleep in your rig, but I'd like to barter the stabling of your horses for a coffee boiler. The bottom of mine has burned through; I noticed a small leak this morning."

"Okay, but comparing your prices and Charlie's, you'll have to kick in three dollars," Luke says.

"Sounds fair; can I see it first?"

Luke disappears into the wagon, and within seconds, he leans out the back and hands it to the livery owner, asking, "What do you think? Do we have a deal?"

The livery owner removes the lid, looks inside, and says, "We do."

"Good! I'm in a hurry to send a telegram. Where's the Western Union office?"

"It's on this side of the street about mid-town."

"And where can I find the newspaper office, a bank, and the best steak in town?"

"The *Wichita Beacon* is our only newspaper. Their office is right across the street from Western Union. The First National Bank is two doors past the *Beacon*. The Longhorn Hotel is across from the bank. They all have big signs and are close together; you can't miss 'em."

With those directions, Luke leads Smokey into the corral, removes his harness, unties Ginger, and watches them walk over to the hay and water. He puts the cash box under his arm and takes off for the Western Union office.

His telegram to Amy says, "Met Jake Cloud today. He's headed to Dodge to offer his condolences and a free dinner. I'm enjoying your food. If possible, send a return note this evening. I plan to leave early in the morning. Miss you, Luke."

The telegraph operator reads it and says, "At five cents per word, that'll be a dollar ninety plus ten cents to deliver it. Your telegram will be in her hands if she's home in fifteen minutes."

Luke pays and asks, "I need a receipt for that. How often do they print a new newspaper?"

"You're in luck. Our newspaper is put to bed on Friday afternoon, printed overnight, and available on Saturday morning. They will occasionally sell out on Sunday afternoons. The churchgoers buy 'em," the telegraph operator answers.

"Good, my mind is hungry for good news," Luke says.

"These days, there's damn little of that; here's your receipt."

Luke leaves the Western Union and walks to the bank, where he exchanges the $400 in gold coins for twenty-dollar bills and asks for a receipt. The cashier makes a receipt but wonders why. Luke then goes to the *Beacon's* office, buys their one-page publication, and takes it to the Longhorn Hotel and Saloon.

Luke had no sooner seated himself when a middle-aged waitress with a big, friendly smile said, "I'm Marge; I'm your waitress. What'll it be, handsome?"

Luke looks up and says, "I'm Luke; what do you recommend, gorgeous?"

"Oooh... WELL! A man your size could handle our "Steer on a Plate." It's a large T-bone, a baked potato with eyes the size of mine, a gravy boat, a pile of green beans, a basket of biscuits with butter and honey, and a large mug of beer. It's two dollars, and I'll refill the mug once for that price."

"Perfect, I'd like that steak well done, no pink."

Marge says, "I'll be right back with your beer. As she walks away, Luke studies her attire, befitting a saloon waitress. She's wearing a fringed, deerskin riding skirt, cowboy boots, and a long-sleeved white blouse that buttons up the front with a black string tie. Marge's beautiful, shiny black hair makes Luke think about the name of her tribe.

Marge sets a large mug of beer down in front of Luke. He thanks her, drinks half of it, and begins reading the newspaper. On the backside, in the lower right corner, as if it wasn't big news, is a small article with the headline: *Tom Addison Missing*. The article is an interview with the Addison, Texas, Undersheriff, Harry Rump. In it, Harry says, "A fire destroyed the Addison Cattle Company and Western Union offices on the evening of June thirtieth. The smell of kerosene and the rapid spread of the fire led the firefighters to believe it was arson. Mr. Tom Addison, the owner of the Addison Cattle Company, who lives at the back of the office, has not been seen. Abduction for a ransom demand is thought possible."

Luke takes a deep breath, exhales, and sits back in the chair. When Marge serves his meal, she asks if he is staying in Wichita or just passing through.

Luke says, "Just passing through. I plan to leave in the morning." And he begins wolfing down the food.

When he's through, Marge says, "Sweetie, you just set a record for consuming that menu item."

Luke excuses himself for eating like a pig by saying, "I've been on hardtack and jerky for several days. I blame my bad table manners on good cooking and a hearty appetite." Luke hands Marge three $1 Liberty coins and says, "We're good."

She says, "Thank you. May I refill your beer?"

"Thanks, I'll pass," Luke says. " It's a huge mug!"

"We serve breakfast at six," she says.

He folds the newspaper, slides it into his hip pocket, and walks out, saying, "I'll be your first customer in the morning."

"Looking forward to it," she shouts back.

When Luke approaches the livery, he encounters a dozen women milling around the corral gate. He climbs over the fence, walks to the wagon, and drops the tailgate. One of the women asks about Charlie. Without much detail, Luke explains Charlie's passing and his wife loaning him the wagon for a few weeks. The women quietly and reverently look down at their feet as if having a moment of silent prayer.

Luke climbs into the back and returns with a board listing each item and the price. He says, "I'm Luke Garrelts, and I'm sorry to be low on inventory, but I'm reducing everything by ten percent. Call it a Charlie Bonner special. I have six long-handled skillets, twenty or more three-piece sets of eating utensils, lots of butcher knives, cleavers, steak knives, ladles, large spoons, spatulas, three coffee boilers, and four boiling pots with lids. I used one of the boiling pots, but only once to make vegetable-beef stew. I'll cut the price on it by twenty-five cents." Five women walk away, and six of the seven stay to buy something before leaving.

The one lady remaining says, "Mr. Garrelts, my name is Jane. Charlie and I have had an infrequent but enjoyable platonic relationship for five years. I'd cook dinner for him, and we'd play card and board games and talk. Charlie was very entertaining. He enjoyed telling me about his wife, her daughter, and the garden. I was never jealous; I was just grateful for occasional male companionship. We only saw each other two to three times a year. I'd appreciate it if you wouldn't tell others about our friendship; it's how rumors start. If you don't mind, I'd like to know how he died."

Luke says, "I'll be glad to do that. But first, I assure you that your relationship with Charlie is safe with me." Luke then tells Jane about accidentally meeting Charlie, where he died, taking him home, meeting his family, the funeral, and the burial.

Jane is weeping; she thanks and hugs Luke and leaves. He walks a short distance to a grocery store to buy apples, carrots, and sugar candies. While the livery owner is locking up, Luke's horses have their heads in the back of the wagon. He walks closer, sees Luke feeding them, and says, "Here's what I owe you for the coffee boiler. Sleep well, and I'll see you in the morning."

Luke takes the coins and says, "I may be at the Longhorn when you get here."

"I doubt that. No one gets up earlier than me."

"We'll see," Luke fires back.

When the treats are gone, he puts the $20 bills from the bank in his old cavalry boots. He retrieves the cash box, places the newspaper and receipts from the bank and telegraph office inside, and stores the box where it would be easy to find among the hardware. If held up, he plans to claim that the cash box receipts are for money he deposited at the Wichita bank and money he had Western Union wire to Dodge. He realizes this ruse only works if the robbers can't read, which is why he thinks it will. He believes the thirty dollars in his wallet should be enough to make them happy and to believe that's all the money he has.

Even though Luke feels safe in the livery corral, he beds down with his rifle and pistol, snuffs the kerosene lantern, and erects an admirable teepee while enjoying Amy's lingering perfume. Luke wonders, *Could Amy have dribbled a few drops on my bedroll when I wasn't looking? I hope so.*

Chapter 9: Luke Trades With The Kiowa
July 8th

It's early Sunday morning on July eighth, and Luke is Longhorn's first customer. The same personable Marge recommends a half-inch thick slice of ham, three eggs, hash browns, biscuits, and coffee for a dollar; it's their breakfast special called "Pork on a Platter." He's out the front door when Marge finds he left another dollar tip, and she shouts, "Hey, big tipper! Come back soon!"

"If I'm ever back, I will."

After breakfast, Luke goes to the telegraph office. Amy answered his note last evening, and it said, "I miss you, too. Jake Cloud is an old friend. Everything is quiet because Wyatt Earp is in town, meeting with Bat. Please be safe. Love you, Amy." Luke rereads her closing, smiles, looks to the heavens, and nods approvingly. He thinks, *Her closing is a strong sign. It tells me her heart is growing fonder, just like mine* is. He folds the note into a small square and tucks it into his shirt pocket.

While Luke prepares the horses to leave, the livery owner fills one of his four canteens with coffee and says, "I like my new coffee boiler. Thanks for the trade. I hope you'll stop when you're back this way."

"I'll make a point of it," Luke says. "Did the bridge over the Arkansas River survive the May flood?'

"If you mean the Douglas Street bridge, it did."

"How much is the toll now?" Luke asks.

"It's free; it's now publicly owned. The city and state got together and bought it."

"I asked because, in the past, I waded across the river to avoid paying the toll. I can't do that with this rig," Luke says.

"Rather than paying the toll, you and everyone who could ford the river did just that. The Douglas bridge competed with smaller upstream and downstream bridges, offering lower fares. Rumor was that the buyers got a hell of a deal."

"Have a good day, and thank you for the coffee," Luke says.

"You have a good day also," the livery owner responded.

Luke is enjoying the fresh coffee and, after an hour, senses nature's unmistakable call. At the first switch of the horses, he stops close to a railroad overpass, puts Amy's telegram in the cash box, and squats next to the rear right wheel. With his back against the side of the wheel, he passes a large T-bone steak, a baked potato with all the fixings, a bowl of green beans, and six buttermilk biscuits. A horsefly bites Ginger on the neck, and she flinches, moving the wagon forward a foot. To avoid falling back into last night's dinner, Luke must lean forward and shuffle his feet to maintain his balance. He wouldn't have given the mishap a second thought if it hadn't been for an embarrassing moment. The brakeman in the caboose of a passing train saw Luke and clapped and whistled because Luke's "Johnson" was on full display.

He climbs into the wagon, laughing, but soon has questions about the *Wichita Beacon* story. Why, after five days, is it not front-page news that Tom Addison is missing? Why hasn't the gun safe been pried open? Why is there nothing about the posse? Why would the undersheriff think someone kidnapped Tom without a ransom note? Though confused, Luke couldn't be happier.

About one o'clock, he's looking for a place to take their noon break when he sees, less than a quarter mile ahead, ten riders and twice as many horses. As he gets closer, he can see they are Indians and appear to be waiting for him. He's having an "Oh, shit" moment, but when he gets close enough to see they're not wearing paint and their weapons are not held in an offensive position, he relaxes his grip on the Henry rifle.

A handsome Indian about his age raises his open hand over his head and lowers it slowly while rotating his wrist. Luke knows the gesture is the universal Indian sign of "I come, or I go, in friendship."

With excellent English for a man wearing only a loincloth, he says, "We would like to trade for some of your kitchen items. We have clothes our women make from buffalo and deer hides; are you interested?"

"Yes," Luke says without reluctance.

"We should get far enough off this road so a cavalry patrol cannot surprise us," the young Indian suggests.

Luke says, "You're safe. Only two days ago, I talked to a lieutenant from Fort Dodge who was responsible for patrolling this road. He was headed back to Fort Dodge and should be there by now. But let's get far enough away to avoid other travelers. I'll follow you."

"I must get approval," the athletic young warrior says. He struts over to an impressive-looking older man whose dress and horse convince Luke he's an important tribal elder. After the older man gives a nod of approval, the young Indian hurls himself onto his horse, nods in the affirmative to Luke, and heads north.

After a quarter of a mile, the group stops and dismounts behind a small bluff. Luke introduces himself, and the young Indian says his Kiowa name translates to "The Third Grandson of Lone Wolf." Luke asks if he could call him "The Third." He gets approval with a nod. Luke then asks if the older man is Chief Lone Wolf and gets another "yes" nod.

The Third says, "My grandfather must be extremely careful. Your government requires us to stay on our Oklahoma reservation unless we receive military permission to leave. They will not approve our request for a leave to hunt buffalo. The only leave they will approve is medical leave. Should the cavalry catch my grandfather off the reservation, he'll be detained in jail until he's tried unfairly and sentenced to many years in a military prison. He would likely die there based on stories from the few who've survived." Occasionally, The Third turns away from Luke, translates their conversation for Lone Wolf, and waits for his reaction.

Luke tells The Third he doesn't have much to trade but will lay out what he has on a poncho. The Third suggests that Luke use half the poncho and let them use the other half. The Indians pack many sizes of the same clothing items, but put only one of each on the poncho. While unloading his inventory, Luke asks The Third where they're going. The Third says, "To a powwow called by Sitting Bull, on the Sioux reservation in South Dakota."

Luke says, "The U.S. Military does not want that powwow to happen. Patrols from every fort in the surrounding states are trying to stop that event. The lieutenant said if they catch you, they will return you to your reservation unless it's your second offense. In that event, you will go to prison; I don't know for how long."

Luke can tell this information is not well-received by Lone Wolf. The Indians follow Lone Wolf about fifty steps and form a circle around him. When they return, The Third says, "My grandfather believes you speak the truth. Only two friends and I will go to the powwow to represent the Kiowa. My grandfather and the others will return home."

Lone Wolf and The Third look over Luke's goods and walk out of earshot to chat with the Braves. After a few minutes, The Third leaves the group and tells Luke they want to trade for all his items. They think a fair trade would be four buffalo blankets, a pair of moccasin boots, and two pairs of men's gloves. The Third assures Luke they have those items in enough sizes, so fitting him will not be a problem. Luke tells The Third that he tried on the knee-length buffalo coat and would like to include it in the trade. The Third says, "I will advise my grandfather of your request."

When The Third returns, he says, "My grandfather thinks the buffalo coat is a fair trade for the information you provided about the cavalry scouting Sitting Bull's powwow."

"He's very generous; please thank him for me," Luke says while looking at Lone Wolf, and Lone Wolf nods at Luke. Luke begins packing his new possessions and admiring their incredible softness and quality. He asks The Third, "Why are you carrying so much clothing?"

"We planned to trade our things for food, lodging, and crafts that other tribes would bring to the powwow. Initially, I thought your kitchenware would fetch a high price there. However, our women will be excited because they consider your things luxuries."

Luke asks, "How did you learn to speak such good English?"

The Third says, "A white teacher on the reservation taught me. My grandfather despises the white man's ways and refuses to learn English. I defied his wishes and attended school; many children do not go today. Grandfather will not speak it, but he understands English better than he lets on."

"Yes, I noticed that. Be safe on your trip to South Dakota. You could be riding into an ambush like Crazy Horse at Wolf Mountain," Luke warns.

"Now that we know they're looking for us, we won't get caught by fat men on tired old horses," The Third says.

They part ways, with both men saying, "Until we meet again." The Third and his two friends head north, Lone Wolf and the others go south, and Luke returns to the road and continues east. The rest of the afternoon is uneventful; the road is good, and Smokey pulls five turns in the harness.

At the intersection of a heavily traveled north-south crossroad, Luke reins Smokey into a commercial operation called "Crossroads Rest Stop." It sits off the road about a hundred paces. He goes inside and notes that it is well-stocked to meet the needs of travelers, but the prices are high. The posted price is $2 per horse for hay and water, and $2 per wagon to camp in the corral. Luke buys two ten-pound sacks of carrots and apples for $2 to go with the remaining sweet potatoes and green beans Doris put in the feed box. After paying for a night's stay, he pulls into the four-rail corral with three prairie schooners and a Conestoga wagon scattered about. He picks a location equidistant from the others.

He turns the horses loose to drink and feed on prairie hay. He creates a tabletop for apples, carrots, sweet potatoes, and green beans by dropping the tailgate halfway. After Luke has cut the treats to Smokey's preference, he says, "Chop-chop-chop!" And they come trotting.

After eating their treats, Luke ties them to the back of the wagon, goes to the Rest Stop's dining room, and has a $3 menu item like the one he had at the Longhorn. After dinner, Luke uses their outhouse, refills the canteens, feeds the horses the sugar treats he bought for a dollar, and climbs into the wagon for the night. Luke thinks, *Twelve dollars for the evening is expensive! However, it's understandable, considering the services they provide. There is value in having around-the-clock security, a dining room, and shops for groceries, drugs, clothing, toiletries, horse feed, tack, and a farrier during daylight hours every day.*

Before falling asleep, he thinks about his time with the Kiowa. He was impressed with The Third and pleased that Lone Wolf took his advice and returned to the reservation. He wonders who got the better of the trade and decides that he did because of the coat. He removes Amy's boots and undresses, pulls on the moccasins, and lies back on a buffalo blanket. The moccasins make his feet feel new. He imagines that Amy is the only thing softer than a buffalo blanket. He lays his rifle at his side, holds his Colt revolver in his right hand, and sleeps well with Smokey at the back of the wagon, providing security.

Chapter 10: The 2-Handles Family
July 9th

After breakfast, Luke meets an Englishman named William Tailor, who is harnessing his horses to a prairie schooner. Luke learns he's traveling west to Colorado with his wife and four children. Luke asks how far it is to Topeka, and Mr. Tailor says, "Close to eighty miles of jolly good road. It was an easy pull for my team."

Luke says, "That's good because I'm in a hurry."

Mr. Tailor asks, "How about the Wichita road?"

Luke answers, "I wouldn't call it an easy pull. Where in Colorado are you headed?"

Mr. Tailor answers, " Denver, my kid brother owns a smallholding near the city. He's been cultivating the soil since your war. We plan to settle nearby, so he and I can work the land together."

Luke says, "Best of luck to you all."

"Thanks, we'll bloody well need it. May the wind always be at your back," Mr. Tailor says while his family is climbing aboard.

It's July ninth, only the fifth day since he left Amy, and it feels like an eternity. After two hours on the road, Luke looks twice to believe what he sees. The prairie schooner in front of him has the name "2-Handles" burned into the tailgate. Luke wonders, *Can it be? Their heavily loaded wagon is moving at less than half of our speed. That explains why I caught up with them, even though I left their farm the day after they did and spent two days in Dodge.*

Luke is eager to meet the people and, if they seem approachable, try to explain spending a night in their barn. He decides he will follow until they stop. He's concerned about how they might react to his confession, so he wants a believable and sympathetic explanation. He decides the truth doesn't sound all that bad and begins considering ways he can strike up a conversation.

After a couple of miles, the 2-Handles wagon pulled off to the side of the road. Luke stopped behind them, filled the horses' water buckets, and pretended Ginger had a hoof problem. He lifted Ginger's left front hoof, held it securely between his thighs, and carefully poked around the horseshoe with his sheath knife.

The father came to the back of his wagon, nodded at Luke, and said, "Nothing serious, I hope."

Luke says, "She's been a little gimpy for the last few miles, but she's a good bluffer. I'm Luke Garrelts. Are you the owner of 2-Handles Ranch?"

"Yes, I am. I'm Joe Stout. I'm traveling with my family to Kansas City."

Luke says, "Joe, meeting you is an incredible coincidence. I have something to confess. A week ago, I spent the night in your barn. No one was around. I desperately needed a place to dry out and rest after being pounded hours earlier by two monster storms. The second was as big and bad as I had ever experienced. Perhaps I incorrectly assumed sleeping in your hay loft would be acceptable. Before leaving, I put six one-dollar Liberty Head coins in a Mason jar on the kitchen countertop. I thought it was fair payment for a bucket of oats, prairie hay, water, and six eggs. Otherwise, I did not touch a thing, but I made some barn swallows and a mother raccoon unhappy. Your livestock all looked fine. I hope you will forgive me for being so bold."

Joe asks, "Did we get any rain?"

"Your farmstead didn't," Luke answers. "The storms were east of it."

"Well, shoot, we need rain," Joe says.

Luke says, "Be careful what you wish for. The first storm was a toad-choker that made flat land look like a lake; gophers were learning to swim. The arroyo that your windmill overflows into would have turned into a raging river and could have endangered the livestock. There was a tornado in the second storm. I crossed its path; it left uprooted trees stripped of their leaves. I'm certain your buildings and animals would not have survived. If it hit a town, I expect to read about it."

Joe says, "This is the first time I remember not getting rain was good news. I'm glad we met, so your $6 in the Mason jar will not be a family mystery. If you stop again, I'll give you a better deal. You must have just missed my mother and father. They live two miles west and come over every other day to check on things. I promised the girls we'd visit their cousins after the wheat harvest. We're on our way to their farm near Kansas City. How'd you come to have Charlie's wagon?"

Luke says, "I met him late afternoon when I left your place. We didn't know each other, but we decided to camp together. To save time, Luke tells Joe an abbreviated version of the story he's told others in the past few days."

Joe says, "Charlie stayed in our barn a few times, but not lately. I think we're further than he prefers to travel now. My girls will be disappointed to hear he died."

Luke asks, "I stayed at the Crossroads Rest Stop last night. Why didn't you?"

"We stopped, but I kept moving when I saw their prices. We stayed a couple of hours past there for half of Crossroad's price," Joe said.

Luke says, "How'd you know?"

Joe says, "We made this trip two years ago. Crossroads is new; that's why I stopped. I was impressed; it's well-stocked. I bought some chocolate for the girls."

Three girls and a barking Collie poke their heads out of the back of the wagon, and Luke says, "Hi, girls. What's his name?"

"Boswald," the girls respond in unison.

"That's a big name," Luke says while smiling broadly.

The oldest girl says, "We shortened it to Bossy."

"Are you having a good time?" Luke asks.

The oldest girl answers, "We enjoy the days, but the nights get SO COLD! We all snuggle up next to Bossy."

Luke laughs and says, "It can get surprisingly chilly on a clear night. I have a cure for that." He goes into the back of the wagon and comes out with three Kiowa blankets.

Joe says, "I can't afford those."

"And I don't want to sell them," Luke says. "I'm just loaning them to the girls until I get your way later this year or early next."

"These buffalo hides are amazingly soft. I wonder how they do it?" Joe says.

"And they're incredibly warm," Luke says.

"I am glad you stopped, but I'm sorry your horse is lame."

"Eh, she's not. She hoped I'd notice her fake limp and switch her with the palomino."

Joe's wife has been quietly listening. She leans out of the wagon and says, "Hi, I'm Mary. Thank you for loaning the girls your beautiful blankets; you're very generous. And, happily, there will be no arguing tonight over who gets to sleep with Bossy."

Luke says, "Joe said you have relatives near Kansas City. I have a married baby sister living in Kansas City. I'm taking a day off in Topeka to rest before seeing her. Since y'all know this road so well, can you recommend a reasonably priced place to stay?"

Mary turns to face Joe with an expression that conveys she expects him to answer Luke's question. Joe says, "At your speed, you can make it to a nice place on the right about thirty miles from Topeka. It's a renovated Home Station that Southwest Stage once owned. I think it's called The Trail Dust Inn.

"I remember the Trail Dust; I just never stayed there. When leaving Crossroads this morning, an Englishman told me the road ahead is jolly good," Luke says.

Joe laughs and says, "It usually is."

"That's my memory, but it never hurts to ask," Luke says. "I haven't been on this road for several years."

Mary says, "These extremely excited girls with the beautiful blankets are, from the tallest, Ester, Sarah, and Mariam. I overheard them introducing you to Bossy."

"Nice to meet you all. In case you didn't hear me earlier, my name is Luke. Again, I must be on my way." He hangs the watering buckets on the hooks at the back of the wagon, climbs up into the seat, and cues Ginger to lean into the harness. Luke hears the Stout girls shouting departing comments, "Thank you, Mr. Luke!"

"Thank you for the blankets!"

"Come see us, Mr. Luke!"

Ginger isn't making her usual pace, so Luke has Smokey pull the last thirty minutes of Ginger's fourth turn. Luke likes that he's less than thirty miles from Topeka. Luke pays The Trail Dust Inn's owner for one night in the corral and sleeps in the wagon rather than paying for a room. Luke ensures his horses have everything they need before finishing his remaining food scraps.

He stretches out on the mattress and tries to relax, but his mind searches for a way to get the money safely into a savings account. His concern is that banks may have the serial numbers of stolen bills, and they'd question how a cowboy got paper-bound bundles of freshly printed bills. He knows that dropping them in front of a cashier and saying he wants to make a deposit would assure him a date with the hangman. Since Jordan is the ultimate beneficiary, she will be interested in advising him on depositing it into a bank account. He's comfortable that Tom's gold coins and the sales to the ladies in Wichita will be adequate spending money. He pulls the buffalo hide blanket under his chin and imagines the Stout girls snuggling up in theirs and how fun it would be if, one day, he and Amy had a family like the Stouts.

Chapter 11: Governor's Wife & Cousin
July 10th

Luke wakes up early and is excited about going to Topeka, the capital of Kansas. However, Ginger is off her feed and even refuses apples and carrots, so it's something serious. Luke knows Smokey can pull the wagon thirty miles to Topeka. To keep an eye on Ginger, Luke ties her to the right front side of the wagon. Because he told Amy he'd send a telegram from Topeka, it's his top priority. His heart is growing fonder by the day, so it's important not to disappoint her, or worse, for her to think he's not serious about her or that her feelings don't matter.

Late morning, about ten miles from Topeka, Luke sees an elegant carriage and a buckboard facing each other as his wagon crests a hill. A man is standing on the buckboard with his pistol drawn, and two riderless horses are behind the buckboard with their reins hanging down. Luke doesn't want to be seen, so he maneuvers the wagon out of sight behind a grove of Osage Orange trees. He grabs his rifle and bandolier, jumps to the ground, and runs down the hill about one hundred and fifty paces while crouching and hiding behind the trees and scrub brush. A split-trunk cottonwood tree about sixty yards from the carriage provides an unobstructed view. A robbery is underway, and Luke can see why the holdup men picked the location. The trees and dense brush have narrowed the road, so it's slightly wider than the big carriage.

The buckboard driver watches as his two accomplices, with pistols drawn, confront two well-dressed women and one man with their hands up. One bandit searches the ladies' handbags, and the other has them remove their jewelry. The well-dressed man gives his wallet to the bandit who pocketed the jewelry. After looking at it for a few seconds, the bandit pistol-whips him, and he falls to the ground. The pistol-whipping-jewelry-thief ties the women's hands and tosses them on the back of the buckboard. He climbs in the back to hold them down and to keep them from falling off.

The robber, digging through the handbags, finds nothing of value and tosses them on the ground. He grabs the carriage horses' bridles below the bits and walks them backward to clear the road so the buckboard can pass. He shoots the horses in the forehead, and they drop where they stand. The horse killer then drags the unconscious man to the rear of the carriage and ties him to a wheel. A small barking dog jumps out of the carriage door window, and the horse killer shoots it. One of the women wails, and her captor grabs a handful of her hair and yells at her to shut up. But both women continue screaming until he puts the barrel of his revolver on the forehead of the lady whose hair he's pulling. Whatever he says to threaten her is convincing because both stop their shrieking at once. The buckboard driver jumps down, mounts one of the two saddled horses, and grabs the other horse's reins. The horse and dog killer climbs into the buckboard seat, says, "All aboard!" and heads in Luke's direction.

Luke comes out of his hiding place to the edge of the roadway. The three men are beyond the range of pistol accuracy, and Luke shouts, "STOP OR DIE!" When the buckboard driver does not, Luke shoots the man in the back of the wagon (the jewelry thief and pistol whipper), hitting him in the center of his chest. He falls between the front and rear wheels, and the rear wheel runs over him. While that's happening, Luke cocks the rifle's lever, ejecting the spent shell casing and reloading the chamber with a shell from the magazine. The bandit on horseback is drawing his pistol and aiming it in Luke's direction, but doesn't pull the trigger before Luke puts a 44-caliber bullet through his heart. In a blur, Luke works the rifle's lever to chamber another round and swings the barrel toward the slowing wagon. The bandit who killed the horses and the dog is leaning back and pulling so hard on the reins that the horse's chin is almost on its chest. The wagon stops fifty feet short of Luke, and the driver raises both hands as high as possible.

Luke says, "Unbuckle your holster with your left hand and toss it close to my feet." With only two fingers on his left hand, unbuckling the holster belt is difficult and slow. Luke waits until the gun belt hits the ground to cut the ladies loose. He tells the bandit, "Keep your hands up where I can see them."

After the women are safely off the buckboard, Luke says, "Now, Mr. Horse and Dog Killer, take off your boots and climb down." Luke asks, and both ladies reply that their injuries are only scrapes and bruises. The dog killer thinks Luke won't notice him reaching for a hidden gun in his boot. Luke sees what's about to happen and says, "Stop, or you'll lose that leg!" When he doesn't stop, Luke shoots his knee joint while holding his rifle waist-high in his right hand. The dog killer drops the gun while doing a nosedive into the dirt. He's writhing in pain and cursing with language that embarrasses Luke, so he asks the women to tend to the man tied to the carriage.

Luke picks up the holster belt and boot gun and tells the dog killer to roll away from the buckboard's wheels, or he'll get run over. The dog killer does as he's told and says, "Why didn't you just kill me, you son-of-a-bitch?"

Luke says, "That would have been merciful; you don't deserve it, and disrespecting my mother isn't smart. Do it again, and you'll see what I mean. I'm going to check on the man your friend pistol-whipped. If you have another gun and decide to use it, my next shot will not be a kill shot but one that will cause far more pain than you have now; you will wish you were dead."

Luke cuts several feet off one of the harness reins on the buckboard's horse and tosses it to the dog killer. "If you want to live, make a tourniquet just above your knee," he advises. Luke then ties the reins of the two riderless horses to the back of the buckboard and leads the horse harnessed to the buckboard over to the luxury carriage. He tosses the gun belt and the boot gun into the passenger compartment.

The man tied to the carriage wheel is conscious, pressing the side of his face with a blood-soaked pad that one of the women made from a strip of fabric torn from her cotton dress.

The lady returning from putting the dog in the carriage says, "Thank the Lord you came along and ended this nightmare. I'm Rosa Anthony, the wife of the Governor of Kansas, George Toby Anthony.[15] This lady is Susan B. Anthony. She's my husband's cousin and the widely publicized leader of the women's rights movement.[16] This good man is Howard Johnson, a Pinkerton security guard hired by my husband to protect us."

"I'm Luke Garrelts, and I'm curious why people of your importance are out here."

Susan says, "It's my fault. I organize speaking events and distribute flyers to encourage voters to pressure their representatives to pass legislation granting women the right to vote. We've been making day trips to small towns close to Topeka."

Luke said, "I've read several articles about your cause and agree with you."

"Thank you," Susan says.

Rosa says, "This was well planned, and I'm suspicious it's the doings of a group of haters who heckle Susan at most of her advertised events. They blocked the road with their buckboard. The driver asked for help with a mechanical problem in the undercarriage. It sounded reasonable, so I asked Howard to help. When Howard was bent over and looking up at the fifth wheel, where the problem supposedly was, the other two rode out of the brush with their guns drawn and threatening us."

Luke says, "When I got here, you all had your hands up and facing them. They thought the typical traveler would not dare to get involved after hearing gunshots and screams and seeing dead animals. You and Susan need to get Howard to a doctor. I'll stay here and clean up this mess. Before you leave, I need to get my wagon. It's back yonder, behind that Osage Orange grove. I'll not be able to see the one with the bloody knee who shot your pup. Let me know if he tries something worthy of losing his gun arm at the shoulder."

When Luke gets to the wagon, Ginger is dead. He takes the hackamore off and has Smokey pull the wagon down to the carriage. The women have finished moving their possessions from the carriage to the buckboard and tied the robber's horses to the carriage. Rosa is in the back of the buckboard with Howard's head in her lap, and Susan is holding the reins. Luke addresses Rosa, saying, "When you get to town, ask whoever brings the carriage horses to bring shovels to bury three horses. A horse that pulled this wagon for thirty years died while I was helping you all. She deserves better than to be dinner for a pack of coyotes."

Rosa says, "In the right front pocket of the first man you shot is my wedding ring and a matching necklace and bracelet set. I would appreciate you getting them for me."

Susan says, "I didn't have any jewelry to give him."

Luke says, "Rosa, I'll give your jewelry to whomever you send back."

A little after one o'clock, Rosa, Susan, and Howard leave on the ten-mile ride to Topeka. Luke figures the buckboard will arrive in Topeka between two-thirty and three o'clock. If everything goes well, help should leave before four and arrive by five. If he leaves within minutes after they arrive, he can get to Topeka by seven.

Luke expects the Western Union office in the state capital to stay open late, or it may never close. Getting a hand-delivered telegram to Amy by seven thirty is probably the best he can hope for.

Luke has four hours to kill. He checks on the dog killer and asks, "How's your day going?"

"Why didn't you let me go with the others?" the dog killer asks.

"If you can't figure that out, you're even a bigger idiot than I first thought," Luke says laughingly.

"If I don't get to a doctor soon, I'll die," the dog killer says. "I don't deserve to die; I have a mother!"

"I saw everything you miscreants did. When your mother reads about you in the paper, whether you're dead or alive, isn't she going to be proud?"

"You bastard, you don't care if I die! What's a damn miscreant, anyway?" the dog killer snarls.

"A criminal," Luke answers. "I told you not to disparage my mother," he says while jamming his rifle's barrel into the dog killer's groin. "I don't care if you die, but I'm certain you will if you don't tighten that tourniquet."

Fighting off the groin pain, the dog killer groans, "I won't do it again." After Luke withdraws the barrel from his groin, he asks, "What the hell does disparage mean?"

"You're too dumb to understand, Luke answers. "And you're still bleeding, so tighten that tourniquet some more."

The dog killer begs, whimpering, "Would you do it for me?"

"Sure, while you stick that knife you have hidden behind your back in my neck," Luke answers.

Luke leaves the dog killer clutching his knee and swearing he will kill the rifleman, the two whores, and the Pinkerton son of a bitch. Getting the harnesses off the dead horses is a difficult job. Luke uses the robbers' horses to drag them off the road a short distance to where burial will be easier. He finds Rosa's jewelry, throws each dead man over a saddle, and ties them securely.

After tidying up the roadway, the dog killer is exhausted from yelling, and wagons appear from both directions. The wagons swing wide to avoid getting close to the dog killer. Luke asks the first wagon driver, "Where have you all been?"

He says, "As soon as we saw what was happening, we held our position. We watched it all play out and warned others to wait until the dust settled. I feel like I had a front-row seat to a one-sided gunfight. I decided it was best to wait because the man, who was cursing and threatening everyone, might try to kill us, given a chance. After you had gathered the dead men and climbed on your wagon, I decided it was safe to come down. That's why you haven't seen anyone for nearly an hour."

"You did the right thing by staying away until it was safe," Luke says. "My old sorrel died. She's…"

"Yeah, we saw her."

"Do you have a shovel?" Luke asks.

"I sure do," the traveler says.

"If you have time, I'd pay three dollars to bury her."

"I'll do it for that!"

Luke says, "If you promise to bury her deep enough that the coyotes can't find her, I'll pay five dollars."

"I'll be sure there are three feet of ground over her."

Luke says, "I'm stuck here until officials return from Topeka, probably three hours from now. I prefer to pay after you've finished the job. Are you okay with that?"

"Absolutely; that's what I'd do in your shoes."

Everyone passing by asks what happened. To keep travelers moving along, Luke says he was not a witness. He volunteered to wait until Topeka law enforcement arrived. Worried that a friend or two of the deceased might show up, Luke keeps his rifle on his lap.

In two hours, the man Luke hired to bury Ginger returns.

Luke says, "That was quick."

The man says, "A friend traveling with us also had a shovel; we buried her properly."

Luke has his wallet out and says, "I'm going to pay you an additional five dollars," and he hands the fellow a ten-dollar bill.

The response is, "THANK YOU, SIR! I'll split this with my friend. Two hours ago, we were flat broke. We need to be going; have a blessed day."

"You also," Luke says. As he had hoped, help showed up just before five o'clock. Luke is relieved to see three men.

The lead man says, "What a mess! I'm Randy Sharp, the governor's groom. Rosa said your horse died, so I brought a shovel for each of us."

"I'm Luke Garrelts. I hired some men to bury her. I've been keeping an eye on that piece of crap with the bad knee. I have a personal reason for needing to leave as soon as possible."

Randy says, "There's no reason you can't go now. Rosa said to tell you to come to the Governor's Mansion and expect to be her guest while you're in town. I'll be in big trouble if you don't show up."

"First, I must find the Western Union office," Luke says.

"It's on Main Street; there's no way you can miss it. The telegrapher can give you directions to the Mansion," Randy says.

Luke offers Randy some advice by saying, "That fellow in the dirt shot the horses and Rosa's pup. He could have a knife, so be careful. Best to tell him to get on the back of the carriage by himself, or you'll leave him here for the coyotes. And I suggest a rope across the back to hold him on. Those two draped over their saddles are secure and shouldn't be a problem, but if they complain, ignore 'em."

Randy says, "So, that SOB killed Skeeter and the carriage horses? I doubt I'll be able to miss any chuckholes on the way into town. Luke, you should go; I'll see you back at the Mansion."

"Okay, thanks, Randy."

Luke gets to the telegraph office at seven-thirty. He knows Amy was expecting a telegram long before now and might be anxiously waiting at the Telegraph office. He hurriedly gets a message to her that doesn't explain the situation in depth. It simply says, "Sweetheart, sorry for sending this so late. I'll explain in K.C. that Ginger passed away this afternoon. I cannot make it to K.C. tomorrow. Send your reply to the Governor's Mansion in Topeka. Love, Luke."

When Luke arrives at the Mansion, Rosa, Susan, and Governor Anthony are waiting on the porch. The women hug and kiss him on the cheek. The governor shakes his hand with both of his while saying, "Mr. Garrelts, I'm George Anthony. Thank you for rescuing my wife and cousin. I've listened to these women tell of your heroics for nearly six hours; I can't wait to hear your version."

Luke says, "Sir, it's been a long day. I'm too tired to think. I need to care for my horse, get my wagon in a safe place, get something to eat, and hit the hay."

Grinning, George says, "Sorry, no hay; our mattresses and pillows are stuffed with goose down." He laughs briefly and continues, "We want you to relax; we've been preparing for your arrival. My butler will take your rig into our stable and care for your horse until Randy returns. Randy is great with horses, and your wagon will be safe. Our cook has kept our dinner leftovers warm, and our butler has prepared a guest bedroom and bath for you. While you're having dinner, I'll have your travel things placed in your room."

"Thank you, sir."

"I would prefer you call me George. I am not big on formalities."

"Me either, George."

The women escort Luke to the dining room and watch as he consumes all the leftovers. He has half of a chicken, a bowl of mashed potatoes smothered in brown gravy, four ears of sweet corn, a stack of sliced tomatoes laced with powdered sugar, a few biscuits, and a gallon of iced tea.

Luke pushes back from the table, and Rosa says, "Where did you put all that? You must have a hollow leg!"

"I haven't eaten since early this morning, and everything was delicious," Luke says.

Rosa says, "Maria, our chief cook, is amazing. Now, let me show you to your room."

They go upstairs, and Rosa shows Luke the room and bathroom across the hall. The saddlebag with his clothing is on the floor beside the bed.

Luke puts his hands in his pants pockets, feels Rosa's jewelry, shows it to Rosa, and says, "I was in a hurry and forgot to give your jewelry to Randy."

"Thank you. I'll sleep better now that I have these," Rosa says.

Luke looks at the bed and says, "I can see I'm going to sleep well tonight. Thank you for your hospitality. I must say good night now before I fall asleep standing."

Rosa says, "There's a chamber pot under the bed and another in the bathroom." The women say, "Goodnight," and they leave.

Luke gets his saddlebag with clean clothes, crosses the hall, and finds a tub half full of warm water and a chamber pot under the hinged seat of an ornately carved oak chair. Upon lifting the pot's lid, he is pleased to discover that it's unused, but doesn't leave it that way. He brushes his teeth, shaves, and bathes before returning to his room. He opens both windows, puts on clean underwear, turns the wick of the kerosene lantern down to extinguish the flame, and falls asleep thinking about Ginger, the bizarre day, and Amy.

Chapter 12: Luke & The Governor Bond
July 11th

Luke is awakened by three knocks on his bedroom door, followed by a man saying, "Sir, a hot bath awaits you in the room directly across the hall." Luke tucks the clean clothes he put on the night before under his arm, cracks the door, sees no one in the hallway, and dashes for the opposing door. Someone has placed every toiletry item Luke has ever used, and some he hasn't, on a dressing table, and now there's a full-length mirror, his first. He lifts the seat of the fancy chair and is pleased to find the chamber pot is empty. Before getting in the tub, Luke looks at himself in the mirror and strikes several poses, flexing his arm and chest muscles.

Once dressed, Luke goes to the stable to check on the wagon and Smokey. Randy is washing the carriage and tells Luke where he can find them. Luke can tell no one has rummaged through the wagon, and the three pebbles are in place. Smokey is enjoying a breakfast of oats and prairie hay. Luke pitches alfalfa into Smokey's stall, then pats his neck and shoulders while bragging about him and talking about his sadness over Ginger's passing. On his way out, he thanked Randy for caring for his horse and wagon.

Randy says, "You don't have to thank me, it's my job."

"My parents insisted I show appreciation whenever someone lent me a hand. It became a habit, so you'll have to get over it. How's the scum who shot Skeeter?"

Randy says, "I overheard Rosa and Susan telling George what happened, so I wanted to kill the bastard as soon as you left for town. He died on the way into town. The sheriff said he bled to death. I tried my best to help."

"No one's going to miss him, but many will miss your beautiful horses and Skeeter," Luke says.

Randy says, "They were a matched pair; they looked like identical twins. We have another pair almost as amazing."

"I couldn't help but notice them yesterday; they're gorgeous," Luke says.

Randy says, "Rosa loved that pup. I hope George can find her another."

Luke thanks Randy again, walks up the Mansion's front steps, and finds George at the dining room table. He's been reading a stack of newspapers, drinking coffee, and waiting for Luke. George looks up and says, "You clean up good. I won't hound you about how you got the best of those ruffians until after breakfast."

While sitting down across from George, Luke asks, "Do you mind that I read your newspapers after you've finished with them?"

"Please do. When you're through, you may keep any you want and give the rest to our butler, Raymond. He uses them to line Rosa's birdcages."

"I haven't met Raymond," Luke says.

"You will," George says.

A well-dressed man wearing white gloves sets down a bowl of scrambled eggs and another with link sausages between the men.

George says, "This man is Bernard, and he'll be offended if you call him Bernie. Bernard, this gentleman is Luke Garrelts."

Bernard says, "I'm happy to make your acquaintance."

"Likewise," Luke says, nodding his head affirmatively.

Bernard leaves and returns with bowls of fried potatoes and biscuits; he leaves and returns the third time with gravy and grits.

George says, "When we're not entertaining, I prefer to eat family style rather than Old South. I don't like someone holding a bowl and watching me take a sensible helping; that's less than I want. Family style is quicker, one's appetite is not on display, and I can see the bowls and know where the second helpings are. Before I forget, you must try the strawberry jam that Rosa ordered. The label claims they make it in New York City."

Luke tries it and says, "It's delicious," but he thinks, *Why does Bernard refill my coffee cup after every sip, even a tiny one?*

George patiently waits for Luke to wipe his mouth with the cloth napkin and place it next to the plate before starting their conversation. He begins by saying, "Rosa and Susan say if you had not come along, I'd be getting a ransom note. The guy who tied their hands said, 'How much do you think the governor will pay to get you all back?' From what they told me yesterday afternoon, you are quite the marksman. Where did you learn to shoot?"

Luke says, "I'm a farm kid from south of Amarillo. For protection, my parents insisted that I carry a small-caliber rifle from the time I began exploring nature. I spent all the money I earned on shells and pestered my parents for more. Everything I killed, Mom cleaned and cooked, and I ate. After reading a poster that Amarillo's Fourth of July festivities would include a shooting competition that paid the winner $25, I got very serious about my target practice. I tried hitting flies on our barn door at ten paces. I know I got close, but I never found evidence of hitting one. Dad made me stop. I shot turkey and pheasant on the wing; quail were hit-and-miss, mostly miss. I never won the Fourth of July competition, but I came close. Before my sixteenth birthday, I joined the North. Based on my performance at the shooting range, I was issued a Sharps rifle. I was surprised at how accurate I became when I trained daily with a boy who used semaphore flags after every shot to relay precisely where I hit the target; I was usually within inches. My instructor told my sergeant my skill was extraordinary, and he transferred me to an elite sniper group; I apologize for bragging."

"So, you were a Sharpshooter; that explains a lot."

"Yes, I was in the 1st United States Sharpshooters Regiment," Luke proudly says.[17]

George says, "Ah, the men in dark green uniforms like Robin Hood, without any light-reflecting metal buttons or insignia."

"Hey, I became invisible when I was up in a tree."

"Tell me about the test you had to pass for acceptance into the Sharpshooters."

"I had to hit a ten-inch-wide target with ten consecutive shots from 200 yards. A Sharps rifle could kill a man at 1,000 yards. They were breech loaders, so I could fire four shots in thirty seconds, while the average Confederate soldier could only shoot his muzzle-loader once. Being camouflaged up in a tree, with a fast-loading rifle that was deadly accurate up to 600 yards, was an unbelievable advantage," Luke says.

Did you see action?" George asks.

"Only at Appomattox. The last battle of the war and my first," Luke says.

"How old were you?"

"I'd just turned sixteen."

"Recruits were supposed to be eighteen. Because of your size, I'm sure you looked eighteen. Both sides needed soldiers and looked the other way when kids wanted to sign up at the recruiting centers. At Appomattox, I was captain of a Light Artillery Brigade, and I had kids that looked too young to be in battle," George says. "I suspect they lost their daddy and joined to avenge his death."

"You had a very responsible assignment," Luke says in a complimentary manner.

"I was in the war from start to finish and was exhausted, relieved, and thankful when it was over. It would have lasted longer if Grant had not been in command. Lincoln picked Grant because, as the war dragged on, he was concerned that some of his generals could sympathize with the Confederacy. Over the long haul, the South wouldn't win because we had significantly more munitions manufacturing in the industrialized East, and we had Grant," George says.

George recalls his battles and the deaths and casualties that resulted from each. While George is lamenting the incredible numbers, Luke reflects on his war assignment. *The military taught me how to get close and pick off Confederate Officers by blending with my surroundings. Those men were probably just as honorable as George.*

It's evident that George's war experience weighed heavily on his heart, and his memories were painful. When he has the chance, Luke looks squarely at George and says, "My miscalculation was thinking the war would be exciting and maybe even fun. What I witnessed at Appomattox changed a part of me forever."

George says, "Wars leave physical and mental scars."

Luke says, "The war was awful, but fortunately, the North had leaders like President Lincoln, General Grant, and men like yourself at the right time and place. Your comment regarding mental and physical scars made me think about Howard. Do you know how he's doing?"

"I checked on him. His face was bandaged, but I could still see swelling and bruising. He said the doctor used a lot of stitches. He was lying down but talkative and seemed to be in good spirits," George said.

Luke said. "That's good news. When I went out to see my horse this morning, Randy said the man I knee-capped didn't make it."

George says, "County Sheriff Jack Nelson came here last night. He said the tourniquet was not wrapped tightly and tied, and he believed the fellow decided to bleed out because he had nothing to live for."

Luke says, "I gave him that leather strap and cautioned him to pull it tight. However, I'm not surprised he cashed in his chips. He knew he'd lose that leg and, given the seriousness of his crime, be hanged or serve a life sentence at Lansing prison. I've seen men die from blood loss; it's a peaceful way to go."

George says, "Jack found warrants on the first two. They were evil men, the type pictured on a dead or alive poster. You have $800 in reward money waiting for you at the bank. Jack will have to go with you to get it. Jack says he'll need time this morning to look through the pile of warrants for the third man. Some warrants don't have a picture, only a drawing based on eyewitness descriptions, and they look like any bearded cowboy. So, Jack must read the warrants with bad pictures to see if distinguishing features, like a scar, tattoo, or missing leg, could identify the dead man. If the third guy is as bad as the first two, and I suspect he is, you're in for a big payday. Jack said you didn't take their money, pocket watches, or cartridges. So, he thinks you're either a choir boy or a preacher."

"I was raised to be honest and warned I would remember and regret every dishonest deed in my old age," Luke says matter-of-factly with raised eyebrows. "It churned my guts to watch your beautiful horses and Skeeter die. I suppose they did that so any onlookers would think twice about getting involved. I saw Howard give one of them his wallet, get pistol-whipped, and collapse on the ground. He must have had something in it identifying him as a Pinkerton. As I'm sure the ladies told you, things got dire after that. I decided the robbers would do anything, so kill shots were necessary. Fortunately, the buckboard came toward me. I shouted for it to stop. I was most concerned about the man in the back of the wagon with the ladies. He's the one who took your wife's jewelry and threatened her with a gun to her head. I feared he would try that again to turn the tables on me, so I shot him first.

Seconds later, I pulled the trigger on the man on horseback who pistol-whipped Howard. He aimed his gun at me, but I got my shot off before he fired. It looked like I hit his heart. On the way down, he fired into the air and was dead when he hit the ground. I didn't shoot the man driving the buckboard, who shot your horses and Rosa's dog, because he was doing everything he could to stop."

"Why not shoot him?" George asks.

"My parents died in a runaway buckboard, so I was concerned that it could happen if I shot the driver. I had him throw his gun belt to the ground and take off his boots because I knew he'd have a hidden gun or knife. I was sure he was reaching for a weapon, so I advised him to stop, or he would lose his leg. He didn't listen, and I shot his knee the second I saw the gun coming out of his boot."

"The woman said you shot from the hip! Where did you learn that?" George says.

"With enough practice, it's not that difficult with a rifle at close range. Can Rosa get another dog like Skeeter?" Luke asks.

"I hope so; she loved that mutt. I sent a telegram to a friend who raises Cocker Spaniels late yesterday. I told him we would take a male in the next litter."

"Good!"

After chewing on two forks full of eggs, George swallows and says, "My first blush impression is that you're capable of much more than selling kitchenware."

Luke finishes a mouthful of eggs and takes a drink of coffee to wash them down, but he doesn't turn loose of the handle, which perplexes Bernard. He inhales deeply, exhales through pursed lips, and says, "I'm not a housewares salesman, and I have no interest in being one. I was on my way to Kansas City to see my half-sister. I crossed paths with the owner of the wagon, Charlie Bonner. We camped together, and he died peacefully in his sleep sometime during the night. Luckily, over dinner, he had talked about his family in Dodge City. The honorable thing to do was to take him home, and Dodge wasn't out of my way. As a gesture of appreciation, Charlie's wife allowed me to use his wagon for a few weeks to make my trip easier."

George says, "Randy peeked into the back of the wagon. He said you don't have much to sell."

To explain why he has no inventory, Luke tells the story of trading with the Kiowa and his reluctance to haggle over their offer for all the merchandise. Then he tells George about loaning the buffalo blankets to the Stout girls only one day later. Luke says, "Those three blankets were more than half of the trade."

"That's a cute story and shows you have a good heart," George says.

"The horses probably think so; they should appreciate that I lightened their load," Luke says.

George says, "Talk about your future?"

"If I'm to achieve my long-term goals of a family, a successful cattle operation, and enough money to do what I want, I must give up cowboying. Besides, the demand for cowboys will decline as railroads and stockyards expand to the outskirts of every major city, making cattle drives shorter. Widespread use of barbed wire will reduce the number of cowboys needed to watch over herds. I could manage a cattle ranch in a rocking chair in my old age if I had a few good men. For probably five years, I've considered selling my wheat farm south of Amarillo, taking out a loan, and starting a small cattle ranch. Cattle should remain profitable because the high price is due to demand exceeding supply. I just never found the motivation to do it. I haven't seen my sister since April last year, but we've exchanged letters almost every month. Two weeks ago, I had planned to visit my sister and stay in the West Bottoms, and if I found work in the stockyards, I'd stay a while."

"To like that area, don't you have to get accustomed to cow manure or not breathe through your nose?" George asks.

"I've been around it so much that I don't notice the smell; however, avoiding fresh cow pies becomes a valuable skill. I've been on seven cattle drives to K.C. and always enjoyed my time in the Bottoms. I was the point man on the last four of King Ranch's drives. Around the campfire, the point man is easy to spot because he's the cleanest. I have a few friends in Kansas City besides my sister."

"I got the sense that your plan of two weeks ago might have changed; is that right?" George asks.

"You're right. My time at Dodge created a problem I've never experienced. I became captivated by Charlie's stepdaughter, Amy. We hit it off and discovered that we shared similar upbringings and values. Since I left Dodge, she has stayed on my mind. She's perfect; someone else will get her if I sit on the fence too long. Would you believe I became motivated to change my life after spending only three days with her? I began thinking about what I needed to do to accommodate her. Before I met her, I had followed my boyhood dreams and was in denial about life's shortcomings as a drover and broncobuster. I refused to believe that the cowboy profession was for young men, even though many of the cowboys on a cattle drive were half my age. I knew cowboying would not allow me to have a family life and the independence I wanted. But I was young and having fun, and I believed there was plenty of time to change my ways. Now, I'm on a short fuse. I have little time to sweep her off her feet, and I'm in the wrong business to offer her the life I imagine a woman like her desires. So, I have a lot to sort out."

Laughingly, George says, "Luke, you just slobbered a bib full! I think you're in love. If so, your problem trumps all of mine."

"George, I want to see her so bad that my time in K.C. will not be more than a week, and I'll be back on the road to Dodge."

George says, "Following your dreams with the right woman and raising children together will result in maximum happiness. Becoming wealthy is simply a product of putting your time and talent to its best use."

George says, "You can easily achieve your long-term goals. I say that because you have the time, knowledge, and ability. If there's some way I can help with your short or long-term goals, please ask."

The Governor's interest in helping him takes Luke aback; he lowers his head and looks down at his hands. When he regains his composure, he removes his tongue from behind his lower lip, raises his head to look squarely at George, and humbly says, "George, I appreciate your kind offer; I will certainly keep it in mind."

George changes the subject, saying, "Based on articles in the *Dodge City Times*, that town must be a wild and woolly place. It's being called the "Wickedest Town in the West.""

Luke explains how he believes Dodge earned that name by saying, "The saloons are where the problems begin. The Santa Fe railroad is enjoying a booming business shipping buffalo hides and cattle. That brings in young cowboys and skinners with money to spend. When a liquored-up kid has his entire paycheck in a $600 poker pot and does not fill an inside straight after the discard, all hell can break loose. The kid accuses a fancy-dressed gambler of cheating, and the argument escalates until it's settled with pistols out in the street. That example is typical of every railway town that ships cattle and has nothing to do with Bat Masterson. In an attempt to reduce violence in the saloons, the city council prohibited concealed guns. That hasn't worked, so they're considering a city-wide ban on firearms. When I settle down, it won't be around Dodge. It'll be closer to where I grew up."

George says, "I read that Wyatt Earp is in Dodge visiting Bat Masterson."

"That must be big news because Amy said the same thing in a telegram I got in Wichita."

Carefully picking his words, George says, "You are an extraordinary young man. From what the women have said and what I can tell, you think logically and make good decisions. Your vocabulary and ability to express yourself are impressive. You're a ranch hand who attended school and likes newspapers; that's a contradiction. The women say you are extraordinarily handsome and well-groomed; I can see that. You don't come across as someone looking for a fight, but you didn't hesitate to put yourself in harm's way to help three people you didn't know. You are not what I expected, and you're very likable. I rarely meet young men with your qualities, and I get around."

Luke says, "That's very kind. I'm flattered. My foster parents wanted me to be well-rounded and prepared me for something more than being a cowboy. If they were still alive, they'd be disappointed."

George interrupts, saying, "When you have children, you'll learn the best you can do is instill good qualities. How they use them and the path they choose is up to them. I can assure you that your parents would be extremely proud."

"I hope so; they insisted I developed good habits, like grooming and manners, and I have tried to live by the Ten Commandments. My record was clean until the war. Then yesterday afternoon gave me more to explain at the Pearly Gates."

"You are a cinch to get in. Since I will be going first, I'll explain the situation to Saint Peter."

"Good; tell him anything you think will help," Luke says, and they both chuckle.

George says, "When we met this morning, you asked about reading my newspapers. That seemed unusual for a cowboy."

Luke smiles and says, "My interest in newspapers came about due to my father's poor eyesight. I'd read the newspaper to him, and we'd discuss articles. Journalists report facts that answer who, what, when, where, and how. They fail to apply the logic that might address the whys. So, Dad and I would discuss the dots that a journalist won't connect. I suppose it was a game we played. That influenced my thinking and why I tend to overanalyze most things."

"Your father didn't want you to be gullible. He didn't want others to be able to tell you what to believe. And especially, to not believe everything you read in the newspapers," George says.

During their discussion, a man enters the dining room carrying an envelope. He waits for the conversation to stop before saying, "I have a telegram for Mr. Luke Garrelts."

"That's me, and I recognize your voice. Thanks for the hot bath this morning; it was a nice surprise. If there's something I can do to help you, please ask."

George smiles and says, "This gentleman is our butler, Raymond James; he manages the house staff and does a great job."

Luke takes the telegram, shakes Raymond's hand, and says, "Thank you, Raymond. It's nice to know who belongs to the voice in the hallway. This telegram is from my girlfriend in Dodge." He reads the telegram to himself, and it says, "The Governor's Mansion! I can't stand not knowing what's happening and must see you. I'm leaving on the train to K.C. this morning. I will arrive on the 13th and have a reservation at the Cattlemen's Inn. Please be safe. I Love You, Amy."

While looking down at the telegram, Luke raises his eyebrows and says, "George, my short-term plan just came together. I need to see Jack, collect my reward, and find a jewelry store that sells wedding rings."

"Well, congratulations," George says. "How did that decision come about so quickly?"

"I can tell from this telegram that she cares for me as much as I do for her. I've been hoping for her to give me a sign, and she just did! She's leaving for Kansas City on the train this morning," Luke says as he grins from ear to ear.

"What's her name?" George asks.

"Amy Bonner; well, her birth name is Amy Bushnell. Her father, Owen Bushnell, died in the Battle of Gettysburg. She became a Bonner when her mother married Charlie."

George says, "Whenever I hear Gettysburg mentioned, two things come to mind; one is very good and one very bad. My good memory is of Lincoln's speech at the dedication of the Soldiers' National Cemetery; only Union soldiers are buried there. His speech was merely ten sentences; he gave it in two minutes. Now, it's considered the most famous speech about the war. That speech became so famous that it has a name, "The Gettysburg Address."[18] Most folks and all school graduates can recite the first sentence that starts with 'Four score and seven years ago.' I was there. Lincoln upstaged the keynote speaker, who talked about the battle for two hours, and today, no one knows his name."

"It proves how much you say is not as important as how you say it," Luke says.

"My bad memory is of a battle called Pickett's Charge.[19] I'll leave out the details and say it was significant because of the number of men involved and the incredible loss of life. The gun smoke was so thick that neither side could see its enemy. The defeat of the Confederacy at Gettysburg was the turning point in the war." Luke sees for a second time that the war is front and center in George's memories.

Then George says, "Before you take off, our new President, Rutherford B. Hayes, is on a whirlwind tour to meet individually with the thirty-eight Governors. They're here for one evening to allow President Hayes and me to get to know each other and discuss Kansas problems. The president before him, General Ulysses S. Grant, is accompanying him. This place will be teeming with military and security types, and while I'm thinking of it, you'll have to leave your gun and knife in your room while they are here. They'll arrive tomorrow afternoon and dine here, along with some of our local dignitaries, and I want you to attend. You will need a suit to attend this event. I have a suspicion you don't own one."

"You're right; I don't."

"And you'll need shoes or calf-high boots, so the pant legs are on the outside. A great shoe and boot store is next door to Westendorf's Clothing. Go there first and take whatever you buy to Westendorf's. I'd recommend Goldman's for a jewelry store because Isaac's prices are fair."

"Thanks, I'll do that. I have a busy day ahead and need to get going." Luke tells George how much he enjoyed the conversation during breakfast and leaves for the stable. Luke notices a buckboard ready to go beside the porch and asks Randy if he could get a ride to the sheriff's office.

Randy says, "Sure, running errands is a big part of my day." Along the way, Luke tells Randy about the warrant money, Amy's telegram, George's invitation to attend the big party, and why he's going shopping for a wedding band, suit, and boots.

After arriving at the sheriff's office, Randy introduces Luke to Jack, saying, "I'd like to stay, but I can't. Good luck with your shopping, Luke."

"Thanks for the ride. I'll see you later," Luke says.

Jack asks, "What are you shopping for?"

"I need to buy a wedding ring and a suit for the president's dinner tomorrow night," Luke answers.

"My wife and I got an invitation to that event," Jack says. "We're looking forward to it. I suppose George told you about the rewards for the first two men."

"He did," Luke says.

"Well, the reward for the third guy is also $400," Jack says. "The damn guy has a bunch of aliases. I know he's the right man because his warrant says he's missing three fingers on his left hand. He only had a thumb and pinky on that hand. A year ago, he was serving a life sentence at the Missouri State Penitentiary in Jefferson for killing a cashier and a customer in St. Louis. He and the other two escapees overpowered their guards. I went to the bank this morning; I hope $20 bills are okay."

"Absolutely!" Luke says. After Jack counts sixty of them, Luke says, "George recommended I shop at Goldman's and Westendorf's. I need help with directions." While getting directions, Luke stuffs the cash in his trousers. He thanked Jack for going to the bank and left for Goldman's Jewelry store.

Luke tells Isaac, "George Anthony recommended I come here to buy a wedding ring; he said you're a square shooter." Isaac goes to the back of his store and brings back a sizeable black-velvet-lined display case with gold rings standing in rows. Luke says, "Amy has small hands. I'd guess her ring finger is about the size of my pinky."

"Then select one from the four front rows, and if it doesn't fit, I'll resize it at no cost," Isaac says.

Luke likes a wide gold band with alternating rubies and diamonds centered around the perimeter. He slides it to the last joint of his little finger and says, "That's close to the right size."

"You have excellent taste. That ring is one of a kind. It's on sale for $90 for today only," Mr. Goldman says.

Luke hands it back without saying a word, and Isaac says, "Because George sent you, I'll let it go for $80."

Luke says, "I'll consider it on one condition."

"What would that be?" Isaac asks.

"If we pass through here in the next few weeks, and she wants it resized, you'll drop everything while we wait.

"Yes, of course," Isaac promises.

Luke pays for the ring, puts it in his inner vest pocket, and sets out for the shoe store next to Westendorf's.

He buys a pair of black, calf-high, elk-skin, square-toed stockman's boots with a low-profile heel for $12 and takes them to Westendorf's. Luke looks at the dressed mannequins and chooses a dark gray three-piece suit that is not formal due to its Western tailoring. He also picks out two white shirts, black suspenders, and a black string tie. Luke thinks the hats and canes are snobbish and decides not to buy either. Luke put on the new boots and the off-the-rack suit. It only requires alterations to the vest and the trousers' waist and inseams.

The diminutive tailor, wearing glasses on the end of his nose, says, "Your bill, with alterations, is twenty-six dollars."

Luke says, "Here's thirty. If you can have it ready by lunch tomorrow, you can keep the change. If it's not ready, I want my money back, and you'll probably hear from Governor Anthony." Luke grins and says, "I'm as serious as a rattlesnake bite. George invited me to a dinner with the visiting presidents and..."

The tailor interrupts, saying, "I'll have it ready by noon tomorrow."

"Perfect, I'll see you then," Luke says. He thanks the tailor, walks to the Western Union office, and sends three telegrams. He addresses the first telegram to Amy Bonner at the Cattlemen's Inn in Kansas City. It says, "Dear Amy, I'm detained by Governor Anthony to attend a dinner party for President Hayes and General Grant on the 12th. I will leave on the 13th and arrive in K.C. before nightfall. Please make a livery reservation for Smokey." His second telegram is to Ray and Virginia Simms at the Cattlemen's Inn in Kansas City, Missouri. It says, "Dear Ray and Virginia, if possible, I would appreciate you upgrading Amy Bonner's July 13th reservation to your largest room with a private bath. I'll be arriving late on that day. I've sent Miss Bonner a telegram addressed to your hotel. I look forward to seeing you all. Luke Garrelts." He sends the third telegram to Jordan, saying, "Dear Jordan, I will arrive late at the Cattleman's Inn on the 13th. I'm available to meet the following day. You pick the time and place. Love, Luke."

After leaving the telegraph office, Luke can't help but notice that the city is dressing up for the arrival of the presidents with flags and banners. He hears a band practicing Hail to the Chief, The Star-Spangled Banner, and Yankee Doodle on an elevated stand at the corner of Main and Kansas Avenue. He figures the parade will pass by on the way to the Mansion and pause for the band to welcome them to the city. Luke sees the *Topeka Blade* newspaper office and buys the morning paper.

Before leaving, he asks a customer, "Do you know where the cavalry troops are from?"

The customer said, "No, but probably Fort Leavenworth, although Fort Reilly is also possible. It seems there are more men in uniform than necessary."

Luke says, "I've heard that since Lincoln, a troop will escort a traveling president."

"They have John Wilkes Booth to thank for that," the customer says.

"But it seems like I've seen over a hundred men this morning," Luke says. "President Hayes has no political history, but Grant must have as many haters as Lincoln. I suspect the excessive military presence has more to do with General Grant than President Hayes, so perhaps both forts sent a troop. Have a good day."

"I suspect you are right. You have a good day also."

Luke wants to find a hotel on Main Street where he can look out of a big bay window, drink coffee, read the paper, and watch the city installing "Welcome" flags. He also enjoys watching pedestrians and guessing their professions based on clothing and demeanor. Luke finds a dining room window just like he hoped for, and he's relaxed and enjoying the stimulation provided by the view, coffee, and sugar.

Luke takes a moment to reflect on his cash requirement and thinks, I spent $80 on Amy's ring, $30 at the men's clothing store, and $12 on boots. I'm going to need plenty of cash for expenses in Kansas City. I should separate my bounty money from the money in the gun safe that I'll give Jordan. So, when I return to the Mansion, I'll put 1,000 dollars of the bounty money in my saddlebag.

He finished a front-page article about the arrival of the two presidents when the following headline had him sitting up straight: "Remains of Tom Addison Found." The article is a report by Addison's Undersheriff. In it, he says, "A week after the fire at the Addison Cattle Company, the town blacksmith opened a locked gun safe that survived the fire. The contents included an engraved Elgin railroad watch, a gold lapel stick pin, and wire-rim reading glasses. The items were confirmed to be Tom Addison's possessions. Mr. Addison's attorney is offering a $1,000 reward for information leading to the arrest and conviction of the person(s) responsible."

Luke thinks, *There is still no mention of missing money or the posse.* He places a fifty-cent coin next to the saucer, folds the newspaper, and tucks it under his arm. He takes a handful of sugar cubes for Smokey and carries his new boots to the front of the hotel, where there's a waiting "for hire" carriage.

At the Mansion, Luke checks for anything indicating someone has been in the wagon, specifically the pebbles between the floorboards. He puts the newspaper and Amy's telegram in Charlie's cash box and fifty $20 bills from the Topeka bounty money in his saddle bag. Luke goes to Smokey's stall for him to pick sugar cubes off the palm of his hand with his silky, soft lips. He tells Randy about his shopping experience and proudly shows him the ring and boots. When Randy asks about the suit, Luke says it requires alterations, so he'll get it tomorrow after lunch.

Luke meets Raymond at the front door. They greet, and Luke tells Raymond he would like to polish his boots. Before Luke can utter another word, Raymond interrupts him, saying, "Sir, one of my footmen is a boot polishing expert. Leave them in the hallway next to your bedroom door before midnight."

"Thanks, I'll do that."

Carrying his new boots, Luke walks around the Mansion's first floor, admiring the artwork, sculptures, oriental carpets, oak tables, and overstuffed leather couches and matching chairs. Luke is studying a large painting of a gorgeous, black-haired woman naked from the waist up, looking over her shoulder toward him and partially hiding her breasts with an arm across her chest. He jumps when George comes up behind him and says, "APHRODITE, she's the Greek Goddess of love and beauty. So, I see you bought boots. How did your shopping go?"

"Good, I think." Luke reaches into his inner vest pocket, retrieves Amy's ring, and says, "When I got to Isaac's, I told him you sent me, so he probably felt pressure to make me happy. Isaac cut me a better deal when he thought I might walk away. Thanks for recommending Goldman's Jewelry."

George says, "That's a beautiful ring; don't let Rosa see it. She thinks I am a penny pincher; that ring is proof." They laugh, and George continues, "So, did you find a suit?"

"I did."

"Where?"

"You recommended Westendorf's, so that's where I went."

"That's a great store; what did you buy?" George asks.

"It's a three-piece suit with a western look, cut, or style, whatever you call it. I'll pick it up tomorrow after lunch. I hope you're not disappointed with my choice," Luke says.

George says, "There's no way you could disappoint me. Those are extraordinarily great-looking boots; are they comfortable?"

"I think so; they're elk skin; feel how soft they are!" Luke replies while handing one of the boots to George.

George says, "Hmm? "The next time I go to Town, I will buy a pair of these." Then George asks, "How about a few games of snooker after dinner?"

Luke answers, "You'll have to teach me the rules. I've seen how it's played, but that's it. In the saloons, the men playing the game drank, gambled, flirted with the women, and swore after every shot they didn't make."

"Snooker is a game of skill and strategy enjoyed by men at all levels of society," George says. "You will figure it out quickly and probably win one after the third or fourth game. My eyesight is not what it used to be," George says.

At the snooker table, it turns out that Luke is giving George lessons. George asks, "Are you sure you have never played this game before?"

"Never," Luke says.

Before taking his next shot, George leans on his cue stick and says, "I want you to consider what I am about to say. Should you and Amy decide to chase your dream of a cattle ranch, I would like to help a little. I will buy your wagon and the palomino. They are worth about two hundred fifty dollars; I'll pay you three hundred. Then you all can take my Pullman back to Dodge."

"That's a very generous offer; however, I want to keep Smokey, and I suspect Doris will not sell Charlie's wagon. Amy and I can ride it back to Dodge," Luke says.

"Luke, not so quick; my Pullman is unique. The Pullman Company made it, especially for my campaign. The front twenty-five feet is for living quarters. The back fifty feet is for my carriage, horses, a groom, and two security types. My carriage is taller than your wagon. There are two horse stalls with feed and water for five days, which is more than we ever needed. There are also sleeping quarters for my groom and two Pinkerton men. It is the safest and most comfortable way to travel. I do not use it now that the campaign is over."

"Holy smoke, who designed that?"

"I did," George said, making a fist and pounding the table to celebrate his accomplishment.

"I can't say no to that, but I won't know our plans until I have Amy's answer to my proposal," Luke says.

"She won't say 'No.' I would bet on it," George says.

Luke says, "I'm not surprised you designed your Pullman. What I'd like to hear is how you got into politics."

"I will keep it short because it's not that interesting. Like your parents, my parents saw that I got a good education. When they died, I inherited enough money that, within reason, I could pursue my interests. Rosa and I moved to Leavenworth, where I was the editor of a daily newspaper and the owner of a monthly farm publication. I enjoyed reading newspapers from all over the state. I was well-informed about current events. I only wrote about issues I felt were important to my readers. I found that if I prepared myself with facts, I could think quickly and speak comfortably in front of a crowd. Those skills made me a good campaigner. Because I was someone who rural folk knew and trusted, a political group asked me to run," George says.

"Any interest in the presidency?" Luke asks.

"Nope, not a chance," George answers.

Luke says, "I need your advice. Tomorrow night, I'll be uncomfortable meeting President Hayes and General Grant."

"Nonsense, those two put their pants on one leg at a time while sitting in a chair, whereas you can do that while jumping out of a second-story window," George said with a big grin.

Luke says, "Funny, but not a confidence builder."

"I apologize; I should not have been so flippant. I've heard that some men shake in their boots when they meet Grant for the first time; some people can't even speak. The General is low-key and calm, speaks softly, and is not vainglorious about his war accomplishments. When he sees you towering over him, he will feel intimidated. You have a very magnetic personality, so my advice is to be yourself. Trust me; you will do fine," George says convincingly.

Luke says, "I would never ask General Grant about this; however, I would like your opinion. During his presidency, Grant seemed to talk out of both sides of his mouth about the Indian Wars. On the one hand, he appeared Indian-friendly because he didn't want trouble in the west, but on the other, he had Generals Sherman, Sheridan, and Colonel Custer stirring up Indian wars."[20]

George answers Luke, "It smelled of a political cover-up to me. The country was in a depression, and it needed economic stimulus. The discovery of gold in the Black Hills of South Dakota was just what the doctor ordered. However, the Lakota's Relocation treaty guaranteed them perpetual ownership.[21] Nothing official ever surfaced, but the government stirred up trouble, and when the Indians fought back, they used that as an excuse to break the treaty. Rumor was that Custer's expedition into the Black Hills was to find a location for a cavalry post. The Sioux kicked Custer's butt because he made some bad decisions, like dividing his troops into three groups to attack the village from several directions. Crazy Horse had enough warriors to overwhelm Custer's men several times over. Newspaper columnists say the 7th Cavalry could not have been annihilated had Custer kept his men together.

"Journalists can create public bias by ignoring the facts; some call it lying. Indians know a lot about that. Public opinion holds sway in the halls of Congress. So, a president can feel compelled to sign legislation against their better judgment or personal feelings. If it goes sour, Washington journalists will cover it up. In summary, politics is an ugly business; men of integrity often serve one term and call it quits."

"That's interesting; it sounds like the Indians need a better representative in Washington," Luke says. "I have another concern eating on me. I know nothing about formal dining etiquette. I'm a bona fide greenhorn; it worries me I'll embarrass you, Rosa, and myself."

"The women plan to shepherd you around and show you the ropes. You'll be Susan's escort and sit between her and Rosa. Watch Rosa, follow her lead, and be patient. You'll find our food is served hot and eaten cold because everyone talks too much," George says.

"Oh, thank God," Luke says.

"You don't have to go that high up," George says. "You only need to thank me." They laugh heartily, and George adds, "Luke, don't ever be ashamed, afraid, or hesitant to ask for my advice."

"Thanks; I hope you will never regret telling me that," Luke says.

It's getting late; George walks around to Luke's side of the snooker table, leans on his cue stick, and lowers his voice so no one nearby can hear. He says, "Luke, there's a good reason you have not read, or will ever read, a newspaper article about the attempted abduction of Rosa and Susan. The experience was traumatic for the women. Susan is constantly on the road and concerned that a newspaper article might give another evildoer an idea. Everyone involved has been instructed not to discuss it tomorrow night or ever."

Luke says, "Good. I don't want to be known for taking out those three. I don't need a young gunslinger hoping to build his reputation by gunning me down. I'm not a fast draw."

"Now, get a good night's sleep and plan your honeymoon. I will see you at breakfast," George says.

"How did you know that was on my mind?" Luke says.

George chuckles. "Because I've been in your shoes."

"Speaking of shoes, Raymond told me to leave my knee-highs in the hallway, and the shoe fairy would shine them; this house is magical."

"Now that you mention it, it is," George says.

Chapter 13: Luke Meets A Famous General
July 12th

In the morning, Luke finds his boots exactly where he put them the night before, looking like the day Amy bought them. He spends most of the morning tending to minor issues with the wagon. If Amy and Doris decide to accept George's offer, Luke wants Randy to be able to tell George that the wagon is a good investment. Luke avoids the first floor because he'd be in someone's way anywhere. The Mansion and grounds are buzzing with preparations for the big event. Randy is busy, so Luke decides not to bother him for a ride to get his suit. A few minutes before noon, Luke asks Randy, "Can I borrow a saddle?"

"Sure, next time, don't ask," Randy says. Luke finds a saddle and a blanket he thinks Smokey will like, and uses the halter Ginger wore when she died.

On the ride to Westendorf's clothing store, Luke enjoys seeing the American flags on every corner and no trash or road apples cluttering the street. His suit is ready and fits perfectly. While the little tailor is carefully folding and wrapping it in paper, he notices they have men's toilet water in several fragrances and asks if he can sample them. The tailor says, "I particularly like the one that smells like vanilla."

Luke splashes a few drops on his hand, sniffs it, and says, "I like it too." He pays for the Eau de Toilet (toilet water), gets the suit, and walks across the street to a barbershop. He only gets a shave and has the barber splash on his recent purchase of toilet water.

Upon returning to the Mansion's stables, he hand-feeds Smokey carrots from Randy's stash of horse treats and gets two heaping pitchforks of hay.

At the front door, Raymond says, "Mr. Garrelts, I'm told our guests will arrive about six. The signal they are arriving will be me playing our dinner chime throughout the Mansion. Rosa requests that everyone be ready to leave for the front porch at the sound of the chime."

"Thank you, Raymond. I will be ready and waiting, but please call me Luke."

"Yes, sir, Mr. Luke. I heard you went to town to get a suit; may I see it?" Raymond asks.

"Sure," Luke says and removes the wrapping paper.

"It is a thing of beauty. There is plenty of time, so may I draw you a bath so your new suit can cover a nice, clean body?" Raymond asks.

"Yes, that would be great," Luke says.

"When it's ready, I'll tap on your door," Raymond says.

Luke lays his new clothes on the couch, strips down, stretches out on the comfortable bed, and stares at the ceiling. He wonders how a boy from Amarillo, with merely an eighth-grade education, can be in the Kansas Governor's Mansion and about to meet President Hayes and Ulysses S. Grant. Luke falls asleep thinking of Amy. An hour later, Raymond's knock awakens him.

After bathing and splashing on his vanilla toilet water, he dresses in his new clothes. He finds that tying a string tie into a bow by looking into a mirror is more complicated than he expected. He reads George's newspapers while waiting for the chime. Before long, he hears Raymond playing the four-beat chime outside his room and leaves for the front porch.

When he gets to the porch, he stands beside Susan and says, "George says you're supposed to help me make it through dinner."

"That is true; let me start by straightening your tie. After tugging at it briefly," Susan says. "That's better. Oh, sweetie, your aftershave smells delicious, like a vanilla sugar cookie. I want to eat you up!"

Luke says, "It's my first bow tie. I got the cookie water at the suit store."

"I could tell it was your first tie. That Cookie water could get you in trouble, if you know what I mean," Susan quips and smiles.

Luke smiles at Susan and thinks, *I hope my cookie water will have the same effect on Amy.*

Excitedly, Luke looks down at seven carriages lining the long half-circle drive. The cavalry troops that lined the city streets now surround the Mansion. Luke is looking for President Grant. He focuses on the lead carriage because it's George's and sees Randy climbing down from the driver's seat, wearing what must be a parade uniform. Randy opens the carriage door and drops a three-step hinged staircase. George steps out first and helps Rosa down. They step out of the way for six soldiers to create a human shield for the president and General Grant.

Luke's first impression is that both men are short. Somehow, he thought all Presidents were tall, like Abraham Lincoln. Luke remembers George saying Grant might be intimidated by his height, and he grins. While guests are exiting the other carriages, Luke only recognizes Jack, who is helping his wife out of the last carriage. The entourage progresses slowly up the front stairs and past the Mansion's staff lined up along a long hallway leading to the living room. To show their respect, the housemaids curtsey, and the footmen bow their heads slightly when the presidents pass. Susan and Luke are the last to leave the porch.

George and Rosa introduce the presidents to their guests. Luke and Susan are together at the end of the line. George introduces Susan as his second cousin. Luke can tell the men knew she would be there because their comments sound prepared. Both heap glowing compliments and commend her for tirelessly petitioning for women's rights. Luke puts one and one together and knows that Susan's presence is not coincidental; she and Rosa planned it.

George introduces Luke as a friend of Susan's and Rosa's who fought for the North at the Battle of Appomattox. Luke thinks each president held his hand for longer than expected and used the time to express gratitude for his service. Luke reciprocates by thanking them individually for their leadership. General Grant asks Luke the name of his battalion.

Luke responds, "The First Sharpshooters, but I only saw action at Appomattox."

President Grant says, "Since you are last in line, I want to take a moment to tell you about the Sharpshooters at Gettysburg. The First and Second Regiments' unique fighting style repelled superior numbers in two separate charges on our flanks. Observers said they won the battle, which turned out to be the turning point in the war. Even Confederate Colonels admit that Gettysburg changed the momentum in our favor. The government should build a memorial on the battlefield to recognize the Sharpshooters. Are you aware that the First and Second Sharpshooters were the most lethal fighting forces in the war?"[22]

"Thanks for telling me that. Is it okay if I quote you?" Luke asks.

"Sure, you can; that's not my opinion; it's a military statistic. People think I like going into battle, but nothing could be further from the truth. That said, Lee's Surrender at Appomattox is my favorite. I will forever be grateful for the chaos you and your fellow Sharpshooters created there," General Grant says.

"What a nice compliment," Luke says as he looks down so President Grant can't see his watery eyes.

Raymond cuts off their conversation by playing the dinner chime, followed by George announcing, "It's time to go into the dining room." Luke thinks, *General Grant is just like George said he would be.*

Susan tugs on Luke's coat tail and quietly says, "You're sitting on Rosa's right and next to me." Luke follows Susan and finds his place card on the corner seat across from Jack and his wife. George is at the other end of the table, sitting eighteen place settings away, with President Hayes on his right and General Grant on his left.

After everyone is seated, George stands and taps on his long-stemmed water glass with a spoon. He waits for the room to quiet down and says, "There will be no boring speeches this evening. You will have ample time to interrogate our distinguished guests after dinner. Rosa and I hope you enjoy your meal; we have enough for seconds." George's comments receive enthusiastic applause and laughter. Rosa and Susan compliment their hero on his suit. Jack introduces his wife, Megan, to Luke and Susan.

Luke looks at all the silverware, raises one eyebrow, purses his lips, and looks sideways at Susan. Rosa sees his reaction, leans toward him, and whispers, "Follow me, and you'll be fine. I'll start on the outside and work toward the plate."

After dessert, Jack and Luke go to the snooker room. Luke applies the techniques George taught him the night before. Jack introduces Luke to Topeka's mayor, three of his five councilmen, State Treasurer John Francis, and Lieutenant Governor Lyman Humphrey. As he shakes Luke's hand, Lyman says, "The governor says you have political potential. So, I'm keeping an eye on you."

Luke has been defeating all challengers at the snooker table. Jack's wife enters the room, faces Jack, and says, "Honey, it is time for us to go. First, we must thank George and Rosa; they're in the living room."

Jack says, "Meg, Luke claims to have never played this game before last night, and he's been wiping the floor with all of us."

Luke says, "George gave me lessons last night." Luke looks at Megan and says, "Ma'am, if I lived in Topeka, I'd be looking for things to do with your husband. He's fun; you're a lucky woman."

"Thank you, but I wish you had told me that privately," Megan says as she winks at Luke.

"Someday, this whippersnapper will be an important man," Jack says.

"I'm impressed. Jack seldom compliments anyone. I'm sorry to break up your fun, but it's getting late. Jack, please hand the stick to Luke so we can thank the Anthonys," Megan says.

Jack and Megan leave for the living room; Luke follows a half-minute behind. George is listening intently to President Hayes. Luke gives George a subtle wave, which he returns, and Luke proceeds to the stable to say good night to Smokey, check on the wagon, and give Randy a hard time about his parade attire. When Randy sees Luke, he says, "In that suit, you look like a politician." After getting the compliment, Luke decides not to mention Randy's parade uniform. Instead, he asks him to talk about traveling in George's Pullman during the campaign and where he keeps it. Randy tells several memorable stories before explaining that it's on a spur the Santa Fe built, especially for George, about a quarter mile away. Luke says good night to Smokey and returns to the Mansion.

Luke can't wait to see Amy tomorrow night and wants an early start in the morning. But he doesn't want to retire without thanking George and Rosa. Luke waits until the last guest has left the front porch. He tells Rosa he has no use for the suit and wants her to have it. He hopes she can give it to someone on the house staff. "Good idea," Rosa says. "It will remind me of you."

Luke says, "I'm looking forward to seeing Amy tomorrow. So much so that it will be difficult to sleep tonight."

"You're lovesick," George says. "And you can't wait to see that ring on Amy's finger."

Rosa says, "You get a good night's sleep. I'll ask Raymond to knock on your door at the first light of dawn. May I see Amy's ring?"

Luke says, "It's upstairs in my saddle bag; it's just a gold band with some small stones, as he cuts his eyes toward George."

George quickly interjects, "I'll ask Randy to have your rig ready to roll by seven."

Rosa says, "Maria wants you to have a hearty breakfast before you leave."

"When it comes to being thoughtful, you two are the best. Honestly, I have never experienced hospitality like yours. This evening was a truly unique and unforgettable experience! Meeting the presidents was amazing, but your beautiful hand-painted ceramic place settings were equally amazing. If I counted correctly, I used nine pieces of silverware and drank from three long-stemmed glasses. Two were for red and white wine, and one had water with ICE! They made the food taste better. I will remember tonight's dinner for the rest of my life."

"I agree, fine dinnerware makes the food taste better, but don't tell Maria that," Rosa says, giving Luke a long hug. She takes one step back and says, "If you hadn't come along, I might not be here. You will always be in my thoughts and prayers."

George says, "Your observation about our fancy dinner is what I expected. I figured you had never attended a dinner like tonight; most people have not. When people experience the finer things, they set their goals higher without realizing it. I hope that happened to you tonight. Now, go to bed and sleep well; tomorrow is a big day!"

Luke says, "I'll take that advice; good night," and walks to a southern-style, wall-hugging staircase to the second floor.

Chapter 14: Luke Gets Amnesty
July 13th

Luke is so excited about seeing Amy that he wakes up every thirty minutes to see what time it is and is relieved when he hears Raymond knocking on the door. Someone has already put hot water in the tub across the hall. When he's through bathing, he's grateful to be pulling on Mr. Strauss's blue denim jeans that Doris bought for him rather than the scratchy wool suit pants.

Raymond meets him at the bottom of the stairs, saying, "The governor is in the dining room waiting for you. If you've packed, I'll load your things in the wagon while you're having breakfast."

"Thank you; just put them under the seat. You find I left my suit in the closet; please take it to Rosa after I'm gone." Luke and George exchange "Good Morning," and Luke sits, as usual, directly across the table from George. Luke tucks a napkin between his neck and shirt while thanking Maria for filling his coffee cup. When George sees Maria's reaction to being thanked, he thinks, *Maybe I should show the staff more appreciation.*

When they finish eating," George says, "I got an idea last night, and I couldn't sleep until I had it on paper and ready for you this morning." George opens an envelope, withdraws one page of stationery, shows the written side to Luke, and says, "This is a safe passage document. It's in my hand, on my official gubernatorial stationery, stamped with the Seal of Kansas, and bearing my signature. It is addressed to Kansas Law Enforcement Personnel and says, Effective July 13, 1877, I, Governor George T. Anthony, grant Mr. Luke Garrelts diplomatic immunity by this document. This Order is in full force and effect while I am Governor of the Great State of Kansas."

George puts his executive order back into the envelope. He hands it to Luke, saying, "You never know when you might find yourself in a situation like three days ago. Without something like this, you could find yourself in a pickle. Should this be ignored, you must get a lawyer and have him send me a telegram."

"You've outdone yourself again. Thank you for worrying about my welfare," Luke says.

The men are comparing their observations and opinions about the presidents when Susan joins them. After she's seated, George teasingly asks Luke if he will propose on bended knee.

Luke says, "I plan to, but if needed, I'll get down on both knees."

"Good answer; there are times when prayer helps," George says, and they laugh.

Susan says, "You'll only have to ask her once. She is one lucky girl, and she knows it."

Luke and George place their napkins beside their plates, excuse themselves to Susan, and walk to the front door. Rosa, Raymond, and Randy are there looking somber. Luke sees his wagon next to the porch steps, and Smokey swings his head toward them when he hears Luke saying, "I'm going to miss you all."

Raymond says, "We seldom host guests as likable and appreciative as you; you're everyone's favorite! The entire staff has been telling me that since you arrived."

Then Randy chimes in, "Getting to know you has been my pleasure; I hope we'll see you again. Last night, when I was getting your wagon ready for an early departure, I noticed your right rear wheel was squeaking. I took all four off and greased them up. I couldn't help but notice that whoever rebuilt this rig knew what they were doing. It's sturdy and yet extraordinarily light. It must be easy to pull."

Luke answered, "Charlie rebuilt it in his barn with advice from a renowned carriage maker."

"He did one hell of a job," Randy says.

Luke says, "Randy, Raymond, I sincerely thank you for everything you've done to accommodate my needs. You helped make my stay very special."

Luke turns to George and Rosa, saying, "Your parting words last night were the perfect goodbye. I wish I had words to express my genuine appreciation for all you've done for me." Rosa is tearing up and can't talk. She hands Luke a sack lunch she prepared herself, and he hugs her tightly.

Susan joins them and says, "If your situation were different, I'd hire you to protect me."

Luke says, "That would be interesting work," and hugs her like he hugged Rosa.

Luke thinks that George looks a little shorter. He looks down and says, "Where are your shoes?"

George says, "Sometimes I suffer with pain in the arches of my feet, and shoes make it worse."

Luke says, "I have something that just might help. He goes to the wagon and returns with the Kiowa moccasin boots. "Try these on," he says as he hands them to George.

George pulls them on, walks around the porch, and says, "These are amazingly comfortable! They support my arches! I want to buy them!"

"I got them in that Kiowa trade, and I refuse to accept a penny," Luke says. "Now, regretfully, I must leave you. I'm 60 miles from Amy. Indians don't say goodbye; they say, 'Until we meet again.' So, until we meet again, my friends." He walks down the stairs, practically jumps flat-footed into the wagon, and begins clicking. Smokey leans into the harness, and they're off for Kansas City. He turns around at the end of the drive to wave goodbye and sees that Maria and Bernard have joined the others.

Luke rethinks his plan to go to Kansas City; *Smokey has shown the ability to maintain six miles per hour by getting a fifteen-minute break after every hour. The question is, can he do it ten times? The wagon has never been lighter, the water barrel is only half full, and the horse treats Randy threw in don't add much. The wagon-to-horse weight ratio Charlie talked about is less than one, and even the freshly greased axles should help a little.*

After an hour, Luke becomes more encouraged because the road is well-maintained and wide enough for approaching wagons to pass without leaving the roadbed. Also, every time he takes a break, there is plenty of lush bluestem grass near the road, and Smokey does better on a full belly.

Luke thinks, *With any luck, I should arrive at the Cattlemen's Inn close to eight. I should be able to unpack, get Smokey to a livery, clean up, and be ready for dinner by nine, which is kind of late. But I won't push Smokey past a comfortable pace, even if it means arriving after eight.*

Luke recollects his promise to Amy on the evening of July Fourth and thinks, *What will she decide after knowing what I did? Since Jordan's words will carry more weight with Amy than mine, I'll not mention Tom Addison without Jordan. I hope Jordan doesn't hesitate to answer my telegram.*

Luke decides his conversation with Amy will be about how he and Jordan became half-siblings and his affection for Jordan and Jesse. If asked why Jordan moved to Kansas City, he'll say, "To forget her past and begin new memories." If Amy asks uncomfortable questions, he'll suggest she can get a better answer by asking Jordan.

The road is good, allowing Smokey to navigate without help, so Luke's brain is free to work on his marriage proposal. He leans back, closes his eyes, and begins rehearsing his ideas out loud so he can hear how they sound. After several attempts, Luke is frustrated and unhappy with everything he's heard. Smokey encounters a steep knoll, and the strain causes him to lift his tail and break wind with such force that Luke feels the blast, causing him to lose concentration. Luke laughs and says, "Smokey, it's lucky I don't smoke, or I'd be on fire right now." Then he thinks, *Doggone it, if Amy says she still loves me after Jordan tells her what I did, I'll whip out the ring, drop down on one knee, and say whatever comes to mind. That's a workable plan. I must stop agonizing over finding the right words and then worrying about how to say them.*

It's noon, and unbelievably, Smokey is passing the 2-Handles wagon. Luke shouts, "Hey, Joe Stout. Are the girls a little warmer at night?"

"Absolutely. Can you stop?" Joe says.

"I planned to stop in thirty minutes, but I'm okay with stopping now."

"Good," Joe says. "I'm sure one of the girls needs to pee."

As they shake hands, Joe asks, "Why aren't you already in Kansas City? And where's your old sorrel?"

"She died; it's a long story," Luke says.

"I have time," Joe says.

Luke says, "But I don't. The girl I want to marry is in Kansas City waiting for me, so I'll give you a shortened version." Luke tells Joe he endeared himself to the governor's wife and Susan B. Anthony by helping them with a problem on his way to Topeka. He mostly talks about meeting Presidents Hayes and Grant.

Joe says, "That's quite a story; can I see that Executive Order?" Luke takes it from an inside vest pocket, carefully unfolds it, and hands it to Joe.

After reading it, Joe hands it back and says, "Damn, if caught robbing a bank, this letter would let you walk away!"

Luke laughs at Joe's comment and says, "Smokey has finished drinking and looks ready to go. I don't want to disappoint my girlfriend, who I hope is anxiously waiting for me at the Champion Hotel, so I'm heading out. When the girls wake up, tell them Mr. Luke is glad to hear that the Kiowa's buffalo blankets are working."

"I will, and I look forward to our paths crossing again."

"They will. I know exactly where you live. When I get settled, I'll find a way to get a message to you, and we can go from there," Luke says.

"I look forward to the day," Joe says.

Luke arrives at the Cattlemen's Inn a little after eight. Amy is taking an evening stroll. When she sees Luke half a block away, she runs to him until she is in his arms. She can't turn loose, which makes it difficult for Luke to unpack the wagon. When everything, except the boots, saddlebag, and rifle, sits next to the hotel's front door, Luke waves to a porter to join them and asks, "What's a fair price to put all this in her room?"

"Twenty-five cents would be fair."

Luke asks, "Does our room have a tub?"

"Yes, a nice big tub!" Amy says excitedly.

Luke asks the porter, "What would it cost to fill the tub half-full of hot water while I'm at the livery?"

"Seventy-five cents would be fair," the porter says.

"Okay, we have a deal; do both, and when I get back, I'll pay you $2." Then he turns toward Amy and asks, "Does Smokey have a place to stay?"

"He does. I paid for three days. The livery is about a quarter mile east on the right," Amy says.

"Good, I know the owner," Luke says.

"Our room is on the first floor; it's number 110, at the end of the hall," Amy says, looking excited and full of anticipation. Luke counters her enthusiasm with a boyish smile and pumps his eyebrows.

Amy says, "Oh, I almost forgot. You have a telegram; I think your sister sent it. Is her married name McMann?"

"Yes, it is. I sent Jordan a telegram from Topeka, telling her I would stay here."

"Is that when you telegrammed the hotel to put me in a luxury suite?"

"Yep." Luke takes a moment to read Jordan's telegram and says, "Jordan wants to meet at her home at ten in the morning. She provided her address."

"Does she know about me?" Amy asks.

"She doesn't, but you're going. I plan to show you off," Luke says.

"Good, I look forward to meeting my future sister-in-law, hint-hint. Luke, there's a photographer in the hotel lobby. When you return, would you do me a favor and pose for him?"

"For you, I'll do it," Luke says, leaving for the livery.

Luke greets Freddy Wilson, the owner of the livery. Freddy says, "Long time no see. I've been expecting you." Freddy opens the corral gate for Luke, then closes it and leaves to help another customer.

Once inside, Luke gets the rifle, goes to the back of the wagon, and gets the saddle bag and boots out of their hiding place. He throws the saddle bag over his shoulder, strokes Smokey's head while saying he's a magnificent horse, and looks around for Freddy. Luke finds Freddy at the forge, heating a glowing red-hot horseshoe, and says, "Freddy, it's good to see you. Smokey pulled the wagon almost sixty miles today. I want him to have all he can eat, like ten pounds of oats and a mountain of hay. His feed bag is hanging next to the feed box. Can the wagon be ready to roll at nine in the morning?"

"Sure," Freddy says.

"I apologize for being in a hurry; I'll see you in the morning."

"If the young lady who made your reservation isn't your sister, I know why you're in a hurry!" Luke takes off for the hotel with long strides.

Amy waits for him at the front desk and says, "The photographer is waiting for you."

Luke says, "Lead the way," and asks about the porter.

Amy says, "I paid him."

"Do you want to be in this picture with me?" Luke asks.

"No, I don't. I want a photo of just you, wearing the clothes from Brotherton's, but you'll have to sit for two flashes, "Amy says.

After the photographer takes Luke's picture, they go to the room. All their gear is along the wall opposite the doorway. Luke lays the boots next to Amy's travel bag and sets the saddlebag and rifle on top. He walks into the bathroom, skims his fingers across the bathtub's water, and says, "The temperature is perfect. I want to get in before it's cold."

"Me too," Amy says excitedly. "But I'm shy, so can we get undressed and climb in the tub in the dark?"

"Sure, I like that idea."

The bathwater is near room temperature by half past nine, so they reluctantly crawl out.

Luke lights a lantern; they get dressed; Amy combs her hair and ties it in a ponytail, and they leave for dinner. Luke locks the door and tries turning the nob. They walk to the registration desk; the doorman, porter, and receptionist stop chatting and turn to acknowledge their presence. Luke asks about Ray and Virginia, and the receptionist says, "They go home at seven."

Luke tells the porter, "The bath water was perfect; you can empty it after we leave in the morning at about nine. We're dining here in the hotel tonight. Please let me know if anyone should inquire about either of us."

Over dinner, they confess how much they have missed each other. Everyone in the dining room sees two people in love. They sit on the adjacent sides of a table for four, hold hands under the table, talk privately, never take their eye off each other, and lean in every few minutes for a brief kiss. Amy says, "You're the first man to steal my heart."

"You're the first girl I ever went to sleep thinking about every night," Luke confesses.

"A great-looking man like you! How can that be?" Amy inquires.

"Well, there are three or four good reasons," Luke says. "My father said he would be ashamed of me if I pursued girls just for romance, so I didn't. In the eight years on cattle drives and bronco busting, I didn't have opportunities to meet nice girls. If I had met one, I would have been too shy and intimidated to engage in conversation. Being single gave me the freedom to pursue that kind of work. And I enjoyed cowboy work so much that I never considered trading it for a wife and family until I met you. Besides my Mother, you're the first girl to show a genuine interest in my well-being. I find you extremely attractive. So much so that I want to kiss you whenever I look at your face," Luke says.

"That's five or maybe six reasons," Amy says.

"I could come up another one or two, but I'd turn bright red telling you," Luke confesses. Amy likes hearing that explanation and asks about his experience in Topeka. He gives her a version with just the highlights while drinking too much wine. When he's had enough wine to gather the courage, Luke tells Amy he loves her. She replies by saying that she is hopelessly in love with him.

Luke says, "Those are the best words I've ever heard." They share a long kiss that has the waitress bringing their check, doing a quick turnaround to avoid disturbing them and ruining the moment.

Luke explains, in detail, how he and Jordan became half-siblings. He tells Amy that Jordan is a fantastic woman and sees those same qualities in her. Amy loves hearing Luke's compliments and can't wait to show her appreciation. She wonders when he will discuss the mysterious family secret that could keep her from becoming Mrs. Luke Garrelts.

When returning to their room, the photographer is looking for them and hands Amy two nearly identical pictures. Amy says, "Oh, I love these! Thank you!"

"Good, I'm happy you're pleased," the photographer says and leaves.

Luke looks at one and says, "That photographer insisted my hat and rifle be in the picture. He must have thought I was an outlaw with a beautiful girlfriend," Luke quips.

"I told him to pose you like that!" Amy exclaims.

"Oh, in that case, I love the picture! Luke confirms. He picks her up and carries her down the long hallway to the door of their room. While holding her with one arm, he unlocks it, looks inside, and says, "Let's go slow."

Amy says, "I'll try, but I can't promise."

Chapter 15: Amy Meets Jordan
July 14th

After a late breakfast, Luke walks to the hotel's registration desk to thank Ray and Virginia for upgrading their room. He explains that he's taking his girlfriend to meet his sister, whom he hasn't seen in over a year. They ask Luke to tell them a little about his sister, and Luke says, "Her married name is Jordan McMann; her husband is J.R. McMann."

Simultaneously, Ray and Virginia say, "Oh my God!" Then Ray says, "She's living among the very well-to-do."

Amy sashays into the room about that time, locks Luke's arm with hers, and asks, "Don't we need to be going?"

Ray says, "Whoa, who is this?"

"A woman I met out front of your establishment last night and can't get rid of," Luke says jokingly.

Amy punches him and says, "Shame on you!"

Virginia says, "Amy and I talked about you for quite a while when she checked in yesterday. You had better be nice to her; she's a keeper. Could you all have dinner with us tonight?"

"Sure, what time?" Luke says.

"Meet us right here at seven?"

"Perfect, you pick the place, and I'll pay," Luke says.

"Nah, we'll flip a coin after dinner," Ray says.

"Deal," Luke says.

They return to their room so Amy can get what she needs for the day, and Luke can get his old boots. Amy says, "What are they for?"

Luke says, "You'll see." At the livery, Smokey is ready to go. Luke rubs his nose, gives him sugar cubes from the breakfast table, and says, "Did you sleep well, boy?" Luke thanks Freddy while lifting Amy onto the seat. He asks for directions to State Line Road, which couldn't have been simpler.

On the way, Luke tells Amy what Ray and Virginia said about Jordan marrying into money.

When they arrive at Jordan's home, she is on the front porch and begins waving as soon as they enter the long private drive bordered on both sides by white fencing. Jordan runs to the wagon while Luke is helping Amy down. Luke raises Jordan off the ground with a hug and introduces her to Amy, saying, "Jordan, I confess that I'm head over heels for this girl."

Jordan says, "It's so wonderful to meet you. I've never known Luke to have a girlfriend."

"Oh, that IS nice to know about the man of my dreams. If you knew the compliments Luke paid you at dinner last night, you'd understand why I'm so excited to meet you." Amy says.

"You can tell me later," Jordan says laughingly.

"Where's JR?" Luke asks.

"He's working. The bank closes at two o'clock on Saturdays, so he holds his weekly staff meeting when the doors are locked. They usually last an hour. I always attend those meetings, but NOT TODAY! JR wants a more impressive bank with more floor space. After his staff meeting, he's meeting with a realtor friend who has several properties to show him. We like to eat at seven, so I know he'll be home before then."

Luke says, "Before I forget, we must leave by five; we're going to dinner with the owners of the Cattlemen's Inn at seven."

"I know Virginia; I see her quite often in the bank. When I saw you entering the drive, I was brewing a pot of coffee. Let's go to the kitchen to get it and then sit on the back porch."

Luke says, "Give me a minute to get a few things." He retrieves the cash box and boots but leaves Charlie's dirty clothing behind.

While leading the way to the kitchen, Jordan looks back at the boots quizzically and then at Amy, who shrugs her shoulders, shakes her head unknowingly, and says, "Don't ask."

Jordan pours coffee from a boiling pot on the stove into a sterling silver coffee pot. She picks up the tray with the 7-piece coffee set and leads them to the back porch overlooking two acres of white-fenced yard with a pond and extensive landscaping. Jordan pours coffee while Luke and Amy watch two men pushing mechanical grass cutters, and two other men are trimming what the cutters miss with hand shears. Amy exclaims, "Jordan, THIS IS BEAUTIFUL!"

"Thank you," Jordan says. "When I started, there was only the fishing pond. I hired people to put the white rock around the edge, build the perimeter fence, and plant the trees and the flower gardens. I'm rather proud of it," Jordan says.

Luke says, "It's perfect. I've read about those mechanical grass cutters, but these are the first I've seen."

Jordan says, "They predate my living here. The person who designed that device was very clever. JR said it was invented in Europe to maintain the estates of wealthy people. They could leave their sheep in the pasture if they owned one."

Then Luke tells Jordan that Amy knows nothing about Tom Addison. He asks her to tell Amy the story she told him last year in April in as much detail as she's comfortable sharing.

When Jordan finishes, Amy is in tears and hugs Jordan, who's also crying. When the time seems right, Luke says, "Amy, I believe in avenging a wrong in the Biblical sense, an eye for an eye, and a tooth for a tooth. So, it was not in me to let Tom Addison kill Jesse and enjoy the fruit of his and Jordan's years of hard work. That would encourage him to do it again. Someone had to take a stand and provide closure for the widows he created." Then, for Jordan's benefit, Luke describes the evening of June 30th with Tom Addison, his getaway, the tornado, meeting Amy's Dad, taking him home, and meeting Amy and her Mother.

Luke gets the *Beacon* and *Post-Journal* newspapers out of the cash box, hands them to Jordan, and waits for her and Amy to read the articles. Amy looks at Luke and says, "I completely understand your motive. Had I known you then, I would have volunteered to be your accomplice. I need to know if you can put that night behind you. I've heard that some men who returned from the war have nightmares, and I don't want that to be you. If you agree not to speak of it again, my love for you is no different than when we woke up this morning."

Luke says, "Amy, I often think about Tom Addison's death because it's still fresh, but I don't regret what I did. I'm at peace; I haven't lost any sleep. Honestly, I sleep better now that it's behind me. I have never experienced post-war nightmares. That said, I promise to never speak of it again." Luke reaches into his inner vest pocket, retrieves Amy's ring, places it on his sweaty palm, drops down on one knee, and holds it for her to see. He clears the lump in his throat and says, "Amy Bonner, will you please marry me?" Amy says yes ten times before Luke can get up, and ten more barely audible yeses as they kiss.

Jordan asks to see her ring, and while holding Amy's ring finger, she says, "Oh my God, this is beautiful; where can I get one?"

"Goldman's Jewelry in Topeka. Mentioning George Anthony's name might get you a discount," Luke says laughingly.

"How do you know the Governor?" Jordan asks.

"It's a long story; let's save it for later, Luke suggests. I need a coffee refill."

While Jordan refills their cups, Luke picks up his old boots beside his chair. He slowly empties the $32,400 into the seat of the fourth chair, then tosses the $400 from the cash box on top of the pile and says, "Jordan, this is for you. It's $32,800 from the gun safe."

Jordan says, "I want you to keep it as my wedding gift. I know you all will do something good with it. If I kept it, JR would buy more stocks and bonds, which I don't enjoy. I'd much rather see you all use it to pursue your dreams."

Luke says, "I wasn't expecting this. I planned to get it into a bank account and transfer it to you over time. I haven't done that because I've been concerned that I might end up in jail if I tried to open a savings account."

Jordan bends over, picks up the key that fell out of the boot, and asks Luke, "What's this?"

Luke smiles and says, "It's the key I used to lock the gun safe."

"Oh, I must have it!" Jordan says pleadingly.

"It's yours," Luke says.

"Good, I need a memento, and this is perfect!"

Amy says, "Put it somewhere you'll see it every day, like in your jewelry box."

"That's a great idea," Jordan says.

Luke says, "This money is likely from a Wells Fargo holdup. What do you think?"

Jordan says, "You may be right. These bundles of U.S. Treasury notes are called packs. There are one hundred notes in each pack. We break the bands and count them before putting them in circulation. Any bank would report to authorities an individual possessing packs with unbroken bands. Even if you removed the bands, this many uncirculated notes would make an inexperienced cashier highly suspicious. When my cashiers encounter a questionable note, they record the serial number and see if it is on one of the lists in my office. They do that out of sight of the customer. Anytime they accept a $5 note or larger, they look in specific areas of the note for something that proves it's legal tender."

Luke asks, "So, the serial numbers on these bills or notes, as you call them, could be on a list at the bank, right?"

Jordan says, "Yes, stolen government notes get reported to the U.S. Treasury. The Treasury sends a report to banks that explains when, where, and how the notes were stolen, along with the denominations and serial numbers."

"So, if these bundles are from a recent robbery, you may not yet have a letter, right?" Luke asks.

"When a pack is counted and banded, they stamp the date on the band; let's look." After looking through the packs, Jordan says, "It looks like they all have the same date, October tenth of last year. Of course, that does not tell us when they were stolen, but I know they don't sit around the Treasury building for long. I've spent a year handling packs like these, and they all go through a security procedure called "chain of custody." The Comptroller of the Treasury has employees in charge of quality control procedures from printing until they're out the back door of the Treasury. These employees attest to the quality and quantity by initialing the band of every pack. It looks like RMC and CBC vouched for all these packs. So, these notes must have been in a train, stagecoach, or bank robbery after leaving the Treasury."

Jordan continues, "Our policy is to give the one and two-dollar notes a pass unless there's no mistake about them being counterfeit. Examples are if the paper has the wrong texture, the color is fading, the ink stains the hands, or all three. Texture is a quality my cashiers easily recognize because they handle money about six hours a day, six days a week. If the paper doesn't feel right, they will give it a closer look. They bring the note to me if they believe it may be counterfeit. If I agree, I send a runner to the sheriff's office, and we detain the customer with coffee and sweet rolls. The law confronts the suspected counterfeiter."

Jordan thumbs through a pack of twenties and says, "As expected, these serial numbers are sequential. I'm sure that's true of all packs, but let's be sure. I'll get a pencil and paper." When she returns, she says, "Give me the first and last number in each pack of the twenties, very slowly, please."

Amy and Luke read the numbers on the thirteen packs, and Jordan says, "These packs are sequential. I only need to check the smallest and largest serial numbers; all the others fall between these two. Let's see if the fives and tens are the same." They repeat the process with the same outcome, and Jordan says, "I'll check the numbers Monday morning. JR and I get there thirty minutes before the bank opens, so I'll have plenty of time. Come to the bank at nine. I'll tell him tonight you're coming so he can clear his schedule for the day."

Luke says. "We should be going. I don't want Ray and Virginia waiting for us, but I must make something crystal clear before we leave. Only the three of us shall ever know about this money. Jordan, you can't tell JR and Amy, you can't tell Doris. In other words, the three of us shall take this secret to our graves. I've had this money in my possession for about two weeks, and worrying about it has never left my mind for more than a few minutes. I can't go on this way. So, I'm begging you; I can't make it any clearer than that. If authorities were to find out, I'd have to leave the country or go into hiding. We'd never see each other again, and authorities would make your lives a living hell while searching for me. The next time I plan to talk about this money will be with St.

Peter. Hopefully, I'll have time to make amends between now and when that time comes."

Jordan says, "Your secret is safe with me, brother."

"And with me, my love."

Luke says, "Jordan, we'll see you at nine on Monday morning. Thank you for telling our story to Amy. I know it wasn't easy." He then turns to Amy, saying, "Let's go, love of my life." Jordan follows them to the wagon, where they have a group hug. While sitting in the wagon seat, Amy gives Jordan a brief history of her father's wagon. Luke says, "See you Monday morning, sis," then clicks his tongue, and Smokey pulls slowly away to avoid jerking his passengers.

Jordan shouts, "I love both of you. See you Monday; be safe!"

After a few minutes, Amy says, "I want to tell Mom that we're engaged. Stop at the telegraph office. I'll make it short and sweet."

Amy's telegram says, "This morning, Luke introduced me to his fantastic sister, Jordan. Later, he proposed to me with the most beautiful ring. Of course, I said, 'Yes!' Love, Amy."

They meet Ray and Virginia in the hotel's foyer, and Amy proudly shows her ring to Virginia. After complimenting Luke on his choice, Virginia says, "Do you all like Chinese food?"

Luke says, "I don't know; I've never had any. I want to try it, but I will expect you all to order my dinner."

"Ditto for me," Amy says.

Ray and Virginia know Amy arrived on the train and assume Luke got there on horseback, so the wagon doesn't come up in conversation. Amy talks about her first train ride, Jordan's home, and the beautifully landscaped grounds surrounded by a white fence. Luke mentions they did not meet JR and asks Ray what he knows about him. Ray says, "The rumor is he's a Harvard grad and has wealthy parents in New York City."

Amy says, "Virginia, Jordan asked us to say, 'Hi.' She's so smart and classy."

Virginia replied, "I agree. Jordan has made a name for herself in the banking business. She came here over a year ago, stayed at our hotel for a while, and moved into a boarding house near JR's bank. Initially, she got a cashier's job because she's easy on the eyes and never meets a stranger. I got to know her because, in our business, I make frequent trips to the bank. She impressed me by simplifying our banking. There's no doubt that the bank's customer base grew because of her. After only a few months, JR had her manage the cashiers and the small and short-term loans department. We've made some loans with her; she's very smart. The large loan managers and accountants report to JR. Jordan manages almost everything else, including janitorial, consumable supplies, keeping the employees happy, and whatever JR doesn't do. They got married about six months ago. JR built his home three or four years ago and only lived there maybe six months when his first wife died from a ruptured appendix."

After dinner, Amy compliments Ray on his restaurant choice: "Tonight was my first Chinese food. I now love Chicken Chow Mein and egg rolls drenched with soy sauce." Ray flips a coin, loses, and Luke offers to tip their waiter.

Walking back to the hotel, Luke says, "The food was terrific, but I couldn't master those horse toothpicks. I was so relieved when our waiter brought me a fork."

Ray says, "They look for folks struggling with chopsticks."

Luke says, "It didn't take them long to spot me. Whose idea was it to put a note inside a cookie? I couldn't read mine because I chewed on it and nearly swallowed it!"

Amy says, "I loved mine; it said, 'Expect new opportunities.'"

Amy Meets Jordan

Virginia asks Amy when they'll be getting married. Amy replies, "I don't know, but the sooner, the better."

In the hotel's foyer, Luke thanks Ray for selecting the Chinese dinner and paying for their meals, and he says, "We get to meet JR on Monday, and we expect to spend the day with him and Jordan. We'll see you all again before we leave for Dodge on Tuesday." The women say goodnight with hugs, and the men shake hands.

Chapter 16: The J&J Is For Sale
July 15th

It's Sunday morning; Luke has nothing on his schedule for the day and is sleeping late. Amy returns from the hotel cafeteria with coffee, pastries, and the morning paper. She says, "You promised not to bring up Tom Addison's death. Since I'm bringing it up, you're not breaking your promise. In this morning's *Kansas City Journal-Post*, there are two articles you must read. One is on the first page, and the other is the lead article in the business section."

Amy hands Luke the paper, and he sees the following front-page headline: 'Five-Man Posse Dead.' The article summarizes an interview with Addison's Undersheriff, Harry Rump: *Our search party returned with the mutilated remains of five men in a posse dispatched on June 30th. They are Moore County Sheriff Hugh Jass, Addison Mayor Claud Bahls, and three employees of the Addison Cattle Company, each with multiple aliases. The bodies were about twenty-five miles north of Addison. The men were swept up and beaten horribly by a tornado powerful enough to uproot mature trees and gouge a meandering, shallow trench nearly a mile long.*

The posse was in pursuit of a person seen leaving the city of Addison immediately after a fire broke out in the Addison Cattle Company office that evening. After receiving no report from the posse for five days, the city dispatched a search party. Finding the bodies and returning them to Addison for identification has been time-consuming. Friends familiar with the men used their clothing and personal items to identify them.

The Texas Rangers investigating the murder of Mr. Addison report that their wanted posters have generated no leads. Until they get one, their investigation is on hold.

"That's good news," Luke says. "I bet all those men had a hand in Jesse's death and the cover-up. Hopefully, one of the three "so-called" employees, whom Jesse called "mad dogs," was the man who shot Jesse."

Luke turns to the business section and sees this headline at the top of the page: 'Tom Addison's Estate for Sale.' The article states: *Due to Mr. Thomas Randolf Addison's having no last will or living relatives, his estate has become the property of the State of Texas. Governor Richard Coke has directed that Mr. Addison's properties be disposed of as soon as possible. The cattle have been sold, but the public can bid on his real estate in a blind auction. The ranch has been divided into thirty 2,000-acre parcels, plus or minus 200 acres. The 1st National Bank of Amarillo will evaluate bids, pick the winners, and schedule closings. Bids will be accepted during regular business hours, from August 1st through the 31st. Winning bids will be posted in the bank lobby on September 5th. Closings will be scheduled to begin on September 17th. Sufficient funds must be available at Amarillo's 1st National Bank or Texas State Bank by October 31st. Interested parties can view a plat of the estate, with each parcel outlined, numbered, and described at the 1st National Bank beginning on Friday, July 20th. No individual can bid on more than five parcels. Properties include all the improvements thereon.*

After reading the second article three times, Luke asks Amy if they can go to Amarillo, look at the map of the estate to see which parcel the J&J is in, and then check on the condition of the improvements. Luke says, "I can make my dream come true with you, that property, and time."

Amy says, "Then let's get going, but before leaving town, I want to be a married woman!"

Luke says, "We can do that tomorrow at the courthouse with Jordan and JR as our witnesses. When we're sure about our departure, I must tell George we will take his advice about using the Pullman."

Chapter 17: They Get Married
July 16th

Before going to JR's bank, they had breakfast at the hotel and walked to the telegraph office. Luke sent George a telegram that said, "I proposed; she said, 'YES!' We will leave on the morning of the 17th. If your offer still stands, we'd love to travel to Dodge on your Pullman. My best regards. Luke."

At the bank, they meet JR, who apologizes for missing them on Saturday and congratulates them on their engagement. Luke asks JR if he has found a property he likes.

JR says, "I did, and it's in a better part of town, and I can build a bigger and more impressive two-story building. My realtor is preparing the offer."

Luke is impressed by JR. He's five foot eight and looks very fit in a dark blue, pin-striped three-piece suit that fits like a glove; even the knot in his maroon silk tie is perfect. JR has thick reddish-brown hair that he combs straight back and a matching beard cut short and trimmed precisely. His wire-rimmed glasses, watch chain, and Harvard class ring are gold, and he speaks with an unmistakable New England accent. His large hand and firm handshake convey to Luke that he is not easily intimidated. He notices that Jordan looks at JR with beaming admiration.

After some usual "get to know you" small talk, Jordan says, "Luke, I'd like to talk to you privately for a moment." They go to her office, and she closes the door. Luke is expecting bad news, and his heart is pounding. Jordan says, "Your demand notes have not been on any of the Treasury's letters since November. If you want, I can deposit it in a joint account after processing them to make it look like they've been circulating for a while."

Luke says, "As I said yesterday, I have never wanted the money to be in your possession, and I don't want it anywhere near JR's bank. I worry that a large deposit could get people asking questions and doing some investigating; I don't want that."

Luke continues, "If Tom's lawyer knew he kept a large sum in his safe, he'd know the arsonist now has it. He might think his best chance to catch the thief is to ask bankers to be alert to a large deposit of uncirculated bills. Do I make a valid point?"

Jordan says, "Here's where your argument breaks down. If Tom's lawyer or anyone close to Tom knew he had a large sum of money in the safe, they would have dragged the gun safe out of the ashes and pried it open the next morning, and they'd have found Mr. Addison's remains right then. But that did not happen. Didn't you tell Amy and me it was a week before they opened the safe?"

"Yes, an article in Topeka's paper said a smithy opened the locked safe one week after the fire," Luke confirms.

Jordan says, "I'm satisfied no one knew about the cash in the safe. Well, some of the men in the posse might have known, but that no longer matters."

"That's an excellent point," Luke says. "It's embarrassing that I fret so much about getting caught that I miss the obvious."

"Anyone in your shoes would do the same."

Luke thinks briefly and says, "You'll think I'm nuts, but it's been safe for two weeks in a pair of old cavalry boots. I think I'll leave it there a while longer."

"You need to do what makes you comfortable," Jordan says. "I appreciate your concern that I do not get involved with handling stolen money. I know JR would agree with you. However, I can recommend what you must do to make the bills safe for spending and depositing."

"Good, I'm all ears," Luke says.

"You must make them look like they've been in circulation for a while; knock off the newness, age them a little, make them look worn. I'd suggest wetting and wadding each note in a tight, little ball by rolling it between your palms and straightening it on a table's edge. If it doesn't look worn enough, do it again. To draw less of a cashier's attention, I suggest making rolls of one hundred notes using rubber bands, just as most banks do. For added protection, ensure there are no consecutive serial numbers. If possible, mix them with naturally worn notes. Before we return, did you read the morning paper?" Jordan says.

"I did, and I asked Amy to go with me to see the J&J. I would love to own it," Luke says.

Jordan says, "Nothing would make me happier than for you all to own it. It would be satisfying to know that someone I care about will enjoy Jesse's and my hard work."

"I'm glad you feel that way. We'd better get back with JR and Amy."

When they rejoin Amy and JR, Amy looks at Luke and says, "JR knows a Justice of the Peace at the courthouse who can marry us in ten minutes. It was your idea, Luke!"

Looking at JR and Jordan, Luke asks, "Will you all be our witnesses?"

"We'd love to," Jordan says.

"Then let's go!" Luke says.

Amy says, "Lead the way, JR."

Herbert Diets presided over their ceremony, filled in the blank spaces on the marriage certificate, and handed it to Amy. She folded and tucked the certificate into her bra, over her heart, while Luke gave the Justice five bucks.

On the way back to the bank, Jordan asks, "So, what's next, big brother?"

Luke pretends he and Jordan didn't have their earlier conversation. He talks about the Addison Estate sale in the morning paper. He says, "The ranch that you sold is for sale. We've decided to give it a look. If the improvements are in good condition and Amy approves, we'll bid on it."

Jordan says, "That's positively exciting. I'll be praying for you all to get it." Luke explains they need to get to Amarillo as soon as possible and should leave for Topeka in the morning. He needs to write to George.

JR is curious why they'd be in a hurry to get to Topeka and asks who George is. Luke says, "Governor George Anthony offered his Pullman to transport my horse and Amy's wagon back to Dodge City. Otherwise, it could take us nearly ten days to get to Amarillo. Now that we have a reason to get there, we shouldn't dilly-dally. Today, I will telegraph George we're leaving for Topeka in the morning."

"How in the world do you know the Governor, and why would he let you use his Pullman?" JR asks.

"Only because I became friends with George and his wife, Rosa. There's nothing political about it, just a favor. Ten miles outside Topeka, I helped Rosa and George's cousin with a carriage problem, and Rosa insisted I stay at the Mansion. The governor was appreciative, and we got along so well that he asked me to attend a dinner party for Presidents Hayes and Grant. Maybe I was invited because Susan B. Anthony, George's cousin, needed a dinner escort for the evening. Anyway, I ended up a guest of the Anthonys for three nights."

After listening to Luke, JR is wide-eyed and says, "Good God, you call the governor by his first name, send him telegrams, stay in the Mansion, and dine with President Hayes and General Grant! May we have the honor of taking you to dinner to celebrate your wedding?"

Amy says, "Yes, a celebration is in order. I want new clothes for my wedding dinner, and I'll be more comfortable meeting the governor and his wife in new clothes."

JR says, "If you can be ready by seven, I'll have a carriage service pick you up in front of your hotel."

"Perfect," Amy says and pinches Luke.

Luke says, "This will be my first-ever experience shopping for women's clothes."

Amy says, "You'll have fun; we'll get you some new clothes too. But first, I want to tell Mom I'm a married woman." Amy's telegram says, "I just married the man of my dreams. We'll be coming to Dodge very soon. Love, Amy."

Luke's telegram to the Anthonys says, "We were married this morning and are leaving for Topeka early tomorrow. We should arrive at about dark. I do not want to create extra work for the staff; we'll sleep in the wagon. We must go to Amarillo to look over a small ranch that's for sale, fifty miles north, near Addison. We're in a hurry and can't stay long, but we look forward to seeing you all. Fondest regards, Luke."

Amy buys two pleated skirts and two coordinated, long-sleeved, pinstriped blouses. Then she talks Luke into buying casual clothes and French-made slip-on shoes so he'll not look like he's fresh off the trail, which he agrees to without complaint. Amy suggests they stop at a barber shop for Luke to get a shave and his beard trimmed while she goes across the street to have her ponytail shampooed and brushed out.

While returning to the hotel, Luke says, "I need to tell Freddy to have Smokey and the wagon ready to roll at sunrise. I'll let you off at the hotel; I shouldn't be long.

At the livery, Luke asks Freddy, "We want to get an early start in the morning. Could you have Smokey fed and the water barrel half full by sunrise?"

Freddy says, "No problem, I'll give him five pounds of oats and enough hay so he can eat all night. Luke, I'm embarrassed to tell you this. The sheriff came here looking for you after y'all left this morning. Someone told him that you are not the owner of this wagon. Until you resolve this, the sheriff has impounded the wagon and Smokey."

Luke says, "I understand how that could happen. The wagon's owner is the mother of the young woman who made the reservation for Smokey." Then Luke asks, "Can you direct me to the sheriff's office?"

Freddy says, "Our sheriff and chief of police have offices in the county jail. The jail is three blocks past the hotel you're staying at, on the same side of the street."

"Thanks; I need to get this cleared up this afternoon. We must leave early tomorrow morning to arrive in Topeka before sunset. So, I need to get going. If I'm convincing, you won't see me again until sunrise," Luke says.

At the Wyandotte County Sheriff's office, Luke explains the wagon belonged to his wife's father, who recently died, and says, "My wife is at the Cattleman's Inn right now; I can get her, if necessary." While Luke explains that, he removes an envelope from an inner vest pocket, hands it to the sheriff, and asks him to read the letter inside.

After reading it, the sheriff says, "I'm familiar with the state seal and recognize Governor Anthony's signature. I apologize for the inconvenience. Is there anything I can do to make your stay more comfortable?"

Luke says, "Thanks for offering, but there isn't. We're leaving for Topeka in the morning to spend a few days with Governor Anthony. If you're through with me, I must return to the hotel. This evening, my wife and I are dinner guests with my sister and her husband, J.R. McMann."

The sheriff quickly returns the amnesty letter in its envelope and says, "Sir, please go and don't be late! I'll tell Freddy you're good to go. I can't think of any reason for JR or the Governor to hear about this little mix-up."

"I agree," Luke says with a knowing smile, taking the amnesty letter from the sheriff's extended hand.

When Amy answers Luke's knock, she says, "You were gone longer than you expected."

Luke responds, "Freddy told me I had to meet with the sheriff about someone complaining that I didn't own the wagon. I told the sheriff it was yours; that cleared it right up, not a big deal." Then Luke tells Amy about his morning conversation with Jordan. He emphasized Jordan's belief that if anyone close to Tom knew he had a large sum of money in that safe, they would have opened it the following day, not a week later. Luke also explains Jordan's recommendations about how to make the bills look like they've been in circulation.

Luke looks at his new clothes on the bed and says, "I've been married for only a few hours, and you're already trying to change me. Hold on; I can see you're about to defend yourself. I was only kidding. I know you're right; I learned how important it is to fit in when I attended the president's big party."

"Oh, come on, you look good in those casual clothes," Amy says. "Can you button me up?"

"Only if I can unbutton you later."

"Only if you promise not to stop at those buttons."

"I promise."

"Perfect answer! If you wonder why I smile so much at dinner, I'm thinking about you undoing my buttons," Amy says.

Amy and Luke are picked up by a luxury carriage and taken to a high-class, members-only restaurant at the top of a six-story building, the tallest in Kansas City. They meet Jordan and JR at street level and walk up the six flights together.

Jordan whispers to Amy to follow her to the Ladies' Room. When they're alone, she gets the derringer pistols out of her handbag and says, "I don't need these anymore, but I think you might have a use for them. I bought them before leaving Amarillo, and although I never used them, I was more comfortable knowing I had them. I kept one in my handbag and one under my skirt."

Amy puts the little pistols in her handbag and says, "How thoughtful, thank you. I'll feel a LOT safer with these."

Jordan says, "Please write me as soon as you know the J&J is yours." Amy says, "I will, but by then, it will be the L&A."

"GOOD!" Jordan blurts out.

While the women are gone, JR orders French Champagne and a tray of oysters on the half shell to toast their marriage and kick off the evening. JR hangs on Luke's every word like he is one of his Harvard law professors.

After the Champagne toast and oyster hors d'oeuvres, Amy and Luke have their first shrimp cocktail and Caesar salad. Then JR coaches them on how to eat a lobster tail garnished with asparagus spears and French-fried potatoes. For dessert, they have cherry pie, fresh from the oven and topped with a generous scoop of vanilla ice cream. Amy notices that the table beside them has strawberries dipped in chocolate and asks JR if she could order a few. They finish dinner and go to a room where a five-man band plays slow music. Amy asks Luke, "Do you know how to dance?"

"Nope," he confesses.

"You're going to try," she insists.

"I'll stand in the middle of the room. You can either stand with me and rock side to side or do whatever you want," Luke says.

After several songs, Amy has Luke's feet doing the two-step. Luke is holding her close, and she asks what he has in his pocket.

Luke confesses that he likes dancing much more than he thought, but suggests they return to the table to be with Jordan and JR.

The two couples chat about the band for a few minutes. Then Luke says, "Sister and brother-in-law, you have made this an extraordinary wedding day for us, and I learned how to dance! We also thank you for the most unusual yet wonderful wedding dinner; we certainly will not forget it. Sadly, we must be going. We have another big day tomorrow." When Luke finishes, everyone is teary-eyed and promises to stay in contact.

On their return to the Cattlemen's Inn, Amy says, "Some delicious creatures live in the ocean."

Luke says, "Yes, but they're ugly as all get out."

In bed, Luke says, "Tomorrow will be a long day, and we must leave early. I told Freddy I would come for the wagon at sunrise. Before I leave for the livery, I'll ask the kitchen to create a breakfast of fruit and pastries that we can take with us. When I return, the grocery store should be open, and I'll get a bag of treats for Smokey. You must be ready to roll within an hour after I leave."

"I can do that," Amy says confidently.

Chapter 18: The Garrelts Go To Topeka
July 17th

Luke brings Amy a morning cup of coffee, says, "Rise and shine, sweetheart," and tells her he's leaving to get the wagon. Before leaving, Amy watches him transfer his bounty money from the saddle bag to the boots with the money from the gun safe.

At the livery, he asks Freddy if Smokey cleaned out his trough, and Freddy says, "There's nothing wrong with his appetite." Luke settles his bill with Freddy and tells him they're leaving town to get an early start for Topeka. After harnessing Smokey, he rides the wagon to a grocery store, where he buys a bag of apples and tosses them in the feed box. Luke has Smokey pull up the wagon beside a hotel exit close to their room. Amy is packed and ready to go. Luke says, "I'm going to the front desk to pay our bill and say goodbye to Virginia and Ray. I'd like you to come with me."

Virginia is at the registration desk and again asks to see Amy's ring. Ray is in the office, hears them talking, and joins them. While Luke is paying their bill, Amy goes to the dining room to get the breakfast Luke ordered. When she returns, the four exchange farewell hugs and kisses, and Virginia is tearing up. Luke looks at Virginia and says, "Until we meet again, dear friends."

Virginia says, "Until then, be safe." Mr. and Mrs. Garrelts return to their room to load their wagon.

Once out of town, Luke says, "We'll stop after an hour to give Smokey a break. I got a bag of apples for him in the feed box. While I'm getting his water, would you get ten apples? I'll cut them in half, and you can feed him."

"You spoil him," Amy says.

"Spoiling him pays dividends for me. I must remember to put the boots in Charlie's secret hiding place. I need to show you where I put three pebbles between the boards. I always look for them before lifting the cover. If they're missing, that's proof someone has opened it."

After Smokey's break, Amy asks Luke about his nine days on the road to Kansas City. "Do you want a quick overview or all the details?" Luke asks.

"It'll take ten or twelve hours to get to Topeka, depending upon Smokey. So, I have time to hear about everyday and the details of your most memorable times. For example, I want to know the exact words spoken by you and the presidents."

"Okay," Luke says.

When he finishes, Amy says, "You should write a book about your experiences. They are quite interesting, and you're a good storyteller."

Luke says, "You find them interesting because you love me. I think anyone else would say they're exaggerated bull crap."

Amy says, "I saw you putting cash from your saddle bag in one of the boots this morning. How much money is in the boots?"

Luke replies, "I didn't expect Jordan to give us the money from the gun safe. So, I kept my thousand dollars of bounty money in my saddlebag to separate it from the gun safe money. That's the money you saw me putting in the boots."

"Why only a thousand dollars? I thought the bounty was twelve hundred?" Amy asks.

"It was, but I used two hundred to buy your ring, new boots, a suit, shirts, suspenders, a tie, and some for a bit of pocket money. There are 33,800 dollars in one of the boots.

"Dang, I'm married to a handsome, wealthy cowboy. That's been my dream since I was a little girl," she says.

"Let's do everything we can to keep it that way," Luke says. "You will charm the devil out of George, Rosa, Raymond, Randy, Maria, Bernard, and Susan if she's still there. They know very little about us. If they ask questions, tell them the facts. I'm not ashamed that I asked you to marry me after only twelve days and married you two days later by a Justice of the Peace in a Kansas City, Kansas, Courthouse. You know enough about me to get by, and vice versa. Feel free to tell them why we're going to Amarillo."

Amy says, "I can manage that. Tell me about the economics of a cattle ranch in case I get asked."

"That's more difficult. I made a mathematical analysis that I'll try to explain. Say we start our cow-calf operation by buying thirty yearling heifers and introducing them to a fine young bull. They will have babies after nine months, just like a woman. And, if healthy, they'll have a baby every year for the next nine to ten years. On average, we're supposed to get fifteen heifers and fifteen bull calves, so let's assume that. The newborn heifers cannot get pregnant for a year. All they can do until their first birthday is eat and become fertile heifers. The bull calves become steers in three months and become steaks around their first birthday; a short life, huh?

In the second year, our original thirty heifers, now called cows, have another thirty babies. So, by the beginning of year three, we'd have thirty cows plus fifteen heifers that together could have forty-five babies. I made a table using those assumptions; the herd would grow from thirty females to a cow-calf herd of 400 in ten years. The bull calves are not in that number because we would sell them. My ten-year estimate of 400 is impossible because cattle die from diseases, predators, accidents, birthing problems, rustlers, culls, and the bulls fighting with each other rather than taking care of business. Herds experience deaths from all of those, with coyote packs being the worst; however, good cowboys can help with those problems."

"Culls; what are culls?" Amy asks.

"Culls are older cows that are no longer fertile, and young cows that don't ever have a calf, or their calves die from lack of nourishment. Some cows get culled due to physical problems, like blindness."

"So, to come up with a more realistic estimate, I repeated the original table and reduced the herd size by thirty percent at the beginning of every year. The herd size dropped to 200 cows and calves by the end of the tenth year. What I found interesting is that the mortality rate is about 50% because the herd size decreased from 400 to 200. So, thirty percent is probably a little too high. We'd have sixty steers to sell in the tenth year, plus twenty culls, worth around $40 a head in Kansas City or Dodge."

"We could live on that," Amy says.

"If we tried to sell the steers and culls locally, they're only worth about ten dollars.

"Don't you suppose Amarillo will have a stockyard within ten years?"

Luke says, "I do. Herd size could affect the price if it's not a large stockyard with many buyers. But I'd drive 'em to Dodge for a better price. I'd probably enjoy an annual 50-mile cattle drive."

"What do you do if you get all bull calves one year?" Amy asks.

"If your goal is to grow the herd, you'd sell the bull calves as soon as you wean them and buy heifers or trade with another rancher who has enough herd cattle and wants steers for his fat-cattle operation."

"How much pasture does a cow with a calf require?" Amy asks.

"Depending upon rain, twelve to fifteen acres."

"How big was the J&J?" Amy asks.

"About 2,500 acres," Luke says.

"At fifteen acres per cow, that's a little over 160 cows."

"We will have to acquire more land as we grow," Luke says. "I look at the J&J as a good start. If we can use the money from the gun safe, we can afford more land than just the J&J. However, if we can't use it, I'll scrape together what I can and get a bank loan."

"What's your goal? How many cows?" Amy asks.

"The demand for beef should exceed the supply for years, which is terrific for cattle prices. My dream is to have a thousand cows. When I extended my analysis, the years beyond ten showed tremendous growth. For example, at the end of the fifteenth year, the herd grew to 700 cows and calves, 200 steers, and possibly seventy culls. My goal is not unrealistic. It's not some dream I had after smoking Lone Wolf's peyote-filled peace pipe," Luke says and chuckles.

Amy says, "A thousand cows would need 15,000 acres! You can't manage that by yourself."

Luke says, "You're right. As we grow, I'll eventually need a ranch manager, miles of barbed wire, and cowboys to ride the fence line looking for broken posts and downed wires. They'll also have to know how to pull calves, brand, castrate, look for diseases like hoof and mouth, shoot coyotes, and look tough enough to discourage rustlers; it's not easy work.

"When the ranch gets that big, my responsibility will be planning and looking at our financial performance, so I'll be more of a numbers guy. The nuts and bolts of my job include ordering supplies, planning roundups, seeing that broken items get repaired or replaced, determining when to sell steers and culls, and acquiring new bulls. I'll pay the bills, bank the income, keep the books, and worry about our profitability. I'll be doing things that aren't fun for a young man, but over time, I'll learn to enjoy watching the ranch grow on paper. I'll be like an orchestra conductor, directing my musicians to maximize their performance. To ensure the ranch operates as I want, I plan to get out among the men weekly to see for myself, listen to what they need, tell them what I've planned for next week, and assure them things are good.

"At King Ranch, the manager would throw a big dinner for us the night before we'd leave on the cattle drive. After dinner, he'd thank us for working for the ranch, tell us where to pick up our pay in Kansas City, and answer questions. Once, I asked him to tell us about his job, and everything he talked about was managerial."

Amy says, "I like that you know what you're getting into and have a very ambitious goal; I figured you would."

"It won't be easy, sweetheart, but it won't be dull either." Luke kisses the back of her hand and says, "You have to trust me."

"Luke, you must not confuse my trust with my concern for your safety. I will always trust you and be concerned about you getting injured. When you're not home after dark, I will worry. I can't help it; it's called love," Amy says.

"That's mutual," Luke says, and Amy kisses the back of his hand.

They arrive before sunset, and, except for Susan, the entire household is on the steps, clapping and cheering like they did for the two presidents. George says, "It's so good to see you again. Get up here so I can hug you all." Luke jumps down, puts his hands around Amy's waist, and gently lowers her to the ground. While standing next to the wagon, Luke introduces Amy to everyone on the porch. Randy, Raymond, and Bernard come down, shake hands with Luke, congratulate Amy, and begin unloading the wagon while Luke and Amy go up the stairs to greet George, Rosa, and Maria.

Luke looks down, sees Randy leading Smokey to the stable, and shouts, "Hey, Randy, I'd like to pick your brain in the morning!"

"Okay, looking forward to it!" Randy shouts back,

George says, "You must be exhausted, but we're dying to know your plans. Let's go into the dining room, where you can brief us over dinner." Luke and George help the women get seated.

The two couples face each other, and Luke says, "We have a plan. There's a property for sale about fifty miles from where I grew up. My half-sister owned it for seven years, and I visited her many times, so I'm very familiar with it. It's roughly halfway between Amarillo and the Oklahoma Panhandle. My sis sold it after her husband died over a year ago. Due to some unusual circumstances, it's now for sale again. It's part of the vast estate owned by Tom Addison. Mr. Addison died without having a will, and he had no heirs, so his ranch became the property of the State. Texas has divided it into 2,000-acre tracts so more folks can afford to bid.

George interrupts, saying, "Tom Addison, didn't they find his remains in a gun safe?"

"I read that a while back, although the two articles in the Sunday edition of the *Journal-Post* didn't mention it.

"Go on with your plan," George says.

Luke continues, "We want to get to the First National Bank in Amarillo as soon as possible. We need to know if the ranch is in one or more tracts and go there to evaluate the condition of the improvements. If Amy approves, we must decide how much to bid. We need to do all of that rather quickly. I plan to sell my wheat farm, and we both have some savings, but we may still need a bank loan. That's a lot for us to do, and the clock is ticking."

Rosa says, "George, these kids need to eat the meal Maria prepared and get to sleep. You're going to bed right now to be sure you leave them alone." George and Rosa leave the Garrelts to eat in peace, but under the watchful eye of Raymond.

Raymond tells Amy, "When George told me Luke was married, I was happy for him. You two seem to be a perfect match."

"Thank you; I agree," Amy says.

Raymond says, "Luke, you all will be in your old room. Have a good night, and I'll see you in the morning."

"Thank you, Raymond."

"Goodnight, Raymond," Amy says. After Raymond leaves, Amy says, "Aren't you glad we're not sleeping in the wagon tonight?"

Luke says, "Yes, I'm delighted. However, when I telegraphed George that we were coming, it concerned me that the guest rooms might be occupied. If they were, George would put us in the most expensive hotel in Topeka. I don't like to invite myself and then find I'm a burden. So, I told George we'd sleep in the wagon in the stable. Smokey loves the stable because Randy stocks his favorite treats. You're in for an experience; our guest bedroom and bathroom are amazing, as is this entire Mansion. After I finish the rest of the food Maria prepared, I'll show you to our room."

Chapter 19: Randy Schedules
The Santa Fe
July 18th

Thirty minutes after sunrise, George is in the dining room reading stale newspapers from cities around Kansas, drinking coffee, and waiting for Luke. When he walks in, George looks up and says, "You look well-rested."

"I feel well-rested. The reception you all gave us last night made us feel welcome and important. Amy was as thrilled as when I proposed. I can't imagine she'll ever forget it." Luke hears a ringing sound and asks, "What's that?"

"That, my boy, is the future. It will let us talk to each other using the telegraph lines, and you will recognize the voice of the person on the other end."

"Ah, it must be a telephone," Luke says.

"Yes," George says. "The device is supposedly experimental, but I predict it will sweep through the country like wildfire. If you ever dreamed of being a telegraph operator, forget about it."

"I read that Alexander Graham Bell was granted a patent last year, and the first telephones would be installed in select places this year," Luke says.

George says, "The Mansion was on the priority list to get one. That ringing is some testing they're doing. I can't use it yet, but I won't have to wait long."

Amy bounces into the dining room wearing her new boots, pleated skirt, and blouse with sleeves rolled up to her elbows. Her long blondish hair is in a tight ponytail, and she has tied a light brown silk scarf in a bow to hold it together. She says, "Good morning, boys," and draws two imaginary pistols by pointing her index fingers at George and Luke.

George smiles from ear to ear and says, "Dang, if you're not as cute as a bug's ear. Sit down here and tell me why you accepted his proposal."

Amy holds her ring a foot from George's face and says, "Look at this amazing ring. The man knows how to negotiate," Amy says.

George laughs and says, "I saw it before you did! You two are perfect for each other!"

"So, what have you boys been talking about?" Amy asks.

Luke says, "You haven't missed much. I told George how thrilled we were with the reception last night, and we were discussing a telephone that's being installed in the living room."

Amy says, "Mr. Anthony, I experienced my first standing ovation last night. They are wonderful for one's self-esteem!"

George says, "We were thrilled to see Luke again and especially excited to meet you."

"How kind of you to say that, Mr. Anthony," Amy says. "Now, when can I see your telephone?"

"It will still be there after breakfast, George says. And please call me George."

"Okay, George."

Luke says, "I wonder when the Santa Fe will make the next run to Wichita?"

George looks at Amy and says, "I asked the man responsible for scheduling my Pullman during the campaign to pull together a schedule for you all. His name is Randy Sharp. Randy has kept up with train schedules, even though I don't campaign anymore. I suppose old habits die hard. Randy said you all can leave as early as noon tomorrow."

Shaking his head affirmatively, Luke says, "We should take it."

Still looking at Amy," George says. "You will arrive in Wichita around six o'clock and be sidetracked until the next day, when you'll hook up to a turnaround train from Dodge. Randy wasn't specific about when you'd leave Wichita, but said it's less than seven hours to Dodge. At Dodge, we decided to give you two days to visit with your mother and sort things out. Randy and Rosa's bodyguard, Howard Johnson, will go with you as far as Dodge. Randy says he can teach Luke everything he needs to know about the Pullman by the time you arrive."

George switches his attention to Luke and says, "Getting the Pullman back from Amarillo takes a week, and I do not want to be without Randy and Howard that long. So, in Dodge, you will meet a Pinkerton man named Ralph Barr, who will stay with the Pullman until it is safely back here. You will not have to be concerned about finding him; he'll find you."

"Taking us to Amarillo must be expensive!" Luke says.

George says, "My governor's budget covers it. After Lincoln, Federal and Kansas legislators approved generous funding for security. The Pinkertons are eager to please, so I make them happy by keeping them busy. You'll be pleased to hear the time from Dodge to Amarillo is eight hours. Randy says that's because it's a new track with fewer curves, hills, and trestles to slow down for."

"George, thank you for having Randy schedule your Pullman to Amarillo. You don't know the load that you just took off my mind," Luke says. Then he reaches up with one finger to remove a tear in the corner of his eye that is about to run down his cheek.

George says, "We're happy to do it. You've more than earned it. Rosa feels extremely indebted to you, so finding ways to help is our way of thanking you. After staying in the Mansion for only three nights, Bernard tells me you have become the staff's favorite houseguest, and most of them have worked for several earlier administrations."

"That's a nice compliment," Luke says. "It makes me swell up a little?"

Amy says, "The train ride to Amarillo can be our honeymoon. And it will be so nice to have two days with Mom; thank you. I want to go sightseeing around Topeka before we leave."

"That won't take long," George says.

Amy asks, "What can we do between now and noon tomorrow?"

Luke says, "I enjoyed watching you shop for clothes in Kansas City, so I think I'll take you shopping in Topeka." Luke looks at George and says, "I thought I saw a ladies' store next to Westendorf's."

"You did; it's called Patricia's. Mrs. Westendorf runs it, and Rosa loves the place."

Amy says. "How soon can we leave? Can I see your Pullman today?"

George says, "Sure, tell Randy what time, and he'll meet you there. It stays locked, but Randy has the keys."

Rosa enters the room and asks, "How are my two favorite love birds?"

Amy answers, "We're great. Your home is amazing. Luke tells me how good you all have been to him and your incredible dinner party for President Hayes and General Grant."

Rosa says, "Honey, your husband is my champion, and those moccasin boots he gave George have been a godsend for George's feet!"

Plaintively, George says, "Pre-Luke, I was her champion. I'll be wearing those boots in my grave."

Rosa says, "I have a request. I'd like us to dine together tonight, and I want Amy to see Luke in his suit. Luke, I haven't given it to Raymond yet. It's hanging in my closet. I'll hang it in your room while you're shopping."

Amy said, "Oh, I can't wait to see that."

George says, "Now, let's have breakfast so these two can get on with their plans for the day." Rosa rings a small bell, and Bernard begins serving breakfast.

Rosa catches a sparkle from Amy's ring finger during breakfast and says, "May I see your wedding ring?"

Amy says, "Of course," and extends her hand to make it easier for Rosa to examine.

"He has excellent taste in jewelry," Rosa says.

"He does," George says and rolls his eyes at Luke. After breakfast, Luke and Amy return to their room, use the bathroom, and then go to George's office to see their first telephone. George demonstrates how the phone will work, and Amy says, "It's peculiar looking but not scary." After a few minutes of looking over the phone, they thanked George and left for the stable.

At the front porch, they look down, and Randy is standing next to the governor's carriage. He shouts, "George says I'm your driver for the day."

Amy says, "That will be fun. I need you to stop at the telegraph office so I can write to my mother." Amy's telegram says, "Mom, we'll arrive in Dodge on the 19th on the Santa Fe and leave for Amarillo on the 21st. I love you, Amy."

Randy takes them to Patricia's Clothing store and falls asleep while they shop. Luke awakens Randy when he drops down the staircase and tosses two packages into the carriage's facing seats.

Luke spoofs Randy, shouting, "Coachman, to the Pullman, with haste, my good man!"

Randy says. "Yes, my Lord...your Royal Highness!"

Amy is so excited about the private quarters in the Pullman that she accidentally hugs Randy rather than Luke. After excusing herself, Randy says, "Anytime you feel like giving me a hug, don't hold back," and they laugh. Randy gives them a complete tour of the Pullman, and Luke is taken by how no detail is overlooked.

Randy says, "Mr. Anthony told me to go with you to Dodge. I'm to ensure everything goes well. There's plenty of time for me to show you the ropes. I wouldn't be surprised if George has a Pinkerton man join us. It could be Howard. He's looking better; the bandages are off."

Luke says, "George mentioned at breakfast that you and Howard would go with us as far as Dodge. Then another Pinkerton man, I think George said his name is Ralph Barr, will ride to Amarillo with us and bring the Pullman home."

Randy says, "The Pullman is George's baby. I often wondered if the Pinkertons were along to protect the passengers or the Pullman. Ralph is a good man; you'll like him."

Luke says, "We're so fortunate. Randy, you would only have to spend one day and a night on the wagon to understand how grateful I am to George."

During dinner, Rosa asks Amy her opinion of Luke in a suit. "Oh, goodness, he looks good enough to eat, but he's not completely dressed," Amy says.

"What do you mean"? Rosa says.

"No gun. That's the only way I've ever seen him." From Rosa's expression, Amy realizes her gun comment isn't appreciated and says, "I could get used to him without it."

George tries to break the uncomfortableness by saying, "After Lincoln, carrying a gun near a U.S. President, except for security guards, is not allowed."

Trying to help, Luke says, "Actually, I prefer not wearing it, but I don't have a choice."

Rosa apologetically says, "I had to learn the hard way that it's a dog-eat-dog world out there. I am sympathetic to your need for it, but I don't like them in the wrong hands. They give a person, with one, power over someone without one." That comment ends the gun conversation, and they return to carving their steaks.

During dessert, Rosa says, "I asked our photographer to take our picture when we finish here, and I expect he'll be here soon."

Luke says, "Could we include your staff? They've been so good to me that I'd like a picture to remind me of them."

"In that case, we'll take two group pictures. One with just the four of us and another with everyone in the house; they'll appreciate that," Rosa says.

Rosa tells Raymond, "Please tell the staff about Luke's request for a group picture."

Raymond says, "Your photographer is in the living room right now, ma'am. Shall I get him?"

Rosa says, "No, we'll go there."

When they get to the living room, Raymond says, "Ma'am, when I told the staff about the group picture, they insisted on having a few minutes to primp, so I gave them ten."

Rosa said, "Okay, we'll use that time to take a few pictures with the Garrelts. Hopefully, George will have his eyes open in one of them."

After taking the pictures, Luke speaks to the hired help, thanking them for their kindness. They applaud, stand in line to meet Amy, and congratulate her on catching Luke.

When the staff leaves the room, George and Luke retire to the snooker room to discuss Kansas's issues. They compare opinions on gun-slingers, lawmen, immigrants, bandits, crooked businessmen, politicians, the decimation of the buffalo, non-white races, the poor, and George's inability to get money to solve state problems. Luke asks George if he's interested in serving a second term. George laments, "Probably not. If a governor doesn't have dependable majorities in the legislative bodies, it's like a captain of a ship without a rudder or an anchor."

The women stay in the living room, and Amy asks Rosa about Susan's passion for trailblazing the women's suffrage movement. When Rosa finishes, Amy says, "I've been thinking about your telephone; eventually, it will change the world.

Rosa says, "Speaking of changing the world, have you noticed the French influence on women's clothing, shoes, and hairstyles?"

"Not until Luke took me to Patricia's today. The saleslady kept pointing out that their fashions were the latest from France. Most of their clothing is for women with money and status, like yourself. They were beautiful, but I'd have no place to wear them. I did find some things I liked, but not until I got to the back of the second floor," Amy says.

Rosa says. "Yes, I doubt Patricia's store would do well in a small rural community. I warn you, all that glitters is not gold. What I mean by that is I appear to be a woman of leisure with no responsibilities. Nothing could be further from the truth. Nothing, I mean nothing, happens without my involvement and blessing. Not to brag, but I am the power behind the throne. I had no concept of the responsibilities a governor's wife had to deal with. I'm more than happy to do it for George. I don't think he knows the extent of my influence and the number of decisions I make. If Luke asks your opinion about him going into governor-level politics, say, 'No,' and stick to it!"

Amy says, "Thank you for that advice, but I can't imagine I'll ever have a reason to use it. Speaking of foreign influence on America, have you read how British-made locomotives and passenger cars will change the speed and comfort of rail travel within a year?"

"I didn't; how do you stay so well informed?" Rosa asks.

Amy says, "Luke and I like to read newspapers together when we can get them. We both enjoy talking, and the morning paper provides topics to discuss throughout the day. When we disagree, the discussion often turns into a debate. I love hearing his opinion on issues of the day; he's knowledgeable and pragmatic."

"That's very close, if not the same thing George said about Luke," Rosa says.

"Would you mind telling me about Luke rescuing you and Susan?" Amy asks. And Rosa gives her a detailed explanation of her fifteen minutes of horror outside of Topeka.

At about ten, Luke and George join the women, and Luke says, "Shopping for dresses and blouses tuckered me out. I must say goodnight to you all and Smokey. I'll take him some sugar cubes so he knows I still love him. After that, I'm going to hit your feather bed," he says to be funny.

Amy does a little curtsey with a head-cocked smile and says, "The evening was perfect, very memorable; thank you so much. I'll follow Luke to the stable and hand-feed him some sugar cubes."

George and Rosa enjoy Luke's and Amy's sense of humor; they nod and grin at each other. Both couples exchange goodnight wishes, and the Garrelts leave for the stable.

Chapter 20: Steer On A Plate
July 19th

The newlyweds are up early, but when George isn't in the dining room, Luke looks for Raymond and asks, "Where's George?"

"Mrs. Anthony told me George is out of sorts this morning. He doesn't want you to leave, and they've decided to say their goodbyes at the Pullman."

"That's the best place to say goodbye," Luke says, telling Maria they will have breakfast in the kitchen and will enjoy her and Bernard joining them. During breakfast, Luke tells Maria that Randy constantly brags about her cooking.

Maria smiles, blushes, and says, "He has a good appetite, and I save dinner leftovers for his breakfast and lunch." Luke figures they have a mutual attraction that Randy hasn't shared with him, which explains the bragging and the blushing. Their conversation with Bernard eventually leads to him describing his long-term plan, which has always been owning a ladies' dress shop.

Amy says, "Bernard, you would be successful because you have a flair for fashion."

"Thank you for noticing, and so do you," Bernard says.

"Why, thank you, Bernard," Amy says and nods.

After breakfast, while they're packing, Raymond knocks on the door and tells Amy he will help carry their things to the wagon. Luke says, "We're ready right now." They carry everything down in one trip. Randy waits on the porch and helps load their things on the wagon. Amy gets in and begins arranging everything to her satisfaction.

When the last item is in, Randy looks at Raymond and asks, "Is this everything?" Raymond nods his head in the affirmative. Then

Randy looks at Luke and says, "Is there room on that seat for the three of us?"

"If you take the reins and Amy sits on my lap, there is. Before we leave, I need a minute." He shakes Raymond's hand and thanks him for his thoughtfulness, the morning baths, and for making his boots look brand new. As they leave, Maria and Bernard join Raymond on the porch to wave goodbye to the Garrelts and Randy.

The Pullman is on a sidetrack a short distance from the Mansion and spotted alongside a loading ramp that rises to the Pullman's big rear door, which is open. Smokey pulls the wagon up the incline and goes inside as though he does it every day.

Randy says, "Smokey is self-confident. During the campaign, I always had to lead our horses in." Luke unharnesses Smokey and gets him comfortable in his new quarters while Amy hands Randy the items she wants to take into the living quarters.

Amy and Randy are looking for places to set things down when she says, "Randy, since yesterday, someone has been here cleaning and polishing!"

Randy says, "That's standard."

Luke hears that and says, "For the Governor of Kansas, I can understand, but no one needed to do that for us."

Randy says, "You underestimate the esteem the Governor has for you. I need your ROYAL assistance to maneuver your wagon into a secure position." Luke looks at Randy through squinted eyes, and Randy says, "I was just teasing; I didn't mean it as a criticism; you should be flattered."

"I am, but don't do it again," Luke says.

"Yes, my Lord," Randy says with an ear-to-ear grin.

"Either you apologize, or I refuse to help," Luke says.

"Luke, I only kid people I like," Randy says.

"Me too, so I forgive you, but stop it anyway," Luke says.

Without another word, they push the wagon to a back corner, where Randy sets the brakes, chocks each wheel, and ties it to three sides of the Pullman. When done, he says. "That's all there is to it."

Luke says, "Let's join Amy." At eleven-thirty, George, Rosa, and Howard arrive in the Governor's carriage with one of Randy's stable hands at the reins. Howard has a small suitcase, George carries a sizable box, and Rosa has a wicker basket.

Luke takes the box from George, carries it into the quarters, and says, "Howard, you're healing up nicely, but you're going to have a scar."

George says, "Rosa told him that women think scars are manly."

Amy looks closely at Howard's scar and says, "Rosa is right about this scar; it's very manly."

Luke says, "This girl flirting with you is my wife, Amy."

Howard says, "Several of the Mansion staff told me about you. You live up to your billing."

Amy winks at George and Rosa, and to tease Howard, she says, "Luke, was that a compliment, or should I slap him?"

They all laugh, and Rosa says, "Thank you, Amy; poor George needs a good laugh. He did not want to get out of bed this morning. He fears never seeing you again; he needs cheering up."

Luke looks at George and says, "Wherever we end up, we will stay in communication. You all are like parents."

"Can you make that a promise?" George asks.

"Absolutely," Luke says.

Rosa says, "We couldn't let you get away without some parting gifts; that's what we've been doing this morning. The box George couldn't wait for you to take from him is a case of French wine from the Mansion's wine cellar. It's the same berry juice we served at the shindig for Presidents Hayes and Grant. I accompanied George during the campaign. I learned not to drink city water without first cutting it with wine. I used equal parts of water and wine. The bouquet of wine masks any odor, and the alcohol kills the bugs that upset my digestive tract. I figured you'd get to Wichita early enough for a nice hotel dinner, so this basket is just for fun. It has several kinds of cheese, crackers, preserves, jellybeans, gumdrops, chocolate bars, licorice, marshmallows, toffee, gum, and other confectionery."

Amy says, "Oh, how thoughtful. We'll enjoy all those fun things; many will be a new experience for me."

George hands Amy an envelope and says, "This is a wedding gift from everyone in the Mansion. You know it's money, so you don't need to open it now."

Amy presses the envelope against her breast, and Luke says, "Be sure to thank them for us and tell them we promise to use it wisely, hopefully, for Texas pastureland."

Amy says, "We'd sure like a copy of last night's pictures."

Rosa says, "Everyone in the Mansion wants a copy. So, I ordered a copy of the two group pictures for all the staff. When you've settled, write me, and I'll get copies to you."

"Speaking of photos, I have two of Luke, and I'd like to give you one." She gets the pictures from her carry bag, hands both to Rosa, and says," The evening Luke arrived in Kansas City, I had a hotel photographer take these. I paid for two and can't tell them apart, so take your pick."

Rosa says, "This one is perfect! It's just how Luke looked the day we met! I love it! Thank you!

They hear the train whistle and then a gentle coupling bump that makes everyone steady themselves. Luke says, "You all had better get off, or you'll be coming with us."

George says, "Raymond told the Conductor to wait for my signal before pulling out."

"You think of everything," Luke says.

George says, "The authority I have as Governor spoils me; however, you're right. Stay in contact, dear friends." He gently touches Rosa's back to direct her toward the back landing and staircase.

At the bottom step, Rosa turns, looks up at Amy, and says, "Take good care of my hero."

"I'll do my best," Amy replies.

George looks at Amy and says, "I hope the property is in good shape and you love it."

"Thanks; whatever happens, we'll let you know. However, we'll not know if our bid is a winner until September 5th," Luke says.

When the Anthonys are off the train, George waves to the Conductor. Within seconds, they hear, "All aboard," and the Pullman begins moving. The Garrelts stand at the back of the Pullman and wave until George and Rosa are out of sight.

Before returning to their quarters, Luke tells Randy and Howard, "We're supposed to get to Wichita at about six. We'd like you to join us for wine and cheese at four and then for dinner." Randy and Howard looked at each other with grins.

Luke looks at Randy and says, "Be sure to knock first."

They lay down on top of the bed for a short nap. Amy's head is on Luke's chest, and she says, "Do you know a good place to eat in Wichita?"

"I do. It's called The Longhorn. It's conveniently located, and I know a waitress there."

"If she's young and pretty, you're in trouble," Amy says and kisses him.

Luke says, "I'd like to tell you a secret about a lady friend of Charlie's in Wichita. I think it helps to understand how rumors get started. But to tell it, I must break my promise to her. I'm comfortable doing that because if she knew Charlie would be helped by telling it, she would say it's okay."

Amy says, "That sounds reasonable to me."

Luke says, "Okay then. I stayed one night in Wichita, and after dinner, a woman named Jane showed up at the livery along with a dozen others. After I sold a few items, they all left except Jane. She confided that she and Charlie enjoyed a platonic relationship for several years. She'd cook, and they'd talk and play card and board games like friends do. I'm convinced that his charming personality was how he got invited to dinner and breakfast at the farms and ranches where he stopped. Most folks probably got excited when they saw his wagon in front of their home."

Amy says, "That doesn't surprise me. Dad never met a stranger, and he loved to talk, so I'm sure his gabby personality cultivated friendships with his customers. His reward was home cooking and someone to listen to his opinions and experiences. Thanks for telling me that. I know a relationship like that will gin up false rumors, which is the stock and trade of a gossip."

They nap for nearly an hour. Amy gets up, washes, changes her clothes, brushes her hair, shakes Luke awake, and sits by a window to watch the countryside pass by. Luke pulls on his boots, brushes his teeth, washes up, and reads the morning paper that Rosa put in the basket of treats.

They wait quietly for a knock on the door. When it comes, Luke shouts, "Come on in." The three men sit at the conference table. Luke uncorks a bottle of wine and fills the four glasses designed to stay upright when a train car jiggles. Amy serves cheese slices on crackers and sets the basket of sweets in the middle of the table.

After uncorking the third bottle, Luke says, "Take it easy on the Governor's wine; it tends to creep up on you."

Randy asks, "Have you opened the envelope?"

"We have. There were twenty-five twenty-dollar bills and a best wishes card signed by everyone."

Randy says, "Let me tell you how that happened. Everyone was going to Raymond and saying they wanted to give you all a wedding gift, but no one had enough money to get something nice. So, Raymond suggested we pool our money. We liked his idea, but when George got wind of it, he suggested we give you money rather than a present. He told us you might be bidding on some property, so cash was a perfect present. I'll bet he rounded it to five hundred by chipping in four hundred or more."

"George was right about giving us cash. When you return, please tell each person that we are thrilled by their gift, particularly George and Rosa," Luke said.

"It's okay to tell the Anthonys that it made me cry," Amy says.

As the train slows into Wichita, Luke says, "On my way to Topeka, I spent a night here in the wagon, in a livery corral, and had dinner at the Longhorn Hotel. If you're hungry, they have a menu item called "Steer on a Plate." It's expensive, but it will fill you up."

In unison, Randy and Howard say, "Good!" They could feel the Pullman uncoupling from the train, and then a team of Clydesdales pulled it onto a short side rail.

It comes to a rolling stop, and they see the brakeman on the back platform turning the brake wheel. When he's through, Howard says, "I'm not a member of the Mansion staff, so

Raymond didn't consider including me in your wedding gift. I insist on paying for dinner."

Luke and Randy look at each other, smiling from ear to ear, and Randy says, "Okay, but I'm going to order that Steer on a Plate anyway."

Luke says, "Howard, we're happy you want to pay, and that will be a generous and memorable wedding gift. The Longhorn is near here; we can walk there in five minutes."

At the Longhorn, Marge, the sassy waitress who waited on Luke twice before, looks at Amy's ring finger and says, "That ring makes me feel better. Handsome here wouldn't give me a second look about ten days ago. Now, I see why."

Amy looks up at Marge and says, "It should make you feel better knowing he spoke highly of you earlier today."

"You just made my day, sweetheart!"

Luke says, "Marge, this little filly is Amy. She disregarded her better judgment and married me in Kansas City four days ago. We're on a honeymoon train ride to Amarillo; these two jokers are our escorts."

Marge says, "Nice to meet you, Amy; it's obvious that you USED your better judgment."

"Thanks, I think so," Amy says.

Luke introduces Randy and Howard to Marge, and they both order Steer on a Plate. When they've cleaned their plates and imbibed the free refill of the giant beer mug, they use their table napkins to wipe their whiskers, and Randy says, "Man, that was hard to beat," and hiccups.

Howard says, "You can say that again!"

"Man, that was hard to beat!" Randy repeats.

Luke says, "This place has an echo."

Amy says, "I know you're full as a tick and feeling no pain, but no belching, please."

Randy says, "Surely you don't expect me to explode!"

"No, but you should burp into your napkin with your teeth together and with your lips tightly closed behind the napkin. That way, you can control the release and muffle the ugly sound."

"I can do that," Randy says. "Y'all have any other etiquette suggestions for me?" he says, using raised eyebrows to keep his half-closed eyes open.

"No," Amy says.

Luke says, "Yes, but it's more difficult to talk about."

"Oh, come on, not among friends," Randy says, followed by a sudden burp and a glance at Amy, frowning. Luke sees Amy's reaction and thinks he should not bring up his issue.

But after a long pause, Luke says, "Okay then, here's the deal: it's your gas. I love you like a brother, so you must hear me out. You seem to have no hesitation in sharing your gas with your friends. When you do, I suspect you save it up to impress me instead of quietly releasing a little at a time. So, I would appreciate you being more considerate and discreet."

Randy's diet is primarily vegetables, giving him an abnormal gas problem, which he does not try to control around men. However, he decides to have some fun with the topic and says, "A silent fart takes out all the fun, so I store them up to impress you. Now, Amy, I don't do that around women, just the guys."

"Boys, boys, please, let's change the subject," Amy pleads.

Howard says, "In a minute, Amy. Randy, I consider you my best friend, but you must listen to Luke."

Randy decides it would be fun to make up a funny story and says, "That may be why the Wednesday night poker guys never invited me a second time. Based on everyone else's behavior, I thought we were playing poker and having a friendly FARTING CONTEST. I tried my hardest to win; I almost soiled myself. I thought they didn't invite me back because they didn't like me showing them up; they were sore losers." Luke and Howard laugh until they wipe tears off their cheeks, and Amy holds her sides.

When Howard pays for dinner, Marge asks about the uncontrolled laughing. Since the group doesn't know Randy's fart story isn't true, Luke wants to save Randy from embarrassment. He tells Marge about a good friend who answered nature's call by squatting near a railroad overpass and being caught with his pants down by a Santa Fe brakeman riding in the caboose.

On their way back to the Pullman, Amy asks, "That story you told our waitress; was that true?"

"Yes, it was about ME! I had been out of Wichita for about an hour on the morning after I had the Steer on a Plate. I was so hurried to answer nature's call that I didn't think about the possibility of a train passing by. I gave the brakeman a story he would enjoy telling; he could see I was past puberty." Their uncontrolled laughing starts over again.

By themselves in the quarters, Luke suggests that if they acquire the J&J, they will likely not return to Dodge for a while. He wants Amy to consider closing her savings account and getting the things, like winter clothes, that she will need.

Luke says, "Keeping money in the Dodge City bank is dicey. I've read articles about the frequency of small bank robberies, which often result in the bank failing, leaving the depositors high and dry."

"Jesse James has made newspaper headlines robbing banks and Wells Fargo's stagecoaches and railcars. Supposedly, he gives the stolen money to folks who have fallen on hard times. The newspapers glorify that noble gesture by calling him the

Robinhood of the West. However, some journalists question whether that's true."

Jesse and Frank James, the three Younger brothers, and a few not-as-well-known crooks were robbing banks from Missouri to Minnesota. Last year, they got shot up while trying to rob a big bank in Northfield, Minnesota; the Youngers got caught.[23] I'm convinced that money in big banks is safer because they can afford security guards and fancier safes," Luke says.

Amy says, "I'll close the account. I only have something like two hundred dollars. Before I met you, I planned to use it for my big getaway. What should I do with it now?"

"Hang on to it and spend it on something your heart desires," Luke suggests.

Well then, I should give it to you; you're something my heart desires," Amy says.

"You know how to make me feel good. Just have fun with it; where did you plan to go?" Luke asks.

"I thought how fun it would be to see modern civilization, like New York City," Amy says. "In terms of culture and modernization, that part of the U.S. is a different country."

"Hopefully, someday you will, Luke suggests. The fact that I haven't decided on a plan to deposit the money safely is gnawing on me. Based on Jordan's advice, there is little risk in spending or depositing the one- and two-dollar bills if we make them look like they've changed hands a few times. So, the fives, tens, and twenties are the problem. I'll try Jordan's idea of wetting and wadding them in Amarillo."

Amy says, "When we get to Dodge, I'll give you the $500 wedding gift from the Mansion staff. They intended for us to buy land with it, so it belongs in the boots with the money we'll use to buy the ranch. Enough talk of money. Do the rhythmic bumps of the wheels hitting the rail joints make our lovemaking more pleasurable?"

Luke says, "Oh...yeah, I suppose so."

Amy whispers, "Don't think I haven't noooo-ticed," she says, sounding like an Irish lassie by speaking each word at a slightly higher pitch in a sing-song manner.

Chapter 21: Returning To Dodge City
July 20th & 21st

Luke, Amy, Randy, and Howard walk into the bright morning sun on their way to breakfast. After finding a table for four, greeting Marge, and ordering, Randy tells them the Pullman will leave Wichita at nine. Randy looks at Amy and says, "It's a seven-hour trip unless Indians attack us."

Amy turns to Luke, winks, and feigns fear by saying, "Oh, Luke, Randy has terrified me! Then she glares at Randy sideways and says, "Randy, don't try to scare me. I'm not some naive, Eastern, goody-two-shoes who grew up playing parlor games with the daughters of the social elite. Indians didn't have success boarding trains from horseback; they gave up even trying as trains got faster. However, your dime western novels keep up the myth with pictures of Indians leaping from galloping horses onto train cars."[24] Amy frowns at Randy with pursed lips and a furrowed brow while Luke, Howard, and Randy laugh at her lengthy retort.

Randy says, "I was expecting a different reaction, but I admit your description of young Eastern socialites is correct. I grew up in Philadelphia and worked eight years as a groom for a highly educated, obnoxious rectum with three like-minded daughters. I took those three hemorrhoids to and from their social gatherings and weekly shopping trips." Randy's rant is momentarily interrupted by the other three laughing at his descriptions.

When they finish laughing, Randy continues, "When riding in the carriage, they entertained themselves by belittling me. While I waited patiently for those pains in the butt, I'd read dime western novels. Since I could only afford a few, I traded them with friends. And you're right; the authors were dishonest about the Indians, but their stories made those pocket-size books extremely popular.

Fortunately, in seventy-five, I heard about a candidate for the Governor of Kansas needing a groom who could also manage scheduling train service for a Pullman car he used in his campaign, so I wrote to him. I'm almost thirty, and my only assets are last week's paycheck and a few clothes."

Luke says, "If I can ever afford a right-hand man to help with my business, Randy, you'll be the first I contact."

Howard hears this and says, "Luke, my story isn't much different from Randy's, so don't forget about me."

"If I ever need two good men or Randy turns me down, you'll be the next person I'll contact," Luke says.

Howard says, "Thanks, I'd like to change jobs. I've been thinking about law enforcement."

"Like police work?" Luke asks.

"Not police work; that's like personal security but on a larger scale. Because I know a little about the law, I'm considering running for sheriff in a rural county. I would tout my Pinkerton employment for a resume."

"I'll keep that in mind; should you ever need someone to vouch for your character, let me know," Luke says.

"I appreciate that," Howard responds.

While waiting to be served, Randy explained that their stop in Dodge would be a relatively quick turnaround. The Pullman will be uncoupled about two hundred yards from the depot. He says, "Uncoupling doesn't take long, so Howard and I need to have our belongings with us to board the passenger car, or we'll have to chase the train to the depot."

"How long will the train be at the depot?" Luke asks.

Randy answers, "Depending upon the season and day of the week, it takes an hour or more to unload people, cargo, and mail and reload the same going to Wichita, Topeka, and Kansas City. Usually, the tender car is replenished with water and wood while people and cargo are trading places. When that's complete, off we go."

Luke says, "Breakfast is on me. Afterward, I'll get a newspaper and say 'Hi' to a friend at the livery. Amy, I'd like you to come with me."

"Okay, but what advice do you have for Randy should he and Howard encounter an Indian raiding party on their way back to the Pullman?" Amy quips.

"I'd suggest he drop to the ground holding his heart with both hands, play dead, and pretend to be bald," Luke says.

Randy says, "I've no comment, but that is excellent advice."

Luke knows the *Beacon* is week-old news, so he skims it and finds the same two articles he read in the Kansas City paper. They walk to the livery, and when the owner sees Luke open the corral gate, he shouts, "I didn't expect you to see you again so soon."

"Since I saw you, I married this little cutie pie."

"HORSEFEATHERS! How did you find her so quickly? Does she have an unmarried twin sister?"

"No sisters...or brothers. Her name is now Amy Garrelts. She's Charlie's daughter. We're going to Dodge to see her Mother for a few days, then heading to Amarillo."

Amy says, "Luke told me about selling housewares in your corral. Did you get a commission?"

"So, Luke does have a name, after all. He was so hurried to send a telegram that we didn't take time for introductions. No, I didn't get a commission or the ten percent discount he gave the ladies. My name is Jeff Addison, and it's nice to meet you."

"I'm Luke Garrelts. Are you related to the Tom Addison who's been in the news?"

"Yes, he was my uncle, and I've spent the last twenty years denying it. My father was Tom's business partner. He died on a deer hunting trip with Tom. The sheriff never investigated it. My wife insisted that I not claim to be his relative. You're on foot, so where's Charlie's wagon?"

"It's on the train. I'm sorry, I don't have enough time to tell you how it got there. When I left you on July 8th, I said I'd come to see you if I ever got back this way. So, I'm keeping my word."

"That's a rare quality," Jeff says. "I'm glad you did."

"We need to get back on the train. My parting advice is, don't cook your coffee boiler dry."

"Good advice; y'all take care," Jeff says as he shakes Luke's hand, tips his hat to Amy, and says, "Nice to meet you, ma'am." The Garrelts return Jeff's parting farewell and leave.

On their walk back to the Pullman, Amy says, "I think Jeff would thank you if he knew the truth."

Shaking his head in disbelief, Luke says, "I'm not surprised Jeff didn't want to claim the old bastard was his uncle. He figured the Texas Rangers would believe he avenged his father's death. It wouldn't be the first time someone did something like that." Amy thinks it's best to let Luke's comment stand alone.

After the train hooks up with the Pullman and leaves for Dodge, Randy finds Luke and says, "I want to give you the keys to the Pullman right now. I worry that I'll get distracted and forget."

Luke takes the keys and says, "Okay, y'all knock on the door when you feel the train first slowing down into Dodge. That should give us time to say our goodbyes."

Around three-thirty, they could tell the train was slowing because the time between the rail joint clicks was getting longer. And soon, they heard a knock on the door. Luke shouted, "Come on in!"

The men enter, holding their travel stuff. Randy says, "Ever since we left Topeka, Howard and I have fretted about saying goodbye to y'all. We've decided we would rather not say goodbye. We want to believe we'll see you again, and soon, we hope."

"I like that," Amy says. They try a group hug, and the men knock each other's hats off. Amy picks up Randy's and Howard's hats, sets them on their heads, and gives each a hug and a peck on the cheek.

As the train backs into the long side spur, Luke says, "Until we meet again, my friends." Both repeat Luke's parting words and leave for the passenger car.

Before closing the door, Randy says, "Hey, y'all, I made up the fart story I told last night. I had too much wine and beer; we were having a good time, so I made it up to entertain you. But I promise to be more discreet with my flatulence. It would be nice if George's horses were as considerate."

They laugh, and Amy says, "It was a very FUNNY story." Randy closes the door as the rear brakeman sets the brake on the Pullman, opens the coupler, and signals to the engineer. The train begins moving slowly, with the men waving their hats and Amy throwing kisses.

A large, well-dressed, official-looking man approaching the Pullman takes Luke's attention away from their departure. He places his hand on the boarding handrail and says, "Good afternoon; I'm Ralph Barr with the Pinkerton agency. I'll be traveling with you to Amarillo." Luke tells Ralph that they will not be leaving Dodge until the day after tomorrow. Ralph says he was aware of that.

Luke says, "Allow me to give you the grand tour."

Ralph says, "I worked for the governor a few times during the campaign, so I know my way around his Pullman."

Luke says, "My wife's Mother lives in Dodge; we'll stay with her. We'll leave most of our things in the quarters and lock them up. I plan to ride Smokey to my mother-in-law's home and return relatively early in the morning with his best friend, a gelding, sorrel, quarter horse named Fury."

Ralph asks, "Would you consider letting me use one of your horses to go to breakfast?"

Luke says, "If you promise to go only to the Dodge House, you can use Smokey. He's been my sidekick for fourteen years. I admit I love him and don't want him waiting for you tied up in front of a saloon."

"I understand your concern, sir. I agree to your terms, and I thank you," Ralph says.

Doris is on her buckboard, wondering why her kids have not exited the passenger car. She decides they must be inside the unusual-looking Pullman, sidetracked a short distance away. She rolls the buckboard beside the Pullman and shouts, "Amy!"

Amy walks out of the living quarters onto the rear landing and says, "Hi, Mom! Come up here; you've got to see this to believe it."

Luke and Ralph finish talking, and Luke leaves to join the women. Luke waits at the door between the front and back sections of the Pullman until Amy and Doris calm down. Luke smiles when Doris reacts to Amy's ring, the living quarters, and Amy's description of Jordan, JR, and the Anthonys. When he thinks the time is right, he greets Doris with a big hug and says, "Doris, I'd like to leave your wagon here tonight."

"That's okay, but I'd prefer you to call me Mom."

"I can do that, Mom." He then looks at Amy and says, "Since there will be a Pinkerton guarding the Pullman, we can leave most of our things here. They'll be locked up. I only need my saddlebag if Mom allows me to use Charlie's grooming products."

"Of course you can," Doris says.

"Good; our Pinkerton man is Ralph Barr. I've got to give him the key to the back half of the Pullman so he can lock it up, then I'll ride Smokey to the farm."

Doris says, "Smokey's saddle and bridle are on the back porch. You're going to ride him bareback through town?"

"I trained him from a two-year-old using only a rope halter. He's never had a bit in his mouth; that bridle on your back porch is a side-pull hackamore. He responds to verbal and non-verbal cues. He understands verbal commands, sounds, and the tone I use. He also reacts to the pressure of the reins, my knees, and whether my weight is right, left, or forward.

"I've never used my spurs on him. I turn my toes in to be sure they don't touch him. What bonds him to me is that he knows I will not cause him pain, and he likes the treats, praise, and affection I shower on him. In a word, he feels "safe" with me.

"Sometimes I use my spurs on Fury, but only a touch. He was nine when I bought him from a man who abused him. After a year of receiving the same treatment as Smokey, he still doesn't completely trust me. I can't bear leaving Smokey here for the night. He'd like to stretch his legs after being cooped up for two days, and he and Fury will enjoy being together again."

Doris says, "You answered my question like Charlie would, with a complete history lesson."

Luke says, "I apologize. I have a great deal of pride in Smokey. You seemed skeptical, so I unloaded on you, and again, I apologize, Mom."

"Hey, what you said was very interesting; I enjoyed your explanation, and now I understand that you two are a team. I hope you and Amy will have that kind of relationship."

Amy says, "Mom, there's no need to hope; Luke and I are already a team. I don't need anything from the wagon. The things I'll need are in the Pullman. We can carry them to your buckboard in a single trip. I want to stop at the bank on the way home to close my savings account."

Luke asks Amy, "Please send George and Rosa a telegram that we arrived safely, and thank them for the wedding gift, the wine, the basket of fun, the Pullman, and Randy's and Howard's help."

"I'll do that," Amy says.

Even though he wants to believe Ralph is trustworthy, Luke arranges several items that Ralph would have to move to snoop around in the wagon. He holds the mattress back to ensure the three inconspicuous pebbles are in place.

Luke sits at Doris's kitchen table, watching Doris frying chicken, Amy boiling potatoes, and making cream gravy. Amy shows Doris their marriage certificate and says, "You'll see that my last name is now Garrelts."

"That's what I would expect," Doris said.

"Interestingly, it's my third; I was born a Bushnell, raised by Bonners, and married a Garrelts."

Doris is unfazed by the name change, but the news of them living down by Amarillo is not as well-received, and she gets teary-eyed and quiet. Seeing that, Amy tries to soften the unwelcome news by saying, "Mom, once we've settled in, it's only an eight-hour train ride to Amarillo. I'll pick you up at the depot, and it's a five-hour buckboard ride to the ranch. I read that the new locomotives Santa Fe will put into service next year will cut travel time by more than half! Before long, Addison will get a depot, so visiting us will take only a few hours. I want you to visit anytime you feel like it and stay until you're tired of us."

Luke hopes Amy's attempt to soften the distance and travel time issues will help Doris accept Amy's leaving. He has a question for Doris, but wants to wait until the women are through cooking and seated so he can have Doris' complete attention. When he feels the opportunity is right, he says, "Mom, I want to ask you something that may take some time to consider. However, it would be nice to have your answer before leaving Dodge, so I need to broach the subject now. I adore Charlie's wagon, and I'd like to buy it. I was offered $300 in Topeka for it and Smokey.

There's no way I'd sell Smokey, but $150 is a fair price for the wagon. Please feel free to counter or say, 'It's not for sale.'"

Doris says, "Nonsense, the wagon will be my wedding gift to you. Luke, a hundred and fifty dollars is more than twice its worth."

"That tells you how badly I want it," Luke says. "Thank you. I wasn't expecting that. I have one more thing to ask. Removing the signs would simplify our lives because so many recognize them."

"Sure, it's yours now," Doris says. "But when you remove the signs, I want them."

In Amy's bed that night, Luke says, "It's going to be hard on Doris to watch you load up your things. She may not feel completely abandoned if you leave some possessions here."

"I agree; I'll leave all my pictures for now and the clothes I don't wear anymore. I'll leave my bed, dresser, and study table so I can use them when I come for a visit. I'll leave my high school awards that Mom's so proud of hanging on the wall, but let's switch my mattress with the one in the wagon. She ordered herself a new one that's on the way."

"That's all very logical," Luke says. "In the morning, I plan to strip the inside of the wagon of everything your Dad installed for the business and take off the signs. What kind of awards are hanging in your room?"

"Oh, they were for academics. I was the valedictorian of my class of twenty-one kids, not a big deal."

"Yeah, it is, smarty pants! Tell me more."

"Okay, remember the tests we took before graduation?"

"Sure."

"Well, I got Honorable Mention in math, reading comprehension, and general knowledge," Amy says.

"How does one earn an Honorable Mention award?" Luke asks.

"Be in the top two percent," Amy says.

Grinning, Luke says, "I must have been in the top three percent. I knew you were smart, but I didn't know you had documents proving it!"

While Amy sleeps, Luke and Doris are up early, chatting and eating pancakes. Before getting Amy's morning kiss, Luke reads Amy's academic awards, saddles Smokey, and leaves for the Pullman, with Fury following close behind at the end of a lasso. Luke wants Fury to adjust to the new surroundings and to see if he's limping. He's pleased that Fury is not favoring that leg. Luke dismounts at the base of the ramp and leads both horses into the Pullman.

While inspecting Fury's hoof, Luke notices Ralph looking at Smokey and says, "It's okay to take my palomino to breakfast. His bridle is a side pull, and he responds best to gentleness. If he doesn't like you, given a chance, he'll leave you stranded. He's smart; he'll come right back to me."

Ralph says, "Thanks for the advice; I'll be on my best behavior," and mounts up and leaves.

Before working on the wagon, Luke checked the position of the items he had placed to indicate if Ralph had snooped; everything was as he had left it. He began stripping the inside of the wagon except for three feet of shelving at the front end on the right side. The back seven feet were bare, except for the mattress. Just as he finished, Amy and Doris arrived, and Ralph returned from breakfast. Amy introduced Doris and Ralph, and they quickly transferred Amy's items to the wagon.

Luke swaps the mattresses and quietly says, "That'll be a nice improvement."

Ralph asks, "If you don't plan on keeping that mattress, my bunk could use more padding."

Doris overhears Ralph's comment and says, "It's yours, Ralph. I ordered a Simmons *Beautyrest* mattress. My old mattress will go on Amy's bed."

Ralph says, "Thank you," and takes the mattress into the back of the Pullman.

After getting her things arranged, Amy says, "It feels homier now."

Luke removes Charlie's signs, puts them in the back of the buckboard, and says, "Mom, I'll put these in the barn."

She says, "Thanks; I plan to mount them along the road. I have a lot of inventory to sell."

"Speaking of inventory, I owe you for the merchandise in the wagon when I left Dodge back on July 5th," Luke admits.

"Please forget about it," Doris says. "Besides, you settled Charlie's debt with Jake Cloud."

"That was only five dollars; I'll find another way to pay you back," Luke says. Then he steps back a few feet, looks at the wagon, and says, "I love Charlie's wagon."

Doris says, "I'm proud to hear you say that. Charlie also loved it; he was always fooling with it."

Luke says, "It took him nearly an hour to explain how he redesigned it. I wish you could have heard George Anthony's groom brag on it."

Luke goes to town on Smokey to send a telegram to the Champion Hotel requesting a room reservation and stops at the train depot to get tomorrow's departure time. When he returns to the Pullman, he tells Amy, Doris, and Ralph, "The ticket agent said we must be ready to roll at seven in the morning, so Amy, we might as well sleep here tonight. I'll put what I took out of the wagon on the buckboard and tie it down. Leave the buckboard by the burn pit, and I'll toss that stuff in when I get there."

Doris says, "Good, thank you, but don't set it on fire. I want to be the one to strike that match."

Amy suggests, "Let's have an early dinner at the Dodge House."

"Okay, but it may not be all that early. You all need to get to the farm so I can unload the buckboard. Mom, would you like some of Rosa's wine and the candy that Amy doesn't want? Maybe you can sell it with your vegetables if you don't like it."

"That's a good idea," Amy says, and she and Doris enter the quarters.

After Amy and Doris leave for the farm, Luke straightens the quarters, locks the windows and doors, and tells Ralph, "You're welcome to take Smokey, but the rules stay the same."

Ralph says, "We got along great this morning. I gave him sugar cubes, and he rubbed his head on me!"

Luke says, "You found his weakness." He tells Ralph about Smokey's dinner habits, swings up on Fury's back, and reminds Ralph to lock up before leaving. Then he says, "We'll probably return rather late tonight. I don't want to frighten you, so I'll tap on the side of the Pullman next to where you sleep."

"Good idea," Ralph says.

When Luke gets to the farm, Doris and Amy have already unloaded the buckboard. He bathes by standing in the horse tank, shaves using his sheath knife, rinses off with fresh water from the windmill's pump, puts on clean clothes, and waits for the women.

At the Dodge House, business is good, but the owner knows Doris and Amy and recognizes Luke from Charlie's funeral, so they are seated quickly. During dinner, Doris asks Luke about the land they hope to buy. Luke explains that his sister owned it for seven years, and he always thought it was a hidden gem. She sold it fifteen months ago to a man who has since died. Before submitting a bid, he wants to evaluate the condition of the improvements and see Amy's reaction, which they need to do as soon as possible.

On the way out of the dining room, Luke sees Ralph, and they wave to each other. Luke tells the cashier to add the big man's dinner to his bill. When they leave, Smokey is tied next to Doris' buckboard. Luke strokes his forehead and talks to him. When Luke walks away, Smokey tries to follow, but can't. Luke notices Ralph took his warning seriously and tied Smokey's reins to the hitching post with two wraps and a double half-hitch. Luke says, "Relax; you'll see Fury and me later tonight."

Back at Doris' farm, Amy and Doris chat in the kitchen while Luke transfers his things from the back porch to the buckboard. Then he goes to the barn to get Fury's horseshoe and puts it in his saddlebag. He sits patiently on the buckboard, waiting for Amy. When Doris finally dozes off, Amy helps her to bed, extinguishes the kerosene lamp, ensures that Daisy is in the house, and closes the doors. She tosses her travel bag to Luke, and he reaches down to lift her onto the wagon.

At the Pullman, Ralph has left his window open. When he hears Luke approaching, he shouts, "You don't need to tap on the siding; I heard you pull up! I want to thank you for buying my dinner."

Shouting at the open window, Luke says, "You are very welcome. After we unload, Amy will be alone for thirty minutes while I take her mother's buckboard home. I don't expect trouble, but I'd appreciate your waiting for me to return. After Luke and Amy unload the buckboard, they close the blinds. When she's safely behind locked doors, Luke gives Amy his revolver and leaves for the farm.

When Luke returns to the Pullman, Ralph opens the loading door, and Fury walks in with Luke in the saddle. The horses snort, nicker, and nod their heads to welcome each other. Luke wonders if Smokey is telling Fury about his evening with Ralph.

After caring for the horses, Luke locks the loading door, opens windows in their stalls, several small side windows, and a large roof vent, and joins Amy in the living quarters. Amy is in a bedside chair in her nightgown, smiling. Luke says, "You'd better jump in and go to sleep; I plan to wake you up at six; that will happen sooner than you think."

"I'll wait for you," Amy says.

"Okay, I'll hurry."

"When we get to Amarillo, will I see your farm?" Amy asks.

"Sure, if we have the time, it's only five miles south of town. But as you know, a wheat field this time of year isn't much to look at," Luke says.

Chapter 22: Luke Stops A Train Robbery
July 22nd

As dawn breaks, Luke prepares to bring back three breakfasts to town. Before he leaves, Doris arrives with two baskets filled with breakfast. Gratefully, Luke says, "Oh, Mom, how thoughtful, thank you! How early did you get up to prepare all of this?"

"Long before that old rooster began crowing," Doris says.

While helping Doris with her baskets, Luke notices a caboose and a Wells Fargo car are on the spur. Luke wonders why George's Pullman is *behind the Santa Fe's caboose.* A dozen Wells Fargo security types are milling around the Wells car, and he suspects they're there to protect a large cash shipment. Luke cracks the door leading to the back of the Pullman and shouts to Ralph, "Time to get up; Doris brought breakfast!" Doris sets out bowls of scrambled eggs, hash browns, bacon, and biscuits, and pours lukewarm coffee from a gallon coffee boiler. When Ralph arrives, they all say good morning to him and dig in.

When finished, Doris gets compliments and thanks from everyone. Luke turns to Ralph, saying, "I need to show you something outside." Luke and Ralph excuse themselves, and when outside, Luke tells Ralph about his concern for the number of Wells security men he saw earlier and says, "I want to talk to the man in charge."

They approach the Wells Fargo car, and Luke asks the first man he meets, "Do you know who is in charge and where I can find him?"

"Rex Lane is the boss. He's inside our car."

Luke shouts into the open door, "Mr. Lane, I'm Luke Garrelts, and I'm here with Mr. Ralph Barr, a Pinkerton security guard! May we speak with you?"

Immediately, a broad-hipped, official-looking man with a dark brown full-face beard stands in the sliding door opening with his arms crossed. He says, "I'm Rex Lane; what can I do for you?"

Luke says, "The two of us and my wife will be in the Pullman following you to Amarillo. Due to the number of security guards milling about, I think you expect trouble."

Rex says, "I can't confirm that, but we did receive information from Huntsville prison about a possible robbery. If this train is attacked, as predicted by an inmate, his sentence will be significantly reduced. The dollar amount of the Treasury bills going to Amarillo, Dallas, and Houston is significant. Since the location of the attack made sense, I decided the likelihood was too high to ignore, and I doubled our standard security measures. We need to kill enough of these train robbers to discourage future attacks on our shipments. Supposedly, they'll be waiting for us at the top of a long incline, the Santa Fe calls Harry's Hill. The engineer said our speed would slow to ten miles per hour. That location is thirty miles from Amarillo. We'll be there about three o'clock this afternoon."

Luke tells Rex that they are willing to help. Rex says, "That would be great. I'll put you all in the caboose's cupola and send the two men I had planned to put up there to the locomotive's cab. That'll make four of my men plus the engineer and boiler stoker".

Luke asks, "Did you ask the railroad to put Governor Anthony's Pullman at the end?"

"Santa Fe's dispatcher did that. He said the Governor is fussy about his Pullman, and knowing there could be trouble, he was afraid to put it next to our car."

Luke asks, "Was Governor Anthony informed of a possible attack?"

Rex answers, "I don't know, but I don't believe he was."

Luke says, "I agree; if he knew, I'd have received a telegram by now."

Ralph says, "I haven't heard from the Pinkerton Agency."

Rex replies, "That's understandable; we play our cards close to the vest when following up on robbery tips. You all return to your car, and I'll alert you when we approach Harry's Hill. Do y'all need rifles or cartridges?"

Luke answers, "No, we're good. We'll expect to hear from you before three o'clock."

As they return to the Pullman, Ralph says, "Your suspicion was right."

Luke says, "The handwriting was on the wall."

Ralph goes to the back of the Pullman, and Luke enters the living quarters as Doris packs the breakfast dishes and prepares to get off the train. She gives Luke a long hug and a light peck on the cheek and asks him to take good care of Amy. Luke tells her not to worry, thanks her again for bringing breakfast and lunch, and says, "We'll see you soon, Mom." Amy helps Doris get the empty baskets to the buckboard, and Luke watches as they have a tearful goodbye. When Amy returns, Luke suggests she transfer her things to the wagon before they arrive in Amarillo.

Still wiping away tears, Amy says, "You have so little; I'll move yours, too."

After Amy finishes loading the wagon, she sits at the table and begins reading a novel she found on a bookshelf. Luke waits until she's engrossed in reading so she will not notice him get the bandolier and walk to the door at the back of their quarters. Before closing the door, Luke says, "I'll be gone for a few minutes to talk to Ralph." But he first goes to the wagon and fills the empty slots on the front and back of the bandolier; it holds sixteen rounds on each side. Then, he gives the bandolier to Ralph, asking him to take it to the dome of the caboose when the time comes.

Luke returns to their quarters, sits on the loveseat couch, and leans forward with his elbows on his knees. He looks down at nothing and processes what Rex Lane told him. He had planned to spend the day thinking about how to get the money safely into an Amarillo bank and writing to Bill Boyer about selling the farm. Until a few minutes ago, they were the most critical things Luke had on his mind. But now, he has a bigger fish to fry, a train robbery that could harm Amy. He thinks, *If attacked, the safest place for Amy is in the living quarters, behind locked doors, on the floor, and under the bed with my revolver. The problem is getting her to do that.* He rubs his forehead, wanting to think about something less worrisome, like writing to his tenant farmer. So, he gets paper and pen and joins Amy at the table.

Luke's letter to Bill explains that he's decided to sell his farm and prefers to sell it to him. If Bill's interested, they need to meet before the end of the month. He is staying at the Champion Hotel.

A couple of hours into the train ride, Luke looks out the window and sees a dozen young Indian braves watching the train pass. They have bows, arrows, and spears, but no war paint, so he knows they're either a hunting party or juveniles out having fun. Since the train's route is not on a reservation, Luke also knows they're breaking a military policy that could result in their incarceration. He knows overweight cavalry soldiers cannot catch them, which may be the game the young rebels are playing.

Seeing them causes him to reflect on the plight of the Indians, and he quickly slides into a meditative state. *He thinks about the many cavalry forts scattered over the plains. They aimed to protect migrating settlers, squatters, railroad contractors, and prospectors. Small patrols were dispatched to find Indians off their reservations; if caught, they were punished, even if merely hunting for game to feed their tribe.*

Initially, the Indians tried frightening trespassers, hoping to run them off the land the Relocation Act Treaties promised. So, the irony was that the military would arrest Indians for doing what they had every right to do.

The U.S. Government's solution to Indian assimilation was to inflict punishment to force them to behave like European settlers. The military forbade them to speak their language, worship their spirits, celebrate their history, wear native clothing, or sing and dance their rituals around a bonfire. When caught off their reservation the second time without a pass, the captive was jailed and, if thought to be a chronic troublemaker or tribal leader, might be killed. He felt it would not be the fate of the small group watching the train pass.

The buffalo was critical for the survival of the Plains Indians. Over thousands of years, they used their creativity to develop unique, almost unimaginable, ways to use every part of the buffalo.[25] When the government decided the solution to resolving their Indian problem was as simple as the elimination of the buffalo, the military began slaughtering them. Additionally, buffalo were killed by skinners for their hides, settlers and railroad contractors for their meat, and New Englanders for sport and entertainment.

The buffalo slaughter intensified after the completion of the Transcontinental Railroad, which occurred ten years earlier. It enabled "Buffalo Bill" Cody to organize extravagant hunting parties for wealthy New Englanders. Since Indians only killed buffalo to survive, they were outraged to find hundreds of carcasses rotting on the prairie. To avenge their anger, they would attack the track-laying crews. But soon, the cavalry began protecting those men, so the Indians could only watch.

The government rubbed salt in the wound by forcing tribes that had been enemies for years to live on the same reservation.

Thinking about all the injustices the Indians had endured was sickening. Before falling asleep, Luke tries to simplify the Indians' past hundred-year saga. He concludes that the U.S. Government had done and would continue to do whatever was necessary to get the Indians out of the way of the nation's westward expansion. Though never stated in Congressional legislation, the goal was genocide by relocation and starvation. All three branches of government were responsible; they caved to pressure stirred up by the dishonest press. As a result, the U.S. Indian population dropped from approximately 600,000 to 237,000 between 1800 and 1900.[26]

Luke lies on the bed and naps until the Pullman jostles enough to wake him. Amy is still reading, and he eats the fried egg sandwich and a slice of apple pie in Doris' sack lunch. He lies back down and takes another catnap. The second time Luke wakes up, he asks, "What are you reading?"

Amy says, "*Pride and Prejudice.*"

"I've heard of it; do you like it?" Luke asks.

"Yes, but I won't finish it before arriving in Amarillo."

Luke says, "I've been thinking about everything we must do before submitting our bids. We're going to be busy. To ensure we'll be safe when depositing the money, I will first test it by taking one of the five, ten, and twenty-dollar bills to the First National Bank. I'll ask a cashier to tell me if they are counterfeit. Hopefully, the cashier will remember me because I've deposited money from my wheat harvests, mustang sales, and cattle drives in an account there for years. Assuming the bills pass the serial number test, we need to decide how much to deposit and, as Jordan insisted, make them look like they've been in circulation."

When Rex knocks on the door, Luke is about to explain his plan for making the bills look used. Rather than waiting for a response,

Rex cracks the door a few inches and says, "We're approaching Harry's Hill."

While getting his rifle, Luke tells Amy, "I want you to stay right here behind locked doors. If you hear gunfire, stay under the bed until I return."

Amy says, "Who is Harry Hill?"

Luke says, "I don't have time to explain. PLEASE do as I ask. I'll leave my gun belt with you; don't hesitate to use the Colt."

Before leaving the Pullman, Luke shouts to Ralph but gets no response. When he reaches the caboose's cupola, he finds Ralph with Rex, the rear brakeman, and the conductor.

Luke asks Rex, "Where have you positioned your men?"

Rex says, "I already mentioned the four in the locomotive's cab with the engineer and boiler stoker. All six have rifles and are protected by the steel plates I had installed. Five are in the passenger car, under orders not to shoot unless there is an attempt to board it. Another four are in the dome of the Wells car, and two men will be with me, the money, and two Santa Fe guards. This is the best prepared I have ever been. If they're at the top of that hill waiting for us, they don't know we were forewarned and prepared for their attack. If the attack group is small, we should surprise and overwhelm them. They'll likely try to board the engine's cab and stop the train. They'll be shocked when they see the amount of rifle smoke coming from the cab and will abort that effort for Plan B, which is to board our Wells car.

The organizers of these robberies recruit ex-cons and ne'er-do-wells by offering a percentage of the haul. They're meaner than a cornered wildcat when sober. The organizers give them plenty of liquid courage while waiting for the train. However, if we can put half of them on the ground, the other half, though stinking drunk, should change their minds."

"Sounds like you have a good plan," Luke says. "I have a suggestion. My concern is for the folks in the passenger car, two cars ahead of yours. If they go to Plan B, which I think you know they will, and they see gun smoke before they get to your car, they're likely to shoot randomly into the passenger car. I want all of us to hold our fire until they've passed the passenger car. If they think it will be easy, they'll not start shooting until we do, so let's let them get close to your Pullman before we open fire."

"Good suggestion; I'll instruct my men to do that."

Before Rex leaves, Amy arrives carrying Luke's gun belt and looking tense. When Luke sees her, he looks down and closes his eyes. He puts his left palm on his forehead, takes a deep breath to calm himself, and looks at Amy. While exhaling through tightly closed lips and puffed cheeks, Luke slowly points his index finger at Rex and calmly says, "Amy, this man is Rex Lane. Rex is a security executive with Wells Fargo. He has good reason to believe this train could be attacked for the cash it's carrying. If that happens, I want you to get behind me as close as possible, unless I tell you to lie flat on the floor. You can help me by laying my gun belt on the floor and handing me cartridges from the bandolier when I ask for them."

Rex says, "Nice to meet you, ma'am. I wish the circumstances were different."

"Me too!" Amy says. Rex thanks Luke and Ralph for helping and leaves.

Very soon, the train begins climbing Harry's Hill and slowing down. The Conductor looks out of the roof hatch using military binoculars and says, "I see a bunch of masked riders. That Wells Fargo car must be full of cash." In another minute, he says. "Mr. Lane was right. The amount of gun smoke from the locomotive changed their minds. They've decided on Plan B, and there are about ten riders on each side of the tracks waiting for us."

Luke cocks the lever to chamber a cartridge and asks Amy to get four rounds out of the bandolier and hand them to him. He puts one cartridge in the tubular magazine beneath the barrel; the rifle now has sixteen rounds and is fully loaded. He puts the remaining three between the fingers of his left hand like he learned to do as a Sharpshooter. Luke says, "Amy, please have six more ready should I ask for them."

Riders are on both sides of the Wells Fargo car within minutes. As Luke hoped, Rex's men held their fire until the robbers began shooting at the Wells car. Luke puts his hat on Amy's head and leans halfway out the window on the right side. After ten shots, in less than a minute, six men are on the ground, and three are fleeing with life-threatening wounds and struggling to remain in their saddles. However, one bandit managed to ride past the caboose. Luke is concerned that he will jump on the back of the caboose.

While putting the rounds in his left hand in the magazine, Luke says, "Amy, hand me the six rounds and point my Colt straight up at the observation door. If it starts to open, shoot up through the roof until it's empty." Then Luke asks the conductor to watch the steps leading up to the cupola, puts the six shells in the magazine, slides over to Ralph's side, and asks, "How's it going on this side, big fella?"

Ralph says, "Take over; I haven't hit one yet." After another ten shots, eight men are on the ground, and the two he nicked are riding away slowly. To be sure they don't live to retaliate, Luke puts a death slug into the center of their backs.

When the gunfire stops, everyone relaxes and says nothing. After a minute, Luke breaks the silence, asking, "Is everyone okay?"

They all say, "Yes," except Amy, who begins firing the Colt revolver at the observation door. The door slams shut with a thud.

Luke struggles to open the door until it's half open, when he sees a body roll out of the way. He opens it fully but doesn't see a body on the roof. Luke closes the hatch and says, "If a bullet didn't kill him, the fall did."

Concerned about another attack, Luke says, "Well done, let's all reload." Amy takes cartridges from Luke's gun belt while Luke slides twelve rounds from the bandolier into the magazine. Everyone stays quiet while Luke looks out of the observation hatch again. As they crest the hill, he sees three riders watching the train pass. He expects they're the ringleaders who supplied the liquor and are waiting for a safe or money bags to fly out of the Wells Fargo car. Luke closes the hatch, sits beside Amy with his back against the wall, and asks, "Are you okay?"

While handing Luke his hat, Amy answers, "I've been better."

When the train resumes top speed, the conductor says, "That was some amazing shooting!"

Ralph says, "It was unbelievable!"

The rear brakeman says, "I was too afraid to watch; I'm glad I didn't soil myself."

Luke says, "Rex will want us to wait here until he finishes a headcount and gives us the all-clear."

In fifteen minutes, Rex shows up and says, "Jesus, Mary, and Joseph, where did you boys learn to shoot like that? I just witnessed the shortest train robbery in the history of train robberies."

Ralph says, "Luke did that fancy shooting. I couldn't stop shaking long enough to draw a bead on anyone. My shots kicked up dirt five feet from where I was aiming. From what I saw, I doubt any of them got away without being hit at least once."

Luke says, "It wasn't all me, Rex. I put a second slug in several whom your men had already hit. I was trained not to hesitate when I had the rifle sights lined up on an enemy. I agree with Ralph; all those who got away have at least one bullet hole and will not live to see the sunset. Which is good; dead men can't tell tales or come after us." Looking at Rex, Luke says, "For Ralph's and my safety, I want Wells Fargo Security to get the full credit for thwarting this attack."

Rex nods approvingly and says, "I'll have to explain the attack in an affidavit for Amarillo's officials and again at the Wells Fargo office. I'm sure Wells will send a copy of it to Santa Fe. I will not mention you and Ralph in either of those."

Looking at the conductor and brakeman, Luke says, "I'm asking you all never to mention that Ralph and I were involved. Can you men agree to that?"

The conductor says, "Yes."

The brakeman says, "That'll be easy for me; my eyes were closed the whole time, so I didn't see a thing."

Luke looks at Amy and says, "When I asked you to stay in the Pullman, I believed you'd be the safest there."

Amy says with a frown and a good deal of attitude, "Well, you scared me when you grabbed your rifle and took off. It's not my nature to wait and worry myself sick, so I followed you. I'm glad I came when I did rather than wait until the gunfire started. I refuse to apologize." Luke knows it's not the time or place to debate the issue. He turns toward Ralph and asks him to inspect George's Pullman for bullet holes after it's decoupled.

At the depot, the conductor has the engineer and brakeman position the Pullman on a spur next to a loading dock with a long, inclined ramp at one end. Ralph opens the back door and asks four dock workers to roll the wagon to the bottom of the ramp. Luke grabs Smokey's and Fury's manes and leads them down the ramp to the wagon. He puts Smokey in the harness and Fury in a halter, which he ties to the right side. He then makes a final check of the living quarters for anything they might have missed.

Ralph has finished his Pullman inspection and says, "I couldn't find any bullet holes."

"Good! I plan to telegraph George and tell him about the attack. Now, I can say his Pullman is fine." Luke gives Ralph the keys to the Governor's quarters and says, "We need to be going. But before we do, if you must file a report for the Pinkerton Agency, can you leave my name out?"

Ralph says, "Since Rex said he'd not mention us in his report, I don't plan to file a report. If asked why I didn't, I'll say that I wasn't involved and tell them to read the report by Rex Lane, Wells Fargo's manager in charge of security on the train."

"Thanks; I hope you have an uneventful trip back to Topeka," Luke says.

"Best of luck to you all," Ralph says.

"Until we meet again," Luke says.

"Until we meet again," Ralph affirms before walking up the ramp and disappearing into the shadows.

As they leave for town, Rex shows up to thank Luke again. Luke says, "I'm glad you trusted Ralph and me enough to let us help. You could have been suspicious that we were planted on the train by the organizers of the robbery."

Rex says, "I recognized the Governor's Pullman when you arrived, and I sent a telegram to his office. I received one back advising that you, Amy, and Ralph were taking the train to Amarillo. We try to stay out of sight as much as possible because I don't want to alarm passengers. I didn't expect anyone to notice I had extra men. I was surprised when you asked to help, and I'm glad you did."

Luke says, "I plan to send the Governor a telegram in a few minutes. Did you suffer any casualties or serious injuries that he will read about in the newspapers? If so, I should tell him."

Rex says, "Two of the four in the dome suffered minor flesh wounds. Stitches and bandages will be all they need. The men up there were taking all the fire, so coming away with minor wounds is extremely lucky."

"Luck could be a factor, but most horses get spooked and jumpy approaching a moving train, particularly with all the gunfire. I suspect those men were too drunk to shoot straight. Imagine the difficulty of hitting a small window high up on the side of a moving train from a nervous horse when you're drunk."

"You make some good points, but I don't think they were expecting a sharpshooter in the caboose," Rex says.

"I didn't ask Ralph, but I don't remember being shot at, Luke says. I want to compliment you on manning the engine. Had they stopped the train, the outcome could have been quite different. We're behind schedule and need to leave. You take care."

"And you," Rex says.

When leaving the railyard, Amy asks, "Why didn't Rex tell George about a possible attack?"

Luke answers, "Rex sent a telegram to the Governor's office. Because the information came from a Huntsville convict, he's not sure it got to George's desk. After going to the bank, I must telegram George about today. I plan to downplay what happened. I'll tell him it ended almost as soon as it started, and there was no damage to his Pullman, which should satisfy his concern for our safety. If I make a big deal out of it, George may have words with Rex, and I don't want that. Also, I need to hire a Western Union courier to take my letter to Bill Boyer."

They arrive at the 1st National Bank just as a bank official and two security guards are about to lock the door. The bank officer introduces himself as Ben Abney and tells them the vault is closed, and the cashiers are gone, so they can't do any cash transactions. Luke explains he hoped to see the Addison Estate sale map. Ben says he'll go ahead and lock the door and open it for them after they finish studying the map.

In only fifteen minutes, Luke makes a crude map, pencils in the salient features he recalls, and copies the descriptions of the physical boundaries of two parcels. Luke thanks Mr. Abney, and they leave for the Western Union office. Luke tells Amy they must bid on two tracts to buy all the J&J. He says he doesn't want either tract if he can't get both, and his bid will stipulate that. Hearing that concerns Amy, but she accepts Luke's decision. Luke says, "It's a little over fifty miles to the J&J. So, we need to leave early."

At Western Union, Luke sends George a note that says, "We arrived safely in Amarillo and are staying at the Champion Hotel. Our train experienced an attack on the Wells Fargo car carrying a shipment of Treasury bills. It was quickly defeated because Wells and Santa Fe were forewarned and well-prepared. We were not in the direct line of fire, and the Pullman suffered no damage. Ralph is a good man; he thinks highly of you, and we enjoyed his company." After paying the telegrapher, Luke tells a courier where to deliver his letter to Bill Boyer.

They check into the hotel and unload the wagon, including the cavalry boots. Before leaving for the livery, Luke removes Fury's shoe from his saddlebag.

Luke reins Smokey to the familiar livery corral. After getting the rig into the corral and releasing the horses to eat and drink, he goes to the blacksmith shop. He gives Fury's shoe to the farrier and says, "Delbert, here's some work for you; it goes on the sorrel's right front hoof." Luke finds Frank Weiner, his long-time friend, and tells him he plans to look at some grassland for sale around Addison. He plans on returning the day after tomorrow, in the evening. He asks Frank to feed the horses early because he will arrive at seven and take both with him.

Frank asks, "Are you going to sell the farm?"

"Yes, to buy the place I want, I'll have to."

"So, is this the sign that you're ready to settle down and give up cattle drives and bronco busting?"

Luke says, "I plan to make it a cattle operation, so I suppose the answer is, 'Not completely.' I'm married now, getting close to thirty, and I want a family. So, I've decided to start working toward the life I hope to have ten or fifteen years from now."

Frank says, "Married, I've wondered when that would happen. Good for you. I remember you and Jesse Booth were friends; is that the place you plan to look at?"

"It is," Luke says proudly.

"I remember that you liked it. The rumor I heard was that Jesse's wife sold the ranch to Tom Addison and moved to Kansas City. They never did business with me, so I didn't know either of them," Frank says.

Luke says, "It's understandable that she would leave Addison. I must return to the hotel; my wife is waiting on me to go to dinner."

In bed that night, they discussed keeping their room reservation and only taking what they'd need for the next two days. Luke says, "We may decide to camp, so I want to be prepared."

Amy says, "I'll leave all my things from Dodge and take only one change of clothes. We need to discuss something, sweetheart. At the time, it bothered me that you shot those men when they were fleeing and could barely stay in the saddle. After listening to your conversation with Rex and Ralph, I now understand you did it to protect our future, so I'm happy you did," Amy says.

"Amy, my love, I apologize for being testy when you came to the cupola. I was unsure how the gunfight would end and didn't want you involved," Luke says. "I was wrong, and you were right. I'm very proud of you; you helped immensely. I gave you an important job because I believed you could handle it, and you did. The best thing God-fearing people can do is put men like them either behind bars for life or six feet underground, forever. I forgive you for following me to the caboose; you saved my life. I hope you can forgive me," Luke says.

Amy confesses, "I know you want to protect me, so I forgive you for being angry at me for not staying in the Pullman. I do not regret taking that man's life. When the hatch opened an inch or two, I could see a pistol barrel coming through the opening. You were in the line of fire, and without thinking, I started pulling the trigger.

"I'm so thankful that you did! I love you!" Luke says.

" I love you, too, and I love showing you that I do!" Amy says.

Luke says, "That's how I'm feeling," and extinguishes the kerosene lantern.

Chapter 23: Amy's First Trip To The J&J
July 23rd & 24th

Luke walks to Frank's livery, inspects Fury's hoof, and compliments Delbert. He harnesses Smokey to the wagon and ties Fury with a halter to the right front side. He stops the wagon in front of the hotel and makes two trips to get his rifle, bandolier, camping gear, ponchos, saddlebag, and old boots. Amy follows Luke to the wagon with her carpet bag, hat, and jacket; she tosses the carpet bag over the tailgate and onto the mattress. Luke looks at his pocket watch and tells Amy, "It's exactly seven o'clock, so we're on schedule."

Amy asks, "How do you know it's EXACTLY seven o'clock?"

"I set it by the clock behind the reservation desk this morning."

"How do you know that clock is EXACTLY right?"

"It's an expensive clock, and I know it is reset by the courthouse bell every day at noon."

"How does the courthouse set its clock?" Amy asks teasingly.

"Okay, I get your point," Luke says as she punches him in the ribs. "However, that is an interesting question. The trains are finicky about leaving on time, so they provide conductors with a 21-jewel *Elgin timepiece.* I think it's interesting that Elgin calls an expensive watch a timepiece; I doubt I'll ever own one. Whoever sets the courthouse clock would be wise to ask the Santa Fe conductor for the time."

Amy says, "What if the conductor used a sundial to set his Elgin?"

They both laugh, and Luke says, "The purpose of the courthouse bell tower is for folks in Amarillo to set their watches and clocks by it. That way, everyone is on time for appointments, business meetings, and store openings. So, for Amarillo, the

Courthouse time is the EXACT time. It doesn't matter that the Addison folk could be ten minutes ahead or behind the folks in Amarillo. Everyone in a town with a train depot must be on the same time. That's why the courthouse, in every town with a train station, has a bell tower." (Author's note: It was common for a bell tower operator to reset the city's clock to match a reliable train departure, i.e., one originating at the location and known to leave on time.)

Amy says, "Now, I wish I hadn't brought it up," and punches him in the ribs again.

They arrive in Addison at six p.m. in the center of town. Luke reins Fury to a stop next to two men on their left, who have been waiting to see the unusual wagon up close before crossing the street. Both men look at Amy; Luke leans forward and says, "Pardon me; was that pile of ashes at one time the office of the Addison Cattle Company?"

"Yes, sir, it's the pile in the middle," the older man says. "Those on either side were vacant at the time. Tom Addison owned all three; he was cremated in the center one; however, some folks prefer to believe he roasted slowly. Texas now owns that pile of ashes."

"The Governor hopes someone will buy it," the younger man chuckles.

Luke says, "You two look like twins born twenty years apart; you must be father and son."

"Yep, we are," the father says. "I'm Bill Cooper, and this fine man is Gary. I own the grocery store, and Gary runs it; we just locked it up."

"How's business?" Luke asks.

"It's down because folks have been leaving town," Bill says. "People have to eat, so we'll find a way to get by, provided the city does. On the brighter side, whoever ended old Tom's life deserves a medal; his demise was overdue. When they opened the safe, they found his watch and glasses and decided the remains must be his; most people celebrated. Hopefully, this town can become a decent place to live, but it won't happen overnight. We need a long list of things; for starters, we must elect honest city and county officials. We'll need a banker willing to make low-interest, high-risk business loans. I can't imagine where we'd find someone willing to do that in this place."

Luke asks, "Did authorities find out who set the fire?"

Gary says, "Nope; three Texas Rangers arrived two weeks ago, on the ninth, and left last Friday. They ran around town interviewing people who'd talk to them. If they recorded anything, the person had to sign a statement confirming that they had told the truth. Well, just about everyone around here had an axe to grind with Tom and worried they might say something to become a suspect, so after a few days, folks clammed up. Before the fire, the folks barely making ends meet were considering leaving. After the fire, most of them took off. Sadly, I was guilty of extending credit to many. So, what are you all doing here?"

"We're considering bidding on property in the big land sale, Luke says. We plan to be around for a couple of days."

"Good; everyone is hoping that selling Tom's Ranch in small pieces will attract young folks with energy, ideas, children, and the need to buy stuff," the father says.

"Where's a good place to eat?" Luke asks.

"The hotel at the end of the street is the only place in town. The owners are Joanna and Billy Ray Barnes. She's a damn good cook and very nice. They have two kids who stay busy helping their parents," the son says.

"Thanks for your time," Luke says. "I hope we'll see you again."

"We'd love to see you all herding six kids around town from store to store," Bill says and laughs.

Luke says, "So would we. We must get something to eat; you all have a good evening." They leave the two men and stop next to the hotel. When Amy goes in, Joanna is standing behind the cash register. She introduces herself and says, "I'd like a steak large enough to make three sandwiches. And if you have them, I'd like a dozen apples, six pickles, six hard-boiled eggs, a large wedge of cheese, crackers for the cheese, and a dozen cookies. Joanna filled the order, Amy paid, and on her way out, she asked, "How early do you serve breakfast?"

Joanna says, "Is six early enough?"

"We'll get here a little after that," Amy says with a big smile.

On the way to the J&J, Luke compliments Amy on her sandwiches and snack choices. "I'll bet you had no idea that Bill Cooper thinks you're a hero," Amy says.

"That was a surprise, but I also heard the city barely has its head above water. While you were getting the sandwiches, I took inventory. Only essential businesses, like the grocery store, hardware store, feed and tack store, and the post office, are open. Except for the post office, I bet they're struggling. Two men were hanging a Western Union sign on the front of one of the vacant buildings, which is good. If we buy the J&J, it would be handy to have a flourishing town only a few miles away; a ghost town is useless."

"The lady who waited on me said they would be open for breakfast at six," Amy says.

In thirty minutes, Fury has them in the center of the J&J farmstead, and Luke says, "Other than the weeds, the place hasn't changed since I saw it last. The house looks to be in good condition. Let's go inside and check it out."

After opening every cupboard and brushing dust off the table and countertops, Amy works the pump handle in the kitchen. When a full stream of clear water comes out, she says, "We could make this place work until we have kids. We'll have to add a room when I have a bun in the oven."

"You have a deal," Luke says. "I want to show you a spring-fed lake where I enjoyed relaxing, swimming, fishing, reading, and napping." They walk outside; Luke points to the northeast and says, "It's right over there." Amy can see only a part of the twenty-acre lake due to clumps of Pampas grass, four feet tall with six-foot feathery plumes, blocking her view. Along the right edge are four mature willow trees; their branches are dangling over the water. At the far end, a healthy stand of cattails stands in shallow water.

When they get close, Amy jumps down from the wagon, runs to the water's edge, and shouts, "Let's go swimming! I bet I can jump in before you!"

"That's unfair; I have the horses to tend to." Smokey and Fury walk to the water's edge to graze, drink, and watch Amy undress behind a clump of Pampas grass. Luke shouts, "Let's camp here tonight!"

"Okay, that'll be fun." Luke strips next to the wagon, runs to the pond, dives when he's ten feet from the edge, and swims up to Amy. She says, "Look down; I can see your feet. Oh, my, you like swimming naked."

She wraps her legs around him, and Luke says, "Dang, I was about to tell you about my plans for tomorrow, but I suddenly went blank.

She giggles and says, "You bad boy."

A moment later, he says, "Now I remember. I'll look at the buildings and pens and ride the fences in the morning. We can ride both properties in the afternoon to be sure the parts I'm unfamiliar with aren't a pig in a poke. We could come back here tomorrow afternoon for more romance in the lake, scare the hell out of bass and the crappie, and leave for Amarillo the next morning."

"Sounds like a plan," she says. "And in the next few minutes, you can add lovemaking to the list of things you like to do here."

After they've dressed, Luke says, "Jesse kept a fishing pole in the crotch of that first willow. I'm going to see if it's still there." He comes back in minutes, carrying a long cane pole and grinning. He shouts, "Amy, do you think a trophy bass will bite on a chunk of cheese?"

"Sure, why not!" she shouts confidently.

Before long, Luke has three two-pound bass flopping in the grass and shouts to Amy, "Do you know how to fry fish?"

"Of course!"

"Good! I'll start a fire and get out my cookware!"

Lying beside Luke in the back of the wagon that night, Amy says, "I'm ready to buy this place."

"That's good," Luke says. "Girl, you cooked the bass to perfection. I wish we could swim and eat bass every night."

"We can tomorrow," Amy says. "Now, say goodnight and pull the blanket over me."

While swimming in the lake the next afternoon, Amy asks, "I forgot to ask if you found anything of interest or concern while making your inspections this morning."

"Very near where I shot the chubby cottontail rabbit, I noticed a small and unusual patch of bare ground. It's almost half a mile west of the house. It's where the shallow ravine, created by those two hills, flattens out. That location wasn't on the J&J, but we'll have to bid on it to get all the J&J's twenty-five hundred acres.

After cutting off the rabbit's head to bleed him out, I was curious about the unusual patch and decided to investigate it. A small, dark brown pool was in the center. Using a long stick, I poked around; it wasn't water. The slimy goo on the stick smelled like kerosene, so it had to be crude oil. If we buy that tract, I'll write to John D. Rockefeller about what I found; his company makes kerosene from oil. Do not mention what I saw. If the wrong person hears about it, we'll have to bid against Standard Oil Company, and we can forget about owning it. I did my best to hide it with branches and grass I found nearby. While covering it up, I changed my mind about the all-or-nothing bid."

"Really, why?" Amy asks.

"Property with oil underneath is worth many times-the value of pasture. I've read that an underground pool of oil can extend in any direction for hundreds of yards. So, if there is a pool of oil, it could lie underneath the J&J as well. That's why I would want the J&J tract even if we don't get the one with the dead patch."

"How interesting. I want our bid on both tracts to be very competitive. Hotel living has become TEDIOUS. I'm ready for a place where we can invest our time and energy!" Amy insists.

After dinner, lying in the back of the wagon, Amy compliments Luke on his cooking skills. He replies, "If you like my rabbit on a spit, you will love my rat on a wire." When Amy sticks her tongue out and makes a gagging sound, Luke laughs and says, "Gotcha! That's payback for ribbing me about saying it was EXACTLY seven o'clock this morning."

Quietly, with a slightly furrowed brow, Amy says, "I deserve that...have I told you lately that I love you?"

"I love hearing those words," Luke whispers. "But actions speak louder than words."

Chapter 24: Returning To Amarillo
July 25th

They leave the J&J at dawn and discuss their breakfast choices on the short ride to the hotel in Addison. Amy introduces Luke to Joanna. Joanna gives Billy Ray their breakfast orders and returns with water glasses, napkins, knives, and forks. Luke asks. "If you have a minute, can you explain why there were so few people in town yesterday afternoon at about six o'clock?"

Joanna says, "Mondays have always been slow because people shop on the weekends, but lately, every day is slow. It's also because we're only half a town. It doesn't make sense for folks to come to town for anything besides mail and groceries. If it's something they can borrow, they'll ask their neighbors. If they can't borrow it, Amarillo is a one-day trip on a horse, two days by buckboard, and three by covered wagon. So, how you make the trip depends on what you plan to bring back.

"There's a young fellow who started a delivery service. He makes twice-a-week runs to Amarillo on Mondays and Thursdays. He boxed in the back of his buckboard to carry more things, and so they wouldn't bounce out. His fee is fifty cents or 5% of the price of whatever he hauls back, whichever is more. We've used him a few times. He stays busy and must be doing well because he bought a second buckboard and hired a boy to drive it." Joanna continues, "I change the menu on the chalkboard almost daily because we buy meats and vegetables from rural folks around Addison. I make a variety of soups, stews, goulash, pot roasts, and similar dishes. We can only serve what farmers have to sell. We signed a twelve-month lease on this building with Tom Addison, which is expiring next month. We're a month behind and can't make next month's payment. So, for us, the handwriting is on the wall. It's time to pull up our stakes and move on. I apologize for being emotional," she says as she tears up and hides her face in her apron.

Luke stands to give her a gentlemanly hug and whispers, "I understand the stress of working hard and being unable to make ends meet. Your business will improve as the shock and talk of the recent fire and Mr. Addison's death wear off."

After a moment, Luke steps back. Joanna looks at him and says, "Perhaps, but it won't pick up fast enough to save us. Addison is now famous in a very negative way. It's natural for people to stay away. It would take an excellent salesman to convince someone to start a business in Addison. Even our schoolteacher decided to leave. She said the town had not paid her for weeks. And if the wind had blown hard from the north on the night of the fire, she and some others would have lost everything. I want my children to get an education; I don't see that happening here. Our most frequent customers were old man Addison and his hired guns. The three hired guns who died in the tornado were NOT good for our business."

"Why was that?" Luke asks.

"If decent folks saw them in the dining room, they'd turn around and walk out. And if any of them had bad luck playing poker, they'd walk out and say, 'Put it on my bill.' But they never paid, and we were afraid not to serve them. Addison wasn't flourishing before the fire, and now it's fallen into the hole it was trying to dig itself out of."

"I'm sorry to hear that," Luke says. When she leaves, Luke turns to Amy and says, "I feel like it'll be my fault if this town becomes a ghost town."

Amy says, "It sounds like it was headed in that direction long before you came along."

Luke hands Joanna a ten-dollar bill at the cash register for their two one-dollar breakfasts and says, "Keep the change."

Joanna holds Luke's hand with both of hers and, before taking the money, says, "Sir, I appreciate your generosity. The Lord will hear about you in my prayers."

On the road back to Amarillo, Luke is noticeably pensive. Amy breaks the silence by asking, "Explain how you plan to determine if the money will be safe to deposit."

Luke says, "I'll tell one of the First National cashiers that you received suspicious-looking bills when you closed your savings account in Dodge City. I came to the bank to find out if they were counterfeit. I'll hand them a crispy $5, $10, and $20 bill and say that I heard the government replaces counterfeit bills."

"Will that be risky?" Amy asks.

"If they're stolen bills, I'll repeat that they were given to you by the State Bank in Dodge. If they say they must confirm my story, I'll say, 'That's fine.' Then, I'll ask the cashier for the balance in my farm account. As a local and long-time customer, I believe they'll be considerate. It's killing me to find out, so I'm going to the bank when it opens in the morning. When we get back, I hope Bill Boyer has returned my letter. Also, I have a proposition for you."

"Oooh, that sounds interesting," Amy says.

"If we submit our bid on August 1st, we'll have to wait until September 5th to know if we've won the bid. That's over a month, so propose we take the train anywhere you want to celebrate your eighteenth birthday."

"Oh, sweetheart, can we go to New York City?" Amy says, almost begging Luke.

"I'll see what I can do," Luke says.

Hours later, Smokey enters the edge of Amarillo, and Luke says, "I'll drop you off at the hotel and take the wagon to the livery. I'll catch up with you in twenty minutes."

Amy says. "I want to freshen up before dinner."

"Me too," Luke says. "You want to share a tub?"

"Sounds like fun!" Amy says.

"It's late, so the high-dollar bath suite is probably available," Luke answers, raising his eyebrows.

"Okay, but I want you to reserve it," Amy says.

Luke returns from the livery, talks to the front desk, goes to their room, and tells Amy their private bath will be ready in fifteen minutes, costing him two dollars.

During their late dinner, Luke reiterates, "I can't wait to go to the bank in the morning. We have the perfect plan to determine if the money is safe to deposit. So, one way or another, it will be a big day. One that will complicate or simplify our effort to buy the properties."

Amy says, "I've given this money a lot of thought, and I think no one knows anything about it...it's mystery money."

"I hope you're right," Luke says.

Chapter 25: Testing The Serial Numbers
July 26

After breakfast, Luke is anxious to get to the 1st National Bank with three of their crisp bills. The cashier tells him none are counterfeit or on their list of stolen bills. Luke struggles to maintain a concerned, puzzled look and refrains from jumping for joy. His whole body relaxes; he thanks the cashier and walks out of the bank, feeling like he's walking on air.

Luke is curious about the bills passing his test and thinks that *Treasury employees prevented a letter with the stolen serial numbers from being drafted or distributed. Whatever the case, the mastermind must have several accomplices to get away with it. What would Tom Addison's role have been? Tom's security guards could easily pull off a stagecoach holdup. Tom could have been contacted by someone in the Treasury who scheduled the routing or had access to it. Tom would pay for the information with "clean" money that the Washington players would share. Tom might pay less than fifty cents on the dollar value of the heist. It was a clever get-rich-quick scheme once the conspiracy players were in place. I'll never figure it out since I know nothing about the U.S. Treasury organization. But now I know that government jobs can pay well if one is crooked enough.*

To be doubly sure about the serial numbers, Luke takes the identical bills to the Texas State Bank. In ten minutes, he walks out with the same feeling of exhilaration. He decides it is time to take Jordan's advice and make the bills appear to have been in circulation. To draw less attention to the size of their deposit, they will open a second joint account at the State Bank. He decides to close his farm account at 1st National and open a new joint account there with Amy. The undecided question was how much money they should deposit in each bank.

Luke wants to draw as little attention as possible when depositing the money. He decides that depositing six rolls of $20 bills ($12,000) into the 1st National and State Banks would tend to make their deposit appear to have come from another bank or be a Western Union money transfer. He decided the 1st National deposit would include the $20 bills from the gold coins, the dead or alive warrants, and the mansion staff's wedding gift.

Luke goes over his decisions with Amy and asks for her opinion. She agrees with his plan. Luke says, "As soon as we can make the bills look like they've been in circulation, I'm ready to take them to the bank. Would you mind going to the Western Union office and asking to purchase a handful of rubber bands for your ponytail? Tell them the ones they use to band money transfers are the right size."

Amy says, "I'll have my hair down and band it up in front of the telegrapher and ask how it looks."

Amy kisses Luke and leaves for the Western Union office. Luke gets out one pack of the twenties, crumples, and rolls five notes into a tight wad while wearing his leather gloves. After straightening them, he isn't satisfied and goes to the hotel bar to buy a bottle of bourbon. He sprinkles bourbon on the bills to soften the cloth-like paper and wads them into a much smaller ball. The notes have lost their stiffness and look well-worn. He straightens each bill by working it back and forth over the edge of the desk and lays it on the morning newspaper. He repeats the process until he has one hundred $20 bills lying on the newspapers he has saved since leaving Kansas City. He puts them in the hot sun shining through the open window.

While they're still damp, he places another page on top, rolls up both pages, and places them back in the sun.

When Amy returns, she shows Luke a handful of rubber bands and says, "He just gave them to me!"

Luke tells her what he's been doing and suggests they enjoy an early lunch to give the money time to dry. When they return, Luke opens one newspaper roll, softens the bills by rolling them up and straightening them out, and says, "These bills look like they've changed hands a hundred times and spent a year in my wallet." He opens the remaining seven rolls of newspapers. After massaging and softening the bills, he puts a hundred in a neat stack, rolls the stack into a tight two-inch diameter roll, and puts two Western Union rubber bands around it.

Luke says, "They smell of bourbon like they were picked up from the floor of a saloon. Also, they have newspaper ink smudges, and the bourbon has left a slight stain. Tomorrow, I'll go to the newspaper office and ask to buy some blank newsprint paper and a couple of rotgut bottles at the saloon.

"What's rotgut?" Amy asks.

"It's distilled after the fermentation of corn. It's ninety percent alcohol, and the rest is water. It's crystal clear, looks like water, and won't leave a lingering odor or stain the bills. That one pack took me over thirty minutes, not counting the drying time. We have five more packs for the State Bank deposit," Luke says.

Amy says, "With two of us working, it shouldn't take too long."

"Maybe not, because I was experimenting. But we can't start until the maid has cleaned our room. Selling the farm and aging the money are the only things on my agenda for the next few days. After breakfast, I'll go to the newspaper and saloon. Wish me luck," Luke says.

"Do you think they may be reluctant to sell you a lot of blank newspaper?" Amy says.

Luke answers, "Should they ask what I'll do with it, I'll tell them we'll use it for packing to protect your breakable dishes and glassware in our wagon. That should make it difficult for anyone to say 'No,' particularly a woman.

"If you can't get the kind of newspaper you want, we'll figure out another way to skin the cat," Amy says.

Looking down and turning his head negatively, Luke says, "I worry about us getting caught. I don't want to raise anyone's curiosity, even a little. "I'll take these newspapers to the burn pit at dawn; I doubt anyone will be up and about that early."

Amy asks, "If we're the first to submit our bids on August first, and they're winners, the earliest we can close is the morning of September 17, is that right?"

"Yes, what's on your mind?" Luke asks.

"I was thinking about when I could start buying things for our first home."

Luke suggests, "An expression my Mother used to warn me about jumping to conclusions was, 'Don't count your chickens before they hatch.' Meaning that it's better not to buy things for the house until we own it."

"Okaaaay," Amy says quietly.

Regarding our bids, we should probably determine what we think is a fair price and make it more competitive by increasing it by as much as ten percent. After seeing it again, I'm excited about owning it. If we get outbid, I plan to ask the winning bidder or bidders if there is a price at which they'd consider selling the property to us, allowing them to make some easy money very quickly.

Chapter 26: An Offer To Sell The Farm
July 27th

After breakfast, Luke stops at the registration desk to pay for the next week. The cashier hands him an envelope from Bill Boyer. Bill's note states that a fair price is $2,700, but if Luke sells to another buyer, he will remove the improvements he made.

At the bottom of Bill's letter, Luke writes, "Your offer is accepted. I prefer to close at the 1st National Bank at ten o'clock tomorrow morning. Please confirm on this note or suggest an alternate day and time." Luke draws a map of his and Bill's farms. He shows it to the hotel messenger, a young boy, but old enough to understand Luke's drawing and the task. Luke tells the boy he must deliver the letter to Mr. Boyer, wait for him to write a response, and return it to the hotel cashier.

Luke asks the kid what he thinks would be a fair payment to do that. He quickly says, "I'll do it for a quarter."

Luke reaches into his pocket, gets a Liberty dollar, and while handing it to the cashier, says, "When this young man returns with my envelope, give him this." The young messenger grabs the envelope from Luke's hand and takes off like he was shot from a cannon.

Luke then goes to the newspaper office and the saloon to get what he needs. To conceal his purchases, he has Amy's travel bag. When the maid leaves their room, he locks the door, opens the window, and gets out the money for their State Bank deposit. "I'll wet, wad, and massage; you straighten and dry; later, we'll stack, roll, and band."

After two hours, Amy says, "This is taking longer than I thought."

Luke says, "We're doing good; we're halfway, and the good news is they will dry more quickly with the rotgut, and there will be no odor, staining, or printer's ink on these five rolls."

While taking a break, Luke lays out the six packs for their 1st National account, plus the $1,900 from various sources, and puts them in the boot for his right foot. He puts the remaining 18 packs, which they don't plan to deposit, in the left boot. By three o'clock, the bills are rolled up in newspapers and drying in the afternoon sun. Luke says, "This isn't fun work, and we'll have to do six packs for our First National account tomorrow. Let's go to dinner and think about what we're doing."

At dinner, Luke says, "When we get back, I want to put my decisions on paper so they'll be easier to remember."

When returning to their room, the cashier says, "Mr. Garrelts, the young courier returned with your letter."

Luke reads it, smiles, and tells Amy, "I'm selling the farm at ten in the morning."

They return to their hotel room, and Luke makes tables for the two bank deposits and the money they have decided not to deposit.

When he finishes making the tables, Luke says, "It's time to unwrap the bills and put them in stacks of one hundred. He shuffles the bills so that the six hundred are well mixed and asks Amy to help him thumb through each stack to ensure no consecutive serial numbers. When they've finished, Luke says, "If Jordan is right, depositing these should go smoothly. To keep from mixing up our deposits, I'll put these six rolls for our State Bank deposit in my saddle bag."

"Good idea," Amy says.

State Bank Deposit	
6 Packs of $20 Bills	$12,000

1st Nat'l Deposit	
Six Packs of $20 Bills	$12,000
Gun Safe Coins	$400
Warrants	$1,000
Wedding Gift	$500
Total Deposit	$13,900

Money Not Deposited		
	Packs	Value
$1	6	$600
$2	4	$800
$5	4	$2,000
$10	3	$3,000
$20	1	$2,000
	Total =	$8,400

Chapter 27: Luke Sells His Wheat Farm
July 28

In the morning glow before daybreak, Luke quietly dresses and takes their rolled-up stack of used newspapers to the burn pit. It's behind the hotel about fifty yards to the southwest; it's thirty feet wide and sixty feet long. One end is for trash, and the other is for garbage. It's six feet deep and one of four city dump sites.

There's only a hint of wind, so Luke throws a lit match on the newspapers and waits for them to burn up. He returns to their room carrying a tray with a pot of coffee, cups, cream and sugar, and pastries. He puts the unused newspapers and the alcohol in Amy's carpet bag. Luke looks at Amy and says, "I'm going to have a busy morning, so I've decided to write down everything I have to accomplish. When I finish, allow me to bore you with my list."

"Okay," Amy says. "And thank you for the coffee and sweet rolls."

After a few minutes, Luke says, "Are you ready to hear my list?"

"I'm ready, shoot," Amy says.

"First, I'll get my deed at the courthouse. I need to be there when it opens at nine; hopefully, I'll be the first customer. Then, I'll beat a path to the bank and make an appointment to close the farm at ten o'clock, when Bill is supposed to meet me. I should have enough time to open a joint account and transfer the money from my farm account into it before Bill arrives. After closing the farm, I need to talk to someone at the bank about submitting our bids. I hope there's a form we can fill out. Then I'll get more of the blank newsprint paper and another bottle of rotgut and return to the hotel to put some wear and tear on our First National deposit."

Amy says, "We should use our full names on our joint accounts. My middle name is Charlene, the female version of Charlie."

"I didn't know that!" Luke admits.

"It's on our marriage certificate!" Amy says.

"I never had a chance to read it because you stuffed it in your blouse so quickly. Never mind commenting on that; I think Charlene would be a great name for our first girl," Luke says.

Amy says, "My getting pregnant is inevitable at our current pace."

"That doesn't worry me at all," Luke says.

"That's good," Amy says.

"I've never had a middle name, Luke says. If I did, no one bothered to tell me."

Amy gets dressed, and they go to the dining room for a light breakfast. Amy can tell Luke is anxious to get going. They discuss the newspaper articles until ten minutes before eight o'clock. Luke gets up, kisses Amy, and sets out for the courthouse using long strides. The courthouse clerk finds his deed surprisingly fast; Luke thanks him and takes off for the bank. The lobby has no customers, and Luke tells the first cashier he meets that he would like to close on the sale of his farm at ten o'clock. The cashier leaves, and after a few minutes, a different cashier tells him the bank president will meet with him at ten. He tells the cashier he wants to close his farm account and transfer the money into a joint account with his wife.

The cashier asks for the names on the accounts, and Luke says, "My farm account is in my name, Luke Garrelts. The new joint account names are Luke and Amy Charlene Garrelts." The cashier asks Luke to print their names on a blank sheet of bank stationery.

While Luke is doing that, the cashier leaves to get his farm account ledger from the vault. Upon his return, the cashier says, "Your farm account has $397.35." Luke asks the cashier to transfer $350 into the joint account, and he'll withdraw the remaining $47.35.

The cashier hands Luke the cash and the new passbook. He thanks the lady and sees Bill Boyer standing near the front door. He gets his attention with a hand wave. While chatting about the farm, Luke says, "In addition to the house contents, I have some things in the bunkhouse and barn that I used for droving and saddle-breaking horses. I may never use them again, but I want them because I have fond memories."

Bill says, "I know what you're talking about. There's some clothing, several pairs of chaps, a couple of bronc saddles, hobbles, a stiff whip, and ropes or lariats, as you probably call them. I'll store 'em in the house until you can fetch 'em.

"I hope they are not in your way because it may be a while," Luke warns.

"If I can find a hand even half as good as you, I'll have him sleep in the bunkhouse. You can take your time getting them; don't worry about it.

At ten o'clock, a middle-aged, well-groomed man in expensive business attire greets Luke and Bill and introduces himself as Hank Pryor, the bank president and owner. Luke hands the deed to Hank and says, "I've agreed to sell this property to Mr. Boyer for $2,700. Hank looks over Luke's property deed and leaves to talk to the bank teller who helped Luke set up the joint account.

When Hank returns, he says, "Everything looks good, so you men can close on the property. Bill, you will sign this document transferring $2,700 to Luke's joint account. At the same time, Luke, you will sign the deed conveying the property to Bill. Bill, you will want to go to the courthouse today to have a new property deed prepared and registered."

When their signing is complete, Bill says, "Joint account? Did you get married?"

"Yep, I did. And I couldn't be happier."

"Any plans for the money?" Bill says.

"I plan to bid on land in the Addison Estate sale," Luke says.

Bill says, "When you left, I remember you were going to Kansas City to work in the stockyards."

"You're right; that was my plan. Before I got to Dodge, I met a pot-and-pan peddler from Dodge City. He passed away during the first night we camped together. To make a long story short, I took him home to Dodge City and fell in love with his daughter."

Bill says, "Good for you; doing the right thing is usually rewarded. I wish y'all had stayed at the farmhouse so I could meet your wife."

Luke says, "She asked to see it, but we couldn't find the time. We arrived Sunday evening and left Monday morning to inspect the property. We returned Wednesday evening, and I traded telegrams with you on Thursday. On Friday, I got everything ready for today's meeting."

Bill says, "You're welcome any time to visit and show your wife where you grew up." Luke thanked Bill; they shook hands and wished each other good luck. Bill departs for the courthouse, leaving Luke and Hank alone in Hank's office.

Hank turns to Luke, saying, "If you plan to bid on a property in the Addison Estate, then I'm your man. The State of Texas has hired my bank to manage the auction. I'm chairman of a five-man committee responsible for reviewing, evaluating, and selecting the winning bids and scheduling closings."

Luke says, "You're exactly the man I hoped to meet. How will closing dates be decided, and what is a fair price for the land in this sale?"

Hank says, "Closings will be scheduled based on the date and time the bid is submitted. If your bid wins, and it's the first one we receive on August 1st, you'll be the first to close. The price someone bids will vary depending on how they value the location, its natural features, the improvements, and particularly how badly the party wants it. We've been telling bidders that good pasture goes for three dollars an acre. Depending upon its size, you can add 300 to 400 dollars for a well-built, two-bedroom home with a kitchen. Add 200 dollars for a typical barn and 50 for a maintenance building. Sheds, coops, brooder houses, root cellars, and outhouses are more difficult to value, so you must use your judgment. Good four-wire fencing is a penny per foot. Add 200 dollars for a well and windmill."

"Thanks; I'll use that information when deciding on my bid amounts, and I'll be here when the bank opens on August first. Do you have a form I can use to submit my bids? This land purchase is my first," Luke admits.

"I don't like using a form, but I'll not bore you with my reasons. It's not a requirement, but I prefer that you allow one of my attorneys to prepare your bid. He will explain the information you must provide. After my attorney prepares your bid, you must approve it by signing and dating it. Before sealing the bid envelope, please allow me to review it. I will only scan your bid to ensure the committee won't reject it because of some legal problem, missing information, or an unreasonable requirement. Lawyers call that checking to see that you've dotted all the i's and crossed all the t's."

"Thank you for that advice. I want to meet with an attorney this morning, if possible," Luke says.

Hank says, "For reasons I'll keep to myself, I'm going to have Ben Abney work with you." Hank picked Ben from his four attorneys on the Bid Evaluation Committee because of Ben's passion for Western novels and because Luke looks like he just stepped out of one.

"My wife and I met Ben the day we got here. The bank was closed, and he was locking the door. He graciously waited while we looked at the property map in your conference room and then let us out, " Luke says.

Hank says, "Let's go to Ben's office." Once there, Ben remembers Luke, and they shake hands. Hank explains that Luke needs help with a bid in the Addison Estate sale and leaves.

Ben says, "I'm glad you found a property you like."

Luke says, "We did, but we must bid on two tracts."

Ben says, "Good! To prepare both of your bids, I will need the tract numbers, the bid amount for each tract, the name of your bank, and the name on the account. If your funds are not in First National, I need your State Bank account number to prepare a transfer order. The committee members are not mind readers, so if you require the bank or a third party to make an accommodation to close, put it in writing and make it easy to understand."

Luke says, "That sounds easy enough. Can I pick them up by the thirty-first?"

Ben says, "Today's Saturday, the twenty-eighth. Due to the estate sale workload, we will be open tomorrow. I only need a day to prepare your bids. So, if you get your information to me on Monday morning, the 30th, you can pick it up on Tuesday, the 31st. I'll review it with you. It sounds like you're in a hurry to close if you win either bid. So, you and Amy should sign, date, and bring it in when we open for business on Wednesday morning."

"That's a good plan; I'll see you Monday morning with the necessary information. Do you know if State Bank will also be open on Sunday?"

"I heard that they will be. Folks who bank there prefer to use an attorney they have known, and most are setting up a special account just for this sale."

Based on conversations with the bank president and his attorney, Luke no longer worries about the bidding process. He stops at the newspaper office and the saloon before returning to the hotel.

While Luke was at the bank, Amy asked the livery to harness Smokey and the kitchen to prepare a picnic lunch. Luke enters their room and says, "I saw Smokey and the wagon out front."

Amy says, "Honey, it's a gorgeous day, so I decided we should go to Lake Amarillo, find a nice shade tree to picnic under, and massage the money in the back of the wagon. I've got everything ready except for your boots and my carpet bag."

Luke says, "Great idea! Give me a minute to put on my city slicker clothes we bought in Kansas City, get my old boots and rifle, and I'll be ready to go!" The distance to the lake is two miles. On the way, Luke says, "Remember me telling you that Jordan said the cashiers don't give the one and two-dollar bills close inspection?"

"I do," Amy says.

"Okay, when we get around to processing the one and two-dollar bills that we may not deposit, I don't plan to soak them with rotgut. I'll rough them up enough to appear slightly used. I'll find time to do that late one evening in the next day or two."

"Dang, I like that idea," Amy says. Why did you decide to wear your wedding clothes?"

"They're lighter, not as hot, and more comfortable in the close quarters of the wagon. Luke answers. "I'm not changing my style, not yet anyway."

They park in the shade of an unusually tall, healthy, windblown mesquite tree near the water's edge. After lunch, Luke gets the boot with the 1st National deposit from under the seat. They find that aging the six packs of bills is nearly a joy in the shade with a cool, gentle breeze flowing off the lake. Because of the limited space in the wagon, they can only process two packs (200 bills) at a time. When they have all the bills rolled up in newspapers and drying, Amy notices no one else is around the lake and suggests they go for a swim. Luke says, "That is good-looking water; let's undress here and make a dash for it."

"I'll be right behind you," Amy giggles. After a refreshing dip, they return to the wagon to dry in the warm breeze provided by the afternoon sun.

Amy looks over the tailgate and says, "Oh, God, two riders are coming, and we don't have on a stitch of clothing!"

"Scoot over so I can get to my rifle, and let's lay the mattress up against the tailgate. I don't think a pistol shot can penetrate the tailgate and the mattress," Luke says. He returns as the riders are within hollering distance and shouts, "Stop right there." They continue riding, and Luke fires a shot that kicks up dirt between them. Then he tells Amy to lie flat on the floor with her head down.

The riders rein their horses to an abrupt stop, and the older rider shouts, "Come out of that fancy wagon, give us your money, and we'll be on our way!"

"I'm afraid not!" Luke shouts back. "We came here for an afternoon swim! We just got out, and we're both naked as jaybirds and drying out!"

"Buck naked, huh? This holdup could get interesting!" the spokesman shouts.

"As long as I'm alive, you two will not see my wife naked. I promise you that! The first to unholster his pistol will lose his hand or, if I miss, be gut shot; that's a slow, nasty way to die!" Luke yells.

"That's big talk for a naked man against two marksman gun hands!" says the spokesman while clumsily dismounting and hiding behind his horse.

"I cannot see what you're doing! Before you do something you'll regret for the rest of your life, allow me to prove my advantage by shooting your saddle horn! If either of you fires a shot, I promise you will be mortally wounded before my ejected casing hits the ground!" Luke warns.

"Again, that's mighty big talk for a naked man!" One second later, the saddle horn explodes. The horse bolts forward, leaving the man standing with his hands up and holding a pistol while the younger man rides away at full gallop.

Luke, more calmly but loudly, says, "I have a notion to kill you, free your horse, and bury you with the saddle and bridle. In a minute, I will throw you a shovel so you can start digging your grave. But first, I will give you a chance to tell me why I should let you live."

Lowering his hands, the would-be robber says, "Look closely at my horse and me; I'm on hard times. I'm worse off than flat broke. I owe the general store eight bucks. The owner won't extend my credit, and I understand why. I have a wife and three kids to feed. My oldest left me standing here just a minute ago. I can't blame him. The Confederacy called me a war hero, but my reward has been to return home and slowly become so crippled that I can no longer do meaningful work. I'm not evil. I didn't intend to hurt you, but I must talk tough and yell to be frightening. I'm not proud of what I do, but what's a man like me to do other than take from those who look like they can afford to give up some of their money?"

Luke says, "I fought in the war and am familiar with your predicament. You are right; we can spare a few sawbucks, so empty that revolver, give us a minute to get decent, and we'll see what we can spare."

"Oh, Dear God, thank you. I'll get my horse while y'all get dressed," the crippled war veteran says and limps away, dragging one leg.

When he returns, Luke is out of the wagon. He hands him four $10 bills and says, "You're in the wrong line of work, friend. You don't know how close you came to meeting Saint Peter today. Go home and tell your family you've decided to turn over a new leaf. Take them to church like a proud father and befriend everyone you meet. Participate in church activities and volunteer your time. Tell those who ask about your condition that every step reminds you of the war. I can assure you that, before long, you will be offered a helping hand by church members, who say to themselves, 'There, but for the grace of God, go I.'"

"Thank you; I'm so very grateful. You are a man with great common sense, a charitable heart, and one hell of a shot. I believe a reward awaits you in heaven," the war vet confesses, struggles to mount up, and slowly rides away.

Luke thinks, *If he only knew.*

Amy says, "Honey, I was scared when those two men rode toward us. You stayed calm and figured out how to get the upper hand; that was an impressive performance."

"Thanks," Luke says.

They get dressed, stack, roll, band, and put the bills back in the boot. They fold the used newspapers, and Amy puts them in her carpet bag. They return to the hotel dining room and speak quietly during the meal. Luke whispers, "You had a good idea today. I wasn't looking forward to processing bills in our room. Being outside by the lake was fun, and we may have convinced a lost soul to take a different path."

Amy asks, "When we've finished abusing the last of the poor, defenseless bills we don't plan to deposit, I don't want to put them back in the boots. I want to divvy them up. I can carry half of them in my beat-up oversized handbag, and you could put yours in the saddlebag. Carrying two old boots around like some rare treasure is suspicious behavior."

"Yeah, I agree," Luke said. "After we make the bank deposits and submit our bid, we'll get the last of the money in spending condition and decide who takes what. After the bank president closed the farm today, he gave me great advice about bidding. I'll tell you all about it in bed."

"Oh, I'll be looking forward to that," Amy says.

In bed, Luke says, "The First National Bank President is a fellow named Hank Pryor. He recommended prices for pasture and improvements. I'll put together a bid estimate for each tract in the morning. Ben Abney, the fellow who let me review the estate map the afternoon we arrived, is an attorney. He will be preparing our bid documents. By Monday, he needs our bid amounts and some basic information to prepare the bids.

Ben said the estate sales have dramatically increased their workload, and the First National and the State Bank will be open in the morning. By late morning, the State Bank cashiers should be overworked and frustrated. Hopefully, they're disgruntled about having to work on a Sunday and will not pay attention to serial numbers if everything else looks good. Those conditions should peak by eleven-thirty, and they'll look forward to their lunch break. That's when we will make our deposit."

"I understand why you want to be devious, and I agree," Amy says.

"Call it devious or just being very careful," Luke says. "I'll be nervous until we are thanked by the cashier for our deposit and walk out with a passbook."

"I plan to be even more devious. We processed twelve rolls of twenty-dollar bills. The bills in one roll smell like bourbon and have smudges of printer's ink. I plan to randomly place those bills with the bills in the other eleven roles. Jordan suggested we use some naturally aged bills. We have ninety-five $20 bills that are naturally aged. I plan to put seven or eight of them on the top of each roll. I'll do that after you fall asleep."

"You think of everything," Amy says. "Now, put out the lamp and come snuggle with me."

Naturally Aged $20 Bills		
Gun Safe Coins	$400	20 Bills
Warrants	$1,000	50 Bills
Wedding Gift	$500	25 bills
Totals	$1,900	95 Bills

Chapter 28: Deciding On Their Bids
July 29

Luke's been working on their bids by the light of a kerosene lamp for over an hour. Amy awakens and asks, "Why are you up?"

Luke says, "Good morning! I've been working on our bids using the bank president's recommendations.

"What do you have so far?" Amy asks.

Champion Hotel and Diner — Amarillo, Texas

The bank president said pasture sells for $3/acre. Jordan and the Anthonys want us to own it, so let's bid $3.50. Tract #19 is only pasture (one-fourth of it is on the J&J).

- 2,150 acres at $3.50/acre = $7,525
- I'd like to round it up to $8,000

Tract #20 has the rest of the J&J and the improvements.

- 1,950 acres at $3.50/acre-------------------------------------$6,825
- Artesian well and lake----------------------------------$1,500
- 2 Bedroom house---------------------------------------$600
- Big Barn with 10 stalls-----------------------------------$600
- Building with Maintenance shop & Storage-------$300
- Roost, Outhouse, Woodshed, Rabbit Cages-------$100
- 4 miles of barbed wire fence at 2 cents per foot--$200
- 2 water wells---$400
- Sum of the above-------------------------------------10,525
- Add 10% to be more competitive----------------$1,053
- Total--$11,578
- Let's round it up to $12,000.

Luke says, "I'll summarize for you; the bank president said ordinary grassland sells for $3 per acre. That's the price he's telling folks who ask, so we need to be higher to be competitive. Because Jordan and the Anthonys hope we get it, I want to bid $3.50, a 17% premium.

Tract number nineteen is 2,150 acres, and tract twenty is 1,950. Tract nineteen has no improvements; it's just a big pasture. Our bid would be $7,525 at $3.50 per acre. Because it has the smelly pool of black goo that I tried to hide, I rounded it up to $8,000. That makes our bid a 24% premium over $3 per acre. If no one else discovers what I believe is oil, we should win that bid handily."

"Tract twenty has all the improvements, including the natural lake. My total for it is $10,525. I added ten percent to make our bid a little safer. Then I rounded that number up to $12,000." Luke hands his work to Amy and asks her to review it for mistakes.

After a few minutes, Amy says, "You're good with numbers. I don't want someone to outbid us. Let's add another $1,000 to each tract. That'll make our total $22,000. Can we afford it?"

Luke says, "Before the closings, we'll have $16,950 in our First National account and $12,000 in the State Bank account. After closing, our State Bank account will be zero. Ben will take $10,000 plus forty dollars to prepare our wills from our First National savings account. That will bring our First National account down to about $6,900, plus we have $8,400 that we haven't deposited yet. So, we'll have around fifteen thousand dollars left over after buying the properties."

1st National Savings Account	
Six Packs of $20 Bills =	$12,000
Gun Safe Coins =	$400
Warrants =	$1,000
Wedding Gift =	$500
Sale of the Farm =	$2,700
Closed Farm Account =	$350
Account Total =	$16,950

State Bank Deposit	
6 Packs of $20 Bills	$12,000

Money Not Deposited		
	Packs	Value
$1	6	$600
$2	4	$800
$5	4	$2,000
$10	3	$3,000
$20	1	$2,000
Total =		$8,400

Luke feels good about their bids and is anxious to see Ben. He says, "We can afford whatever you need to set up housekeeping and for me to buy a starter herd of heifers and an eager young bull. After that, would you be okay with investing some of the money in our savings account to help the city? It's a way to pay back for our good fortune and a smart investment in our future."

"Doing that would be very noble of you," Amy says. "But don't forget my birthday trip to New York City. That could be an expensive trip."

"I haven't forgotten about it, and we can afford it. You enjoyed the train ride from Topeka so much that I picked Randy's brain to understand what it costs to travel on a train. My numbers are rough and intentionally on the high side. I based the cost estimate on the assumption we'd be gone for three weeks. I assumed it would take five days to get there, ten days to tour the city, and five days to return home. Randy said to use $20 per passenger per day plus a dollar per meal. So, for both of us, I used $50 per day for ten days, that's $500. Everything I've read about New York tells me it's high-priced, so I assumed $25 per day for a hotel room and

$20 per day for our food. $45 per day for ten days is $450. So, train, food, and lodging are almost a thousand bucks, and I'd guess we'll blow twenty to thirty dollars a day on sightseeing: that's another $300. If we spend twice $1,300, it's worth every penny. I'm excited about seeing New York City. And, if we have time, I'd like to take a side trip to Boston or Philadelphia; those cities and New York are chock-full of American history, and they're the birthplace of the American dream."

Amy says, "I love that you are always thinking of me. In addition to being smart and handsome, you're a splendid husband. Now, come back to bed and snuggle with me before sunrise."

Luke says, "Since we're not going to State Bank until nearly noon, you can sleep in, and we'll have a late breakfast at about eleven."

Amy says, "A late breakfast is called brunch."

"Well, la-de-da," Luke says.

After a quick snuggle, Amy falls asleep, but Luke lies awake, worrying about what he'll do if the State Bank deposit goes badly. He decides to recheck the rolls to ensure they meet Jordan's advice about keeping a cashier from becoming suspicious. Luke gets out of bed slowly and quietly so as not to wake up Amy, and gets the saddlebag. He removes the six rolls of $20 bills and meticulously goes through each. They are all just as he planned, and he puts them in Amy's carry bag and returns to bed.

They sleep until ten, have a buffet brunch at eleven, and take the hotel's courtesy carriage to the Texas State Bank. They open a joint account with a $12,000 deposit. The bank is buzzing with activity, and the cashier they get appears overwhelmed. He asks another cashier to help him count the money. Neither man comments on some bills having a faint bourbon odor and ink stains. The bank presents Luke and Amy with a gold-embossed passbook. The only thing that made Luke a little nervous was that the two cashiers recounted the money three times. He decides it must be the bank's procedure to recount a deposit until they get the same number three times.

When they leave, Amy says, "Look at our deposit book; we have $12,000!"

Luke says, "Not so loud, sweetheart. Everyone in town doesn't need to know. I was wrong about the bourbon and ink drawing attention. I think they had the opposite effect; they gave credibility to the money being well-circulated."

Amy says, "I feel good about our deposit; I want to celebrate. Can we walk back to the hotel so I can do some window shopping?"

"We had a conversation only three or four days ago about counting your chickens before they hatch, Luke says.

"With or without you, I'm going to window shop," Amy says.

Teasingly, Luke says, "Sweetheart, honestly, the J&J already has all the windows we need."

Amy punches Luke in the ribs and says, "Smart aleck."

Luke laughs and says, "Window shop as much as you like, but please don't buy anything until we own the J&J."

Amy says, "I will agree to that."

Luke says, "I'm going to celebrate with a bottle of Hires root beer; would you like one?"

"No, thank you," Amy says.

"I'm going to get a bottle at the hotel and finish reading Mary Shelley's *Frankenstein* this afternoon at my favorite table in the dining room.

"Do you like the story?" Amy asks.

"It's even less believable than a Western dime novel," Luke says.

"Does that mean you don't like it?" Amy asks.

"I like it okay; it's just not believable, Luke says. I think the author had a horrible nightmare, woke up, and wrote a story about it."

"Go to the hotel, get your root beer, and book. I'll window shop for a while, and then I'll nap. I love you," Amy says.

"And I love you," Luke says. We can celebrate our banking success after dinner while snuggling."

"Ooooh, I'm looking forward to that," Amy says as sexy as she knows how while rocking her shoulders and giving Luke her come-hither look.

Chapter 29: Ben Gets Their Bid Data
July 30th

It's Monday morning, and Luke gets to the bank at nine. Ben is in a meeting, so Luke chats with a customer about the need for rain. When the cashiers open their cages for business, the customer excuses himself. Ben sees Luke, hurries to join him, and says, "Sorry to make you wait. I didn't expect to be in a meeting this morning." Luke hands Ben a folded page of hotel stationery and says, "Amy wrote this. Please draft both bids using our full names and note that we have joint bank accounts.   Ben reads it and says, "Having your accounts set up by the end of this week is good, but it's not necessary; August thirty-first is your deadline.

Champion Hotel and Diner — Amarillo, Texas

Dear Ben:

Our bid for tract 19 is $9,000 and tract 20 is $13,000.

By the end of this week, we will have accounts in First National and State Bank in the names of Luke Garrelts and Amy Charlene Garrelts.

For closing, please take all the money out of our account at State Bank; the First National Account will cover the remainder and our Wills.

Sincerely,

Luke and Amy Garrelts

"I read about that on your Customer Communications board, Luke says. "Tell me a little about how you will process all the bids.

"Okay, after the bank closes on August 31st, the committee will separate the bids by tract number. The next morning, we'll start with tract number one and open every bid for that tract. If the highest bidder has funding to cover the closing and requires nothing unacceptable, we proceed to tract number two. We hope to work through all thirty tracts the next four days and post the auction results on the morning of the fifth."

"You're going to be busy," Luke says.

"We're prepared to work some long hours if need be. There will be some tracts without a bid and others with only one or two bidders. I expect the tract 15, with the ranch house and buildings, will take the most time", Ben says.

Luke says, "Should a problem arise regarding our bids, I'd like to know. We're staying at the Champion Hotel."

"I'll be sure that doesn't happen. Your bid documents will be ready tomorrow at one o'clock," Ben advises.

"We didn't want all our eggs in one basket, so we have another account at State Bank. Amy has the passbook, and I don't remember the number. I'll have it on Monday," Luke explains.

"Good," Ben says, putting Amy's letter in a folder with "Garrelts, Luke & Amy Charlene" on the front and dropping it in a file in his desk drawer. Luke is slow to leave; before he takes a second step, Ben says, "I put this file in our safe every night before we lock up."

"Good; I was wondering about my problem if someone was to get their hands on it," Luke says.

Ben says, "Before you leave, I'm curious if you read dime western novels and what you think of them?"

"I bought one but never finished it," Luke said disapprovingly.

"Why not?" Ben asked with a concerned look.

"It wasn't believable," Luke says with conviction. "Most of the action is exaggerated."

In his defense, Ben says, "I'd have no way of knowing that. I'm a city slicker from Boston, a college boy, a family man, and a banker. I enjoy reading those stories and fantasizing about that lifestyle. I have a sizable collection. I asked for your opinion because you look like the men pictured in them. I hope you do not mind that Hank and I talked about you. I said that I thought you carried yourself like a man who doesn't fear anything. Hank agreed and thought you appeared to analyze and size up your surroundings. We decided that you seem to anticipate that something unexpected could happen at any time. I've noticed you keep your right hand within inches of that Colt's pistol grip."

Luke says, "I know that I unconsciously do that, but I didn't know it was so noticeable. It's due to a behavior developed from eight years of driving cattle through some rough country and four years as the point man. Rarely did a day pass that something worrisome didn't flare up. Rather than dozing off in the saddle, I learned to stay alert, use all my senses, think fast, and react quickly. Without realizing it, vigilance became a habit. I'm aware that my mind scrutinizes every situation to evaluate the worst that could happen and how I should respond."

Luke continues, "I have a love-hate relationship with this pistol. It changes depending on where I am. In my work, it's necessary for survival; however, I get unwelcome looks in banks, the hotel dining room, and when walking into most stores."

"Don't blame your gun for those askance looks and stares; they're due to more than the gun. No one would look twice if you came into the bank wearing a business suit with a gun on your hip. In your case, they're also looking at that huge sheath knife that I'd guess is sharp enough to shave with; is it a Bowie knife?" Ben asks.

"Yes, I do, and yes, it is."

"It's also because you're tall and very fit. You look like you're over six feet tall. Adding to your persona are the knee-high cavalry boots, big hat, vest, neck scarf, fringed Indian-made gloves, and spurs. You are intimidating, except that your short-cut facial hair accentuates your face rather than covering it up. You don't chew tobacco, have all your teeth, smell good, wear clean clothes, and have a welcoming smile. Your good attributes are what throw people off. You are a contrast in style, but I like you just as you are."

Ben continues, "Somewhere in my blathering is why you are so intriguing and why people look long and hard trying to figure you out. I'm also guilty of that, so I understand why you feel like people stare. To be redundant, you're exceptionally well-mannered, well-spoken, well-groomed, and very likable; the word admirable comes to mind. Those qualities are unexpected, based on how you dress and what most people would guess is how you make a living. You are a paradox, Luke Garrelts."

"If I ever get out of the business of punching cows for a living, I will reconsider how I dress," Luke says. "Until then, I'm glad you like me as I am," and grins.

Ben says, "I overheard our female employees whispering about you after you left yesterday. Their comments would make you blush. A man whose persona can put both good and evil men on edge, yet women find alluring, is truly unique. The first time we met, I thought you could cause trouble. If Amy hadn't been with you, I'd have said, 'We're closed.' Now that I know you, you're much more polished than expected. I'm being repetitive, so I should shut up. I hope you don't think I'm an ass-kisser."

"Of course, I don't. But I am impressed by your well-bred, clean-cut, good looks. Your stylish dress, likability, and the esteem Hank holds you in. What I would give to have your education, job, respect in the community, and an understanding of all those law books that fill the wall behind you," Luke says.

Ben says, "Thank you for the compliments. I see you ARE a very accomplished and polished ass-kisser. I'll have your bid ready tomorrow morning at ten," and they laugh while shaking hands.

"Perfect, I'll see you then," Luke says while walking away, liking Hank and Ben and feeling good about Ben preparing their bids.

Chapter 30: Ben Has Their Bids Ready
July 31

Luke is in the dining room, waiting for Amy before ordering breakfast. He's finished reading yesterday's newspaper and is thinking about his morning activities. He plans to pick up the bid documents from Ben, bring them to the hotel for Amy and him to sign, return them to the bank for Hank's review, and then hold on to them until tomorrow morning. Then, it strikes Luke that Ben may need to witness their signatures. So, when Amy joins him at breakfast, Luke says, "I don't know, but we may have to sign the bids in Ben's presence, so you should go to the bank with me."

Amy says, "Okay, but I'll need an extra twenty minutes."

"You got it," Luke says.

They arrive at the 1st National Bank at 10:30. Luke asks Amy if she remembers Ben. Amy smiles, nods toward Ben, and says, "Sure, we met the afternoon you sketched the Addison properties we're bidding on. He stayed late just for us."

Ben says, "And I remember you. It's nice to see you again. Please sit down and get into your signing posture. You'll sign and date duplicate copies of the bids and transfer orders for the two tracts you're bidding on."

Ben says, "You'll be surprised by your documents resembling a newspaper. My secretary prepared them with a new mechanical device called a typewriter. Hank bought three of them, and they've dramatically improved the speed at which we can prepare documents. We may be the first in town to have them, but eventually, every business will have at least one."

Luke says with amazement, "You have typewriters! I've read they're as scarce as hen's teeth. How were you able to get them?"

"Hank said he knew somebody who knew somebody. They were expensive; Hank has us put them in the vault at night."

"Can we see one before we leave?" Amy asks.

"Sure, I'll ask Carolyn to demonstrate it for you," Ben says.

Amy looks at the signature page of the first bid document and asks, "Ben, do I sign and initial with my three names?"

"Yes, the documents identify you as Amy Charlene Garrelts, so you must sign and initial that way."

Luke notices a distinct change in Ben and thinks, *Ben is more patient and charming, less businesslike and hurried. I think he wants Amy to be comfortable and to like him. I'm glad I asked her to come along.*

After executing the bids, Ben says, "I hope you will be successful. I would enjoy seeing you all occasionally."

Luke says, "September fifth will be a dark day if we find out we've wasted our time. Hank gave me some bidding guidelines, which we used. But then we rounded up each bid rather significantly out of concern over losing something we've set our hearts on. How much do I owe you?"

"Nothing. The bank is getting a small percentage of the bids to oversee the sales. Hank hopes the estate sale will bolster the bank's image. He knows there will be more people who do not buy a property than those who do. Hank doesn't want his reputation tarnished by losing bidders growling about having to pay for something they didn't get. That's why he's asking bidders to let him have a look at their bid before sealing it. And why he's offering free legal help to prepare or clean up a bid."

"It's a very customer-friendly policy," Amy says.

"I'll tell Hank what you said, Ben says. He'll like that term."

Luke says, "That reminds me that Hank suggested we have him review our bid to be sure it satisfies all the rules."

Ben slides the two copies of the documents into separate mailing envelopes. He hands them to Luke and says, "Submit one copy from each envelope tomorrow; the others are yours."

Luke asks, "Do you make Wills?"

"I do!" Ben answers.

"We'd like to have separate wills that would give us the right of survivorship, and our children would receive equal shares after we're gone."

Ben says, "That's a standard will, which Carolyn can easily duplicate using others I've done. I'm on the bid evaluation committee. If you win your bids, your wills can be ready when you close, thanks to Carolyn and her speedy typewriter."

"We want you to prepare wills even if we don't get to buy the properties. What do they cost?" Luke asks.

"They're twenty dollars each," Ben says.

Luke says, "Okay. Oh, I almost forgot. Amy, Ben needs the number of our State Bank account." Amy hands Ben their passbook and watches him retrieve their envelope from his file drawer. In the upper left-hand corner of her letter, Ben writes SBT-ZEG-DX9.

When Ben hands Amy's passbook back, she says, "What you wrote on the corner of my letter looks weird."

Ben says, "I wrote your account number using a code I developed. It adds an extra layer of security, and it's fun."

"I like that. How does the code work?" Amy asks.

"It's a security code; I can't tell you," Ben answers.

"Oh, all right," Amy says.

Ben says, "Let's go see Carolyn's typewriter. Her desk is down the hall on the right." Ben introduces everyone and asks Carolyn to type their names. While Carolyn loads a sheet of paper into the machine, Ben says, "It only prints in capital letters."

Within seconds, Carolyn prints their names and the alphabet, pulls the page out of the typewriter, hands it to Amy, and says, "You can keep it."

Amy says, "Thank you; your machine is amazing, but it's kind of noisy."

Carolyn says, "At first, to show them off, Hank put us near the entry, but when the cashiers complained about the noise, he relocated us back here. I prefer to be back here, where everyone who comes to the bank isn't gawking at me and the machine. It's nice to meet you all, but I must get back to work. This estate sale is putting calluses on my fingertips. Have a nice day."

Ben, Luke, and Amy thank Carolyn for the demo, and Ben leads them to Hank's office. Before leaving, Ben introduces Amy to Hank, glances at Luke and Amy, and says, "I'll see you two in the morning."

After Hank and Amy express their pleasure in meeting each other, Hank reviews the bids and transfer orders and says, "Ben has done his usual good work, and they're executed correctly." He puts them back in the envelope, writes his initials in the lower corner using a fountain pen, and blows on the ink to dry it.

Luke says to Hank, "Thank you for your time and advice. You're a busy man, so we should excuse ourselves and let you get back to more important activities."

"Nothing is more important than our customers; they're number one. I wish you the very best of luck with your bids. You now have friends in the banking community. If you ever need a loan, I hope you'll consider First National your first choice."

Luke shakes Hank's hand, saying, "We absolutely will." While leaving Hank's office, Luke tells Amy, "Banking makes me hungry."

In their next step, they hear Hank, who weighs 250 pounds, say, "Banking has that effect on me, too."

Walking back to the hotel and unable to be overheard, Luke says, "After lunch, we need to discuss how to divvy up the money we're not going to deposit right away."

Amy says, "I'm glad you think the money is safer in my handbag and Smokey's saddlebag than in an old cavalry boot underneath our dirty laundry. I've been giving some thought to how we divide it."

After lunch, Luke dumps the last packs on the floor and says, "Have you noticed these bills smell like feet?"

Amy bends over to get her nose closer and laughingly says, "They sure do!"

They separate the packs by denomination, and Amy says, "Let me take a shot at divvying these up. (Refer to the tables at the end of Chapter 26 for Bills Not Deposited.) Since it was my idea, I'll make choices that give you less to carry around. To prove that point, I'll start by taking four of the one-dollar packs, three of the two-dollar packs, and all four of the five-dollar packs. That leaves you with two packs of ones, one pack of twos, three packs of tens, and one pack of twenties. I'll have eleven packs, and you'll have seven."

"While it's fresh on your mind, let's write down what you said," Luke says.

"Good idea," Amy says. They sit side by side at the desk; Amy repeats her decisions, and Luke makes a table.

Amy's Divvy Money			Luke's Divvy Money		
	Packs	$		Packs	$
$1	4	$400	$1	2	$200
$2	3	$600	$2	1	$200
$5	4	$2,000	$5	0	$0
$10	0	$0	$10	3	$3,000
$20	0	$0	$20	1	$2,000
Total	11	$3,000	Total	7	$5,400

"That plan works for me," Luke says. "I'll carry a pack of ones in my wallet and slide the other six packs down my boots next to my ankles. Should some fool hold me up for my wallet, I'll let him have it. As I spend my small bills, I'll exchange my tens and twenties at First National for ones and twos, or I can trade with you."

Amy thinks about her strategy momentarily and says, "I'll hide the four packs of five-dollar bills in the lining of my handbag. I'll put all the ones and twos in telegraph envelopes addressed to us at the hotel. They'll look just like those three over there on the desk. I'll put a rubber band around every stack of three envelopes and keep them at the bottom of my bag. The average bear of the woods will never suspect there is money in them. My plan may not be perfect, but if we're not going to deposit the money, it is better than carrying it around in old boots."

"I trust you'll keep that handbag close, Luke says. You'll have $3,000 in it!"

"Don't worry, your pretty head. My plan is okay, and I can change it if I come up with a better idea."

"Have you thought of making a money belt?"

"I haven't, but that's an excellent idea," Amy says. "Let's tidy up and put these back in the boot until we're ready to work them over."

Before dinner, Luke suggests they take a twilight walk along the main street. Luke is relaxed and in a good mood because his plan has come together flawlessly. "We should do this every evening," he says.

"I wish the stores were open so I could shop," Amy complains. Luke looks at her with a raised eyebrow, and she says, "Hold your breath; I know what you're about to say."

They have a quiet dinner and retire early. Luke can't sleep and gets out of bed because he's concerned about the seven packs of one and two-dollar bills they will be spending around town. He gets them out and works on them into the wee hours. When done, he puts them back in the boot and returns to bed.

Chapter 31: Submitting Their Bids
August 1

Luke can't sleep thinking about their First National deposit. To be sure they didn't screw it up, he gets out of bed, lights a kerosene lantern, and takes the seven rolls of $20 bills out of the boot. He confirms that six rolls have 100 bills, and one roll has 95. He checks that the serial numbers are not consecutive, that the slightly bourbon-smelling and ink-stained bills are intermingled randomly in all the rolls, and that six or seven naturally worn bills will be on top when the cashier removes the rubber band from each roll. He decides his worry is for naught, tosses the seven rolls into Amy's carry bag, extinguishes the lantern's flame, and returns to bed until sunrise.

A little before eight, they leave for breakfast; Amy carries their bids and the deposit money. When the courthouse clock strikes eight o'clock, Luke sets his watch, pumps his eyebrows at Amy, and says, "I'm on EXACT Amarillo time."

Wrinkling her nose and grinning, Amy says, "Which was determined by a one-eyed fellow using a sundial in a rainstorm." Luke rolls his eyes and doesn't comment. While waiting on their light breakfast of poached eggs on toast with coffee, Luke reads the articles with eye-catching headlines to Amy from last evening's paper. They leave for the bank at a quarter to nine and see Ben, from a distance, sweeping the boardwalk with the bank door wide open.

Ben greets them, saying, "Good morning. You all go to my office; I'll be there in a few minutes."

The Garrelts return Ben's greeting, leave him sweeping the bank's boardwalk, and wait in his office.

When Ben joins them, Amy hands him their bid envelope. Ben writes the date, time, and initials on it and says, "You both need to put your initials next to mine."

When they're through, Luke says, "Before leaving, we need to make a deposit."

Ben says, "I see a cashier who has opened his cage."

Amy places the seven rolls of $20 bills in front of the wide-eyed cashier and says, "By our count, all of these should be 13,900 dollars."

The cashier says, "Bank policy requires that I count this with a witness. Another cashier should arrive shortly."

Luke says, "No problem, we're in no hurry." He watches as the cashier talks to Hank, who looks at them and nods in approval. A calm rapidly spreads through Luke, and he appears as relaxed as if he were making a $5 deposit.

In about twenty minutes, the cashier returns and says, "You were right; it's exactly $13,900, which I've added to your account. If you have your passbook, I will update it." Luke hands their passbook to the cashier.

Once outside the bank, Amy asks, "How much is in this account now?"

Luke says, "I don't have to look. I peeked when he handed it to me to be sure it was right. We have 16,950 dollars. When I set up our joint account, I transferred $350 from my farm account and added $2,700 from the sale of my farm."

"We don't look that rich," Amy says.

"And we should keep it that way. I've been wondering about how to explain our wealth. Would anyone believe I won a gold mine in a poker game that became a bonanza?" Luke asks.

"Why not?" Amy asks.

"Well, I'm a lousy poker player and know nothing about gold mining," Luke says.

"Just say you were dealt a royal flush and sold half of it to a mining company," Amy suggests.

Luke says, "Good idea, but seriously, you must try to end a conversation when someone asks about the source of our wealth. But if pressed, let them think I have a generous benefactor like Pip had in Charles Dickens' *Great Expectations*. Let's pretend I have a wealthy hermit uncle named Fred, living in New York City with nothing better to do with his fortune than squander it on me. And that's all you know about him. But don't play that card unless you absolutely must."

"I can easily sell that," Amy says.

They stop at the newspaper office to buy more blank newsprint paper, then go to the Western Union Office. Luke telegrams George and Rosa, informing them that they have bid on two tracts and will be happy to get either one. Amy asks to buy a dozen of their message envelopes and a half dozen rubber bands; the telegrapher insists they're free to their good customers.

At the hotel, Luke says, "I'll be glad when the bills we're going to divvy up are processed so I can stop worrying about being caught with packs of uncirculated bills."

"Ditto," Amy says. "But I've changed my mind about throwing the boots away. I'm going to keep them as souvenirs of this experience."

"Consider them a gift from me," Luke says. "And speaking of gifts, I plan to go to the depot tomorrow to plan for your birthday trip."

"Can I come too? It's not a surprise birthday gift, so I'd like some input."

"Sure, I'd like you to come with me," Luke says. "Regarding our divvy money, I roughed up the one- and two-dollar bills last night so we could spend them without concern. That leaves only eight packs of five, ten, and twenty-dollar bills to process this afternoon.”

Amy says, “Let's get started.”

They've become so skilled at making uncirculated U.S. Treasury notes look worn that they finish the eight packs by late afternoon. Amy says, “I'm so excited about going to the train depot tomorrow that I won't be able to sleep tonight.”

“I'm glad you're excited. I'm going to sleep very soundly because I won't be waking up worrying about processing more treasury bills,” Luke says.

“I'm so glad we have that behind us,” Amy says.

Chapter 32: Bad News At The Depot
August 2nd & 3rd

At Santa Fe's depot, the ticket agent explains that a railroad strike has shut down all the rails going north and east of Chicago, so tickets for departures to New York are not for sale. Amy asks the agent to recommend popular pleasure trips. He replies, "The Transcontinental Railroad to Sacramento, California, is very popular. Folks rave about the beautiful scenery and tell me the weather is perfect. You can take the Santa Fe to Kansas City, the Kansas Pacific to Omaha, Nebraska, and the Transcontinental to Sacramento; you're there in seven to eight days, depending on when you leave. Or you could go to New Orleans through Dallas and spend a little time in both Cities. The Missouri and Kansas folks are taking the new KP line to Denver. I could drop you off at Dodge, and you could take a coach to Denver."

Amy says, "I'm from Dodge, and I took a Southwest stagecoach to Denver with my parents a few years back. I promised myself I'd never do that again."

Luke says, "Thank you for the suggestions. I doubt we have enough time for the Transcontinental trip, and I'm not sure New Orleans is a good place to be in August. We'll take one of your departure schedules and think about it."

On their way back to the hotel, Amy is disappointed and quiet. Over lunch, she says, "I've come up with an idea to replace New York, but it isn't going to sound nearly as exciting. I'll send Mom a telegram inviting her to Amarillo to celebrate my birthday. I think she'd enjoy seeing the property. I know I'd like to see it again."

"If having your mother here to celebrate your birthday makes you happy, that makes me happy," Luke says.

The following day, August third, Amy sends Doris a telegram inviting her to Amarillo for her birthday, and as an incentive, she'll reimburse her for the round-trip ticket. Amy returns from the telegraph office and says, "Luke, if we buy the properties, I want to rename the ranch the L&A. I've played around with brands and decided on this." She hands Luke a scrap of paper with the brand she designed.

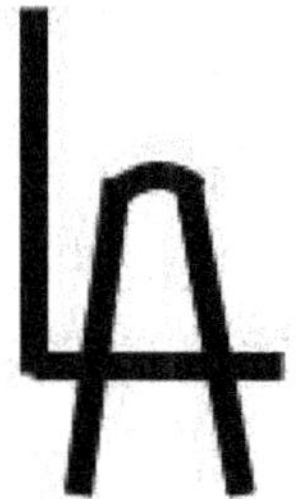

Luke quickly says, "I like it; it's simple, yet hard for a cattle rustler to forge by branding over; it's decided."

That evening, a Western Union courier delivers a note from Doris to Amy. It says, "I will leave Dodge on the seventh, and you will not reimburse me for the ticket. Love, Mom."

Chapter 33: Doris Arrives In Amarillo
August 7

Amy and Luke walk two blocks to the train depot to meet Doris at three o'clock. The women are excited, so Luke steps back to give them time to reunite and settle down. Amy asks Doris if she wants to see the property they bid on. Doris enthusiastically says, "Yes, of course!"

Luke has been listening; he interjects, "Okay, but you all will not go alone. I recall seeing a Western Union sign on one of Addison's buildings. I'll try to send a telegram to the hotel this afternoon. We can make it to Addison by six if we leave EXACTLY at seven in the morning. Stay there for the night and run up to the J&J the following day."

"Good idea," Amy says. "Let's stop at Western Union on our way back to the hotel."

The porter sets Doris' luggage next to her; Luke thanks and tips him and tells Doris and Amy, "I'll get the big one and let you all carry the two little ones."

Doris asks Amy, "Why did Luke emphasize the word EXACTLY?" Amy tells the story on the way to the Western Union office, and Doris thinks it is cute. Luke has been listening to Amy's explanation and says, "Mom, your daughter knows how to win an argument."

"She was on the debate team during her last school year. She and another girl won the state competition in Wichita. I've never been able to talk her out of ANYTHING that she sets her mind on," Doris whines.

Luke says, "I'm slowly learning that."

Luke is pleased that the Western Union office in Addison is open for business and sends a telegram to Joanna Barnes at the

Addison Hotel. He requests reservations for two rooms for two nights, one single occupancy and one double. They continue walking to the hotel, and Doris excitedly says, "I'm looking forward to seeing the property, and it will be nostalgic riding on the wagon!"

Luke says, "You all have a lot of things to talk about. Amy can handle the reins, so I'll ride in the back on Amy's mattress and wake up to switch the horses and try to be useful. That will give you all plenty of time to enjoy each other's company."

When they reach the Champion Hotel, Amy says, "Mom, I checked you in this morning, so we just need to get a key before going to your room."

Luke sets Doris's big suitcase on the bed, and Amy suggests that her mother rest until dinner. Doris says, "I'm too excited to sleep. Could you give me a quick tour of Amarillo before dinner?"

"Sure, but wouldn't you like to unpack and freshen up first? When you're ready, knock on our door directly across the hall; I'll be ready to go," Amy answers.

While the women are touring, Luke receives a confirming telegram from the Addison Hotel. He goes downstairs to the hotel dining room and asks Reba, the head waitress, if the chef could prepare three sack lunches while they have breakfast between six and seven. Reba says, "I'll make those sandwiches myself." She is concerned they may not return and asks, "Will you be returning soon?"

"Yes, in the evening, three days from now," Luke answers.

"Oh! Great! I'll be waiting for you," Reba says.

Luke thanks Reba, goes to the livery, greets his friend Frank, and tells him, "Amy and I are taking her Mother up to Addison to see the property we've bid on. It's a full day to get there, so I'll be here at 6:30. I'm taking both horses; I'll harness them. I'd like you to put twenty pounds of oats in the feed box and fill the water barrel."

"Will do," Frank says. When do you plan to return?"

Luke says, "Late in the day, three days from now."

Frank says, "Have a safe trip; I'll stay open until you return." Luke thanks Frank, shakes his hand, and goes to the grocery store to buy ten pounds of apples and the same amount of carrots.

Luke tells the women at dinner, "I received a confirming telegram from the Addison Hotel. We'll meet here for breakfast at six. The kitchen will prepare our lunches, so decide what you'd like and be ready to place your order. We're all set; we'll leave EXACTLY at seven o'clock in the morning." Amy and Doris look at each other while laughing.

Chapter 34: Doris' First Trip To The J&J
August 8th –10th

Luke has the horses and wagon waiting in front of the hotel at seven. Amy and Doris come out with small travel bags and the lunches Reba prepared. Luke says, "Give me a minute to get my things." He returns with his saddle bag, rifle, bandolier, and used flour sacks with the apples and carrots.

Luke looks at Amy and says, "If you see or hear anything that could be trouble, whistle loudly; the sooner, the better, because I could be asleep. Another precaution for tomorrow at the homestead: I want to ride the property's perimeter before returning to Addison. That's a little over a ten-mile ride, so it'll take about an hour. I'll leave my gun belt with you. Should ANYONE ride up, you fire two shots and reload. If you feel threatened or uncomfortable, fire twice more by pulling the trigger as fast as possible, reload, and defend yourself like in the caboose."

Luke's comment leaves Doris wide-eyed, wondering what happened in the caboose, but she doesn't ask. Instead, she asks Luke, "What will you be looking for?"

Luke answers, "Nothing in particular; I'm curious to know if others have been riding the fence lines and if I missed something when Amy and I were up here last month." But secretly, Luke is only going to where he found the dark brown, bubbling pool of goo nearly a half mile away. He is eager to know if there are signs of anyone prowling around it. If they took samples, there would be footprints.

Luke says, "Doris, our routine is to stop after either horse has pulled for an hour. We rest and water them for fifteen minutes, and I will switch them after two turns in the harness. We take a hour's break at lunch. They appreciate stopping at a grassy area. Sometimes, that can be a short distance off the road. I'll give each of them a bucket of water and the apples and carrots in the feed box. They don't get the oats until evening; you should appreciate me doing that."

Knowing that oats make them flatulent, Doris says, "I do."

Luke says, "By sticking to that, they will get us there more quickly and not be overworked." Following those comments, Luke hands Doris his pocket watch and asks, "Would you mind keeping the time and calling the breaks? It's an important job."

"I'd be happy to do that," Doris says.

Luke says, "Thank you," and goes to the back of the wagon, climbs in, and gets comfortable. The trip is uneventful, and the horses have the wagon in Addison at a little after six o'clock without Amy ever whistling.

They get their bags, go to the front desk, and Joanna says, "Hi Luke, hi Amy; I'm surprised y'all are back so soon. By the way, thanks for the telegram."

Amy says, "This pretty lady you have not met is my Mother, Doris Bonner."

"So nice to meet you. I'm Joanna Barnes; my husband is Billy Ray. We have two boys, seven and nine. You'll run into them sooner or later. Please tell me if you see them doing anything you disapprove of."

Luke leaves to unload their bags, and Amy tells Joanna, "Since we saw you, my husband and I bid on two Addison tracts. Until we know our fate next month, we're staying in Amarillo, my husband's hometown. Doris rode the train from her home in Dodge City to be here for my birthday in about two weeks. I wanted to show her around the ranch. We're going to do that tomorrow."

Joanna says, "I hope you all get the land because the town needs young folks like you. Please sign our guest register and provide your full name and address. Today's date is the eighth. The daily room rate is one dollar per occupant, and we ask that you pay in advance," Joanna says.

While signing the register, Amy noticed that the last two entries were by the Texas Rangers. She asks Joanna, "I see you haven't had a customer in a while. Shouldn't the estate sale draw interested buyers to stay for a few nights?"

"Maybe it's because they have three more weeks to submit their bid. But times are tough; getting a loan approved isn't a cinch, and interest rates are high. Or maybe it's because Addison's recent history has them afraid of staying here. It's probably due to a little of all of those," Joanna suggests.

Amy pays Joanna for two nights while Luke unloads the wagon. They carry their travel stuff to the rooms. Luke says, "You all stay here and relax. I'll take the wagon to the livery." When Luke returns, they decide to eat and retire early.

At dinner, Luke suggests they meet for breakfast at nine. Since the properties are only three miles away, they can sleep an extra two hours.

At breakfast, Amy asked Joanna if she could prepare three light lunches. Joanna says, "Sure, but all I have is roast beef."

"That'll be great!" Luke says.

Joanna looks at Luke and says, "I'll make one of them big." Luke smiles, looks at her, and nods approvingly several times.

Luke intentionally finishes breakfast before the women and goes to the livery. He harnesses Smokey to the wagon and ties Fury to the back with a rope halter. They leave for the J&J Ranch at ten o'clock and arrive in thirty minutes. Luke rummages around in the barn and maintenance shed and inspects the windmill, corrals, chicken coop, small cages, and root cellar. Amy and Doris meander around the property, and Amy describes her plans for giving it a woman's touch.

Doris has something complimentary to say about everything. Amy says, "Mom, you don't need to make me feel good about our decision to buy this property. Luke and I know it needs work, but we're excited about living here. By working together, we can make it a great place to raise a family. Luke is so much more than a good-looking cowboy. He's as smart as any college graduate and a devout Christian who is generous, confident, brave, funny, and loves and respects little 'ole me."

"If he can afford this much property, you left out rich," Doris says. Amy tells her that Luke sold his wheat farm to become a rancher. Amy doesn't want to deceive her mother by mentioning Luke's make-believe hermit uncle. Doris assumes Luke must have owned a sizable farm, had some savings, and perhaps gotten a loan.

Amy says, "I want to show you Luke's Lake. Hey, I think I just named it! It's picturesque and tranquil." They take the wagon the short distance to the lake so the horses can graze on tall, thick grass and drink fresh, cool water. Amy says, "We swam there two afternoons and spent both nights in the wagon, parked not ten feet from this very spot. Luke caught, cleaned, and dressed three big basses that I pan-fried. Pointing, Amy says, "Luke says he will put my garden over there alongside the overflow from the lake, where his sister, Jordan, had her garden. Luke says I can divert the overflow once a week to irrigate it."

When Luke finishes his inspections, he sees the women have taken the wagon to the lake's edge. He finds them sitting under one of the giant weeping willows. Luke unbuckles his gun belt, hands it to Amy, and says, "I want you all to stay right here; I won't be gone long." He swings up on Fury's bare back and rides off.

Doris says, "The lake is lovely; it begs you to get in."

"That's exactly how I felt the first time I saw it," Amy says.

Doris furrows her brow and says, "However, sleeping here in the wagon seems risky to me, but then, young love knows no peril."

Amy says, "When I'm with Luke, I feel safe. He is extraordinarily skilled with a rifle and a pistol. His horses know to warn him if anything approaches the wagon, day or night. He endeared himself to Governor Anthony by rescuing his wife, Rosa, and his cousin, Susan B. Anthony, from a plot to kidnap and hold them for ransom. He single-handedly prevented a train robbery on the Santa Fe going to Amarillo."

"I'd love for you to tell me more," Doris says. I got hints about something big happening in Topeka from your telegrams. Naturally, I was curious; however, I felt asking was prying, and I didn't want Luke to think I was a snoopy mother-in-law."

Amy says, "I will proudly explain those events. Governor Anthony told Luke that Susan feared copycats and didn't want the story in the papers. So, the Governor used his position to keep it out. Luke asked me not to tell anyone, but I know you will not repeat it." Amy tells Doris, word for word, the story Rosa told her about the attempted kidnapping. Then, she shares Luke's observations of President Hayes, General Grant, and Susan B. Anthony. Amy gives Doris a brief and carefully worded description of the train robbery, and Doris asks Amy to explain Luke's comment about what she did in the caboose.

When Amy finishes, Doris realizes Amy has matured well beyond her eighteen years. And Doris's opinion of Luke has just gone from very impressive to DAMN! She thinks, *Now, I understand his confidence and why Amy feels safe in his presence and head over heels in love.*

Luke never intended to ride the fence lines. His interest was solely in checking out the small area without vegetation. He approaches the patch from downwind, halts Fury a hundred feet away, dismounts, and smells the air to reassure himself that the faint odor of kerosene is coming from it. Luke surrounds the dead area with more grass, shrub branches, and dead tree limbs until he's satisfied it's well-hidden and looks like a nature-made barrier preventing a passerby from riding into it. He's elated that he saw nothing showing someone had been investigating the area. He's been gone almost an hour and decides to get back to the women.

Luke finds Amy and Doris right where he left them and says, "Are you all ready to head back to town?"

"We are," Amy says.

Doris asks, "Find anything that concerns you?"

Luke says, "Nope, everything looked better than good."

Doris says, "That's what I noticed. At one time, this place got a lot of loving care. I can see why you all want to buy it; Amy can't wait to call it home!"

After dinner, for something to do that evening, Amy and Doris walk Main Street. Doris asks about the three burned-down buildings. Amy tells Doris that an older man and his grown son said the big pile of ashes in the middle was Tom Addison's two-story office. Amy explains that the land they're bidding on is available because Mr. Addison died without a will or known heirs. By law, his entire estate became the property of the State of Texas. The property they were on today is just a sliver of the man's 64,000-acre ranch. Texas divided the Addison Ranch into two-thousand-acre tracts and stipulated that a bidder could buy no more than five tracts.

"I wondered why you called it the J&J. When I saw it burned on a board over the barn door, I knew why," Doris says.

"If we buy it, that board comes down. I'll flip it over, burn L&A on the backside, and nail it right back up," Amy says as she draws the brand in the dirt with her finger.

Doris says, "Can you put it inside a heart?"

Amy asks, "I suppose so, but wouldn't that look like something Luke would carve on the trunk of an oak tree when he was sixteen and I was six?"

Doris says, "You're right. Let's get back to the hotel. I'm feeling sorry for Luke having to follow us around town." Though tired, Doris has difficulty sleeping due to replaying Amy's stories about Luke's heroics.

When the women are safely in the hotel, Luke talks to the infirm livery owner about getting the wagon in the morning before eight. Luke learns that the old man is looking for a buyer. Thinking about his discussion with Frank Weiner, Luke says, "I know a man who could be interested. How much would you want?"

"Due to my health, I'll seriously consider any fair offer," he says.

"Okay, I'll let him know," Luke says and leaves.

The women are in the dining room at seven a.m. and order pancakes for three; Luke joins them a few minutes later. After a quick breakfast, Luke leaves for the livery. Joanna brings their lunches for the trip home to the table. Amy pays and thanks Joanna, and she and Doris carry their things from their rooms to the hotel's porch in two trips. Luke pulls up in front of the hotel, loads up, and they individually thank and tell Joanna goodbye. It's after eight when they leave for Amarillo, and Joanna is surprised to see Amy holding the reins and Luke in the back of the wagon, but she says nothing.

On the ride back to Amarillo, Doris tells Amy, "After breakfast, while Luke was getting the wagon and you were packing, I got an earful from Joanna. I was surprised to learn that the man the town was named after was a genuine bastard." Doris repeats Joanna's story about Tom Addison's cremated remains being found in a steel gun safe that survived the fire. Then she says, "I found it interesting that Mr. Addison's glasses and watch confirmed the remains were his."

Amy asks, "Did Joanna have an opinion on why someone would want to murder Mr. Addison?"

Doris says, "Oh, my goodness, yes! Her husband, Billy Ray, said most of the town hated the man and worried he might not have suffered enough. Joanna said two Texas Rangers stayed at their hotel and tried to investigate the arson and murder for two weeks. She believed the Rangers hoped that sworn statements would lead them to a disgruntled local. Since most folks had a run-in with the old man Addison, they clammed up, refusing to cooperate. The Rangers left town empty-handed."

Doris tells Amy another of Joanna's stories. She says, "A gravedigger told Billy Ray that an attorney hired him to bury Mr. Addison. The Texas Attorney General froze Mr. Addison's assets. So, they buried his ashes like a pauper. Only the funeral director, the attorney, and the gravedigger were present. There was no funeral service. The gravedigger tossed a child-size pine box into a shallow hole. Mr. Addison's ashes are in an unmarked grave where the city buries indigents and gunfight losers. I told Joanna that Mr. Addison's funeral was appropriate."

They arrive in Amarillo after eight and are thankful that the livery and the Champion Hotel's dining room have remained open. Reba knew they would arrive late and asked the chef to wait for them. They have dinner in the dim yellow light of a kerosene lantern in the middle of their table. They thank Reba, and Luke leaves a generous tip.

Doris was unusually quiet during dinner, and Luke sensed her behavior toward him was different. At the time, he thought, *Doris must be tuckered out from traveling for three days.* In bed that night, Luke says, "I thought Doris was noticeably tired tonight. At times, she seemed to stare a hole through me."

Amy says, "Mom had three busy days. But also, while you left us under the willow tree yesterday, I told her about you saving Rosa, Susan, and Howard, and she wanted to know about what I did in the caboose. Mom listened to those two stories without asking a single question. I think I overwhelmed her. She told me she didn't sleep very much last night."

"Well, from our telegrams, she had to be curious. I don't like secrets, so I prefer she knows, but she must keep it under her hat."

"I'm confident she will; otherwise, I would not have told her. Put out the flame and come here, you irresistible man!"

"I'll be right there!"

Chapter 35: Vacationing In Chicago
August 11th – 21st

After breakfast, Amy asks Doris, "Would you help me make a list of the kitchen things I'll need? There's a nice store at the other end of town with everything one would find in a well-equipped kitchen. We could go there and see what's new and what I can't live without. I don't need to shop for furniture because Luke didn't sell his furniture with his wheat farm."

Doris says, "Okay, that sounds like fun."

They leave, and Amy says, "I want to show you Leroy's Clothing store; it has a man's name, but he sells the kind of women's clothing I like. And I want to show you a revolver at the Colt store that I'd like to have at the ranch."

They shop at all three stores but buy nothing. On their return to the hotel, Amy says, "Thank you for helping me with my list. Luke wants me to help Addison's economy by buying things for my kitchen after we live there, so that's my plan. However, I'm concerned they may not have what I want or even be in business when I'm ready."

Doris says, "You could write a letter explaining your timing and attach your list. I bet they'll write you back."

"Do you remember the name of the store?" Amy Asks

"I do; it's called Kitchen Things," Doris replies.

"I like your idea; I will write to them," Amy says. "Changing the subject, is there a city you think would be fun to visit for a few days? Consider it an all-expense-paid vacation, courtesy of Luke. My only conditions are that we travel by train and we're back here for my birthday."

Doris says, "On the train coming here, I enjoyed seeing the country. I want to do more of that. Let me think about your vacation offer. I'll have an answer by lunch," Doris says.

Luke, Doris, and Amy meet for lunch, and Amy says, "Luke, we can't get to New York City, but I'd still like to take a birthday trip. This morning, I asked Mom to pick a city she'd enjoy spending a few days in. But I insisted that we be back in time to celebrate my birthday. She's been thinking about where to go."

Immediately, Doris interjects, "I've decided it would be fun to go to Chicago, where cattle go to become steaks and roasts! We'd see a lot of country while getting there!"

Luke says, "That's an excellent choice, but you're on a short fuse to do it. You all must go to the train depot when we finish here."

At the depot, Amy tells the ticket agent they want to go to Chicago; they can leave as early as tomorrow, but must return by the twentieth. The ticket agent surprises them, saying, "If you can leave tomorrow afternoon at five, you're in luck. Due to the strike, the B&O Railroad decided to run its idle express trains from Chicago to cities in the southwest. Those trains serve the major cities between Chicago and New York City. In that part of the country, the overnight passenger trains have the Pullman sleeper, dining, and lounge cars. Next week is their maiden run from Chicago. Your travel time will be shorter because an Express Train only transports people, mail, and light cargo; it does not carry livestock or heavy freight. It also makes fewer stops due to having a large tender car. Because it's a short train, it has a good top speed, but the problem with going to Chicago is slowing down for old tracks and bridges; elevation changes also reduce the average speed."

"What's the route?" Doris asks.

"Through Oklahoma City, St. Louis, and several jerkwater towns in Oklahoma, Missouri, and Illinois. In St. Louis, it stops for three hours. People with motion sickness welcome that stop. They have time to get off, stretch their legs, and clear their heads," the ticket agent replies.

"Neither of us has that problem," Amy says.

"You're lucky; motion sickness is bad. Some people spend a good deal of their time between cars, vomiting!" The agent briefly studies his schedule and says, "You'll arrive in Chicago at seven a.m. on Wednesday the fifteenth. To get you back, let me see (the agent takes a long pause). Okay, you'll leave Chicago on the eighteenth at six in the evening and arrive at Amarillo on the morning of the twenty-first at eight o'clock. Your return train is also a B&O. It has the same Pullman cars and runs the same route."

Amy says, "That would work. What do you think, Mom?"

"I'd very much like to do it," Doris answers.

"How much for three round-trip tickets?" Amy asks.

The ticket agent does some figuring and says, "Two hundred ten dollars, including your meals."

Amy asks excitedly, "Do these trains have the Pullman Palace cars, like on the Transcontinental Railroad?"

"No, not that luxurious, but they're very nice."

Amy blushes and asks, "Are the sleeping compartments big enough for two people?"

Speaking in almost a whisper and enunciating so Amy can practically read his lips, the ticket agent says, "I can't speak from experience."

Amy says, "I don't carry that much cash. Can you reserve the tickets until later this afternoon?"

"Yes, but company policy requires me to sell reserved tickets after we sell out. I very much doubt that will happen. This recession and the labor strike in the northeast have been hard on the rail business."

Amy says, "One more thing: we will need room reservations in a nice hotel for the nights of August sixteen, seventeen, and eighteen?"

"I can do that," the ticket agent says. "We like to book our passengers at the Palace. It's near the depot and the docks. It's pricey but worth every penny."

"How much for two rooms?" Amy asks.

"A room with a double bed is ten dollars per night per person, and you'll pay at check-in," he answers.

"That sounds perfect!" Amy says.

Amy and Doris return to the hotel and find Luke reading at his favorite table by the window overlooking Main Street. Amy asks, "What are you reading?"

"*Pride and Prejudice,*" Luke answers.

"Do you like it?"

"Yes, but I'll think twice before having five daughters."

"Where did you buy it?" Amy asks.

"At a little bookstore next to the State Bank, I bought two other novels recommended by the *Amarillo Times.*"

"What did you get?"

"I also bought *Wuthering Heights* and *Sense and Sensibility.* Would you believe women wrote the three I bought? If you include *Frankenstein,* which I bought two weeks ago, that's four!"

Doris says, "I'm not surprised."

Amy tells Luke about their experience at the depot. Luke says, "I'll go purchase your tickets, but I want you to consider postponing your birthday party to the twenty-second. You'll probably need some recovery time; that trip will wear you out."

"Good idea, I'm okay doing that," Amy says.

Luke says, "While you were at the depot, I decided I would be an anchor you all would have to drag around Chicago. So, I plan to visit The Third while you're gone. The Kiowa reservation is only a two-day ride due east of here, and I'll enjoy seeing him again."

"I thought you might not want to go," Amy said. Would you try to get Mom and me a pair of those moccasin boots like you gave George?"

"Sure, I need you to outline your right foot on a newspaper page. The registration desk should have scissors to cut them out. I'll get 'em if they're available in your sizes," Luke says.

Luke asks Amy to keep his book until he returns from the train depot and leaves in a rush. Doris says, "You have the most agreeable husband. Does he ever tell you no?"

"He hasn't yet," Amy says.

"Chalk up another endearing quality," Doris says with a smile and raised eyebrows.

When Luke returns to their room, Amy isn't there, and he goes across the hall to Doris's room. Amy answers his knock, and Luke hands her the tickets. She returns his book, and he asks, "How much money do you plan on taking with you?"

"Mom and I were discussing that very question. Can we catch up with you at seven for dinner?"

"Sure." Luke returns to the dining room to continue reading and receives two telegrams.

Amy says, "Mom, when Luke and I were considering going to New York City, he suggested I wear a money belt. So, I bought a thin elastic belt and some fabric. I could use your help making it."

Doris asks, "Okay, how much will you put in it?"

"Until we get to Chicago, we'll not need much money. I'm considering carrying only ten one-dollar bills and a few coins in my handbag. I'll give you the same amount to cover your expenses. Our room for three nights is $60, and I'm going to guess that food will be more expensive than here, so $20 per day for each of us is $120. A guided tour of the city, at $5 each, and three shows, at $5 each, is another $40. All in, that's $220. I'm going to ask Luke for $250. So, the money belt should be just big enough to hold twenty-five ten-dollar bills."

Being very familiar with the thickness of that number of bills, Amy says, "It should be thin enough to wear comfortably beneath my underwear and not be noticeable."

That afternoon, while they're making the money belt in Doris' room, Amy leaves and returns with the derringers Jordan gave her. She says, "Mom, Jordan gave me these little pistols for protection before I left Kansas City. I'm giving this one to you. Please put it in your handbag and practice retrieving it quickly; do not hesitate to reach for it when needed. Two women traveling alone look like easy targets."

Doris says, "Thank you; I've often thought about buying one. It's so cute."

Amy returns to her room before dinner, shows Luke the money belt, and says, "I plan to put $250 of my divvy money in it."

Luke gets thirty $10 bills from his boot and says, "I know you don't have any ten-dollar bills, so take these. I don't want them back. I can't wire you money because I'll be somewhere between here and wherever. Don't you have your Dodge City bank account money hidden somewhere?" Luke asks.

"I do," Amy says.

That can be your emergency funds," Luke says, grinning.

"Good thought; except for a roll of one-dollar bills, I'm going to leave you with the rest of my divvy money, but I want it ALL back when I return," she says.

"And with five percent interest, I suppose?" Luke says with a strained look.

"That's not a bad idea," Amy says with a smile.

At dinner, Luke surprises them with his decision to have Ralph Barr escort them around Chicago. Amy says, "That's a great idea; I like Ralph. How did you find him?"

"As soon as you left for the depot, I telegraphed George, asking where I could find Ralph. He told me that Ralph works out of the Pinkerton office in Topeka. Before I could telegraph Ralph, he sent a telegram saying he was available and wanted to know when and where. You know George had a hand in that."

Doris says, "A well-dressed, physically imposing man like Ralph will be nice to have around. Until I knew his nature, he frightened me."

Amy looks at Doris and says, "I agree, he'll be great, but bring your derringer anyway."

Luke says, "Now that I know your travel schedule, I'll have Ralph meet you at Chicago's depot. He'll hire a rental carriage, so don't be reluctant to tell him where you want to go. I'll tell him to get a room across the hall from you all. After a while, you won't notice he's following you around."

Doris says, "You think of everything. I like that about you."

The following day, Luke reserves the hotel's courtesy carriage to take them to the depot. He helps get their baggage on board and follows while they investigate the three Pullman cars. They get excited about the toilets in the sleeper and lounge cars and laugh at the "DO NOT FLUSH" signs.

While holding her face, Luke kisses Amy and says, "Please be careful."

He then hugs Doris and says, "Mom, keep an eye on her for me."

"You know that I will," Doris says.

Luke leaves them very excited and exploring the Pullman cars. They arrive in Chicago on schedule, and each greets Ralph with a hug and a "Good to see ya." Ralph has reserved the Palace Hotel's courtesy carriage, and he and the carriage driver stow their baggage on the back.

The Pullman cars made their trip relaxing, so they were not travel-weary but excited about seeing the city. Amy tells Ralph, "After checking in and unpacking, we'd like you to take us on a city tour."

Ralph says, "I'll get the rental carriage and wait for you in the lobby." Ralph has the carriage driver take them to State Street, in the financial and commercial heart of the city. They're impressed by the clean paved streets and multi-story stone buildings.

That evening, they dined at the Palace with Ralph two tables away, keeping a close watch. They are indecisive about which freshwater fish entree to order. Doris says, "Gosh, there are two kinds of salmon, three kinds of trout, two kinds of walleye, and bass, and none are expensive." The waiter suggests they order the walleye steak because it's a house favorite. It's an inch thick, six inches in diameter, and served with a salad, baked potato, and green beans.

As they leave the dining room, Doris says, "Ralph, the Walleye Pike is a whale of a lot better than our mud-hole-grown catfish." Ralph also had the Walleye and heartily agrees with her opinion.

Amy says, "The Boston Philharmonic is playing in the Grand Ballroom; we should go." Without asking for their agreement, she buys three tickets in the first row of the mezzanine floor. Ralph falls asleep during the performance.

On their second day, Ralph takes them to the docks, where they're awed by the incredible size and number of ships. They enjoy shopping at the import stores along the wharf.

In the middle of the afternoon, Doris says, " Ralph, I'd very much like to see Chicago's biggest slaughterhouse." It's several miles from town, and the smell tells them when they're getting close. The processing facility is massive, but the stockyard is mind-boggling. The women gasp when they see cattle as far as they can see and must shout to hear each other over the high-pitched mooing.

That evening, Amy convinces Doris that a Chinese restaurant is fun. Doris thinks the food is tasty, but can't master chopsticks. Amy tells her Luke had the same problem. Doris says, "So, we have a flaw in common." After dinner, they attend a twelve-act vaudeville show. They see a magician, a juggler, an acrobat, a ventriloquist, and several singers, dancers, and comedians.

They decided to walk back to the hotel. Ralph follows closely on foot, and the rental carriage follows Ralph by fifty feet. The women look around the hotel lobby for things of interest. Doris sees a nearly life-sized poster of Wild Bill Cody, dressed in buckskins, with a Springfield rifle. An adjacent stand holds a four-foot square card saying: William F. Cody, Buffalo Bill, and his troupe will perform Ned Buntline's *Scouts of the Prairie* at the Olympic Theater from August 13th to the 18th. Tickets are available at the registration desk for matinee and evening performances. Doris waves to Amy and points at the big poster. Amy gets there quickly and says, "I read about that show; I think it would be fun."

Doris says, "I do, too."

Amy says, "Let's find out if tickets are still available." The desk clerk tells Amy she has a few unsold seats for the two remaining two o'clock matinees. She tells the clerk, "For us, it's tomorrow or nothing." The clerk says, " I have two adjacent seats in the center of the mezzanine for four dollars."

"I'll take those, and I need one more seat nearby," Amy says.

"Okay, I have one seat five rows behind the first two seats and six seats to the left," the clerk says.

"Is it also two dollars?" Amy asks.

"Yes," she answers.

Amy hands the woman a $10 bill, gets her change, and looks around for Ralph. She can't find him immediately because he's making love to his cigar behind a tall, leafy potted plant in the corner of the room. She tells him about buying tickets for the three of them to see Buffalo Bill Cody perform at the Olympic Theater at 2 p.m. tomorrow. Ralph says, "Thank you, that will be fun, but I could have waited outside."

Amy replies, "Nonsense."

Amy asks Ralph to join them for lunch at an Italian café on day three. They have ravioli and lasagna with Chianti wine, followed by a cannoli pastry filled with strawberry cream cheese for dessert. After lunch, they attended the Scouts of the Prairie showing; Ralph stayed awake during the show.

After the show, Amy tells Ralph, "We enjoy your company, and we'd like you to join us this evening for dinner."

"Thank you, I would like that," Ralph says.

That evening, they dine on Chicken Cordon Bleu at a French restaurant, and, at Amy's insistence, they attend the play *Romeo and Juliet*. On the ride back to the hotel, Amy tells Doris, "I liked all the shows we've seen, but tonight's Shakespearean play was by far the best."

Doris asks, "Did you read the story in school?"

"I did, and many of Shakespeare's other plays. My teacher had a collection of his famous writings, and she let me read them before and after school," Amy answers.

"All this time, I thought you left early and stayed late to be with your girlfriends."

Upon returning to the hotel, Ralph senses they are tired after being on the go since they arrived. He suggests they sleep late, check out at eleven, and let him treat them to brunch in the hotel. Ralph says, "I'd like to give you a tour of the four-mile by one-mile burned-out area of Chicago's famous 1871 fire. That area is still rebuilding."

Ralph has them at the train depot at five-thirty. They thank Ralph for showing them a good time and give him big hugs and pecks on the cheek. Ralph says, "You all have been a delight to be with and very entertaining. Be sure to tell Luke hello. He's the most amazing man I have ever met, but don't tell him I said that."

Doris looks at Ralph and says, "That makes two of us."

They are supposed to leave Chicago at six p.m., but due to a mechanical problem, they do not leave until 10 p.m. After the Oklahoma City stop, the women are alone in the lounge car playing five-card draw poker between nine and ten p.m. on the twentieth. Doris is rehashing and gushing about everything she saw, ate, and experienced for the first time. Then she talked about the things that amused and amazed her and ended by saying, "I'd like to come back when I can stay longer."

Amy says, "I agree it's a fantastic city, but before we return, we should take the Transcontinental Railroad to San Francisco in the Pullman Palace cars. I read they are more luxurious than the fanciest New York Hotels. The depot manager said travelers claim the scenery is spectacular and the weather is always perfect."

Doris says, "Let's start saving our money now."

As Doris finishes speaking, a well-dressed but disheveled middle-aged man staggers into the lounge car. The alcohol and swaying of the train require him to progress to their table by holding on to chairs and tables. Amy quietly says. "Get your derringer in your shooting hand."

The drunk faces the women's table. They are on either side of him, looking up, expressionless. He says, "Ladies," and burps with closed lips and puffed cheeks, "Put all your money under the table." He looks down at his feet and steadies himself by putting his hands, palms down, on the table. He hiccups and exhales with breath that reeks of bourbon.

Because he doesn't have a gun, Amy winks and nods at Doris and says with a fearful voice, "Oh, kind sir; we don't want trouble. We'll do as you ask. Give us a moment to get our money from our handbags." The women whip out their derringers, cock them, and Amy says, "I'll shoot for his heart; you shoot where he pees."

Doris says, "Okay, on the count of three, one... two..."

Waving his arms frantically, the drunk slurs, "Whoa, I'm just messin' with y'all! Kindly point those pea-shooting mouse pistols in a different direction!" He hiccups so hard that his eyes close for a few seconds, and his head bobs twice. He tries to make a better presentation by running his finger through his hair, hitching up his pants, and straightening his tie.

"When you're gone, we'll put our mouse guns away. Our advice is don't come in here trying to be funny," Amy says.

The drunk heads for the sleeper car and tries to open the door by pushing it out. Before realizing the door opens inward, he investigates his dilemma by bending over to look through the keyhole. When he's gone, they laugh loudly, and Amy says, "We surprised him."

Doris says, "Yes, but he won't remember us in the morning."

Amy gets a concerned look and says, "I'm afraid Luke will be disappointed when I tell him Ralph got to see Buffalo Bill in *Scouts of the Prairie.*"

Doris says, "Then I suggest we not mention it."

Amy says, "I have a way of always spilling the beans. So, when I do, I'll say I didn't enjoy it, which would be truthful."

Doris says, "I thought it was corny. I don't believe the Indians fought wearing full ceremonial headdresses while dragging them on the ground. The Indians call white men paleface. Did you see how pale the Indians were? Except for Buffalo Bill, most actors didn't appear fit enough to fight old ladies."

Amy says, "I agree, but the fancy-dressed city slickers were lapping it up. What surprised me was the ratio of women to men attending all the shows we saw. I'd say there were almost twice as many women as men. Luke was surprised that women wrote the four books recommended by the newspaper. It seems that women authors are writing more novels than men."

Doris theorizes, "How can a brilliant and ambitious woman express herself? Women aren't welcome in the businessmen's fraternity."

"But Jordan got in," Amy says.

"Yes, but she married the bank's owner; that's different. Being an author is a respected vocation for women seeking fame and fortune. If they want anonymity, they can use a *nom de plume*. That is French for using a name other than your own."

"I didn't know you paid attention to such things," Amy says.

"I believe in women's right to vote and the removal of the barriers that keep women from working in male-only professions. For example, I'd like to have a woman doctor," Doris says.

"Me too," Amy says.

"I appreciate a man's need to feed and shelter his family. However, after the war, tens of thousands of women who lost their husbands were desperate to feed and shelter their children. If they got a job, it didn't pay enough to live with dignity. To survive, many married an older man or one unfit for war. They were lucky if he didn't rape them and beat their children," Doris says disgustingly. "I felt lucky to marry Charlie, a true gentleman. I can't imagine an all-male Congress will give women the right to vote any time soon." (Author's note: The 19th Amendment to the Constitution, giving women the right to vote, became effective forty-three years later and ten years after Susan B. Anthony's death.)

Amy says, "How many cards do you want?"

Doris says, "Four."

"Are you trying to fill a flush or a straight?"

Doris says, "I'm thinking a full house or four of a kind."

"Good luck with that," Amy says with a big smile.

"This trip is the best time we've ever had together," Doris says.

Amy says, "I agree, but I know there are even better times ahead."

Chapter 36: Luke Meets With The Third
August 12th – 21st

As soon as Amy and Doris leave Amarillo on B&O's Express Train for Chicago at five p.m. on August twelfth, Luke begins making plans for Amy's birthday party and, hopefully, getting a telegram to The Third. He's already decided to travel by horseback to the Kiowa reservation because he can get there by the end of day two, whereas the wagon would take four days.

Luke immediately goes to the Western Union's office and finds out they have an office on the reservation. He asks the telegrapher for directions, and he's given a map. Luke thinks, *I must squeeze in a trip to the reservation and return in time to meet Amy and Doris on the 21st. If The Third can answer my telegram by tomorrow, the 13th, I could leave the next morning, on the 14th. I could arrive at the Western Union office late afternoon on the 15th. I could stay two days with The Third and leave on the morning of the 18th. I would return here on the evening of the 19th and have a day to spare. That plan will work.*

Luke telegrams The Third, saying, "I have been thinking about you and would like to visit for a day or two. I have nothing important to talk about. I need to leave here on the morning of the fourteenth and should arrive by late afternoon on the 15th. I need directions to your teepee from Western Union's office. I hope to buy buffalo moccasin boots and coats for my wife and her mother, and I would enjoy a bird hunt. If you are interested and have the time, respond to Luke Garrelts, Champion Hotel, Amarillo, Texas, by tomorrow, the thirteenth, if possible."

Luke goes to the hotel's dinner late because he wants to talk to the cook about making a cake for Amy's birthday party on the twenty-second. When he's the lone customer, he asks Reba if he can meet the cook. Within a few minutes, a stocky, fortyishlooking fellow wearing a white, finger-smudged cook's apron secured by a frayed and dangling bow perched on his belly follows Reba to Luke's table. He looks down at Luke, frowns, and says, "I'm Rudy; Reba says you want to meet me. If I've come out here so you can complain about my cooking, save your breath! I've heard it all! But since I've come all this way, go ahead, vent your spleen!"

"Whoa, big fella. My name is Luke Garrelts. My wife and I are staying in the hotel and have been steady customers for three weeks; ask Reba."

Reba looks at Rudy and says, "Six meals a day, every day. They're your best customers."

"Thank you, Reba," Luke says. "Rudy, I have a problem I hope you can help me with."

"What's your big problem?" Rudy asks.

Luke answers, "My wife and her Mother left this afternoon for Chicago. They'll be back on the twenty-first, and my wife is expecting a birthday party on the twenty-second, ten days from today. I need to find a baker who can make a cake with frosting and candles and write Happy Birthday Amy. Can you do that?"

"Sure; how big of a cake do you want?" Rudy asks.

"Big enough for three people to have a big slice and still have half leftover."

"White cake or chocolate?"

White," Luke says.

"What's her name?" Rudy asks.

"Amy."

"So, I only put Happy Birthday Amy on it?"

"That's right," Luke says.

"How do I spell it?" Rudy asks.

"H-A-P-P-Y..."

"Stop! I can spell happy birthday," Rudy says with attitude.

"A-M-Y; you need to be more specific," Luke says.

"How many candles?" Rudy asks.

Luke thinks for a moment and answers, "Twenty-one."

"What kind of frosting?" Rudy asks.

"Chocolate would be great!"

"Okay, so where do I deliver it?"

"Right here. I'm going to make a dinner reservation for seven o'clock. Reba, could you bring the cake out after dinner?"

"Sure, I'll be happy to," she says.

Rudy says, "My cake price is two dollars and fifty cents, but that's for a buck-naked cake. After I add the chocolate frosting, the writing, the candles, and your spelling insult, your price is three bucks, and I require payment in advance."

Luke smiles and says, "Reba, please add four dollars to my bill for the cake." Then he turns to Rudy and says, "If that cake doesn't show up, I'll come looking for you." Luke says with a wink and a smile, leaning forward and acting like he's going for his Colt.

Rudy says, "Hold on, I understand how important it is to you. Reba, write everything this Luke Garrelts fellow and I agreed to about his wife's birthday cake on your pad."

Luke says, "If you have a minute, I want to compliment you on your steaks. You serve THE BEST STEAKS I've ever had. I'm curious how you do it. If there's a secret, I'd like to know it."

Rudy's facial expression changes from a permanent partial frown into a bit of a smile, and he says, "A customer ordering a two-dollar steak expects me to give it special attention. There's not one thing I do that makes it so memorable. It's a process, and I refuse to take shortcuts even when covered up with orders. If it's not perfect, it's chopped up for stew meat.

"My butcher knows I want one-pound ribeye and sirloin steaks that are an inch and a half thick with narrow veins of fat throughout. I can cut them in half for those ordering a half-pounder. I can't make a one-inch-thick steak juicy enough.

"I handle so many steaks that my fingers know the age of the meat, and I grade it on a scale of one to three. The amount of tenderizing depends on the grade number; a three gets the most.

"I brush it with salt and tenderize it by puncturing both sides with a lightweight hammer I had the blacksmith make with six tines that are a half inch long. The meat is close to half-chewed before it hits the grill. I am careful not to over-tenderize. Chewing is necessary to free the juices that saturate the taste buds.

"I want the grill hot enough to leave burn marks and sear the meat. Searing locks in the juices. I can tell if the temperature is right by holding my hand a few inches over the grill. The heat of the fire changes with the hardness of the oak and hickory I use. I have a hand crank to raise and lower the grill over the fire, allowing me to have the desired temperature. I can also control fire and smoke with wood chips, which I keep in a bucket of water.

"Unless the customer orders it well done, I want the middle to be slightly pink. Because there are so many variables, knowing when to flip the steak is a skill that takes a while to learn. After the flip, I brush on a family recipe of bacon fat, butter, salt, pepper, and several of my secret ingredients. My customers say my steaks produce great burps."

"Oh, I do enjoy the burps," Luke says.

"That is not all, Rudy says. I insist my steaks are served hot. To help ensure that, I heat the plate over the grill. Cowboys with only a few teeth and taste buds all shot to hell from chewing tobacco all day; come in for my steaks."

"You've turned cooking a steak into an art form," Luke says.

Reba believes Rudy has finished and reads the birthday cake specifications from her order pad, and Luke says, "That's correct."

Rudy says, "I appreciate your interest and compliments. Reba will tell me when the next steak order is yours, and I'll be sure you get a thick, tender cut."

"Rudy, I may leave for the Kiowa Reservation on Wednesday morning. If I do, I will not see you again until the nineteenth or twentieth."

"I'm glad you're paying for the cake in advance," Rudy says.

"I'll be fine; I have friends in high places there."

"Like how high?" Rudy asks.

"High as Lone Wolf," Luke replies.

"Oh, that is quite high. But beware of hot-blooded renegades. Better not let them see your thick head of hair, or it'll hang on a war lance in front of some young buck's teepee."

Luke says, "I appreciate your concern. But I spent years herding cattle from South Texas to Kansas through Indian territory and managed to keep my hair, so I'm not worried. I'll think about one of your steaks on my two-day ride back."

"Good; I look forward to Reba telling me you're in the dining room. Have a safe trip," Rudy says and returns to the kitchen.

The next day, Luke takes the horses for a fifty-mile workout. When he returns, there is a telegram from The Third saying, "I'm looking forward to your visit. I will take you on a bird hunt that you will not forget. After you find the Western Union, anyone can tell you where I live." Luke spends the rest of the day preparing for the trip and goes to bed early.

Luke leaves Frank Weiner's livery early on the morning of the fourteenth. Fury has the packsaddle with the camping gear and provisions. Other than being hot, the day is unexciting, but during the night, a starving bobcat kitten sneaks into camp. It's just a few weeks old, sniffing at everything, hoping to find something to eat. It stumbles through the cookware, and the rattling awakens Smokey and Luke.

Luke hand-feeds the kitten tiny pieces of jerky and pours canteen water into his frying pan. When the kitten is full, it sits and stares at Luke. Luke slowly reaches out to pet the little fur ball with the swollen belly. When Luke gets on his bedroll, the cat curls up beside him. Luke rolls the cat over on its back and says, "Well, young man, you've had a tough life. If your momma comes looking for you tonight, please tell her how good I've been to you."

In the morning, the kitten is pawing at the packsaddle. Luke opens it, feeds him one of Rudy's buttermilk biscuits broken into small pieces, and pours water into the skillet again. Luke breaks camp and sets out for the Western Union's office. The kitten follows the best he can by clumsily jumping over and through grass twice as tall as he is. The little guy cannot keep up, and Luke worries he'll be lunch for an eagle or hawk, so he turns back and puts him in one of the packsaddle pouches. The cat rides there for the rest of the day, and Luke gives him a small snack and water every time he stops to rest the horses.

Luke has been following the telegrapher's map, and at about six o'clock, he sees an Indian village. He asks a boy practicing with a bow and arrow where he can find Western Union's office and the teepee of The Third Grandson of Lone Wolf. In good English, he tells Luke the general area of the telegraph office and says, "That teepee is easy to find; it's twice the size of the others."

The Western Union office and the Bureau of Indian Affairs are in the same building. It's dilapidated and surrounded by a few other shacks that appear vacant. Luke sends a telegram to Amy at the Palace Hotel in Chicago. It says, "Dearest, I hope you are safe and having fun. I'm on the Kiowa reservation. If you need me, send a telegram to this office. I'll leave directions to where I'm staying. I plan to leave here on the morning of the eighteenth. I miss and love you, Luke."

The Third's teepee is remarkably easy to find, and Luke shouts, "Is anyone home?"

The Third ducks down to exit the teepee; he looks at Luke, still in the saddle, and says, "It is good to see you again. It pleased me you wanted to visit."

Luke says, "I'm glad that you're glad," and dismounts, shakes The Third's hand, and gets the cat out of the packsaddle. Holding him up at eye level, Luke says, "This little fellow wandered into my camp last night. His mother must have died because she could have easily followed his trail. Do you have children?"

"I have two boys."

"Do you think they would want him?" Luke asks.

The Third calls for his boys, and they come running in seconds. They're excited to get the kitten, and they name him Luke. The Third suggests they go inside. Luke meets The Third's wife, whose Kiowa name translates to Morning Flower. After getting comfortable reclining on a large buffalo hide bag filled with goose down, Luke asks about Lone Wolf. Luke is pleased to hear he is in good health, but saddened that Lone Wolf is frustrated by Washington's refusal to meet to discuss tribal issues. Luke hears the tribe is not producing enough food, and the military has cut the provisions promised in the treaty as punishment for infractions. Luke says, "It saddens me to learn that your people are hungry and suffering."

The Third says, "Grandfather will want to talk with you. He is constantly searching for answers to our problems."

Luke said, "I was hoping I'd see him."

"Good, I will tell him you are here. How long can you stay?" The Third asks.

"Two more days, if you're okay with that," Luke says.

"More would be better," The Third says.

"I must get back to Amarillo for my wife's birthday."

"Were you married when we first met?" The Third asks.

"Nope," Luke answers.

"That's what I assumed."

Luke says, "I gave up the single life in Kansas City on the sixteenth of last month. I'm no longer selling kitchenware, but I still have the wagon. I had a wheat farm south of Amarillo that I sold about three weeks ago. About two weeks ago, my wife and I bid on a small ranch less than three miles from Addison, Texas. I hope to make it a cattle ranch."

"You do not let the grass grow under your feet," The Third says. He pauses pensively and asks Luke, "Would you consider keeping a small herd of buffalo for the tribe? A buffalo feast at our annual Sun Dance would create excitement and improve the tribe's morale. The elders would regain their enthusiasm for passing hundreds of years of ceremonial rituals, songs, and dances to our children."

"I can do that, but I would like some assurance that the tribe will not get into trouble with the authorities," Luke says.

"That is a risk the elders would be willing to take. We could invite other tribes to participate. The military tends to stay at a safe distance when our numbers are large. They don't have enough men to deal with an angry crowd," The Third confidently says.

"I'd be happy to pasture buffalo for you, but you'll have to find them first, Luke says. Let's start with at least six females and a young, eager bull."

"I will see what I can do, The Third says. "The skinners should be willing to help us find a few calves since we pay the most for their buffalo hides."

"How was the powwow?" Luke asks. The Third tells Luke that the cavalry kept Sitting Bull's powwow from happening. But their trip wasn't all for naught because the women were excited to get the kitchen items. Luke tells the stories of how he loaned three of the four buffalo blankets to three young girls and gave the boots to the Governor of Kansas.

The Third asks, "You've been married only a month, and your wife let you leave for a week to visit me?"

Luke says, "My wife and her mother decided to see Chicago. I didn't want to go. I've been living in a hotel for nearly a month and needed a change of scenery. I thought seeing you and keeping you from being productive for a few days would be fun." Then Luke asks if they have boots and coats like the ones he got in their trade.

The Third says, "Morning Flower says filling your order is not a problem. When I got your telegram, I asked her to check our inventory."

Luke gives The Third the cutouts of their feet, which appear identical, and says, "I'd like for the boots and the coats to be as nearly the same as possible; I think you know why. Coats that fit Morning Flower would be perfect."

The Third says, "Sadly, our only revenue is from selling the things our women make. Our problem is getting buffalo hides. We pay skinners a better price than they get from buyers at the train depots. They'll come here first if the reservation is not too far out of their way. To get a pass to leave the reservation for anything other than a medical emergency is impossible. So, we lie about medical emergencies and use the opportunity to find skinners."

After dinner, Lone Wolf shows up with his peace pipe and a beaded buffalo scrotum holding peyote. Lone Wolf talks to Luke in the Kiowa language, and The Third translates. Lone Wolf expresses his frustration over the U.S. refusing to meet to address his grievances. Luke learns that Lone Wolf has picked The Third to succeed him. Unaccustomed to anyone telling him "No," Lone Wolf tells The Third that he will take Luke on a walking tour of the reservation after breakfast. The Third relays Lone Wolf's invitation to Luke, and Luke looks at Lone Wolf and nods to show his acceptance.

The tour covers several miles and takes over three hours. Luke gets disapproving looks from every face. He believes it's because he looks like someone the U.S. Government sent to make their living conditions worse. Before long, Luke becomes uncomfortable making eye contact. Lone Wolf tells Luke that his people have been stripped of their culture and forbidden to pass on their customs to the next generation. At one time, the buffalo provided all their needs. They no longer have buffalo grazing on the reservation.

Luke is concerned that the children are not in school on a Thursday. Newspapers claim that Indians consume alcohol in excess, and frequent empty bottles suggest that this may be true. Luke thinks, *Men of Lone Wolf's generation exemplified Charles Darwin's theory of the Survival of the Fittest. They now sit without expression, seemingly lost, dressed in white men's clothing, and lacking the motivation to honor the presence of their leaders. The Third and his grandfather must be embarrassed for me to see these downtrodden, aimless men who, before reservation life, were proud providers and protectors of the tribe.*

While on tour, Luke reminisces about his Father's attitudes, opinions, and teachings regarding the Federal Government and the Indians. *Myron said there were two facts that few people were aware of. Indians were not proficient enough in English to understand the legal language in the treaties, and politicians and newspapers conspired to make the public believe Indians were unprovoked savages.*

Dad was incensed by newspaper articles portraying Indians as ruthless. The truth was that both sides were, but military atrocities like the Massacre at Sand Creek didn't make headlines.[27] After Sand Creek, in retaliation, the Cheyenne and

Arapaho Indians raided squatter families. They killed the adults and took their children: the girls for breeding stock and laborers, and the boys for hunting and fighting. However, the newspapers remained silent about the cavalry massacring Indian settlements and shooting women and children fleeing for their lives. The news media never revealed the broken treaties or the policies and punishments used to control the Indians, nor the effect they had. The absence of honesty in reporting stoked intense Indian anger.

Newspapers created fear by describing Indians as primitive, ignorant, and bloodthirsty pagans who lived in groups called tribes. There were numerous tribes, each with its unique language and culture. Communication between the tribes combined some language with hand gestures. Except for a few, tribes didn't have a written language; they passed on their tribal history through storytelling. Their homes, called teepees, were conical-shaped structures made using buffalo hides and long, straight poles. Their wealth was based on the number of ponies they owned. They fought with other tribes so frequently that battle casualties caused the number of women to outnumber the men significantly. Men who could support more wives had them, and some had many.

Warriors and boys trained daily with weapons in hand-to-hand combat; older men dealt with outsiders and supplied the tribe with various game, including elk, deer, rabbit, pheasant, quail, turkey, duck, goose, and fish. The women and girls were responsible for all the other tasks.

They had unusual first names, such as Soaring Eagle and Morning Star, but no surnames. They worshipped spirits believed to have control over a specific aspect of nature. They danced around a bonfire at night, chanting incantations to their spirits. Before living on the reservation, they migrated with the buffalo that sought greener pastures. Their horses dragged everything they owned on a travois, built using the poles and buffalo hides from their teepees.

In summer, the men wore only a loincloth and moccasins. Their straight, coal-black hair flowed down their back, often adorned with an eagle feather. They painted their faces, bodies, and horses when preparing for battle and rode bareback. They fought with crude weapons like bows, arrows, tomahawks, spears, and knives.

Their weapons used flint rock for the cutting edge. They would strike a piece of flint with repeated glancing blows by a harder stone to form the desired shape with a nearly razor-sharp edge. Although appearing crude, compared to weapons made of steel, they were lethal in the hands of a skilled warrior trained in their use from childhood.

Indian culture was so drastically foreign to northeasterners that they could not relate to people for whom time had stood still. Newspaper articles about the Indians caused Whites to be indifferent to their mistreatment and suffering.

Dad lectured me about the Relocation Act of 1830. It gave President Andrew Jackson and his successors the authority to acquire tribal lands in the east in exchange for poor-quality land west of the Mississippi. He was suspicious that the government purposely crafted one-sided treaties to the detriment of the Indians.

Tribes were forced to leave their homes with only what they could carry, walking great distances in harsh conditions. The most infamous Indian relocation spanned twenty years and involved 60,000 members of the "Five Civilized Tribes." It became known as the "Trail of Tears." The Cherokee named it that due to their immense suffering and loss of life."[28]

The Kiowa were nomadic and roamed South Dakota until being forced to relocate to southwest Oklahoma only ten years earlier, in 1867. Four years later, in 1871, the U.S. Congress passed legislation forbidding treaty-making with Indians. This act took away any leverage the Indians had to improve their living conditions. Eventually, the Federal Government broke every Indian treaty it had made since the Revolutionary War.

The government stripped away part of the land provided by the Relocation Act to make space for the massive immigration of European farmers. The Indians believed they could discourage settlers and railroads by attacking them. A frustrated Federal Government hatched the evil plan to eradicate the Indians by killing the buffalo. Though never written into law, it was the policy. General William Tecumseh Sherman, famous for his march across Atlanta during the Civil War, led a successful campaign to eradicate the Indians by starvation. [29]

While Sherman killed the buffalo, General Sheridan, also of Civil War fame, attacked the people directly. His standing orders to Custer were to kill all the warriors, capture all the women and children, destroy all camps and material goods, and kill all the ponies.[30]

Before the tour, Luke only had feelings of resentment toward his government. After Lone Wolf's walking tour, the memories of his stepfather's teachings, and what he knew to be true, those glowing coals became a raging fire.

Luke tells The Third, "Please explain to your grandfather that Davey Crockett, the Kentucky Congressman who famously died defending the Alamo, believed the Relocation Act violated the 5th Amendment to the Constitution by taking property without fair compensation. Mr. Crockett said the Relocation Act conflicted with prior treaties approved by the United States that guaranteed the Indians' possession of the land in perpetuity.[31] So, legally, Indians could not be forced to agree to treaties requiring them to relocate to inferior land. Also, tell him my stepfather, a well-read, fair, and honest man, was severely critical of the government for taking back portions of the land promised in Relocation Treaties. He believed the Indians reacted as anyone would. Many believe the government has treated Indians unfairly and illegally; I am one of those."

On the second night, after the peace pipe had made several rounds, Lone Wolf and The Third spoke for a while. When they finished, The Third looked at Luke and said, "I told my grandfather about our conversation and that you know President Hayes. He would like you to consider speaking to him on behalf of the Kiowa. Grandfather is impressed with your knowledge and speaking skills. He likes that you now have first-hand knowledge of the severe punishment the tribe must endure for violating the military's unreasonable assimilation policies. He also believes you understand that the military intends to eliminate the Kiowa by any means necessary. He believes you have a good heart, speak honestly, and are respectful and respected."

Luke says, "Washington has done much to be ashamed of. I'm suspicious the military has not made President Hayes aware of their actions and your circumstances. The man I met seemed fair and thoughtful. After taking office, he met with all thirty-eight governors in their state capitals to learn about their problems and solutions. I believe the president cares about all people. I must carefully consider your grandfather's request. I need a little time to make my decision."

The following day, The Third takes Luke on a bird hunt. They bring back enough pheasant, turkey, and grouse for The Third to drop off over half of the birds at a tribal food dispensary. It's Luke's last night on the reservation, and The Third tells Luke they will dine in Lone Wolf's teepee.

Lone Wolf's teepee is not taller but has a much larger diameter than The Thirds. It is so much larger that it requires vertical interior poles supporting each roof pole at its midpoint. Lone Wolf's teepee can accommodate a large group meeting of the tribe's elders. The surprise is that the wives of The Third, Lone Wolf, and several tribal leaders spent the afternoon preparing birds from their morning hunt. The dinner party is obviously in Luke's honor because Lone Wolf has invited four sub-chiefs. Luke is sure The Third has told Lone Wolf that he will accept Lone Wolf's request.

After dinner, to get his attention, Luke looks at Lone Wolf, extends his hands wide open, and says, "I told your grandson I would write to President Hayes and those responsible for Indian Affairs. I will do my best to communicate the need to find solutions to the tribe's living conditions. If I can get a meeting, you and several of these men will have to travel with me by train to Washington. I must have your agreement that you will do that. Though hopeful, I do not know if my words will be powerful enough to accomplish the changes you desire." When Luke finishes, Lone Wolf nods his head in approval, which proves he does understand English. He then extends his open right hand, which Luke grips and shakes firmly, solidifying their agreement.

Lone Wolf motions to his wife. She leaves and returns with two women, similar in size to Amy and Doris; one of the women is Morning Flower. They are wearing buffalo coats and carrying moccasin boots. With both hands, Lone Wolf motions from the girls to Luke. The Third says, "My grandfather gives you these gifts in friendship."

Blurred by tears of emotion, Luke looks at Lone Wolf and gestures his appreciation. Luke taps his chest over his heart with his right hand in a fist. Then he extends his open hand with his palm facing Lone Wolf while nodding in approval. Lone Wolf nods, showing that he understands Luke's gratitude, and returns the gesture. The Third is pleased that his grandfather and Luke have developed a strong friendship.

Ten young girls entertain the assemblage by singing and using sign language to tell the history of the Kiowa. The Third tells Luke the song is hundreds of years old. Luke thanks Lone Wolf for the excellent evening and his home-brewed cactus drink. Lone Wolf grins, and The Third does not translate for him. Luke shakes Lone Wolf's hand and the sub-chiefs, bowing his head slightly each time to show respect. Luke thanked the ladies for the delicious feast and asked The Third to help him with the gifts.

On the way to The Third's teepee, Luke says, "So that you will know that I am a man of my word, I will send you a copy of each letter I send to Washington. I know you will read them to your grandfather. You must remind him to be patient; the U.S. Government moves at the pace of a hibernating bear."

While Luke is packing on the morning of the 18th, The Third tells him he will ride with him to the edge of the reservation. From there, two braves will escort him to Amarillo. Luke says, "I consider you a friend, and I have a personal question I would like to ask. If it's none of my business, please say so."

The Third asks, "What is it?"

"I have never heard you mention your parents," Luke says.

The Third says, "My mother died of smallpox when I was three. My grandmother told me that European immigrants brought cholera and smallpox to America. Those diseases killed thousands of Indians, half of the people in some tribes. My grandparents raised me because my father was a warrior in our tribe and led many raiding parties. He died in a raid by the 4th Cavalry at Palo Duro Canyon in '74."[32]

Luke says, "That raid was famous because the military killed and captured fourteen hundred Indian ponies."

"That's right," The Third says. Then he asks, "What was your childhood like?"

Luke pauses briefly and replies, "I have no memory of my birth mother and father. I suspect my childhood, up to age fifteen, was better because my aunt, on my mother's side, and her husband raised me. They were well-established wheat farmers, but they weren't wealthy. I was their only child, and they insisted I follow Christian rules of behavior. I knew they wanted the best for me, and I did my best to make them proud. When I was fifteen, they died in a runaway buckboard that flipped over on them. I have always loved horses and hunting. So, whenever I had free time from wheat farming and my chores, I hunted or worked at a livery in Amarillo."

On the ride to the reservation's Western boundary, they compare childhood experiences and find a good deal of similarity in what they did to entertain themselves growing up. Before parting, Luke says, "I'll write to President Hayes next week. Your wife gave me your address, and she has mine. Please do not hesitate to write if you have an idea about how my Washington letters can be more powerful, or describe a new tribal abuse, or if I've left out a significant detail that is unknown to me."

The Third says, "That is a good plan, my friend," and uses the sign Luke created to express his emotion about their parting.

Before riding on, Luke repeats the sign, and his voice cracks in mid-sentence when he says, "Until we meet again, my friend."

Luke arrives in Amarillo on the evening of the nineteenth. As soon as the city comes into view, his escort disappears without a word. Luke stops at the depot to inquire about the train from Chicago. He's told it would arrive four hours late, at about noon.

The next morning, August twentieth, one day before Amy's birthday and two days before her party, Luke enters the hotel dining room and asks Reba if Rudy might have a minute to talk.

Reba sees the coats and boots, knows they're important, and goes to get Rudy. When Rudy arrives, Luke asks, "Have you baked the cake?"

Rudy says, "No! I'll do that on the morning of her party! Is that what you wanted to talk about?"

"No, I have another favor to ask, Luke says. These boots and coats are presents for my wife and mother-in-law at the birthday party. I would like to surprise them and hope Reba and another waitress could bring out the cake with these presents. Could you make that happen?"

Rudy says, "When Reba comes out of the back carrying the cake, she can wear Amy's coat. Hildred can take a break from helping me and follow Reba, wearing your mother-in-law's coat and carrying the moccasins. After Reba sets down the cake, they will give them the presents."

Luke is pleased that Rudy is eager to help and says, "That'll be perfect, thank you."

Rudy says, "How much did you have to pay for these?"

"Nothing; Lone Wolf gave them to me, but that doesn't mean they're free. They're a prepayment for getting him an audience with President Hayes."

"You do have friends in high places!" Rudy says.

"I only know these men through mutual friends, and I don't hold sway with either of them," Luke insists.

Reba asks, "Describe the coat I will give to Amy?"

Luke says, "They're identical; it makes no difference."

"Good, that makes it easy," Reba says.

Luke says, "Okay then, I'll pick up Amy and Doris at the depot at noon tomorrow. So, beginning at lunch, we'll be back in the dining room, morning, noon, and night. This birthday party is going to be one Amy will remember.

Rudy asks, "I'm curious about something. Do you like your eggs the way I cook 'em?"

"I like a soft yoke. Once the white is cooked, tip the skillet and spoon a little hot grease over the yoke," Luke says.

"If you want 'em basted, you should have said so!" Rudy says.

Luke says, "Okay, baste them from now on. "

"So, after three weeks, I'm finally going to cook your eggs how you like 'em!" Rudy says and leaves, talking to himself.

Luke looks at Reba and says, "Rudy is a crusty old bugger."

Reba says, "Are you kidding? I think Rudy respects and likes you because he never cursed at you. Secretly, he wants to please you."

"I suppose that's true, though I think he came close to cussing the time I started spelling Happy Birthday Amy," Luke says. They laugh so hard that Reba holds on to Luke's chair for stability.

Luke orders his regular breakfast and returns to his hotel room after having two basted eggs, fried potatoes, biscuits, and coffee. He decides to catch up on some badly needed sleep.

The following day is Amy's birthday. After breakfast, Luke bathes, puts on his best, and reads *Wuthering Heights* in the dining room until eleven-thirty. He takes the hotel's courtesy carriage to the depot and asks the driver to wait. Luke walks through the depot to the tracks, looks north, and thinks he can see a speck of black smoke on the horizon. Before long, the train's shrill whistle fills the air. It comes to a slow stop with a bell clanging and steam hissing. Luke hurries onboard to find Amy. She's looking out the window for Luke, but a passing cloud of steam makes it impossible. She turns around when Luke says, "Happy birthday, beautiful." They share a kiss and a long hug that lifts Amy off the floor.

Amy asks about her birthday party, and Luke says, "I've planned a quiet dinner at the hotel for tomorrow night."

"Good. Were you able to get the moccasin boots for us?"

"Yes."

"Where are they?" Amy asks.

"You'll have to wait until tomorrow night," Luke answers.

"Oh, okay."

Luke says, "Hi, Mom; how was the trip?"

Doris says, "The most fun I've ever had!"

"Really, that good?" Luke asks.

"Absolutely!" Doris answers. "And Ralph was great. Thank you for hiring him."

Luke says, "I'm glad to hear that. I asked the hotel's carriage driver to wait, but I'd rather not keep him waiting too long."

Over a mid-afternoon lunch, Luke tells Amy he decided to take her shopping instead of buying a birthday gift she might not like. Amy says, "Good idea; there are clothes at Leroy's Western Wear that I've had my eye on, and I want a revolver I saw at the Colt store."

"Why a revolver?" Luke asks.

"My derringer is cute, but a dang drunk insulted me by calling it a pea shooter and a mouse gun! And it's only a single shot; I want a double-action, six-shot revolver on the ranch. I'll need to protect myself from things that crawl and walk, whether on four legs or two. I know exactly what I want. It's called a Shopkeepers Special. It's small, so it fits my little hand. It's the only one at the Colt store. The owner said he could order me one if he sold it."

Luke says, "If he hasn't sold it, filling your birthday order could be a piece of cake."

"Let's go as soon as the stores open in the morning," Amy says.

"Okay, Luke says.

Amy asks, "Mom, would you want to come with us?"

Doris says, "I need the rest of this afternoon and all of tomorrow to rest up for your party. I want to be at my best."

Amy agrees, saying, "I know what you mean, Mom. Our trip tired me out, too. I plan to spend the rest of the day recovering." She turns toward Luke so Doris can't see her, sends him a coded look, and Luke gives her a knowing smile.

Amy says, "Sweetheart, before I let the cat out of the bag, I want you to know we saw Bill Cody's *Scouts of the Prairie* production and took Ralph with us. I kept his program as a souvenir of the evening." Showing it to Luke, she says, "See how handsome Mr. Cody is, and look at the gorgeous outfits the Indians are wearing. I don't want you to regret not being there to see it. You should know the truth: Bill's show was NOT authentic. Their dialogue was corny, sometimes laughable, and they often stepped on each other's lines. While Mom and I were quietly chuckling, everyone else was clapping and hanging on every word."

Luke says, "Yeah, the theater critics say it wasn't worth the money, but Wild Bill packs the house every night. The folks in Chicago and the Northeast don't know it's not factual. I've seen a few Military scouts in my day, and none wore tailored buckskins without tobacco spittle all over the front, and were either clean-shaven or had neatly trimmed beards. This picture of overweight, potbellied Indians so pale they could pass for a white man and wearing headdresses that drag on the ground is not an accurate picture of a real Indian warrior."

Doris looks at Amy and says, "Now he's thrilled he didn't go with us. If Luke had attended three two-hour shows of orchestra music, comedy, and talent acts, as well as *Romeo and Juliet*, he might have changed his mind about the mind-numbing effect of whiskey. I'm going to my room; I'll catch up with y'all tomorrow evening."

"Sweet dreams, Mom, Amy says. When Doris leaves, Amy says, "Sweetheart, Mom and I had the time of our lives. Ralph was the perfect escort for us; what a nice man. Mom likes him a lot, I think. I'm ready for bed."

"Me too," Luke says. Then he wonders, *Hmm, Ralph and Doris. Am I possibly a matchmaker?*

Chapter 37: Shopping For Birthday Gifts
August 22nd

Amy returns to their room after a 7 a.m. bath reservation. She flops on top of Luke and says, "It's time to get up and take me shopping!" After dressing, she crosses the hallway to Doris' room and knocks softly.

Doris says, "Who is it?"

"Your daughter, do you want to reconsider going birthday shopping?"

Doris says, "I'm afraid not; you all go have a good time. I'll see you in the dining room at seven. Buy something you like that I can afford, and I'll pay you back."

"Hey, coming here was enough of a gift," Amy says. She returns to her room, gets the "Do Not Disturb" sign, and hangs it on Doris's doorknob. She buys a newspaper at the front desk and enters the dining room.

Reba says, "You're up early."

"Luke is taking me birthday shopping this morning, and I couldn't sleep. He'll be here in a few minutes."

"Congratulations! Would you like a cup of coffee?" Reba asks.

"Yes, thank you," Amy answers.

When Reba returns, she says, "Tell me all about Chicago."

"Okay, but that will require a lot of time. It's huge and modern, with lots to do and see. Luke says we're having my birthday dinner here tonight."

"Yes, Rudy and I are looking forward to your party. He plans to give you all a complimentary bottle of wine," Reba says, and excuses herself to wait on another customer.

When Reba isn't waiting on customers, she stops at Amy's table to hear more about her experiences in Chicago.

Before Amy can finish the newspaper headlines, Luke shows up. They have a light breakfast and discuss his trip to the Kiowa reservation. Amy loves his stories about the baby bobcat and the bird hunt dinner. She is concerned that writing monthly letters on behalf of the Kiowa will waste Luke's time, but she keeps that opinion to herself.

On their way to the Colt store, Amy says, "I will need at least a hundred rounds for target practice out behind the hotel by the burn pit; a hundred and fifty would be better." Luke suggests they buy another hundred for inventory at the ranch. At the Colt store, the owner, Don Johnson, greets Amy at the front door. She introduces Luke to Don, a war veteran with a stump and a crutch. Luke thinks, *Mr. Johnson must have a closet full of brand-new boots for his right foot.* Luke tells Don that Amy wants a Colt Storekeeper Special with a belt and holster for a right-hand draw.

Don says, "I know the one she wants. She's had her eye on it for a while. It has a nickel finish and a pearl handle and comes with a beautifully hand-tooled holster and matching belt."

After trying to fit her, Don tells Luke, "Because of her little waist, I'll have a bootmaker trim the belt and add a few more holes. It just so happens that he is involved in making a holster for a customer of mine, so let's give him three days."

Luke says, "That works. I'll pay you today, and she can pick it up on Friday, right?

"Yes, Friday for sure," Don confirms.

"Perfect; add five boxes of thirty-eighths to my bill. Does she need to bring the receipt?" Luke asks.

"I prefer to do business that way. Sometimes, people change their minds after they leave, or one of us has a bad memory. A receipt takes care of that," Don says.

Luke pays and finds Amy shopping for a small-caliber rifle. He gives her Don's receipt and tells her to present it on Friday to get her purchases.

She says, "Luke, eventually, I'll need a rifle."

Agreeing, Luke says, "Okay, in time, but learn to use your six-shooter first."

"That's not going to take long. I'm a decent shot; I need a little practice," Amy says.

When they leave the Colt store, Amy skips with small steps beside Luke. He looks down the street and says, "Is that Leroy's over yonder?"

"It is!" Amy says excitedly.

"Funny, I never noticed it before," Luke says with a puzzled look.

"I hope Leroy still has the clothes I saw when Doris and I shopped for my kitchen the day before we left for Chicago."

"You worry me that you will be devastated if we don't get Jordan's ranch," Luke insists.

"I won't be because you will offer the buyer a quick profit for selling it to us. But if he doesn't, we'll find another place. So long as I'm with you, nothing can discourage me. Can you please walk a little faster? I can't wait to show you the clothes I want."

When they get to Leroy's store, Amy introduces Luke to Leroy, a balding man with a big smile and a well-trimmed, full-face, white beard. Leroy tells Luke, "It's nice to meet you; I've been curious about the lucky man who married this interesting girl." While Luke responds to Leroy's compliment, Amy scurries about the store to find the clothes she wants. She returns to Luke and Leroy with a deerskin jacket with fringe on the sleeves and around the bottom, brown dress boots with short cowboy heels, and three long-sleeved, embroidered blouses.

Luke tells Leroy to put them on his bill, and Amy says, "I'm going to need work trousers, like the kind you wear, made by Mr. Strauss. I want the blue ones that stop at your waist and have those little copper rivets. They don't make them for girls. But Sidney said he could tailor them to fit me for twenty-five cents."

Luke rolls his eyes and says, "Okay."

Amy asks, "Where is Sidney?"

Leroy answers, "He's in the back tailoring a suit."

Amy finds the smallest pair of pants and goes to the dressing room. She returns, walking on the pants' legs and holding them tightly around her waist with both hands. Sidney comes from the back of the store, neatly dressed but slightly bent over. He looks at Amy and says, "You're back."

"I am, Amy says. "Remember telling me you could tailor these to fit me?'

Sidney says, "Of course," and shows Amy where to hold the pants. Then, he goes about gathering the excess fabric and pinning it.

Sidney steps back to see if he likes what he sees, and Amy says, "I'm not going to wear suspenders, so I want the buttons cut off. You'll have to sew on some loops for me to run a belt through."

Sidney says, "Okay, show me where you want the belt loops."

"Using the fabric that you cut off. Cut six pieces an inch wide and two inches long. Attach them equally spaced around the waist." Amy shows Sidney where to place them.

When she leaves the dressing room, she finds a belt the size of her Colt belt, hands it and the trousers to Sidney, and says, "The loops must be wide enough for this belt to go through with a little room to spare. Other than that, use your best judgment."

Sidney says, "I'm afraid I must charge you fifty cents for alterations."

Amy asks Leroy, "How much do the waist-high trousers cost?"

Leroy says, "With Sidney's fee, they'll be three dollars."

She says, "Okay, I'll take three of them and the belt."

Amy continues shopping by meandering around the shop. Luke looks at Sidney and asks, "When can they be ready?"

"Three days," Sidney says.

Luke says, "Perfect. I need to apologize to you and Leroy. When my wife shops, she gets excited and doesn't realize she can be a little pushy. She's a little more so today because we're shopping for birthday presents, and her party is tonight. It appears she's had her heart set on these clothes for a while."

Leroy overhears Luke's admission and says, "She's been in my shop several times. I don't forget cute girls like her; she's a lot of fun to watch. You're right; she is more energetic today. However, young women these days are less reserved than women of my generation. I see it every day and find it amusing and rather charming.

Sidney says, "I've read articles by women who think they should vote in our elections. The next thing you know, they'll want to hold office. Imagine what our life would be like if that ever happened."

"You men probably think I'm an easy touch," Luke says. "And you'd be right."

"I think of you as a very fortunate man," Leroy says.

When Amy returns, she's wearing a light tan gaucho hat and a matching cloth jacket and asks, "What do you think?"

"It goes with your hair. It's you," Luke says.

Amy says, "Bad news, Sidney, this jacket fits perfectly." The men, including Sidney, have a good laugh while smiling.

Amy turns to Leroy and says, "I will wear the hat and jacket back to the hotel. You should write to Mr. Strauss and suggest he make women's trousers."

Luke interrupts, "Before writing that letter, Leroy, can you write up our ticket? We need to be going."

Leroy says, "I'm ahead of you. All in, it's thirty-eight dollars."

Luke opens his wallet, gives Leroy four ten-dollar bills, and says, "We're even." Then he tells Amy, "This man with the pins stuck in his coat sleeve says he can have your trousers ready by Friday."

"Perfect, the same day I get my revolver!" she says.

Luke says, "Amy, you're starting to talk like me. If you'll hand me her packages, Leroy, we'll be on our way."

Amy says, "Thank you, Leroy. Sidney, I'll see you Friday."

As the Garrelts walk out the door, Sidney turns to Leroy and says, "That man has his hands full."

Leroy says, "Yes, he does, and it's obvious he enjoys it."

The birthday dinner, cake, and gift presentation are perfect. Amy and Doris are beyond pleased with their gifts and celebrate by drinking too much wine. Doris asks Luke, "Why were there twenty-one candles on Amy's cake?"

Luke says, "I didn't want Rudy and Reba to think I was robbing the cradle."

Amy says, "Mom, with all respect, this has been my favorite birthday."

"Well, your father and I never had the money to do all this," Doris says.

Luke says, "I must come clean. I didn't pay for the moccasins and coats. They're gifts from Lone Wolf. He smoked too much peyote and lost his better judgment."

Doris looks at Amy and says, "If we asked, I bet Luke could pull a rabbit out of his hat!"

Slurring her words, Amy says, "Oh, yeah, whenever I ask for a bunny rabbit, he runs to his hat."

Luke says, "You all have had too much wine and will be miserable in the morning. You need to be sleeping it off."

Doris hiccups and extends her right arm to maintain her balance and keep from falling backward. Through squinted eyes with raised eyebrows, she says, "You just made a couple of good points, my boy. I like your plan."

Luke turns to Reba and says, "Would it be all right if I paid my bill in the morning and picked up the rest of the cake?"

"Sure," Reba says.

"You were great; thank you for making the evening special. Add six dollars to my bill; four are for you and two for Hildred."

"THANK YOU. We enjoyed serving you all."

Amy and Doris are wearing their buffalo coats and boots and propping each other up. Luke picks up their shoes, gently pushes them toward the door, looks at Rudy, and asks, "Herding these two won't be easy. Do you have any rope?"

Grinning, Rudy says, "You could leave 'em here and get 'em in the morning."

"They'd never let me live it down," Luke says. "The evening was perfect; thank you!"

"We enjoyed watching you all have fun," Rudy says.

"Good, I must go; I just lost sight of the buffalo coats," Luke says, hastily leaving the dining room for the hotel's lobby. The women seem unsure where to go, so he takes them by the hand and leads them to their rooms.

In their room, Luke asks, "How was your eighteenth birthday party?"

"Like I told Mom, it was THE best! I love the clothes and the gun you bought for me today. And I got so excited when Reba and Hildred walked out of the kitchen wearing our coats and carrying the cake and boots. I doubt I will ever forget that!"

Luke says, "This winter, you'll say it's the softest and warmest coat you've ever had." Amy falls asleep mid-sentence, saying, "Everything was perfect, sweet...."

Chapter 38: Amy Meets Doc Holliday
August 24th

It's 7 a.m. on Friday, and Amy has been helping Doris carry her luggage to the lobby. Doris asks the registration desk attendant to keep an eye on her stuff. While walking to the dining room, Amy explained that she had told Luke they needed private time together over breakfast. Once seated in a quiet corner, they say good morning to Reba and order poached eggs, buttermilk biscuits with honey, and coffee.

Doris says between bites and sips of coffee, "You were always a happy child, but I've never seen you happier. I now have proof that you could not be in better hands. To me, Luke meeting your father the afternoon before he passed was an act of God."

Amy says, "If Luke and Dad hadn't camped together, Luke would have ridden right through Dodge just like he did in seventy-four. Luke was that rare man who would bring Dad home; God knew that about him. And then I couldn't help falling in love at first sight."

"I watched that happen and was happy for you," Doris says.

Amy holds Doris's hands, looks into her eyes, and says, "Mom, you can never repeat the story that Rosa Anthony told me or the attack on the Santa Fe train. If the wrong people got wind of either, Luke could end up like Jordan's first husband, Jesse. You've never been one to gossip, so I felt safe telling you. No matter how tempting it is to brag about your son-in-law, you must not."

Doris says, "Don't worry; my lips are sealed. I want to leave you with something to consider. Assuming you and Luke have several children, wouldn't it be nice to have some help? I'd like to live here, but not with you all. I'd sell my farm, and, with your approval, I'd like to build a cottage overlooking Luke's Lake."

Amy says, "Mom, I would love that, and I think you can count on it happening."

Before eight, they leave the dining room, and Luke is waiting in the lobby. The wagon and horses are out front, and Luke says, "I've already loaded your things. If we make ourselves smaller, I think we can all sit on the box," and they do.

It's a short trip to the depot. So, only seconds after Smokey has them moving, Doris tells Luke how much she appreciates his generosity and how it has made her stay memorable. She says, "I don't have enough time to express how much I enjoyed the Chicago trip, Amy's birthday party, and the Kiowa clothing. However, getting to know you made the trip even more special. And I've been so impressed by you, and I appreciate your concern for Amy's safety. You're a principled young man, a rare quality, for sure. I'm proud and thankful that my only child is in such competent hands. I'll pray for you all to get those properties. It would be a wonderful place to raise a family."

Luke says, "Doris, having you here the last three weeks has been good for Amy; that's important to me. I've enjoyed your company, getting to know you better, and seeing how much Amy and you have in common. We'll have an answer on the properties in a couple of weeks. If you get a telegram on September fifth before lunch, you'll not need to open it because it will be Amy saying that our bids were good."

Doris asks, "Why did you bring Fury?"

"I thought you'd want to say goodbye to both," Luke answers.

"You're right, I do," Doris says.

At the depot, Doris pets both horses, brags about their remarkable stamina and behavior, and tells them goodbye. Following that farewell, the three transferred Doris' belongings to the passenger car in one trip. Doris hugs Luke first and says, "I couldn't ask for a more admirable son-in-law."

"And I couldn't have a nicer mother-in-law," Luke says. Doris and Amy have a tearful goodbye. The train pulls away from the station at eight-thirty. Luke has his arm tightly around Amy's shoulders as she continues waving until she can no longer see her Mother.

They return the wagon to Frank's livery. Frank can see that Amy's usual enthusiasm is noticeably lacking and says, "I'll take care of the horses; you all go on." Luke thanked Frank, and they walked back to the hotel.

Amy sits quietly alone in their room for over an hour. She's thinking about how long it will be before she sees her Mother again. She suddenly remembers she can pick up her birthday gifts and snaps out of her doom and gloom. She finds Luke reading in the dining room and tells him, "I'm leaving to get my birthday presents. You don't need to come with me."

Luke says, "Thanks, I'm at a place in this book where it's hard to put it down; you be careful."

At Leroy's, Sidney shows Amy that he sewed on seven belt loops rather than six. Sidney shows her a loop he didn't use and explains how he cut the strip of fabric a little wider and twice as long. He folded the strip lengthwise and sewed the open sides together. Sidney says, "I thought an extra loop in the middle of the back would keep the waist material underneath the belt. Try on this pair; I'm anxious to know your thoughts."

"Okay, where's my belt?"

"Right here," he says, and hands it to her.

Amy exits the changing room on her toes, looks into the full-length mirror, and says, "Sidney, they're perfect; you're a MASTER SEAMSTER!"

Sidney says, "I hoped you would be pleased, but I didn't expect to get a title." While Amy watches, Sidney stacks the trousers and belt, wraps and ties the package with string, and hands it to Amy.

He says, "I liked your idea about women's trousers so much that I asked Leroy if I could write to the company. I mailed it yesterday and told them it was your idea."

"I'm going to enjoy these; thank you so much. I love knowing where I can buy more of them. I'm going to the Colt store to pick up my birthday pistol after I leave here. If you hear a small war, do not approach the trash pit behind the Champion Hotel from the west."

Amy says, "Sidney, just saying thank you is not enough. I want to hug you, but don't forget about that sleeve full of pins."

"I won't. I wish all my customers were as charming and excited about my work as you are." After the hug, Amy leaves Sidney standing by the front door, blushing and watching her hurry toward the Colt store.

Amy hands Don the receipt and says, "Luke said I was to give this to you."

"Yes, but in your case, it wasn't all that necessary," Don says.

"Why is that?" Amy asks.

"You and your husband are not my run-of-the-mill customers," Don says.

"I hope that's a compliment," Amy says.

"It is, to be sure," Don says. I saw you pass by and go into Leroy's store. Now that your hands are full, I worry you have too much to carry. You could wear the holster belt and gun, but perhaps you should return tomorrow for the bullets."

A well-dressed customer, but relatively thin and noticeably pale, has been listening to Amy and Don's conversation and asks Amy, "Where are you going, Ma'am?"

"Just two blocks to the Champion Hotel."

"I'd be glad to help with your purchases; I'm staying there."

"Thank you so much; my name is Amy Garrelts. My husband and I are staying there while we wait to hear the verdict on our bids in the big land sale."

"My name is John Holliday. My friends call me Doc because I have a degree in dental surgery."

"Where did you study?" Amy asks.

"At a small college in Philadelphia, I doubt you would have heard of it," Doc answers. "Are you going straight back to the hotel?" Doc asks.

"Yes, I'm through shopping for the day," Amy says.

Doc says, "Don, I will help Amy return to the hotel with her purchases. Please double-bag her shells. I'll be back tomorrow to evaluate the changes to the quick-draw holster." Doc turns to Amy and says, "I'm guessing you bought some new clothes today."

Amy says, "Three days ago, I bought three pairs of Mr. Strauss' work pants at Leroy's store. I had them altered to fit like men's trousers. I plan to wear them on our ranch."

Doc says, "I know Sidney; he tailored a suit for me."

Amy says, "Sidney does good work." It looks to me like you may be wearing the suit he made."

"I am," Doc answers.

Don puts Amy's pistol in the holster, wraps the belt around it, and hands it and the cartridges to Doc. Doc turns to Amy and says, "Let's go, little lady."

On their walk back to the hotel, Amy says, "Are you a traveling dentist, Mr. Holliday?"

"I'm a professional gambler and practice a little dentistry on the side."

"Do you plan to stay in Amarillo?" Amy asks.

"No, my companion, Kate, and I are looking for a new place to call home. The Fort Griffin Sheriff ran me out of town for killing a man in self-defense. We rode the stage for two hundred fifty miles and arrived here a week ago. Just so you'll know, the man drew a concealed gun. I threw a boot knife at him. Unfortunately, it stuck in his heart. The other men at the table testified I acted in self-defense, but the sheriff ran me out of town anyway."

"That sounds like a day in Dodge City," Amy says.

Doc says, "We're leaving for Dodge in a few days. The rumor is there are big poker pots in Dodge, but being handy with a gun is essential for self-preservation."

"Is that why you may buy a quick draw holster from Mr. Johnson?" Amy asks.

"It is," Doc answers.

"I can tell you about Dodge City. I lived there from birth until I married thirty-four days ago, but who's counting?" Amy says, with a big smile that exposes her adorable dimples.

"Is it as wicked as the papers say?" Doc asks.

"Only in the saloons, but we have quite a few."

"Is there a hotel you would recommend?" Doc asks.

"The Dodge House is said to be the nicest, but there are others," Amy answers.

As they enter the Champion Hotel, Amy says, "Mr. Holiday, my husband is probably reading in the dining room. Let's go see if I'm right."

Amy interrupts Luke's reading to introduce him to Doctor John Holliday, known as Doc by his friends. She explained that they met in the Colt store, and Doc helped carry her purchases back to the hotel.

Doc sets the gun belt and cartridges on the table in front of Luke and asks him, "Did you surrender your gun to the authorities in Dodge?"

"No, but it is illegal to carry a concealed gun. The *Dodge City Times* reported the city council has considered prohibiting carrying firearms, whether concealed or in plain sight," Luke says.

"What is your business?" Doc asks.

"I worked for King Ranch for eight years as a cattle driver and broke saddle broncs on the side," Luke answers.

"You look red-blooded, physically fit, strong as an ox, and tough as nails. Are you a poker player?" Doc asks.

"I'm not and don't care to learn. I'm prejudiced because I've seen men drink too much at the end of a cattle drive and leave all their pay on the poker table," Luke says.

"I'm familiar with what you're saying," Doc says.

Luke says, "When I met you, your suit, demeanor, handshake, and greeting convinced me you were an educated man. From our handshake, I knew you were not a working man because of your soft hands," Luke says.

Doc says, "You are very observant. My suit still looks good because it's only two days old. Dentistry and poker are my work, but neither tends to strengthen nor put calluses on my hands. I offered to help Amy because Kate and I saw a little of her birthday party on Wednesday evening, so I thought you all might be staying here."

Amy says, "Mr. Holliday may buy a quick draw holster from Mr. Johnson. Perhaps you should consider one of those, sweetheart."

Doc says, "Mr. Johnson and his bootmaker friend are collaborating with me to make a unique holster. We've been at it for over a week. In my profession, I spend hours at a poker table. A gun belt around my waist and a holster on my hip get extremely uncomfortable. Another problem is that my revolver is difficult to unholster without standing up. My new holster will solve both of those problems. It's roughly positioned over my belly, with the barrel pointed at a forty-five-degree angle to my left side. We're still fiddling with those details. Another unique feature is that we added a shoulder strap to keep it in position. I call it a side-draw holster. We have just completed the third design change, which I hope will be the last.

"Not being an experienced poker player, I doubt you've witnessed the situation where a loser has imbibed too much liquor. That will occasionally end in gunplay. So, if I see signs of a player becoming upset, nervous, and sweating, I will hold my cards in my left hand and drop my right hand on the tabletop, where it's only inches from the gun handle. A man going for his pistol will lean forward slightly and reach for his gun as he stands up. I plan to have my Colt forty-five cocked and pointed at his face before he can touch his pistol.

"I should be going. When I left our room an hour ago, Kate was sleeping, and her laudanum bottle was empty. So, I stopped at the pharmacy before going to the Colt store."

"Before you go, I have one quick question. Is there anyone you know in Dodge?" Luke asks.

"No, not really. I told Wyatt Earp I'd meet him there. Wyatt worked on the police force for a while, made a name for himself, and left," Doc says.

"Did he, ever!" Amy says.

Luke says, "We know Bat Masterson. I read that Bat and Wyatt are friends. You may run into Bat. If you do, please tell him Amy Bonner married Luke Garrelts."

"Will do; I must be going. You'll see me and Kate around the hotel for a few days; then we'll be on the train to Dodge," Doc says.

Amy says, "Good luck to you, Mr. Holliday, and thank you for assisting a damsel in distress."

"Good luck to you all," Doc says and leaves. Halfway to the second-floor staircase, Doc stops to cough hard and wipes blood-stained saliva from his mouth with a white handkerchief.

Amy says, "Oh, honey, you will not believe my trousers. Thank you for letting me get them."

"I had no idea that men's pants could make you happy," Luke says.

"Usually, it depends on who is in 'em," Amy says. "By the way, where is my divvy money?" she asks.

"Since I got back from the Kiowa reservation, it's been in my old boots under some underwear in the corner of the room."

"Well, you picked a safe place," Amy says. "Now, I must find a way to repay you for your trouble." She gestures to Luke, suggesting what's in store for him by looking seductive, raising eyebrows, and smiling.

Luke says, "Tomorrow morning, I'll give you some shooting tips behind the burn pit. Now, let's have an early dinner so you can re-hide your divvy money and repay me for keeping it safe."

Between the day Doris left Amarillo, August 24th, and the announcement of the successful bidders, September 5th, Luke and Amy can only wait nervously and fill their time with reading, letter writing, window shopping, and target practicing. What happened at the 1st National Bank the following day would be discussed for years.

Chapter 39: Luke Stops A Bank Robbery
August 31st & September 1st

The morning began like most August days in the Texas Panhandle. It's hot, dry, dusty, and without much hope of improving. It's the bank's last day to accept bids for properties in the Addison Estate sale. Amy is asleep, and Luke is in the dining room reading the local newspaper provided by the hotel and drinking coffee. Sugar glazing and crumbs from a cinnamon roll litter the dessert plate before him. His fork and knife lie diagonally across the plate, signaling to Reba that he has finished.

Luke empties his coffee cup and, remembering Amy's etiquette advice, burps quietly into his napkin, folds it, and gently places it along the left side of his plate. He refolds the newspaper and puts it in the center of the table for the next customer. Then he sets off for a morning walk along Main Street, as he does whenever Amy doesn't join him for breakfast.

It's a little after eight-thirty; folks are indoors, out of the heat and bright morning sun. Luke's in no hurry and stands in the hotel's doorway momentarily. While deciding which direction he'll take, four rough-looking riders pass him so aimlessly that it gets his attention. Luke decides to follow them, keeping over a hundred feet of separation. He wonders if they are in town to stock up on supplies. *That's not logical because everything is closed except for the hotel they just passed. The dusters they're wearing could be to conceal something. They're here for some reason; until I know, I'll keep an eye on them.*

The riders stop after another fifty paces, and Luke quickly sidesteps into a recessed doorway. Three men dismount in front of a closed hardware store, two buildings from the 1st National Bank. The men on foot wrap one rein around their saddle horn and give the other to the man on horseback. Looking repeatedly in both directions, they walk to the bank's door and position themselves on either side.

Luke knows they are not there to make a deposit. He thinks, *Good Lord, at three dollars per acre, the bank vault could have over two hundred thousand dollars to settle estate sales.* Luke returns to their second-story room as quickly and quietly as he can. He encounters no one on the way whom he can warn about the pending bank robbery.

Amy is in bed reading, and she watches as Luke grabs his rifle and bandolier. He leans over the bed and says, "The First National is about to be robbed. You stay here until I return." He takes the back stairs and loads the rifle as he runs behind the buildings to a breezeway he knows is past the front of the bank. He crouches and sneaks toward Main Street. Fortunately, a fifty-gallon oak whisky barrel has been placed at the front corner of the building to catch rainwater runoff from the roof valley directly above. He feels safe because the barrel provides an excellent hiding place with an unobstructed view of the bank, and he's sure a revolver bullet cannot penetrate even one side of it.

While waiting, Luke drops onto one knee, chambers a round, and fills the magazine tube. He's less than fifty paces from the bank's front door, which he watches by looking through the narrow gap between the rain barrel and the building. The three men on the boardwalk are nowhere in sight, and the front door Ben usually leaves open is closed.

The man on horseback leads the three riderless horses to the front of the bank. He's looking for anyone approaching the bank and is noticeably nervous. The four horses are also uneasy and move around enough that Luke's view of the bank's door is intermittently blocked.

Luke thinks, *If the robbers get away with twenty-five percent of the bank's money, Hank will reduce our joint account by the same amount.* Then he hears a single pistol shot from within the bank. Ben exits the front door, slips on the boardwalk, and skids to a stop like he's sliding into home plate. The rider unholsters his gun and points it at Ben, who raises only one hand. Luke can hear Ben pleading for the gunman not to shoot. Luke knows Ben's life is in imminent peril, and he must take a kill shot.

Just as Luke pulls the trigger, the three men in the bank run out carrying feed sacks. Luke's bullet hits the robber on horseback in the center of his chest, and he falls into the dirt. Luke chambers a round while leaving the rifle in the firing position and looking for his next target. The scene is chaotic; the horses are excited and bumping into each other; one misses stepping on Ben by inches.

One robber kneels behind a courtesy bench provided by the bank. He's trying to find who shot their lookout, but he can't. He points his pistol at Ben, who's begging for mercy. Luke is confident he must shoot at once to save Ben's life. The robber's head is the only body part visible, and Luke takes the shot.

The last two robbers look like clowns trying to grab a single dangling rein that flips from their grasp as the startled horses rear up out of fear. Once they grasp the rein, they have difficulty holding the money sack and getting their foot in the stirrup of a frightened horse stepping sideways. When finally saddled up, they flee in opposite directions.

Luke runs to the center of the street, decides the rider going south is his best opportunity, and hits him in the center of his lower back. The rider drops the feed sack and falls out of the saddle, but his left boot becomes trapped in the stirrup. The horse is at full gallop, and the robber's head slaps the ground with every stride.

Luke chambers another round while turning back toward the north. The robber has turned onto the side street beside the Champion Hotel and is no longer in Luke's line of sight. Luke runs to one of the frightened horses prancing sideways near Ben. He flips the hanging rein over the horse's neck, grabs the saddle horn, and swings onto the saddle with one hand and his rifle in the other. The bandolier is over one shoulder and across his back and chest. He digs his spurs into the horse's flanks, and while turning west at the hotel, he sees a man mounting up in front of the sheriff's office.

After a mile, Luke's horse closes the gap, and the robber is within rifle range. He puts the reins in his teeth and tries to get the man in the rifle sights, but he's lying forward over the horse's neck, making himself an impossibly small target. Luke's horse is tiring, and the robber is pulling away. Luke realizes he must shoot, or the rider will get away. After several shots into the horse's rump, it stumbles and rolls over the rider.

Luke dismounts but doesn't bother checking the man's pulse because it's evident that his neck is broken. He picks up the feed sack and knows he must relieve the dying horse's misery.

Using his revolver, Luke shoots the near-death horse in the middle of its forehead, halfway between its eyes and the base of its ears.

The man Luke saw mounting up in front of the sheriff's office rides up, looks down, and says, "There's something you don't see every day."

Luke asks, "What's that?"

"The damn guy is on his stomach and looking straight up. That isn't easy to do when you're alive!"

"Yeah, his horse rolled over him several times at runaway speed."

"I'm Sheriff Dick Pryor, and you need to hand me that money bag before someone thinks you're the one who stole it."

Luke looks at Dick's badge, hands him the feed sack, and says, "I've seen you around town. I'm Luke Garrelts, and I need to return to the hotel. My wife will be looking for me and will be nearly panicked if she can't find me."

"You can go," Dick says. "Would you stop by my office and tell my deputies I need help and a horse to get this man to the undertaker?"

"Sure. Before I go, I need to ask a favor. For my wife's and my safety, I don't want to be known as the person who stopped the bank robbery. I don't want to be the target of a family member or friend seeking revenge. I got involved because we have money in the bank for the estate sale.

"I understand, and I owe you that," Dick says. "However, I'll need to get a statement from you. Could you come by my office later this evening?"

"Okay, just you and me, right?" Luke says.

"Yes."

As Luke rides away, the Sheriff mutters, "How incredibly lucky for this Luke Garrelts to show up when he did. Otherwise, my brother Hank and his depositors could kiss this money goodbye."

Luke hasn't ridden far when he sees two men approaching, notices their badges, and stops long enough to tell them he left the Sheriff with a dead man a half mile back. Luke says, "The Sheriff asked me to go for help. It looks like you all saved me the trouble." The men hastily leave, and Luke figures they will sling the dead man over one horse and ride tandem back to town on the other.

Luke rides the robber's horse to Frank's livery. To not be seen, he avoids Main Street, and, luckily, everyone has gathered in front of the bank. Luke is surprised Frank is there and says, "Frank, I'm so glad you're here. I need a favor."

"Just name it," Frank says.

"This horse belonged to one of the dead bank robbers. I had planned to turn him loose in your corral. Would you tell Sheriff Pryor someone left him tied to your gate?" Luke asks.

"I can do that," Frank answers.

Luke walks behind the buildings to the hotel, goes in the back door, and up the back staircase to their room. He puts his rifle and bandolier in the corner and goes downstairs to find Amy. She's by the front door, looking worried; he's not surprised. When Amy sees him, Luke says, "Please don't say a word until we have privacy. Let's go to the dining room. I doubt there's anyone there right now."

They walk to the back of the dining room. Seeing no one, Amy asks, "Is this private enough?"

Luke says, "Yes, but keep your voice to a whisper anyway."

Amy says, "I saw you, a full gallop, following a man carrying a feed sack, and you were riding a horse that wasn't Smokey or Fury."

Luke says, "Yes, you did. It looks like you're mad at me, but don't be. I was careful not to put myself in danger." Luke quietly explains what happened and how they would have been affected if the robbers had been successful. She tells him she understands why he got involved, but his life was worth more to her than money in their bank account. Luke knows it must sink in before Amy will forgive him, so he suggests they go to the bank to hear Ben explain what happened there.

At the bank, they talk to Hank privately in his office. Hank explains that Ben is at the doctor's office. He says, "Ben was hit in his upper left arm and had a nasty flesh wound. I used my belt to make a tourniquet to stop the bleeding. I'm sure the bullet missed the bone."

Luke tells Hank that Dick has a sack of money. Hank looks straight up, inhales deeply, exhales through tight lips and puffed cheeks, and says, "Wonderful, that's the third sack; the other two are in the vault."

Luke says, "I'm curious about what went on inside the bank."

Hank says, "I can only repeat what Ben told me before he passed out. I was chatting with my brother Dick in front of the sheriff's office when we heard a shot that sounded like it was from the bank. Dick went to his office to alert his deputies and to get his horse. I took off for the bank but stopped when I heard rifle fire. I was nearly run over by a man I didn't recognize. And seconds later, I had to scramble to get out of YOUR way.

"I was the first to reach Ben. He was in pain and jabbering. I did my best to calm him down. He said it was fortunate that other bank employees were late and that he was alone. Ben doesn't like being late, so he sets his watch ten minutes ahead. He opened the bank before our security arrived; that will be a policy change. The robbers knew about Ben's habit of sweeping our front walkway before opening the bank at nine o'clock.

"Ben said three men overpowered him when he unlocked the door. They put a gun to his head and told him to open the vault in two minutes, or he was a dead man. He said they were like pigs at a trough, so busy filling the feed sacks that they paid him no attention.

"Ben thought he could run outside and alert anyone on the street. A bullet ripped through his upper arm when he was halfway through the door. Ben didn't expect the horses. He tried to avoid them but lost his footing on the boardwalk. The rider drew his pistol, but the excited horses made it difficult for the rider to get off a shot. When the rider was in position, the smile on his face made Ben think he would enjoy killing him. Ben said a bullet hit the rider in the center of his chest.

"The horses were panicking while the three inside the bank ran out. One robber knelt behind our courtesy bench and couldn't find you, so he aimed at Ben. Ben said he knew he was a goner. But at that moment, the man's head exploded, splattering brains and blood over the front of the bank. The other two men had great difficulty mounting their frightened horses. The first to mount up went south; the other went north. Ben heard the third rifle shot but didn't know the results. He didn't realize the shooter was you until he saw you in the street, aiming your rifle at the robber riding north.

"Without putting your foot in the stirrup, you mounted one of the robbers' horses beside the boardwalk with one hand on the saddle horn and a rifle in your other. He said you appeared to fly onto the horse's back and disappear into a cloud of dust. Ben said the experience was like he had read about once in a Western novel."

Luke says, "Ben had a traumatic experience, so some exaggeration is not unusual. He was in agonizing pain and didn't know the severity of his injury. He might have thought he would bleed to death. I saw that behavior in the war."

Hank says, "Ben told me all that while I put my belt below his armpit. Ben fainted when I pulled it tight enough to stop the bleeding, and four men carried him to the doctor. I don't know how to thank you for stopping those thieves."

Luke says, "Here's how. I asked your brother to keep my name out of this, and he said he would. I want you and Ben to do the same. Tell Ben not to name me as the shooter. If someone claims they saw me, ask Ben to deny it. He could say something like, 'I saw the shooter, but I didn't recognize him.'"

Hank assures Luke, saying, "I will, and so will Ben. We owe you for saving Ben's life and my bank. I would have had to postpone the estate sale indefinitely until First National depositors could adjust their bids or find funds to cover their loss."

After dinner, Luke and Amy walk to the sheriff's office. Dick is alone; he sees Luke and says, "Luke Garrelts, I cannot thank you enough for stopping those men. I've seen y'all around town; Reba told me your names and why you're here. But y'all are too law-abiding for me to have met before now." Dick looks at Amy and says, "I'm Dick Pryor, the Sheriff of Potter County; my older brother, Hank, owns the First National Bank. We are grateful to your husband for stopping the bank robbery." Then Dick looks at Luke and says, "I'm too tired to take your statement tonight. Cleaning up the mess those bank robbers left has tuckered me plumb out. Would you be available tomorrow morning?"

"Yes, but could you take my statement in the privacy of our hotel room?" Luke asks.

Dick says, "Sure, I can do that."

"Good, take the back stairs up to the second floor. We're in room 207. Don't knock if anyone is in the hall," Luke says.

Dick says, "Regarding your earlier concern. Anyone near the bank would have run for cover when the shooting started. It isn't likely that anyone other than Hank, Ben, and I saw you. If your name should surface, I'll deny it was you. I told my deputies you were on a morning ride and happened to arrive at the right time, so I asked you to tell them where to find me.

Dick winks at Luke and says, "When I stabled my horse this evening, Frank Weiner showed me a horse someone left tied to his corral gate. Turns out, it was a robber's horse. Frank also had the horse that went south. A good Samaritan found it about a mile from town; the robber didn't make it that far. It's been a busy day for the mortician; he'll get paid out of the money the county receives from selling their possessions. The county gets to keep what's left over. If there's a bounty, I'll be sure you get it."

Luke says, "If there is a bounty, can you not mention my name?"

Dick says, "That's standard policy; otherwise, no one would get involved. However, killing a famous outlaw is damn hard to keep quiet, and the lawman or citizen may become as famous as the outlaw."

Dick looks at his boots momentarily and says, "You know, on second thought, I don'tneed an affidavit from you. You can talk me through what happened; then, I'll draft a statement of my observations of the man who did the shooting."

Luke suggests they meet at eleven, and Amy will get their lunch. The sheriff says, "That sounds good, but I insist on paying."

Luke says, "Can't do that. Reba starts a daily ticket for us at breakfast; we add to it during the day, and I settle our bill after dinner. Amy will get lunch as she and I do when we have lunch in our room. Reba will add it to our bill, as always. I don't want our routine to change."

"I understand your caution," Dick says.

"Thanks, we'll see you tomorrow morning," Luke says, and the Garrelts return to the hotel.

The following day at eleven a.m., Dick knocks softly on door 207. Amy opens it, greets Dick, and sits on the bed. The men shake hands; Dick sits at the small table. Luke pulls a chair from the corner of the room close enough to speak quietly. Dick takes paper, pen, and ink from a specially designed case, tries to get comfortable, and says, "Luke, begin when you first realized they were up to no good. I don't write fast, just one thought or sentence at a time. I'll say, 'Okay,' when I'm ready for the next."

Luke starts talking about when the four rode slowly past him on Main Street, and ends when he handed Dick the feed sack full of money. Luke says, "What I know about what went on inside the bank is second-hand information. Hank told me what Ben told him while lying on the boardwalk before he fainted."

Dick says, "I'll get Ben's statement when he feels up to it."

Amy knows their conversation is complete and excuses herself to retrieve their lunch.

Dick finishes putting away the writing materials, and they talk for a while about the repercussions had the robbers been successful. Amy returns in ten minutes and kicks softly on the bottom of the door. Dick opens the door, and Amy enters carrying a big tray. Dick says, "What do you have there?"

Amy says, "Two lunches and two slices of apple pie. The sandwiches are for y'all, but the pie is mine."

Dick asks, "You want to trade?"

Amy says, "Not for a sandwich."

Dick laughs and asks Luke, "How did you remain calm and shoot so accurately when all hell was breaking loose?"

Luke says, "I credit my military training and working as the point man on one-thousand-mile cattle drives. The ranch manager probably chose me because I was a Sharpshooter in the war, had three years of drover experience, had demonstrated my ability to handle responsibility, and was several years older than the boys working for me. I led the cattle drive by riding an eighth to a quarter of a mile ahead of the herd. I evaluated potentially dangerous situations daily and decided how best to confront or avoid them. Deciding to stop or turn a herd of two thousand longhorn cattle should not be made on a whim. I made my best decisions when I stayed calm and clear-headed. I couldn't panic and be impulsive or indecisive, and freeze. A few times, the lives of men and cattle were at stake."

Luke continues, "I'm concerned those dead men could have family members who would seek revenge if they knew where to find me. I want to live a quiet life with Amy on a cattle ranch without worrying about someone shooting me in the back."

Dick responds, "I understand perfectly. I've already described the man who shot those men to a reporter; rest assured, that man is not you." They simultaneously push back from the table, stand up, and stretch their legs, backs, and shoulders. Dick says, "I'm curious about the day you arrived in Amarillo. That was the day of the unsuccessful Santa Fe train robbery. I know the Wells Fargo security boys got the credit, but I heard a story about a young fellow who shot the hell out of those road agents."

"I heard that same story. Who told you?" Luke asked.

"A Wells Fargo man named Rex Lane. I took his statement at the depot. He said a stranger traveling on the train volunteered to help. He believed this stranger killed or nicked a robber with every shot. In only a few minutes, fourteen men were on the ground, either dead or dying. Another five, still in the saddle, were so badly wounded from multiple shots that they would bleed to death within an hour. He said it was the most remarkable shooting he had ever seen. When I asked who the shooter was, he said there wasn't time to get acquainted before the attack, and the stranger took off as soon as the train arrived in Amarillo. He gave me a description that would fit anyone."

Luke thought briefly and said, "Fourteen men on horseback from a moving train? That sounds like a story in a Western novel." During their exchange, Dick looks over at Amy. And each time he does, she looks down and away, so he can't make eye contact. Dick thinks, *Amy's behavior confirms my suspicion.*

Dick says, "Before I leave, you should know that the City of Amarillo, First National, their depositors, and Potter County are indebted to you. It's a shame that you'll only hear words of gratitude from Hank, Ben, Ben's wife, and me."

Luke says, "I was protecting our savings account. I deeply appreciate you saying that with Amy present. Maybe she'll forgive me now."

Amy says, "If you were in Ben's condition, I'd be very angry with you."

They shake hands; Dick leaves, and Amy hugs Luke long and hard and says she's incredibly proud of him. Luke says, "I'm glad Dick convinced you I did the right thing because I hate the feeling I get when I think you're mad at me."

Amy says, "Everything you told Dick made me realize you were probably the only man in town who could stop that robbery. I believe you don't get into those situations by accident. Years ago, our minister talked about divine intervention one Sunday morning. He believed nothing ever happens by accident. He said our Creator is in control and is all-knowing. So, He knew what would happen at First National and with Rosa Anthony. He made sure you were there, and He felt responsible for protecting you."

Luke says, "I didn't feel anything spiritual like the hand of God pushing me to go for a walk. A morning stroll is my routine after having breakfast alone, so it's merely a coincidence that I happen to be there."

"Ah-ha, I wanted to go to breakfast this morning, but I couldn't get out of bed, Amy says. Think about that."

Luke raises his eyebrows at Amy's comment, pauses, and says, "That was just a coincidence. I know what compels me to get involved. When I sense trouble, particularly gunplay, my anger toward men who would harm those less capable of defending themselves takes over. I know they'll repeat it if they get away. So, turning my back and walking away is not an option. My confidence is due to my Sharpshooter training, combat experience, exceptional vision, and a Henry rifle's accuracy and firing capacity. Those things give me a distinct advantage over the ordinary gunman. Not to boast, but they're not in a fair fight."

Amy adds, "I've been in a few scrapes with you and heard some eye-opening stories about how you jump into action. Your physical fitness, the ability to remain calm, quick thinking, and unequaled marksmanship are incomparable advantages. God knows that, so He uses you for good."

"Perhaps so," Luke admits.

Chapter 40: Winning Bids Are Decided
September 5th

Other than greeting Reba, they have an unusually quiet breakfast due to coping with the anxiety of possibly getting unwelcome news at nine a.m. Amy breaks their silence, saying, "My heart's thumping, my hands are sweaty, and my mouth is dry; how are you feeling?"

"Not that bad, but like you, I'm worried. I did my best to hide the thick, dark goo, but if someone who knows what oil looks like stumbled upon it, neither of our bids was big enough. It's almost nine; let's go find out."

They're a few steps out of the hotel's front door when Amy asks, "Where will the winning names be posted?"

Luke answers, "The list will likely be on the board where they post customer communications. It's on the wall left of the cashiers' cages, right between the big windows. When we go in, let's walk straight to it."

Amy says. "I agree."

Sheriff Pryor sees them leaving the hotel and whistles. He hurries to them, limping painfully on his left leg, tips his hat to Amy, and whispers to Luke, "Missouri has a $1,400 dead or alive bounty on the four. I'm having their pictures taken today and sending them to Jefferson City in tomorrow's mail. I expect the money to arrive by wire transfer in the next few weeks. There shouldn't be an identification problem because they are unmistakable from their wanted posters. Once a crook has been in state prison, their picture in the next wanted poster is quite good."

Luke inquires, "What about the man shot in the head? Could you get a picture of him?"

Dick answers, "We did, but it wasn't easy. It looked like your bullet hit just above the right ear. Surprisingly, his face below the bridge of his nose remained intact, but the top of his head, including most of his brain, was never found. I think a couple of stray dogs found them first. The mortician arranged his face, and I put his hat on him; he looked enough like his poster. What will seal the deal is that his wanted poster said he had an ace of spades tattooed on the back of his left hand, so I made sure that hand was up by his face."

Luke asks, "What do you know about them? Were they from around here?"

Dick says, "They're not local; their warrants said they were bank robbers convicted of murder. It would seem they were good at their trade, given the size of the bounties. Probably Jesse James copycats who holed up in the Ozark Mountains in Arkansas. I searched their pockets and saddlebags and found a Fort Smith newspaper article about the Addison Estate sale. These misfits were likely a gang hired by someone with brains and a talent for planning robberies. The planner must have read about First National handling the closings of the properties and knew the vault would be full of cash near the end of August. He undoubtedly had someone watch the bank long enough to realize Ben's habit of sweeping their boardwalk before business hours and before security arrived."

Luke remains quiet, and Dick thinks for a moment before saying, "Coincidentally, the little town of Addison had a wealthy founder named Tom Addison. Locals knew he was as crooked as a dog's hind leg, but no one was brave enough to do anything about it. His reign came to a gruesome end when he was put in a locked gun safe in his office, and the building was set on fire. That night, a tornado killed the pursuing posse of five men who were Tom Addison's employees, or should I say, henchmen. Talk about cleaning up a town. What are the incredible odds of that happening?"

"I read about that; were those responsible ever caught?" Luke asks.

"Nope. I heard the Rangers gave up trying," Dick replies.

Luke explains, "If we win our property bids, we'll be here until closing on the seventeenth. That's almost two weeks from now, so the reward could be here by then. If not, I'll make a special trip back for that much money."

Dick says, "Okay," and returns to his office, kicking yesterday's sunbaked road apples underneath the boardwalks.

Luke and Amy reach the bank's front door at nine a.m., just as two security guards are unlocking it. They greet the guards, saying, "Good morning," and walk hesitantly toward the customer information board. There's no bounce in Amy's step. Her pace and posture suggest she's expecting bad news and is in no hurry to hear it.

Hank has been waiting for them and shouts from across the room, "Y'all got the properties you bid on!"

"Oh, thank God! Amy blurts out. She hugs Hank and says, "My brain has lived in that house for the last month. How soon can we close?"

"You can be the first on the seventeenth if you want," Hank says.

"So, nine o'clock on the seventeenth?" Amy fires back.

"How about nine-thirty?" Hank says.

"We'll be here with bells on," she says.

They see Ben; his left arm is in a sling, and he's walking toward them. Ben says, "It's good to see you all."

"Likewise," Luke says.

Ben hugs Amy with his right arm, shakes Luke's hand, and says, "Luke, the last time I saw you, I was lying on the boardwalk and lucky to be breathing."

Luke says. "Let's go into your office, close the door, and talk quietly."

Ben closes the door and says, "How's my hero been since the robbery?"

Luke speaks slightly louder than a whisper, saying, "I'm not a hero; tell me about your arm."

Looking squarely into Luke's eyes, Ben says, "It gets a little better each day. You have no idea how grateful I am to you to still be among the living."

"Ben, you're embarrassing me. How many days of work did you miss?" Luke asks.

"Six, today is my first day back. Look, I'll stop kissing your ass with gratefulness when you stop acting like saving my life is not a big deal. My wife, Beverly, would strongly disagree with you."

Luke says, "I see her point, and I'll admit that because I liked you, I pulled the trigger sooner than for someone I didn't know. So, being nice to people can pay off in ways you'd never suspect. Hank told me everything you told him before you passed out."

Ben says, "Dick told me the newspaper article was intentionally light on details; he wanted it that way. How did you know they might rob the bank?"

Luke answers, "When they passed me on Main Street, they looked like trouble. I was suspicious about why they were in town, so I followed them. When they stopped two doors from the bank, and three of the four dismounted and walked to the front of the bank, there was no doubt about their intention. I was concerned they would shoot their way out of town and take the life of an innocent bystander to dissuade anyone from becoming involved. I was wearing my Colt and wanted more firepower, so I returned to the hotel for my rifle." Then Luke asks, "Tell me why you came out of the bank?"

Ben answers, "Well, the three in the bank were so engrossed in filling their feed sacks, I thought I could make it outside and yell, 'Bank robbery' at the top of my lungs. I had no idea a fourth man and four horses were at the front door. I got shot trying to open the door; then I slipped on horse pee on the boardwalk. When the guy on horseback pointed his gun at me, all I could think of was to put my hands up, but my left arm wouldn't. That bastard was excited about the opportunity to finish me off," Ben says, followed by a forced, breathy laugh.

"Your situation looked so dire; I knew I had to take a quick kill shot," Luke said.

"You nailed the bastard, and I thank God you did," Ben says as Amy pinches the back of Luke's arm. "He hit the dirt, the horses panicked, and the three in the bank came out carrying bulging flour sacks. One crouched behind our bench and, unable to find who shot the lookout, pointed his gun at me. I believe he was less than a second from pulling the trigger when his brains splattered all over the bank."

"That headshot was the only shot I had," Luke says.

"I thanked God for a second time," Ben says, and Amy pinches Luke again. "I didn't know the shooter was you until you ran out in the street. I saw you fire at the robber headed south and figured you got him because you turned to aim at the guy headed north. When you didn't fire, I knew he must have turned west at the hotel. I watched you leap on the horse near me and follow him out of town. Hank told me you stopped him, too. How did you do that?"

Luke answers, "At first, I could gain on him, but after a mile, my horse was tiring more than his, so the gap between us was getting bigger. He was a small target because he rode with his head down on the side of the horse's neck. I didn't want to shoot the horse, so I held my fire until I realized he'd get away if I didn't. The horse went down in an awkward forward roll that broke the robber's neck."

"Oh, man, I'd like to have seen that," Ben said.

Amy decides it's a good time to inform Ben of their plans and says, "We plan to leave for our new home after we close on the seventeenth."

"That's good to know; my wife wants to be here to meet Luke."

Ben follows them to the front door; Hank joins them and asks, "Are you going to the properties?"

Amy says, "A team of wild horses couldn't keep me away."

Ben says, "That does not surprise me. Hopefully, I'll get to see the properties one day. I look forward to seeing you all at closing on the seventeenth."

"At nine-thirty sharp!" Hank chimes in.

After exchanging "thanks and goodbyes," Hank and Ben watch as they return to the hotel. Amy is holding Luke's hand, walking sideways, and looking at him in awe. Ben says, "That man saved my life twice."

Hank says, "That man saved my bank, which is pretty damn close to saving my life."

Chapter 41: Closing The Properties
September 17th

Luke and Amy go to their soon-to-be home between September sixth and the sixteenth to clean up, fix up, and prepare for moving in. They take down the J&J sign, burn L&A on the back, and nail it back up. Luke finds time to write to John D. Rockefeller to describe the dark pool that smells like kerosene and feels oily. They swim every afternoon and either go to town for dinner or pan-fry bass, crappie, or catfish filets by Luke's Lake.

Luke cleans out the barn, and they spend their last three nights cuddled up in the wagon in the barn with Smokey and Fury. On their last night, Luke says, "Ten days ago, I could not have imagined being this happy and optimistic about the future. You, my dear, deserve all the credit for making that happen."

"I feel the same way about you," Amy says. "Every night, before going to sleep, I think about what you and I can do with this land, and it excites me."

Luke says, "I bet you like sleeping in the barn."

"I do," Amy says. "Having the horses nearby makes me feel a lot safer. Without wind gusts rattling the wagon, I don't wake up as often. And I darn sure don't miss the night critters prowling around making weird noises."

"I haven't noticed any difference," Luke says, smiling broadly.

"How could you?" Amy says, "After making love, you sleep like Rip Van Winkle."

"You should, too; Smokey is all the lookout we need," Luke says.

"He is a good sentry," Amy says.

Luke and Amy return to Amarillo on the evening of September sixteenth. They get to the bank the following morning at nine-fifteen. Ben greets and escorts them to a large room with an oak table surrounded by a dozen chairs and says, "Hank and my wife will join us in a few minutes. Hank will have your documents, and Luke, be forewarned that my wife will be extremely nervous about meeting you. I'm to blame for making you into a giant."

"I'm sorry to hear that," Luke says. "I promise not to say *Fee fi fo fum*. I'll behave like I'm introverted and shy."

"You're already that way, so be careful not to overplay it," Ben says laughingly. You all arrived a little early. I'm sorry we weren't quite ready for you, but it's better to be hours early than a minute late."

Amy winks at Ben and says, "You share that opinion with William Shakespeare."

Ben asks, "Yes, I do. So, where did you study?"

"Dodge City," she says.

"Does Dodge have a college?" Ben Asks.

"No, I didn't go to college; only through the eighth."

"You could fool me," Ben says.

Luke chimes in, "She's smart. Her bedroom wall has academic accolades under wood-framed glass attesting to that!"

"Those only prove that I'm a good guesser," Amy says.

Hank and Beverly enter the room. For privacy, Hank closes the door, using his butt, and places three nearly identical stacks of papers on the table. While everyone stands, Ben introduces his wife, saying, "Beverly, this gentleman is Luke Garrelts. He's the remarkable man who saved my life TWICE! And this LOVELY young lady is his wife, Amy."

Tearfully, with a weak, trembly voice, Beverly says, "Sir, I feel honored to be standing next to you. Since that awful morning, I have thanked God every day you were there (Amy pinches Luke). I've tried so hard to find words to express my gratitude. I no longer believe there are any good enough."

Luke says, "I think you just found them." He bends down and hugs Beverly while the others quietly process what they have just heard.

Hank breaks the silence by stepping toward the conference table, clearing his throat, and pulling out a straight-backed, oak armchair for Amy. Luke sits down in a chair next to Amy. Hank looks at Luke and Amy, clears his throat again, points at the stacks of papers, and says, "These documents legally convey the properties you all are buying. Ben will explain them and show you where to sign and date them. There will be no surprises and no unanswered questions. We keep nothing from you and will remain here until you are satisfied. I apologize for your having to share one ink pen. Those darn things seem to walk out of the bank by themselves." Hank's joke falls flat as, other than Ben, the rest aren't familiar with the bank's mysterious disappearing fountain pen problem.

Ben slides three stacks of documents before them and says, "Hank thought we should make triplicate copies, which he'll explain later. Ben describes the purpose of each document, waits until they've read them, asks if they have questions, and shows them where to sign and date.

Except for the deed, Luke only reads the first few paragraphs of the other documents, and he rarely asks a question. Amy follows Luke's lead. The closing goes without a hitch. After executing the documents, Ben announces, *"The deed is done."*

Amy whispers to Ben, "Shakespeare's Macbeth." Ben looks at her with raised eyebrows and winks.

Hank says, "Our standard procedure is to give the buyer two copies of their closing papers. They file one copy at the county courthouse; the second is theirs. We have prepared a third copy of the closing documents in your case because your two properties are in Moore County, and the county seat is Addison. My concern comes from a fire that occurred there. It didn't spread, but with different wind conditions, it could have. Addison's future is somewhat uncertain, so I thought it best to keep an official duplicate copy here at First National."

Luke says, "That's an excellent idea, thank you."

The new property owners get up to leave, and Hank says, "It's unusual for a husband and wife to own property jointly. And for such a young couple to buy a property of this size without a loan."

Luke says, "Fortunately, we received generous financial assistance."

Ben chimes in, "They're also legally smart. They have identical wills that grant the last to die the exclusive right of ownership, and when both are gone, their children share equally; it's rare for folks to think that far ahead."

Luke says, "When my foster parents died, their wills made it easy for me to take ownership of their farm. I read that a jointly held deed and a marriage license were enough for Amy to claim my share and vice versa, but I wanted wills like my parents had that would convey our property to our children, if we ever have any."

Amy whispers in Luke's ear, and Luke says, "Forget my 'if we ever have any' comment." Everyone congratulates them with long hugs and handshakes.

Beverly asks Amy about their properties. When Amy finishes, Beverly asks if she has what she needs to set up housekeeping. Amy says, "Luke asked that I buy what I need for my kitchen from a store in Addison called Kitchen Things. I wrote to them, and they replied that they could fill my order. We were there from the sixth until yesterday. Luke put down enough earnest money to hold the things I picked out. Luke kept the furniture from the wheat farm, which he sold to Bill Boyer. Frank Weiner, the livery owner on Main Street, has offered to bring it to us. Frank and Luke's friendship goes back to when Luke was a boy, over twenty years ago. Frank is considering buying the livery and blacksmith business in Addison. Frank thinks a slower-paced location would be a nice change. So, the plan is for Frank to look it over when he delivers Luke's furniture and some horse training things."

Sheriff Dick Pryor knocks on the door, interrupting everyone's conversations. Hank opens it and says, "Come on in, brother, we're finished here."

As he enters, Dick closes the door for privacy and says, "I hoped I'd find you all here. Luke, the bounty arrived late yesterday. I put it in our account here at First."

"Good; that saved me a trip. Ben, could you do me a favor?

"Of course," Ben says.

"Would you get with Dick and transfer it to Amy's and my joint account with no one else involved?"

"Sure, that's not much of a favor," Ben says.

"Thanks, I appreciate that because we need to be going," Luke says.

Dick says, "Before you go, I have something I want to get off my chest, and this is the only audience I can share it with. To build suspense, Dick holds his hands up head high, slowly looks around the room, making eye contact with each person, and says, "The morning of August thirty-first will be talked about for years and could become legendary. Luke, your character in the legend, will eventually get a hero's name, like Colt, maybe Henry Colt. Over the years, your story will become exaggerated by storytellers who love to gild the lily. Eventually, it will be said something like this: a mysterious, courageous, dashing young cowboy stopped a million-dollar robbery at the First National Bank of Amarillo. He rode into the fray on a palomino stallion with the reins clenched in his teeth. He had a Colt revolver in his left hand and a Henry rifle in his right that he fired with deadly accuracy and chambered cartridges one-handed."

Dick continued, "Ten men were left dead or dying when the smoke settled. Three survivors fled, each with a bag of the bank's money. They were pursued at full gallop by the daring young man. The county sheriff followed minutes behind and found the three robbers dead a mile out of town and a hundred yards apart. When he returned with the bank's money, the concerned depositors asked, 'Who was that man?' The sheriff replied, 'When I arrived, he was riding off alone into the setting sun.' Eventually, that story will end up in a dime novel with a title like *The Lone Rider.*"

Ben interrupts Dick, saying, "I want you to repeat that so I can write it down."

"I will, but I first want Amy and Luke to know that we have sworn to defend Luke's anonymity. Only Doc and the people in this room will ever know the name of that legendary hero. I threatened Doc the day it happened. One last thing: Luke, when I retire, would you consider running for Potter County Sheriff?"

"I appreciate your confidence; it would be an honor, Luke says. "But not possible because we'll live in a different county." Luke looks at Ben, smiles, winks, then looks at Dick and says, "Dick, your story has enough exaggeration to be in a pocketbook novel."

Ben says, "I agree!"

Hank asks, "Are you going to your new home today?"

"We are. And we need to be on our way. The wagon is at the hotel, loaded, and ready to go. If you crave a day of hard work or fishing, please come see us."

Amy follows up, "If you come to fish, holler our names before approaching the lake. We'll need a few minutes to get decent if we're swimming."

Everyone laughs, and Luke says, "Hank, Ben, thanks for helping to make Amy's and my dreams come true. Turning to

Beverly, he says, "Beverly, I'm thankful to have been able to help your husband and my good friend; that day will always be special for me. "

Hank says, "Many banks fail following a robbery, so thank you for protecting my financial future. I wouldn't have gotten the money back if you hadn't stopped them."

Beverly says, "Thank you for saving my sanity."

Dick said, "Thanks for saving the city's reputation. Before you go, I have one last question. I've told myself repeatedly that I shouldn't ask, but my curiosity won't let me do that. Why would Richard Coke, the Governor of Texas, be interested in knowing if you were among the winning bidders?"

"I could guess, but at the risk of being wrong, I won't. That reminds me, Amy, we must telegraph George before leaving town."

As they leave the conference room, Amy says, "Until we meet again." Everyone repeats Amy's farewell.

When the Garrelts are walking toward the wagon, Dick says, "The George he mentioned is George Anthony, the Governor of Kansas. When they arrived, I noticed the Pullman's uniqueness and asked Santa Fe about it. They said George Anthony owned it. I hope no one put political pressure on the bank's evaluation committee."

Ben quickly said, "No; Oh, GOD, NO! The Garrelts outbid their nearest competition by about ten percent! But I suppose Governor Anthony could be the source of what Luke called 'generous financial assistance.'"

Dick asks, "Did Luke say that?"

Ben answers, "He did."

Shaking his head in disbelief, Dick says, "Dang, he's even politically connected! It's time to break up this Luke love fest."

The Garrelts walked to the hotel to thank and say goodbye to the staff who made their stay enjoyable. They find Reba and Rudy in the kitchen and ask them to visit the L&A when they need to relax. Then they stopped at the grocery store for grub and horse treats and at Western Union's office to telegraph Doris and the Anthonys.

Luke and Amy leave Amarillo with Amy sitting in Luke's lap. They excitedly plan their next few days, discuss baby names, and try to guess the delivery date. The Garrelts are as happy as God intended, but Hank's comment about Addison's uncertain future weighs on Luke's mind.

After a few miles, Luke says, "I want you and Luke Junior to rest on the mattress for the rest of the trip." He reins in Smokey to stop. Amy says, "Thanks, we appreciate your concern." She carefully walks sideways to the back of the wagon. Luke daydreams about growing their ranch and the city using Tom Addison's ill-gotten gains. Luke thinks God should know his intentions, so he looks up and addresses the heavens, saying, "Dear Lord, favor me with time and health, and I promise to do everything in my power to redeem myself for violating your commandment."

Luke asks Smokey, "Do you think He was listening?" Hearing his name, Smokey turns his ears toward Luke and whinnies robustly. Luke says, "I hope you're right."

Chapter 42: Ten Years Later
August 21st, 1887

Luke's boundless energy and passion for growing the L&A ranch and the City of Addison, as well as improving living conditions in Oklahoma's Indian Territory, are widely known. He has organized and staffed the L&A to accomplish those things, leaving him time to travel with Amy; their life is good.

Luke Garrelts, Junior, nicknamed "L.J.," is nine, and his brother Charlie is seven. It's Amy's twenty-eighth birthday, and she's in her fortieth week of pregnancy, hoping for a healthy baby girl to arrive today.

Jordan and J.R. arrived two weeks ago. However, due to his concern that the bank could not survive without his leadership, J.R. returned to Kansas City five days ago. The boys met Aunt Jordan and Uncle J.R. for the first time the day they arrived. That was because they had not visited the L&A since L.J.'s birth. Luke and Amy always stayed with Jordan and J.R. for a few days whenever they passed through Kansas City on their travels. During those stops, Luke would tell Jordan about growing the L&A, and she was anxious to see it for herself. The birth of her first niece or third nephew gave her the reason to convince J.R., who is work-obsessed, to make the trip.

L.J. and Charlie are practicing roping a wooden stick figure resembling a calf. Luke is giving the boys a tip about rolling their wrists to make the lariat open into a bigger circle. The boys try Luke's suggestion with immediate success. Luke says, "One day soon, you boys will be wranglers."

L.J. asks, "When Randy and the ranch hands leave on the cattle drive to Amarillo, can we sleep in the bunkhouse?"

"Better ask your Mother," Luke advises.

The boys run into a sprawling, one-level, adobe-style home, yelling, "Mom, Mom!" Amy has been in labor for several hours while reclining on a buffalo hide couch. Their Aunt Jordan is in the matching chair, drawn close to Amy. The boys wait patiently for their Mother and Aunt to finish their conversation.

Amy explains to Jordan that the couch, chair, and several other pieces scattered around the house are gifts from The Kiowa Chieftain, whom Luke calls The Third. They were delivered after Luke got the Department of the Interior and the Bureau of Indian Affairs to make decisions that changed living conditions for all the tribes in Oklahoma's Indian Territory. The Kiowa Tribal Council made Luke an Honorary Chief. His Indian name is *Paka tu Shires*, which translates to 'Man of Honor.'"

"How was Luke able to get meetings in Washington?" Jordan asks with a puzzled look.

"He wrote a monthly letter to President Hayes, with copies to the Secretary of the Interior and the Director of the Bureau of Indian Affairs. He had done that for years, but he never got a reply until George Anthony suggested he send a copy to the editor of The *Washington Post*. A few months after Luke's letters appeared in the paper, he got invited to Washington, D.C. by the Indian Bureau to discuss his Post Articles."

When Amy pauses to get comfortable, the boys plead their case. She approves, and they run to the kitchen, where Maria has made a stack of tortillas. They grab two apiece, run back to tell Luke their good news, and then resume lassoing the wooden calf.

Luke looks to the west at a cluster of pump jacks and walking beams moving up and down, pumping black gold, and mutters, "Thank you, Mr. Rockefeller."[33]

Luke sees Joe Stout riding in from Addison. Joe says, "Howdy; I see you're admiring your oil field."

Luke says, "Those structures have sprung up like mushrooms. The new production equipment is made of steel and called pump jacks. I originally agreed to give Standard Oil one hundred acres to drill on; now, they want another hundred acres. Our attorney, Ben Abney, Junior, whom we call B.J., thinks we can negotiate a better deal on the full two hundred acres."

"Nice problem to have," Joe says.

The boys are not close enough to hear all the conversation, but they can tell that their Dad and Mr. Stout are reminiscing about something that happened long ago. After Joe rides off, L.J. says, "Dad, we heard you and Mr. Stout laughing about something. What was it?"

"Yes, we were," Luke said.

"Will you tell us about it?" L.J. asks.

Luke looks down, thinks for a few seconds, and says, "Okay, but I doubt you boys will be impressed or find it funny."

Charlie interrupts, saying, "That's okay; we want to hear it."

Luke wants his story to have a moral. He says, "This happened on the wheat farm where I grew up. I wanted to do something I could brag about to my friends, but it was a painfully bad idea. I was fourteen, and Smokey was two. I wanted him to jump over a four-rail fence. Smokey lost his courage and skidded to a stop short of it. I flew over his head into the fence, broke my left forearm, and had bruises from head to foot. If you try that, start with a much shorter fence, maybe one with only one rail."

The boys look at each other disappointedly. L.J. says, "But Dad, we heard you mention Grandpa's wagon and Kansas City."

"Oh, you're right; we did talk about that. Ten years ago, I was as nervous as a cat in a room full of rocking chairs. Except for your birthdays, I think that day was the best day of my life. I had driven Grandpa's wagon to Kansas City from Dodge City, and your mother met me there by taking the Santa Fe from Dodge. We went to Aunt Jordan's home so that Mom could meet her. That afternoon, I gathered all my courage, took a deep breath, got down on one knee, and asked your Mom to marry me right in front of Aunt Jordan," Luke says.

"Why were you nervous about asking Mom to marry you?" Charlie asks.

"If she had said, 'No,' I would have begged with tears in my eyes and humiliated myself in front of Aunt Jordan. Someday, you'll find out that asking a girl you can't live without to marry you is stressful."

"Why is it stressful?" LJ asks

"I doubt you will understand, but since you asked. The stress is due to the worry or fear that the person you love may think you are not right for them and say, 'No.' You'll try practicing what you want to say, but it'll never sound good enough. When you finally work up the nerve to ask her to marry you, your hands will be sweaty, your throat will be dry, and your heart will be pounding. You probably will not have eaten for a day or two, causing you to be lightheaded and feel like you might faint or throw up."

L.J. says, "Heck, I'm not getting married."

Luke says, "That would be a mistake, L.J. You'll get through it by being brave. When she says, 'Yes,' you will experience joy that you'll remember for the rest of your life."

Disappointedly, L.J. says, "Dad, I was hoping to hear a story I could tell my friends. Charlie, let's go swimming with Smokey and Fury." The boys coil up their ropes and hang them around the wooden calf's neck.

The boys call to their horses in unison by saying, "Chop-chop-chop." Within seconds, Smokey and Fury trot out of the barn where Grandpa Bonner's wagon is stored. The horses are followed close behind by four greyhounds Luke uses to hunt coyotes that stalk his calves. The hounds can reach a speed of forty miles per hour and often return with coyote hair in the corners of their mouths and blood on their coats.

The horses stop inches from Luke and the boys, dropping their heads, hoping for a treat. But they're satisfied with L.J. and Charlie patting their foreheads and talking to them. The hounds gather around Luke with their tails wagging frantically in anticipation of going on a coyote hunt.

L.J. weaves his fingers together to make a stirrup. Charlie inserts his left foot, and L.J. lifts Charlie until he's high enough to swing his right leg over Smokey's back. Then L.J. grabs a handful of mane and slings himself onto Fury's back. Luke watches with pride as they ride a short distance to their Grandmother's cottage that overlooks the lake. Luke built it for Doris after Charlie was born.

The boys dismount next to the porch. Doris walks out and asks, "Are you boys going fishing or swimming?"

"Swimming, but maybe both," L.J. says.

"How's your Mother?" Doris asks.

L.J. answers, "Mom's lying down. Aunt Jordan thinks we should get our brother today."

"Mom's going to name him George," Charlie says, wrinkling his nose.

"I should get down there," Doris says.

Luke can see the boys talking to their grandmother. He goes inside, leaving the hounds at the screen door whimpering for his return, and asks Amy how she's feeling. After getting a not-so-great answer, he says, "I regret having to go to town and possibly not being here for our third child's birth."

Jordan asks, "It's Sunday; what will you do on a Sunday?"

Luke answers, "A couple of things, but primarily, it's the double ribbon-cutting ceremony at two o'clock for the new school and church; they're only fifty feet apart. The City Council asked me to talk briefly about both projects. Scheduling their grand openings after church is the best time to gather a crowd. The trend is for businesses to open for a half day on Sundays, after church, and be closed on Mondays. At church, I'll remind folks about the event. So, I need to leave here no later than ten-thirty.

"If he's open, I want to stop at B.J.'s office to find out if Jim Baird accepted our offer for his ranch. If Jim has, I've decided to ask Howard Johnson to resign as sheriff and manage it. I'll have him report to Randy until he can handle it; then, he and Randy will report to me. I'm satisfied they'll work well together; they're very good friends."

Luke continues, "B.J. will ask me to approve changes to any L&A contracts he's reviewing. I'll walk Main Street until the ribbon cutting and chat with folks. After the ribbon cutting, the City Council and the Planning Committee have a joint meeting. The purpose is to kick around possible solutions to articles in last month's *Honest Opinions*. I must be there because I'm on the Council and the Planning Committee and expected to present issues and our proposed solutions at tomorrow night's City Council meeting. I've seen the meeting agenda; we'll probably adjourn before we get through it, so I'm doubtful I'll be home by dinner time. You all don't wait for me; leave a plate of leftovers. In my infinite wisdom, I figured you wouldn't feel like having a birthday party anytime soon. So, after you and our baby are back up to speed, we'll celebrate your birthday at the R&R Steak House. Whenever I see Reba and order one of Rudy's amazing steaks, I have memories of your eighteenth birthday party."

"That was a good party," Amy says. "Would you have time to pick up a few groceries?"

"Sure," Luke answers.

"Thank you, my list is on the dining room credenza," Amy says.

The grocery list is next to the ten-year-old pictures at the Governor's Mansion. Luke looks at them and says, "I'll call the Anthonys and J.R.; is there anything I should tell them?"

"Yes, tell them whether we get a George or a Charlene; this baby will be a fighter. This little devil has been punching and kicking me all morning. It feels like my bladder is their punching bag."

Jordan says, "Luke, please tell the Anthonys their church is beautiful, and J.R. that I miss him and will see him a few days after Amy delivers my niece."

Before leaving, Luke kisses Amy's forehead and says, "Try not to have our baby until I get back. If you all need help, everyone is on alert. Six men finished the night shift and are asleep in the bunkhouse. Two are extending hog wire fencing around your new garden project. Randy and three men are in the barn putting up hay, but they'll be castrating calves this afternoon in the corral."

Jordan says, "Doris and Maria have experience far exceeding theirs. What do those men know about birthing babies?"

"Heating water, I suppose," Luke says with a smile.

Amy says, "Don't worry, sweetheart; I've heard the third time is a charm. I'll be fine. You go to town, be careful, and come home safely; I love you."

"To be clear, I wanted you to know help is available if you all need it. I didn't expect our hired hands to help with delivery. I expect they are as useless as I would be at delivering babies other than baby calves, colts, piglets, and lambs." Luke says. "I must get going; I love you."

After Luke is gone, Jordan asks, "Why would Luke go to those ribbon cuttings? Who is B.J., and explain *Honest Opinions?*"

Amy answers, "Okay, but I'll need a little time. An eight-year school with a qualified schoolmarm attracts young couples with children. Growing Addison and helping his friends succeed are

Luke's passions. But he is also serious about our boys getting a good education. Our school was a dilapidated small house on the edge of town. When the boys came home with stories about it being too small, cold, drafty, and wet when it rained, Luke decided he'd build a new one. The parents met secretly with the City Council and got their approval to name it *Garrelts School*."

When Doris comes in, they trade greetings, and Amy says, "Mom, I'm explaining to Jordan why Luke must be in town today. Then Amy turns to Jordan and says, " Luke needs to be present for the church ribbon cutting because he headed up the fundraising. When the Anthonys visited, Luke was just over halfway to his goal. Right after the Anthonys left, Luke announced the church building fund had met its goal. Everyone knew who made that happen. He'll thank the church contributors, especially George and Rosa, in absentia, for their considerable contribution toward saving our souls." They all chuckle.

"Regarding the school ribbon cutting, Luke didn't want to brag about his school, so he asked the schoolmarm, Mrs. Miller, to explain how the new school would provide the kids with a better learning experience.

Doris says, "He was good at public speaking ten years ago. His extemporaneous comments at Charlie's funeral were heartfelt with some humor; in a word, they were perfect. I've been to town with him quite a few times. He patiently talks to anyone who chases him down to inquire about a civic project or to put a bug in his ear about their pet project. He impressed me with being good with people, numbers, organizing, planning, and problem-solving. He's an entrepreneur, businessman, and politician who manages an oil and cattle empire in his spare time. He's come along way, and success has not gone to his head."

Jordan asks, "How many businesses are you and Luke involved in?"

Amy takes a deep breath, exhales, and says, "Oh, my. Well, quite a few. I'm not sure if I can remember them all. Luke first helpedFrank Weiner buy and relocate to a livery and blacksmith shop in Addison. He purchased several vacant city buildings owned by the State of Texas. People thought he was nuts. Luke would write to men he regarded highly, hoping they would consider a business opportunity in Addison. Luke would tell them what he thought could be successful and what he'd do to help them get started. I'm sure the chance to own a business, be the boss, and be more financially secure was compelling. I also believe that their trust and respect for Luke made the decision easier. With his friends, Luke makes business deals with a handshake. To help someone start a new business, Luke might co-sign a bank loan, invest his money, be a non-managing partner, or lease a building; whatever it takes. Typically, there isn't much in it for us, but that's not Luke's concern. His goal is to help his friends be successful. He knows everyone benefits from having one more successful business in town.

Amy continues, "Not long after we bought the ranch, Standard Oil showed up. Luke sold them the right to drill for oil on the acreage surrounding a surface leak he found. You can see exactly where it is. They fenced it, built several steam-powered contraptions to pump oil, and, within a year, we had extra money to invest. We used it to buy more land and to fund Luke's ambitions for Addison."

Jordan says, "There were only a couple of oil pumps here when L.J. was born, but now there's a bunch of them!"

Amy says, "The demand for oil keeps growing because women are giving up wood and candles for kerosene stoves and lanterns. Luke says Standard Oil distills kerosene from crude oil, like grain alcohol is distilled from fermented corn."

Amy says, "You asked about B.J. When Ben and Carol Abney came to see us, Luke complained about getting bogged down in contracts. Ben suggested that Luke talk to his oldest son, Ben Junior, who graduated from Ben's alma mater, the University of Pennsylvania, months earlier with a law degree. I'm sure you know why we call him B.J. Initially, Luke offered B.J. free office space, furniture, and a monthly salary. He drafts or reviews our purchase, sales, employee, and contractor agreements. Luke will review contracts with him if he's not tied up with another customer. Luke says our legal work is less than half of B.J.'s business. He's doing so well that Luke has him on a retainer, and he bills us for his time.

"Luke is good with numbers and keeps meticulous business records. He keeps his ledgers and operating cash in a large gun safe in the office next to our bedroom," Amy says, winking at Jordan.

Jordan asks, "He has a bunch of irons in the fire. How does he find the time?"

Amy answers, "Luke has hired enough talented, dependable, conscientious people to do whatever he wants with his day. Randy Sharp, formerly Governor George Anthony's groom, manages the ranch hands. He also purchases supplies and advises Luke on staffing needs, personnel issues, work plans, and other important matters. Luke had our lumber company add an office to Randy and Maria's home. They live next to Mom's cottage by the lake. Maria was Rosa Anthony's chief cook. Governor Anthony officiated at Maria and Randy's wedding in the Mansion.

Amy continues, "Our bunkhouse can sleep up to twenty. Maria has two ladies from town pick up food at Cooper's grocery store every morning and prepare two big meals. If the headcount isn't correct, they turn the leftovers into sandwiches for the stragglers. Luke stops by the grocery store on Friday and pays the bill. Randy and Maria have two daughters, almost the same age as our boys. Maria and I plan to be matchmakers when the time is right.

Amy repositions herself to be more comfortable and continues, "For the town to become more well-known and attract new residents, Luke talked the council into a Fourth of July barbecue picnic with fireworks. Folks can spend the day buying, selling, or trading their handicrafts on Main Street. Getting to know their fellow citizens has helped the community. It was a brilliant idea. He and Randy pit barbecue a steer, which volunteers make into sandwiches and serve with potato salad, beans, cake, and tea. It's advertised as 'Addison's July Fourth Powwow.'"

"Holy smoke, who pays for all that?" Doris asks.

"Luke supplies the beef, and the city has fundraisers during the year to cover the rest, Amy says. "Fundraising didn't quite cover it this year, so Luke did."

"Luke has convinced many friends that Addison has good business opportunities. He has kept every promise he made to those who took his advice, and they have done the same.

"One example is Hank Pryor opening a branch bank for his grandson to manage. Another is Reba and Rudy married and bought the Addison Hotel from the State with a loan from Luke. It's now the R&R Hotel & Steak House. The Third's eldest son runs the Kiowa trading post. People have come from Amarillo and all around Addison to buy their crafts. Howard Johnson, the Pinkerton man with Rosa and Susan when they were nearly abducted, was elected.

County Sheriff. No one knew Howard, so Luke attended every one of his stump speeches to endorse him.

"George wasn't elected to a second term and left the Mansion in January '79. Luke traveled to Topeka at the end of '78 to talk to George's employees about opportunities in Addison. That's how he got Randy, Maria, and Bernard; a few others, like Howard, trickled in later. That would not have been possible without the oil money.

"When Randy and Maria came here, they lived in a tent until Luke, Randy, and the ranchhands built them a home. Bernard has a ladies' clothing store; he has an eye for fashion and is extraordinarily relatable. Bernard rents a building from us and lives in the back. Luke made Bernard an interest-free fifteen-year loan based on the price he paid the State. In a few more years, Bernard will own the building!

"Raymond James, George's butler, manages the train depot. He lives in a home our ranch hands built near the depot. Dick Pryor, Amarillo's former sheriff, decided not to run for a fifth term after his wife's death. He and Luke became partners in a store called Guns and Ammo. Dick lives in the back and is sweet on a widow he hired to help run the store. Joe Stout and Luke are partners in the Feed and Tack store, and one of Joe's sons-in-law runs it for them.

"Ralph Barr and Luke are partners in a store that sells farm tools and hardware. Ralph is the Pinkerton man who accompanied us on the Pullman from Dodge to Amarillo; he lives on the store's second floor." Then Amy asks Doris, "Mom, is it okay if I tell Jordan that Ralph is sweet on you?"

Doris answers, "Jordan, Ralph wants to be my third husband. What do you think of that?"

Jordan says, "I met him. He is a very nice man and handsome. Have you accepted his proposal?"

"I told him I needed time. I will eventually surrender to his charms. Right now, I'm enjoying the chase," Doris says.

Jordan says, "I'm happy for you."

Amy says, "Ralph is practically part of the family."

Jordan asks, "Why is Luke so ENTHUSIASTIC about Addison being successful? Perhaps DRIVEN would have been a better word choice."

"Luke thinks he's earning redemption," Amy says.

Jordan quickly asks, "Redemption for what?"

Amy says, "That's difficult for me to explain and maybe harder for you to understand. Luke looks hard on the outside, but inside, he's as soft as a marshmallow. His nature is to respect and help anyone of good character, which he believes is God's expectation. The afternoon of my Father's funeral, the Fourth of July in 1877, we discussed our religious beliefs on the front porch of Doris's house. Luke said his father told him a man worthy of the Kingdom of Heaven does not lie, cheat, or steal. Luke said he promised his father he would only do those things if necessary to protect himself or his loved ones. That seemed like a high standard, and I decided Luke exceeded my second hurdle for marrying material right then."

"What was the first hurdle?" Jordan asked.

"Being extraordinarily handsome," Amy answered. "At the risk of sounding selfish, Luke spends more time in town helping others than with me, but I've learned to live with that because, at night, he's mine. His only character flaws are that he is fearless and a workaholic."

Jordan says, "I agree Luke is fearless and stays busier than a one-armed paper hanger."

Amy says, "After I became aware of Luke's tendency not to shy away from dangerous situations, I asked him why. He said there were two reasons. One was his inability to turn his back on a situation where ruthless, violent men would harm innocent people. The other reason was that his skill with firearms gave him a considerable advantage. I recall he said something like, 'The men I confront are not in a fair fight.'"

Amy continues, "Ben Abney wrote a story based on Luke's heroics in one of those ten-cent Western novels called *The Lone Rider*. The hero in the story is a man named Henry Colt. I have a copy of it on my credenza. It's an exaggerated story about how Luke stopped an attempted robbery of the First National Bank of Amarillo in '77. You're welcome to read it, but I forbid you to tell anyone who the story's hero is."

"I forgot I was supposed to explain why Luke needs redemption. Before we married, Luke told me, OH, MY GOD! PLEASE... stop kicking!" Amy pauses for a minute, and the baby stops. She says, "Luke didn't say, 'stop kicking.' I'll start over; before we married, he told me he didn't regret anything he'd ever done; however, that changed during my first trip to Addison. Mom, does the name Tom Addison ring a bell?"

"Yes, his office burned down; they found some personal items that confirmed his remains were in a gun safe," Doris says.

Amy says, "That's right, and Luke was responsible for the fire. Before judging him, you must talk with Jordan. She'll explain how her husband, Jesse Booth, was assassinated at the direction of that vile, greedy, ruthless man. Luke did something no other man dared to do. Mr. Addison's death brought closure for Jordan, several other widows, and their family members.

"Luke told me he never regretted avenging Jesse's death. He said it was gratifying and calming, but those feelings changed. Here's how that happened. Luke wanted my approval before bidding on the J&J property. Therefore, we needed to know its condition, which could sway my interest and affect our bid amount.

"After talking to citizens and merchants, Luke became concerned that he had upended the lives of the people of Addison to the extent that it could end the town's existence. I was in on several of those conversations. People believed the fledgling little town could not flourish if Tom Addison stayed in control, but they questioned its ability to survive without his money. West Texas ghost towns are not uncommon. Most thought the fire that killed Tom Addison and the tornado that killed the mayor, sheriff, and Tom's three convicts gave those men the justice they deserved.

"In late July of '77, after we decided how much to bid on the two properties, I asked Luke if we could afford the land and a starter herd of cows." Amy winks at Jordan because she knows, at the time, they had plenty of cash to do that. Amy continues, "Luke said we did and asked if I'd be okay with investing whatever we could spare to help the town prosper. He argued that a town with successful businesses offering goods and services was a worthy investment. I told him it was a noble cause, and I would support him. "What Luke has achieved in the past ten years is remarkable. He believes God or Saint Peter is judging him and keeping score. Luke studied the Bible and learned about Paul's letters to the Romans, where he quoted Christ, 'Never avenge yourself; vengeance is mine, and I will repay.'

"I'm sure Luke believes he's in trouble with the Lord and hopes his civic projects and kindness to others will be redemption enough for his act of vengeance against Tom Addison. He takes pride in helping others and derives satisfaction from it, so his guilt is a positive thing for the community. I think Luke is eligible for Sainthood; I can't believe the Devil would want him."

Jordan teases Amy, saying, "There already is a Saint Luke." Then she gets emotionally serious and says, "Luke helped me more than I can describe. I was a woman obsessed with revenge, to the point of being mentally handicapped. Luke provided me with closure for Jesse's death that I could never have achieved through the legal system. When my father read about bad men in the Fort Worth newspaper, he'd tell me, 'In the absence of good men, evil flourishes.' Luke is one of the good men Dad had in mind. I also know Luke has a good heart and strongly believes in God's word. And Amy, I agree wholeheartedly with what you have said about my big brother."

Amy says, "Luke's passion for the city's growth never diminishes. Within a few weeks of finishing a project, he'll lie awake and stare at the ceiling. I've learned what that behavior means, and it's never worth losing sleep. When we talk, it's always the same. He's heard of a city problem or a need and is trying to determine the best way to solve it. When he decides what he wants to do, he asks me if it's okay because his solutions almost always take money. I always say, 'Yes,' and he goes to sleep. The problem is that the cycle starts over within a matter of weeks. I've decided he's on an endless search for ways to repay a debt that no one knows he owes. Each project gives him the sense that he's inching closer to redemption for that night in June of '77. Does that make sense?"

Jordan said, "That helps to explain what I observed when I went to town with him a few days ago. I was curious about what he did there. I was concerned that someone might recognize me, but I saw no one I remembered or who remembered me. We were in town for most of the afternoon. Everyone could recognize Luke from a distance, and they'd run him down to discuss city politics, problems, solutions, and projects.

"Folks wanted to press his flesh and ask his opinion on various subjects. I was surprised by his knowledge and understanding of local and non-local issues. Folks know he cares because he asks questions and can rephrase their concern concisely, so they know he's listening. My observation is that he adopts their concern. I say that because everyone thanked him for his commitment to improving the city. That behavior seems extraordinary for a farm kid who was a Sharpshooter in the North-South War at age sixteen."

Amy sighs and says, "Jordan, there are two reasons for what you saw. First, he is a voracious reader; his office bookshelf and newspaper subscriptions are proof of that. Second, six months ago, the mayor had astroke and couldn't speak. Since Luke was a city council member, the other councilors asked him to complete the mayor's term as Mayor Pro Tem. Luke agreed and asked Ralph Barr to complete his councilman term. Luke will probably get roped into running for mayor next year."

Jordan says, "You still haven't explained what Luke called *Honest Opinions*."

Amy says, "Oh, that's a fun thing that Luke has the school kids involved in. Luke has wanted a weekly newspaper for years. During our second year here, he bought the pile of ashes that had been the Addison Cattle Company's office. He rebuilt it, but no one was interested in renting it due to its history. So, Luke bought a Sherwin printing press, hoping to turn it into a newspaper office. He advertised for an editor and even asked George for help. A few interested parties showed up, but they thought the town was too small to support a newspaper.

"Here's where the story gets good. Our new schoolmarm, Mrs. Miller, knew how to set type. She asked Luke if she could use the press for schoolwork; of course, Luke said she could. After losing sleep for a few nights, Luke asked Mrs. Miller if she would help the kids print a monthly newspaper. He wanted the kids to be the paper's reporters. He asked Mrs. Miller to teach them the fundamentals of reporting, turn them loose to gather information, interview residents, and help them write their articles. It became the talk of the town, with businesses and individuals paying to advertise their products. The kids sell it for two cents, and they keep a penny. So far, they have managed to cover the cost of paper and ink and have a little in the bank. The kids are so proud.

"Bernard's Fashion Shop is next door. Luke began paying Bernard to collect the advertising and sales revenue, purchase supplies, and maintain the books. Bernard is now setting the type and operating the press rather than Mrs. Miller. So, Luke got his newspaper, after all. When the kids took it home to show their parents an article they authored, some learned that their parents couldn't read, so they used it to teach them. Everyone is a winner; it's like breeding puppies. *Honest Opinions* is just another of Luke's many success stories."

Jordan asks, "How did it get the name *Honest Opinions*?"

"Mrs. Miller wanted the kids to name it," Amy says.

Doris, who has been quietly listening for quite a while, says, "They came up with a clever name."

Amy says, "Folks tell me they like *Honest Opinions* because it's only local news. The kids don't care about politics. Citizens who care about Addison now know more about the town's problems and the planned solutions. The City Council says it helps them prioritize budget money. One of the kid reporters is responsible for interviewing the Mayor every month! The title of that article is *What's Happening*."

Jordan says, "Do you think Luke knew that kid reporters would generate ideas to feed his passion for improving the town?"

"It's possible; he's clever in that way," Amy says.

Doris says, "Jordan, we must find time for you to tell me about Tom Addison."

Jordan says, "I look forward to an opportunity to do that, but it will have to wait until this baby decides the room in Amy's belly is no longer adequate."

Amy says, "Jordan, that cannot come soon enough. Mom, this conversation was long overdue. I'm so relieved and happy to have aired it out." Jordan and Doris quietly reflect on Amy's comment.

Doris says, "I have one question. Why do you keep Luke's old boots on the back porch? They look like the ones he wore to Dad's funeral. I remember you buying him a new pair at Brotherton's after the funeral."

Jordan looks at Amy, winks, and says, "It looks like you're using them for rag storage."

Amy says, "You're right; I am. And Mom, those boots bring back memories that I cherish. If I throw them in our waste pit and set fire to them, my memories will go up in smoke."

Jordan winks at Amy and says, "I know what you mean. I keep things in my jewelry box to remind me of people and events."

"Mom, you put my high school academic awards on the kitchen wall of your cottage. Is that any different than me keeping Luke's old boots?"

"You're right. I'm going to go talk to Maria and sort out our responsibilities when this reluctant baby decides to join us."

Jordan asks, "Doris, I have a question before you go. What is your impression of the trip you took on the Transcontinental Railroad to San Francisco last year?"

Doris says, "The scenery, the weather, and the city were incomparable."

"I must get J.R. on that train. We don't go anywhere because he stays so busy. What's the point of making money if you don't take the time to enjoy it?" Jordan laments.

Amy says, "Luke often talks about that trip. Because of that, I think J.R. would enjoy it too. I suggest you buy the tickets without asking; he'll find the time. Travel stimulates my curiosity and awakens my senses, making me feel more alive. Travel is fulfilling and relaxing. J.R. could probably use some time away from his job. Seeing something is ten times better than reading another person's impression. I read that a trip around the world is considered equivalent to a college education."

Doris leaves for the kitchen; Amy and Jordan smile at each other with raised eyebrows. When Doris is out of the room, they quietly compliment each other on keeping their promise to Luke and doing it without lying to Doris.

Amy asks. "Do you ever get to see Ray and Virginia Simms?"

"Virginia comes into the bank at least once a week. I'm not in the customer part of the bank that much, but when I am, we chat. Ray has become the top auctioneer in the Bottoms and cries two or three weekly cattle sales. Our bank promotes an annual charity auction. Ray volunteers to be our auctioneer. The money raised is used to offer college scholarships that renew for three years if the recipient keeps a B average."

Amy asks, "What does Ray auction at that event?"

"Businessmen and city and county officials who volunteer to perform six hours of work on a mutually agreeable Saturday. Last year, the Equestrian Club bought JR and his two VPs to clean horse stalls for six hours," Jordan answers while laughing.

Amy says, "I can't wait to tell Luke about this. He's the organizer and president of a Moore County organization that helps people who fall on hard times. Usually, the club supports widows and orphans, but sometimes it's an entire family. Luke is always looking for fun ways to raise money. The idea of auctioning businessmen and public officials is perfect. That idea may solve the community fund-raising problem he's working on. It would keep him busy promoting a fun project and engaging the community leaders. Thank you, Jordan, thank you!"

Jordan says, "You triggered my conscience when you told your mother how refreshing it was to clear the air about something you hadn't talked about with her. There's something about Luke and me that you and I have never discussed in the ten years we've been sisters-in-law. However, Luke may have already told you."

"You all have a secret I don't know about? Amy asks.

Jordan answers with a question, "Have you ever asked Luke about his family tree?"

"No, never," Amy says. "I didn't because it wouldn't have made any difference. My father was German, and Doris was Irish. I had always assumed they came to America for a better life. Luke never asked about my family. What he knows about my father, he learned from Doris."

Jordan says, "I guessed that you probably had not asked Luke, and I'm glad his genealogy doesn't matter. I want to share a piece of our family history. But before I do, you must agree to ask Luke about it, but not until I have returned to Kansas City. I know he would never keep the truth from you. I want you to hear it from Luke so you can tell him it would have made no difference if you had known on the day you met. Say you will do that, and I'll tell you about a pact we made when we were not much more than kids."

"Sure, I'm not afraid of asking Luke anything. You've piqued my curiosity; please continue and hurry. I'd like to hear this deep, dark secret before this baby decides it's time to come out," Amy says.

Jordan says, "Our Mother, Naomi, was full-blood Cherokee. Naomi and Pheobe, Luke's stepmother, were sisters. Luke's Father was an Irishman, and his genes watered downour Mother's Indian genes so much that Luke looked like any European. My Father was of English and German descent, and I inherited the same genetic pattern of looking European.

"I find it remarkable that at ten years of age, our Mother walked over one thousand miles from Northeastern Alabama to Fort Gibson in Oklahoma with her sister Phoebe. They buried both parents along the way, and another four thousand didn't make it. Due to their resistance to being relocated, President Martin Van Buren had the military use force. Our mother told of the horrors of 15,000 people forced to leave their land at the point of rifles with bayonets. The Cherokee named their forced march "The *Trail of Tears.*"

"At age twelve, I wrote to Luke using information my father knew about his adoptive family's last name and their location. Luke showed up only two weeks later. He rode Smokey over three hundred miles to Fort Worth. He said his stepparents had died earlier that year in a buckboard accident. Luke hired a neighbor to sharecrop his land and planned to enlist in the war before getting my letter. I tried to talk him out of the war, but it was useless. He stayed with us for several days and constantly questioned my father about our mother. Luke found two things so interesting that he took notes. They were her memories of walking the Trail of Tears and her decision to leave the reservation. There were hard truths in her memories.

"As this country expanded to the West, there were few single white women, so it was common for European immigrants to marry Indian women. Consequently, thousands like Luke and I were scattered across the Plains, but life among racists was not easy. Luke and I discussed the treatment experienced by Indians, even for European-looking half-breeds who identified as Indian. So, we made a pact not to discuss our roots with anyone. Sweeping our kinship and ethnicity under the carpet didn't mean we were ashamed of either. We agreed to it because we thought it would simplify our lives. We now know that was a good decision because we didn't have to experience the cruelty of being an Indian in a white man's world."

Amy says, "Now that I know, I'm even more proud of you all. Thank you for telling me. I will find a way to discuss family trees with Luke after you return to Kansas City. He will never know we had this discussion. I'll tell him I better understand his motivation to do some of his projects, which makes me love him even more."

Jordan says, "That's a good plan."

Amy says, "It wouldn't have changed my mind about marrying him if he had told me he was from Mars. Does J.R. know your little secret?"

Jordan says, "He doesn't. I liked J.R. from the moment I met him."

Interrupting Jordan, Amy confesses, "Oh, I know that feeling!"

Jordan continues, "J.R.'s Eastern upbringing was initially a concern because I thought folks in that culture were prejudiced toward everyone. When he didn't inquire about my family or first marriage, I assumed that was because they were dead. Since I looked, talked, dressed, and worshiped like a European, I think J.R. believed I was. I am half-European. J.R. has never said or done anything to make me think he is prejudiced toward Indians. However, I'll be forthright if he ever asks about my heritage.

"Amy, I chose to get into this discussion because your situation differs from mine. Luke has shown great empathy for Indians. Due to his roots, he naturally developed an interest in their struggle. I thought you would better understand his motivation by knowing our heritage, hearing about our twenty-year-old pledge, and understanding our reasoning behind it.

"Over the seven years that Jesse and I were married, Luke would visit for a week each year and talk for hours about the abuse of the Indians. Luke's stepfather, Myron, had ingrained in him feelings of sympathy for the oppressed and less fortunate.

"Myron disdained the government's theory of Manifest Destiny, which was the belief that God wanted European settlers to spread across the West and displace the Indians.[34] When you told me thirty minutes ago that Luke successfully petitioned the government on behalf of the Kiowa, I was not surprised."

Amy says, "What you have said explains many things. It's no accident that Luke has a small herd of buffalo and delivers a few to the Kiowa reservation for their annual Sun Dance. Also, there's a Kiowa trading post on Main Street; the yearly Fourth of July celebration is called a Powwow. One of Luke's best friends is a Tribal Chieftain, and Luke is an honorary Sub-Chief with a Kiowa name. That's why he dedicated much of his time and talent to writing and traveling to Washington, D.C., for nearly three years.

"A while ago, I mentioned Luke's monthly letters to Washington. The letters did not generate interest until George Anthony recommended that Luke send a copy to the *Washington Post*. After several of them appeared in the paper, Luke was invited to present his case to the Department of the Interior. That meeting triggered several more trips to Washington, and he took Chiefs, Sub-Chiefs, and military officers to testify. Their presentations had examples of broken treaties, newspaper articles of massacres, the government's Indian death statistics, eyewitness testimony, and military documents and records exposing abusive policies and punishment.

"In his presentation, Luke argued that George Washington believed Europeans were like visitors in the home of the first people to have inhabited America for centuries. Specifically, Washington said the Indians were "prior occupants" and should be considered foreign nations rather than subjects of the state.[35] In the archives, Luke's attorneys found George Washington's letter to the Cherokee Nation in 1796. The letter promised the Cherokee that if they did their part of the treaty, the government would enforce it and ensure their survival. Washington said, 'To not do so would be a stain on the character of the nation.'[36] But that isn't what happened after Washington left office in 1797. Indian attorneys claimed the Relocation Act of 1830 broke Washington's promise and violated the Fifth Amendment's right to fair compensation for the government's property exchange. They filed lawsuits accusing Congress and the Supreme Court of violating the U.S. Constitution by failing to keep every treaty since George Washington's time and for nonperformance of the Relocation Act Treaties. If you wonder how I know all this in such detail, Luke practiced his speeches to Congress on me. I became familiar enough to tell him when he left something out.

"The squeaking wheel gets the grease, is the best way I can describe what happened. The government said, 'We've had enough of your petitioning and lawsuits; if you shut down both, you win.' As I said earlier, that changed reservation life for all the tribes in Oklahoma's Indian Territory. Luke didn't get everything he wanted, but the Bureau of Indian Affairs agreed to new positions in the organization that only Native Americans could hold. So, Luke hopes that, with time, change can come from inside the organization."

Jordan says, "The painting of Luke on your bedroom wall must be from a few years ago; gosh, he was handsome!

Amy says, "Rosa Anthony had it made for me. She had hired an artist to paint George and her from a photograph taken with them on the mansion's front porch. She also had him paint Luke from a picture I gave her the morning we left Topeka on the Pullman. A photographer at the Cattlemen's Inn took that picture the evening before I met you. I asked Luke to sit for two shots. I gave Rosa her pick. Rosa's painting of Luke is life-size, and I understand why. He has more whiskers because Rosa told the painter to make him look rugged and intimidating."

Jordan says, "I love the picture." After a minute of listening to Amy deal with labor pain, Jordan says, "I'm going to see if Maria has fresh coffee; can I bring you a cup?"

"Thank you, no," Amy says with a groan. When Jordan is gone, Amy rolls off the couch to the floor, gets up clumsily, and pushes the big Kiowa chair Jordan had been sitting on twenty feet to its usual place. She stands motionless momentarily and shouts, "Jordan, my water just broke! Tell Doris and Maria the baby is on the way! Meet me in the baby's bedroom!"

After six more hours of labor, Amy is nursing little Charlene and says, "Daddy got the little girl he wanted."

Doris says, "When didn't Daddy get what he wanted?"

While Amy was in labor, Luke was in town making his stops. The news around town was about cattle rustlers rounding up calves in weaning pastures. Luke remembers Randy saying he started weaning the late spring calves yesterday, so the L&A is a prime target."

Luke gets home just before dark, sees Randy, and shouts, "Has Amy delivered?"

"Yes!"

"What did we get?"

"I'm not telling; you'll have to find out for yourself. Go on; I'll unload the buckboard."

"Thanks; it's only groceries. Please do me a favor and see that Bonner has what he needs for the night. How many calves are in the weaning pasture?"

Randy answers, "60...I'll take care of Bonner; you get on in there!"

Luke runs to the long hallway with six bedrooms, all of them along one side. He finds everyone in the third bedroom, two doors from their bedroom. Doris hands Luke their newborn, and Amy says, "Say hello to Charlene!"

Sitting beside Amy on the bed with the boys kneeling before him, Luke kisses his daughter's forehead every few seconds and talks to Charlene with his eyes full of tears, as is everyone's. Charlene studies her father's face with wide-open, bright blue eyes. Before falling asleep, she grips his little finger, looks into his eyes, and smiles. Luke senses something uniquely special about their first encounter.

Luke tells Amy about the board meeting, ribbon cuttings, Jim Baird accepting their offer, and the phone calls to J.R. and the Anthonys. Then he says, "I'm working the morning shift in the weaning pasture for Roger; he has dysentery. Oh, I almost forgot. The phone company will start running a line to us next week."

Amy says, "We'll be right here in the morning. I moved the baby bed here so you'd be far enough away that her crying wouldn't wake you. Be careful out there; I love you."

"I love you, and I thank you for this beautiful baby girl who looks like you right down to her blond hair, blue eyes, and a turned-up nose," Luke says.

Doris is sitting in a Kiowa-made rocking chair in the corner of the room, listening; she adds, "I love that their birthdays are the same; that's one less date for my old brain to remember."

Jordan says, "Luke, you sitting on the bed and surrounded by your family is a picture I will never forget."

Maria says, "Luke, you have a beautiful daughter."

"Thank you, Maria. But she's no more beautiful than your girls," Luke says. He hands Charlene to L.J., turns to Amy, and says, "I'm going to get some dinner, do some paperwork, and prepare to spend the morning scaring coyotes away from the weaning pasture. You have made me extremely proud; thank you. You now have one more birthday party that will be easy for us to remember in our old age. Hopefully, Charlene will let you get some sleep; I'll see you in the morning," and Luke leaves for the kitchen.

Chapter 43: The Weaning Pasture
August 21st, 1887, Continues

After a cold dinner of Maria's tasty fried chicken and garden vegetables, Luke sheds the business suit and hand-tooled cowhide gun belt and holster, a gift from The Third. He puts on clean yet well-worn and comfortable work clothes. He goes to his office and reads until almost midnight. When he decides it's time to get out to the weaning pasture, he thinks about what to take if he's there until sunrise. He opens the closet door and gets his Henry rifle, bandolier, Colt Peacemaker, buffalo coat, a soft rag, and a small can of gun oil. He wipes the dust off the rifle's barrel and gunsights and goes to the back porch to fill a canteen and get the horses' poncho.

Luke walks to the forty-acre weaning pasture. The calves were weaned from their mothers a day and a half ago. He easily finds Rodger, tells him why he's there, and asks Roger to leave the calves with him for the night. Luke decides the best place to hide is in the center of the field in the tallest grass. He's on the west side of the creek that carries overflow from the lake with his name.

The calves are all together in the southeast corner of the pasture, where the fence corner extends into the shallow edge of the lake. They're standing belly-deep in water, looking for their mothers and bawling mournfully. Luke puts on his Kiowa coat, spreads the poncho over the grass, sits to avoid the saddle hole, wraps the ends around him, and takes a few minutes to lubricate the rifle's moving parts. When finished, he works the lever action to ensure the mechanism operates smoothly without sticking. Then he loads the magazine and chambers a cartridge. He didn't ask Roger to stay because he doesn't expect his hires to be gun hands, although he knows some are.

Luke holds his solid gold pocket watch, an Elgin 21-jewel timepiece, with the hands facing the moon; it's after one in the morning. After listening to Cicadas rub their legs together and calves bawling for an hour, Luke sees something at the northeast corner of the pasture. He can make out the silhouettes of men on horseback in the moonlight. Two men dismount and cut the four strands of barbed wire, nicknamed the Devil's rope, on the right side of the corner post. They pull the wires from the opening so the calves and their horses can pass without becoming entangled. Luke lies back, disappearing into the grass. They pass him on the opposite side of the overflow stream, riding slowly toward the calves.

After they pass, Luke picks up everything, wades across the narrow creek in two steps, and runs to the corner with the downed wire. The bawling calves drown out what little noise Luke makes running through the grass.

Luke drapes the horse poncho over the corner post and the two bracing posts at 45-degree angles. He positions the poncho's saddle hole so he can look and shoot through it. Luke folds and wraps the Kiowa coat around his upper body to have four layers of buffalo hide to absorb a bullet. He kneels behind the corner post and leans to the right to look through the saddle hole; he feels well-hidden and waits. The moon is not full, but there is sufficient light in the clear night sky to see at a distance.

Soon, the calves come into view, and Luke estimates there are about thirty in a tight group. The rustlers are close behind, but spread out. Luke thinks, *I need to have all the rustlers close enough so I can fire five to six accurate shots in thirty seconds.* Luke changes position so that the left half of his body is behind the center post. He removes his hat so the top of his head is behind the bracing post. With his chest and abdomen protected by four layers of buffalo hide, he feels well-prepared for the impending shootout.

When the calves are about to walk past Luke through the opening on his right, he opens fire. Before the rustlers can return fire, the two closest to him fall from their saddles. Luckily, their horses run out of Luke's line of sight. The other four see the flashes coming from the corner post and decide, rather than fleeing for safety, they will kill the shooter or die trying. They begin firing pistols at the corner post, and Luke centers himself behind it. Their shots are wildly inaccurate due to the distance and being on horseback. The two riders on his right decide to flank him, and he drops them when they come into view with three shots in rapid succession. The last two men are now front and center and too close for him to stay put, so he rolls to his left six feet from the corner post. Lying in the grass, Luke is hidden behind the poncho hanging over the left brace post. The rustlers finish emptying their pistols only thirty feet from the poncho. When Luke hears repeated clicking, the sound of empty cylinders, he sits up and shoots one man in the center of his chest. The last rustler has holstered his pistol and is retrieving his rifle from its scabbard when Luke pulls the trigger on him. Before falling off his saddle, he says, "Clever bastard," causing Luke to smile.

The frightened calves and riderless horses are running toward the lake. Luke stands behind the post center, looking carefully at each body; one is moaning. Within minutes, Randy rides up bareback, followed by ranch hands streaming in one and two at a time. While sliding off his horse, Randy asks, "*Qué pasa*, boss?"

Luke begins loading the rifle's magazine out of habit and explains to Randy, "In town today, I heard stories about rustlers stealing weaning calves from ranches in the county. I put two and two together and figured we could be next. I knew Charlene wouldn't let me sleep, so I came here.

"You can mend the barbed wires, but leave the rustlers where they lay until Howard sees them. The smell of blood will attract coyotes, so you'll need to leave a few men here to protect the bodies. I'll bring the hounds to help. The men guarding the bodies must keep a safe distance because the one over there moaning may last until sunrise, but not much longer."

Luke asks Randy if all the off-duty men are present. After taking a head count, Randy tells Luke that they are. Luke addresses his hired hands loudly, saying, "Men, Sheriff Howard Johnson will be here in the morning. He's an ex-Pinkerton man and an old friend of Randy's and mine. If he asks questions or wants a statement, cooperate fully, but only talk about what you've seen since getting here. Don't guess what happened before you arrived; I'll report on that. I want to hush this incident up in case these rustlers have friends. Other than Sheriff Johnson, don't talk to another soul about this. If I find out that you have, I'll fire you. If someone in the house asks about gunfire, say a pack of coyotes was stalking the weaning pen, and I fired shots to scare them off. Roger, Amy might ask how you're feeling. To not worry her, particularly in her condition, I told a white lie. I said you weren't feeling well, so I volunteered to fill in for you."

"Gotcha, boss. There's no sense worrying, Amy," Roger says.

Luke advises Randy, "Be sure the hands working the night shift hear this message in the morning."

Randy replies, "Will do, but why weren't we asked to help?"

Luke answers so that all will hear, "I don't want anyone injured and unable to work. For this ranch to run smoothly, everyone needs to be healthy. I'm going to get the hounds and come right back." He walks to the barn, gets the hounds, and leads them back to the weaning pasture. He tells the men fixing the fence, "The dogs will only sniff the bodies. They'll try to find the scent of a coyote. If they pick up a trail, they'll take off; trying to stop them is nonsense. They'll eventually return to the barn." After giving that advice, Luke goes to the bunkhouse for a few hours of sleep.

The following morning, after her breakfast, Luke coos Charlene until she falls asleep. Then he leaves to check on his greyhounds. Luke finds them less energetic in the barn due to their lack of sleep and early morning excitement. Each dog has a couple of bloody toes, indicating they were probably in a chase, but nothing to prove they were in a fight. Luke cleans and dresses the bloody toes. Randy shows up with Howard and two of his deputies at about ten o'clock. Luke gives them a walk-through of the events in the weaning pasture and insists that the deputies not talk about where they found the rustlers. After the deputies leave for town, Howard, Randy, and Luke go to Randy's office. Luke draws a picture of the pasture with the position of the bodies, and Howard takes his affidavit. When Howard finishes taking Luke's statement, Randy asks, "Howard, I heard you telling your men you thought the rustlers were the Burks. What do you know about them?"

Howard says, "The Burk gang is three brothers and three brothers-in-law with a hideout across the border in Mexico. They engage in numerous illicit activities, but their specialty is cattle rustling and rebranding. Their warrants say they're wanted dead or alive. Don't quote me, but I believe the bounty on each man is $300 unless it has increased recently. Luke, how did you know the rustlers would try your weaning pasture next?"

Luke explains, "I didn't, Howard, but given the facts, it seemed logical. I was in town to attend the ribbon-cutting for the school and church. I heard stories about rustlers stealing calves from weaning pastures. Randy had started weaning some calves the day before, so they'd bawl all night. Any rustler worth his salt knows the sound of opportunity, and you know the L&A had to be on their list. Yesterday afternoon, Amy delivered a beautiful baby girl; we named her Charlene. I knew she wouldn't let me sleep, so spending the night with bawling calves was a good trade-off. I suppose Charlene should get the credit for stopping the rustlers. If the rustlers are the Burk's outfit, give Randy the reward money. And Randy, I want you to divide it equally among yourself and all our employees, both men and women."

"Thanks, boss!" Randy says enthusiastically.

Luke looks at Howard and says, "Can you report that this Burk gang died someplace other than on my ranch?"

"That's not a problem," Howard says, "The Burk gang is wanted dead or alive, so my report will simply say that an anonymous bounty hunter delivered them to my office."

"That's perfect," Luke says with a handshake and slap on Howard's shoulder. "While I was in town on Sunday, I stopped at B.J.'s office and learned that Jim and Martha Baird accepted Amy's and my offer for their ranch. Do you recall that I once told you if I ever needed two good men or Randy turned me down, you'd be the one I'd call?"

"I sure do," Howard says.

"You're an excellent county sheriff, and I'd like to think I had a hand in helping you get elected," Luke says. "But now, I need your help. I'd like you to resign and come to work for me, managing the Baird Ranch. I plan to call it the Little L&A, though it's not so little. Naturally, you'd have to live there. I've heard it's a roomy house. They raised four or five children in it."

Luke says, "You would report to Randy until you get both feet on the ground. When that day comes, you will report to me. I will double your sheriff's pay because the job is twenty-four hours a day and seven days a week. Every year, at the end of January, you'll receive a bonus of one percent of the previous year's total profit for both ranches, excluding the oil revenue. That is total revenue minus all expenses. Of course, you can quit anytime and give up your bonus. Your bonus this year will be prorated based on the number of weeks you're employed. If you want a herd, I'll allow you to keep a hundred branded cows with mine, and my bulls can service them. You must brand your calves before weaning them."

Luke continues, "This morning, I asked Randy what he thought about you managing the Baird ranch and temporarily reporting to him. You'll be glad to know he wholeheartedly supports the idea. There will be many decisions for the two of you to make, but I'm confident you will do that. However, should you ever feel you're out on a limb by yourselves, talk to me; I'm always available in the evening. On the last Thursday of each month, we will meet in my office at three so you can brief me on your problems and plans for the next month, and vice versa.

"This is a family decision, so I'll wait two weeks for your answer. If you accept, the County Commissioners will want you to stay on until they find your replacement. I can apply a little pressure, so keep me apprised of their progress. The Baird ranch closing is September 30th; that's a Friday. So, I need to hire someone by then or manage it until I do."

Howard says, "I'd love to work with you all, so I want to say yes. However, you're right; I have a wife and kids to consider; it's also a significant life change for them. I must spend a day or two on the property and discuss my concerns with Randy. It would be ideal if Randy and Maria could join June and me for a one-day visit."

Randy says, "That's an excellent idea. I want to understand its size and get a feel for possible problems," Randy says.

Howard confesses, "Randy, I have much to learn; I hope my questions won't try your patience."

Randy confesses, "You needn't worry about my patience. If we pull together, the load won't be as heavy, and I think we can have fun doing it. You'll find that working for a fair man like Luke is a dream job."

Luke says, "I'll talk to Mr. Baird about you all getting a tour of his ranch this week. I'm going to see him tomorrow. He signed the offer B.J. drafted, but I want to shake his hand while looking him in the eye.

"Howard, so there's no misunderstanding, B.J. will draft my offer as an employment contract. It's a one-year agreement that renews automatically on January 1st unless you give me written notice on or before December 1st that you want to renegotiate or terminate employment. That's the same for everyone working for the L&A. Randy has a paymaster overseeing weekly employee pay. We have several pay classifications, all based on a daily rate. The exceptions are you two; you're both on a fixed weekly salary.

"While you all have different ranches to manage, I expect you to coordinate the allocation of the ranch hands to maximize efficiency. No ranch hand will consider themself to be employed only by the L&A or the Little L&A; they are employees of both. Frequent rotation between the ranches will prove the point and create a more flexible workforce. I want you all to build one team, not two.

Luke continues, "Both of you will be allowed to take ten days of vacation each year, with pay." Both men look at each other and grin from ear to ear. Luke adds, "I expect you not to use your vacations until you are both comfortable with the team you have built. The other restrictions are that you schedule your vacation days during our slower periods, and you can't both be off at the same time. Please consider going somewhere you can relax and enjoy your family, which is why I wanted to do this. Randy, in your case, Maria will need to coordinate with Amy, but that will not be a problem. Do you have any questions?"

Howard says, "Luke, your plan strikes me as thoughtful and very tempting. If you can get us a tour of the Baird ranch this week, you'll have my answer a few days later and a month before your closing.

"Perfect, say hello to June for us," Luke says. They shake hands and leave Randy's office, each man feeling good about the meeting. Luke returns home to check on Amy, Charlene, and the boys. Randy finds Maria to tell her about Luke and Amy buying the Baird ranch, asking Howard to manage it, but reporting to him for a while, as well as his raise and ten days of paid vacation. Howard returns to the sheriff's office and then home to discuss Luke's surprise job offer with June and his children.

Chapter 44: Epilog - 1897

Between 1887 and 1897, L&A Enterprises matured into a substantial oil and cattle operation. This extraordinary growth was primarily due to Howard discovering another pool of dark goo on the Little L&A, having the same odor as Standard Oil's pump jacks and storage tanks. Rather than selling the mineral rights to Standard Oil, Luke asked L.J. and Charlie to form Garrelts Oil Production Company. Recently, their extraordinary success has been headlined in newspapers and on the cover of magazines from New York to California.

The burgeoning demand for beef, plus Luke's, Randy's, and Howard's leadership, has driven the expansion of the cattle operation to over 250,000 acres and a herd of 3,000, more than four times the size of the Addison ranch. The property east of Luke's Lake resembles a small village housing family members and married employees. Ralph and Doris are married and living in Doris' cottage. The old bunkhouse serves as a recreation center, where men can relax with a beer and enjoy playing card games, billiards, dominoes, and darts. The new bunkhouse resembles a hotel, complete with live-in cooks and housekeepers.

Luke's enthusiasm, commitment, and business sense are primarily responsible for Addison's population of over 4,000 city dwellers. The town has a train depot, a water tower, a sanitation department, a volunteer fire department, a chief of police, and three deputies. Luke has been reelected Mayor of Addison twice and is twelve weeks from retiring. In his second four-year term, he and Hank Pryor built a limestone bank with second-floor office space for L&A's executive officer, an accountant, four clerks, and B.J.'s law and real estate business. That building is between the new R&R Hotel and Steak House and next to, and architecturally matches, the police and sheriff's offices.

Luke is forty-eight, and leaders of the Texas Legislature have tried to persuade him to run for Governor. Recalling Rosa's advice, Amy told Luke, "You do not have my permission to run for governor," which settled the question.

Standard and Garrelt's Oil Companies pump 700 barrels per day of crude to a tank car loading rack on a Santa Fe spur located halfway between the ranch house and Addison's train depot.

L.J. is nineteen and married to Randy and Maria's eldest daughter, Hannah. George Anthony presided over their wedding in the church he and Rosa built. The kids are halfway to getting Luke and Amy, their first grandbaby.

L.J. and Charlie have matured into extraordinary young men. They will graduate with bachelor's degrees from the University of Texas at Austin within a year. L.J. with a Business Law degree, and Charlie with an Accounting degree. Upon graduation, they will work in the office space above the bank alongside Luke, Luke's accountant, his clerks, and B.J.

Randy and Howard manage over one hundred employees, including veterinarians, blacksmiths, mechanics, cowboys, cooks, former Pinkerton security guards, and skilled craftspeople. Luke insists that Indian applicants get hiring preference.

Luke's and Amy's current project is a community center that's supposed to open in a month. It was initially Amy's idea. Over time, she has developed Luke's passion for improving the city. She believed a theater with an elevated stage, seating for 300, curtains, and concessions would attract traveling shows, hopefully a Shakespearean troupe. Luke's interest was in having a bigger and more impressive gathering place for City Council meetings and ceremonial and social events.

Amy got the idea to build adjacent offices for two physicians and two dentists. While construction was in progress, she wrote to medical schools, hoping to recruit doctors by enticing them with a monthly income based on the number of subscribers to her medical plan. She offered free office space, equipment, and an initial supply of medicines and consumable supplies to get started.

Amy's medical plan provided unlimited access to medical doctors and dentists in exchange for a monthly fee. She found that mothers were eager to sign up, but getting their husbands to agree to a monthly payment took much more persuasion. Amy is optimistic that, with time, her idea will work, but until then, she plans to subsidize the doctor's monthly payments. The women in town are promoting Amy for the next mayoral election. It's less than three months away; her winning appears to be a sure thing; she's running unopposed.

Amy and Luke finally found time for their long-deferred vacation to the East, spending six weeks in New York City, Philadelphia, and Boston. While there, Luke caught a "history bug." He now enjoys educating others about "America's Birth" whenever asked about his trip to New York City.

Charlene, now known as Charlie, is fascinated with horses, cattle, and guns. She has a twenty-two caliber, pump-action Winchester and a chestnut Arabian gelding with white socks and a blonde mane and tail; she adores both. Charlie has loved horses since she was five and rides with no fear. Amy cringes watching her baby ride bareback at full gallop. However, Luke sees his daughter as becoming one with the gelding's athletic, powerful, rhythmic stride. With Luke's mentoring, she and her brothers will run L&A Enterprises one day.

Luke and Amy's passion for improving the health, wealth, and happiness of their children, employees, and the citizens of Addison is undiminished. Despite a single act of vengeance and rather sizable body count, St. Peter sees faithful Luke's moral integrity, resulting in a better life for all. Luke's odds of passing through the "Gates" are improving.

THE END

Endnotes

1 https://www.okhistory.org/publications/enc/entry.php?entry=NO001

2 https://en.wikipedia.org/wiki/Kansas_City_Stockyards

3 https://en.wikipedia.org/wiki/Names_of_the_American_Civil_War

4 https://www.history.com/topics/black-history/thirteenth-amendmen

5 https://en.wikipedia.org/wiki/Psalm_23

6 https://pestifier.com/how-fast-can-a-wasp-fly/

7 https://case.edu/ech/articles/w/wagon-and-carriage-industry

8 https://www.jacobbromwell.com/pages/our-story

9 https://en.wikipedia.org/wiki/BatMasterson

10 https://education.nationalgeographic.org/resource/texas-becomes-state

11 https://www.legendsofamerica.com/oregon-trail-danger-hardship/

12 https://en.wikipedia.org/wiki/Battle_of_Wolf_Mountain

13 u-s-history.com: U.S. population, 1790-2020

14 En.m.wikipedia.org: American bison – Wikipedia

15 https://en.wikipedia.org/wiki/George_T._Anthony

16 https://www.womenshistory.org/education resources/biographies/susan-b-anthony

17 https://en.wikipedia.org/wiki/1st_United_States_Sharpshooters

18 https://en.wikipedia.org/wiki/Gettysburg_Address

19 https://en.wikipedia.org/wiki/Pickett%27s_Charge

20 https://www.smithsonianmag.com/history/ulysses-grant

21 https://en.wikipedia.org/wiki/Black_Hills_land_claim

22 https://militaryhistorynow.com/2021/06/08/the-u-s-sharpshooters-meet-one-of-the-civil-wars-deadliest

23 http://www.northfieldhistory.org/the-bank-raid/

24 https://en.wikipedia.org/wiki/Dime_Western

25 Google: allaboutbison.com ›what-part-of-the-bison-was-used

26 American Indian Mortality in the Late Nineteenth Century

27 https://www.nps.gov/sand/learn/historyculture/index.htm

28 Google, Wikipedia: Trail of Tears

29 history.com/news/shermans-war-on-native-americans

30 https://www.history.com/topics/american-civil-war/philip-sheridan

31 https://www.crf-usa.org/bill-of-rights-in-action/bria-21-1-c-indian-removal-the-cherokees-jackson-and-the-trail- of-tears.html (See the section titled Jackson and Indian Removal)

32 https://en.wikipedia.org/wiki/Battle_of_Palo_Duro_Canyon

33 https://ethw.org/Pump_Jacks

34 https://www.history.com/topics/westward-expansion/manifest-destiny

35 Google: George Washington: First Author of Federal Indian Policy

36 Google: George Washington: First Author of Federal Indian Policy